Rhino What You Did Last Summer

ROSS O'CARROLL-KELLY
(as told to Paul Howard)

Illustrated by
ALAN CLARKE

PENGUIN BOOKS

PENGUIN BOOKS

Published by the Penguin Group
Penguin Books Ltd, 80 Strand, London WC2R 0RL, England
Penguin Group (USA) Inc., 375 Hudson Street, New York, New York 10014, USA
Penguin Group (Canada), 90 Eglinton Avenue East, Suite 700, Toronto, Ontario, Canada M4P 2Y3
(a division of Pearson Penguin Canada Inc.)
Penguin Ireland, 25 St Stephen's Green, Dublin 2, Ireland (a division of Penguin Books Ltd)
Penguin Group (Australia), 250 Camberwell Road, Camberwell, Victoria 3124, Australia
(a division of Pearson Australia Group Pty Ltd)
Penguin Books India Pvt Ltd, 11 Community Centre, Panchsheel Park, New Delhi – 110 017, India
Penguin Group (NZ), 67 Apollo Drive, Rosedale, North Shore 0632, New Zealand
(a division of Pearson New Zealand Ltd)
Penguin Books (South Africa) (Pty) Ltd, 24 Sturdee Avenue, Rosebank,
Johannesburg 2196, South Africa

Penguin Books Ltd, Registered Offices: 80 Strand, London WC2R 0RL, England

www.penguin.com

First published by Penguin Ireland 2009
Published in Penguin Books 2010

1

Penguin Ireland thanks O'Brien Press for its agreement to Penguin Ireland
using the same design approach and typography, and the same artist,
as O'Brien Press used in the first four Ross O'Carroll-Kelly titles

Typeset by Palimpsest Book Production Limited, Falkirk, Stirlingshire
Printed in England by Clays Ltd, St Ives plc

ISBN: 978-1-844-88177-2

www.greenpenguin.co.uk

Contents

'We may see the small value God has for riches
by the people he gives them to.'
Alexander Pope

Prologue

The old man looks up at us, over the top of his reading glasses, and says the *cunillo* is wonderful.

Erika lifts her glass and goes, 'Happy New Year,' but I'm too in shock to return the toast. So her and the old man end up just clinking glasses.

'It will be,' he goes. 'It will be now.'

I look at *him*, then back at her. I don't see it. I don't see any resemblance at all. Or maybe I don't want to see it. It's one of those shocks that's, like, too big to take in all at once.

I stand up. Except I don't actually *remember* standing up? Let's just say I find myself suddenly standing up.

He turns to her and goes, 'Oh, here comes the waiter – have you decided what you're going to have?'

She's practically popping out of that black satin bustier, but of course I'm not allowed to even notice shit like that anymore.

I've got to get out of here. I stort walking. I hear *him* call me. I hear *her* call me as well. But I keep going.

I walk out of the restaurant, out of the hotel and out onto the street. It's snowing – coming down pretty heavy, in fact.

I get in the cor, turn the key – still in a daze – and point her in the direction of actual Barcelona.

I put my foot down and I'm suddenly tearing along all these narrow cliff roads in the pitch dork with the snow blinding me, not giving a fock – if I'm being honest – whether I even crash?

But then my phone suddenly beeps. It's, like, a text message from Sorcha, saying that she and Honor are thinking about me and that they're hoping that we beat Ireland A. She obviously knows fock-all about rugby, but it's still an amazing message to get and I kill my speed, suddenly remembering everything I have to live for, and realizing at that moment exactly where I'm headed.

What happened back there in the restaurant has made me realize that I need to be with my family. I need to see my own daughter and I need to find out if there's still a chance with Sorcha. I focked things up there like only I know how. But I need to know if there's still something there. Because it's with her and Honor that I actually belong.

I notice a set of lights in my rearview and somehow I *know* they belong to Erika.

Soon I arrive at the border crossing. The dude operating the barrier can't believe it's me. His eyes are out on practically stalks. 'I hear eet on the reddio,' he goes. 'It hees true? We score a try hagainst Island?'

I nod. 'We also kept them to less than a hundred points,' I go, which *is* the bigger achievement.

'A try hagainst Island!' he goes. 'You are hero to all of Handorra!'

He waves away my passport. No interest in even seeing it. I look in the mirror and watch Erika's lights approach.

'Dude,' I go, 'can you do me a favour? I'm trying to give this bird behind me the slip . . .'

He's there, 'Ha crezzy fan, yes?'

I'm like, 'Something like that. Can you make sure there's some kind of paperwork she's got to fill in? As in, a lot of it?'

'For you,' he goes, lifting the barrier for me, 'effery theeng hees poseeble.'

I put the foot down and off I go again, snaking through the Pyrenees, and I'm suddenly having one of my world-famous intellectual moments, thinking about how much your life can change in the space of an hour. It's like, there I was earlier tonight, being carried around the pitch shoulder-high, the hero of a – pretty much – country, which I've now left behind and will probably never see again. *And* it turns out that Erika's my sister.

My mind drifts back to a day, whatever, six, seven years ago, the day her old dear's divorce from Tim became final. Erika was majorly upset. I called around, supposedly to offer my sympathies, and we ended up going at it like two jailbirds on a conjugal visit.

I snap back to reality, realizing, very suddenly, that the border guard won't be able to hold her for long – not with her chorms. And not in that bustier.

I put the foot down again.

It takes, like, two and a half hours, but I finally reach the airport. It's, like, two o'clock in the morning when I pull up outside the main terminal building, throwing the rental cor in a set-down area, not even bothering my hole to return it, just leaving the keys in the basically ignition.

I realize that I don't even have any baggage. All my clobber's still back at the aportment.

I peg it in and check the departures board, my eyes going up and down what to me is just a mass of letters, waiting for two words to jump out at me: Los Angeles. There they are.

LA. The Windy City. Call it what you want – but that's where I'm headed.

I miss Honor so much that when I think about her, it feels like I'm having a hort attack. And, if I'm being honest, Sorcha too, even *if* she's with an auditor now.

The flight leaves at, like, 7.00 a.m. I order a first-class ticket using my old man's credit cord – the least he owes me in the circumstances.

3

There's, like, a major crowd hanging around the actual departure gate. As I get closer, I realize that it's the Ireland A team. They must be going out on a chorter.

Suddenly, roysh, they're all turned around, looking straight at me, all in their blazers and chinos. We're talking Keith Earls. We're talking Jeremy Staunton. We're talking Johnny Sexton. I'm expecting words like *traitor* to be suddenly bandied around like there's *no* actual tomorrow? But someone – might even be Roger Wilson – storts clapping, roysh, then one by one they all join in and before I know it the sea of Ireland A players has suddenly ported, and I'm being given a guard of honour through the departures gate.

It's actually just what I need.

But it's as I'm reaching the end of the line that I hear her voice. 'Ross!' she goes.

Of course, I should keep walking – I don't know *why* I don't? Maybe because I hear one or two wolf-whistles from the Ireland A goys. I turn around. She's obviously been crying, from the state of her boat.

She goes, 'Please don't go!'

I'm there, 'I need to get my head around this – time, space, blahdy blahdy blah.'

'Do you think *I'm* not confused?' she goes. 'Do you think *I'm* not angry? How can I ever trust my mum again?'

I go to turn around. 'I'm going to spend some time with my daughter and my – still – wife.'

'*I* could come with you,' she goes. 'We could get to know each other.'

I'm there, 'Maybe down the line. Right now, I need to get my head straight – see Sorcha, maybe find out if there's still . . .'

'A chance?'

'I was going to say a sniff. But yeah.'

She suddenly throws her orms around me, buries her head in my chest, then on go the waterworks. Out of the corner of my eye, I can see one or two of the Ireland A players looking at me, obviously thinking, whoa, rather you than me, Dude.

I rub her bare back and tell her she should be wearing more. She pulls away and looks at me, rivers of mascara running down her face, and says she left the restaurant in such a hurry, she forgot her coat.

I kiss her on the forehead and her hair smells of, I don't know, almonds and dandelions. I feel a sudden and familiar tightening in my trousers and, hating myself, I quickly turn away from her and tell her that I'd love to stay longer, but I've got, like, a plane to catch?

1. Right back where we started from

'How do you like them babies?' he goes, pointing at his shoes with a rolled-up copy of the *Wall Street Journal*. 'John Lobb custom brogues. Want to know what they cost?'

I actually *don't*.

'Four! Thousand! Dollars!' he goes anyway.

Of course, I just shrug, because it doesn't matter *how* good the Toms are – a man wearing a bluetooth earpiece is only five-eighths of a man.

Still, it's not up to me to tell him.

'Cillian!' Sorcha goes. 'We're supposed to be showing Ross around the house – *not* what you're wearing?'

This isn't, like, jealousy or anything, but I've never worked out what she sees in this tosspot.

I mention – being nice more than anything – that it's some pile of stones and straight away he has to mention that Beechwood Canyon is one of *the* most prestigious addresses *in* the Hollywood Hills.

It's only focking rented anyway.

'Madonna used to live, like, up the road?' Sorcha goes. '*And* Forest Whitaker. And who else, Pookie?'

Pookie? Jesus!

He's there, 'Aldous Huxley – *if* that name means anything to you, Ross,' pretty much *looking* to be decked?

They lead me out into this, like, huge entrance hallway. 'It's essentially a classic, 1930s-style Spanish villa,' *he* goes. 'Ten thousand square feet. Twelve bedrooms. Sixteen bathrooms.

Eight-car garage. Pool. Spa. Home theatre. *Four* bars. Three-hundred-and-sixty-degree views . . .'

I pull a face as if to say, you know – wouldn't exactly be *my* cup of tea?

Then they lead me into the kitchen, which Sorcha mentions is – oh my God! – the kitchen she's, like, *always* wanted?

The whole gaff is like something off *MTV Cribs*, in fairness to it.

She's there, 'It's got, like, a gourmet centre island,' which I can see for myself, 'with, like, three Sub-Zero refrigerators, an *actual* chef's Morice stove, a Fisher and Paykel double-drawer dishwasher *and* a built-in Nespresso . . .'

'It's a limited edition one as well,' *he* goes. 'You can't buy them in the shops,' and then, for no reason at all, he storts doing these, like, stretching exercises. This is a goy, bear in mind, who never played rugby.

'Oh my God,' Sorcha goes, 'I haven't even asked you about your flight.'

I'm like, 'Yeah, the flight was fine,' pulling up a high stool. 'Bit wrecked after it.'

'Have you decided yet what you're going to do for a carbon offset?'

It's amazing. I've known Sorcha for, like, ten years – been married to her for, what, three and a bit? – and she still knocks me sideways with questions like that.

'Because what you *can* do,' she goes, 'to pay off your emission debt, is set up a standing order with one of those companies that plant trees on your behalf. That way you can fly *and* drive with no, like, guilt at all.'

'I already do,' would be the wrong thing to say, so instead I just go, 'Cool,' cracking on to actually *give* a fock about, I suppose, world affairs.

8

She asks me if I fancy a coffee and I tell her I'd actually prefer to see Honor, if I could.

'Bad news,' *he* suddenly goes, 'we've just put her down.'

Sorcha's like, 'Cillian!' and he's there, 'Sorcha, if you wake her now, she'll be awake for the night. And I told you I've got that report to read on the high default rates on subprime and adjustable rate mortgages and their likely impact on the US economy.'

Adjustable rate mortgages? I'm thinking, he's *getting* decked – I don't give a fock how much Sorcha likes him.

But then *she* goes, 'Ross hasn't seen his daughter for, like, three months, Cillian. He's just flown for ten hours,' and then she turns around to me and she's like, 'Ross, come on . . .' and she leads me back out into the hall and up this big, winding staircase.

Honor's is the fourth bedroom on the right. I push the door, but when I catch, like, a glimpse of her curls in the light from the window, I end up just, like, filling up with tears and I have to actually turn away. All I want to do – I don't know why – is peg it back down the stairs and out of there. But Sorcha grabs me in, like, a clinch and whispers that it's okay, I suppose I'd have to say soothingly, in my ear. 'Take your time,' she goes, running her hand through my hair, so I take a few seconds to, like, compose myself, then I turn around and, with her orm around me, Sorcha sort of, like, slow-walks me over to the bed.

I get down on my knees and watch her tiny sleeping face. She's so beautiful. 'I can't believe how much she's changed,' I go, 'even in that time.'

Sorcha tells me that she still looks like me, which she doesn't. She's actually a ringer for Sorcha, but it's still, like, a really nice thing for her to say?

I stroke her little cheek and go, 'I've missed you so much,' and she actually opens her eyes for, like, two or three seconds, then closes them again.

I turn around to Sorcha and go, 'I better let her sleep,' and Sorcha's like, 'Why don't you come back in the morning? You can take her for the day?'

I ask her if she's sure and she's like, 'Ross, I feel – oh my God – *so* guilty for taking her away from you,' and I tell her not to be stupid, then I tell her – because I obviously didn't want to say it in front of *him* – that she looks well herself, as in *really* well, as in really well to the point of pretty much incredible?

She says it's possible to be practically vegan in LA and that she's been pretty much existing on mango slices and tempeh sausage patties. She says she also can't believe how much she underestimated the power of the blender.

I tell her I'm not just talking weight-wise. I'm there, 'You're, I don't know, *glowing*? The States has always suited you,' remembering how well she always looked when she came back from her Jıer and how it always made me feel guilty for doing the dirt on her while she was away.

She smiles and says thank you. She smells of buttermilk moisturizer and in normal circumstances – you *know* me – I'd try to throw the lips on her there and then. But I don't, because, well, I think deep down I know that the reason she looks so amazing is that *I* haven't been in her life.

'Hey, what are you doing tonight?' she suddenly goes.

I'm there, 'I was just going to head back to the hotel – basically crash.'

She's like, 'Okay, you're *not*? I'm going to take you to, like, *the* best hot dog place in – oh my God – the actual world.'

See, she knows I'm a focker for the hot dogs.

'You haven't lived until you've tasted these,' she goes.

We head downstairs and she tells Cillian she's taking me to Pink's. And even though he tries to play it cool, roysh, you can tell he's *not* a happy bunny? 'I thought you were tired,' he goes to me, showing me his entire hand. It's like playing poker with your focking granny.

I'm there, 'I think I'm getting my actual second wind.'

'Well, I'll come as well,' he goes, but Sorcha's there, 'Er – and leave Honor on her own? Cillian, you said you had work to do. We'll only be, like, an hour. Two at the most,' and I make sure to give him a big shit-eating smile on the way out the door.

We're heading for, like, North La Brea, but Sorcha tells me I can switch off the SatNav because she, like, *knows* the way? I ask her what she thinks of the cor – we're talking a BMW 650 convertible – and she goes, 'How did you even rent this – you don't have, like, a licence?' and I laugh and tell her that I borrowed JP's.

She's there, 'Oh my God, you could get into *so* much trouble for that,' then she shakes her head, roysh, as if to say, same old Ross, he's never going to change – thank God.

The queue for hot dogs is up the focking street and around the corner, but it's good because it gives us, like, an hour to catch up. 'Like, *all* the celebrities come here?' Sorcha goes. 'I saw Famke Janssen here a few weeks ago and I'm pretty sure Mila Kunis. And my really, really good friend Elodine – Honor goes on, like, playdates with her daughter, Jagger? – she saw Brody Jenner ordering a pastrami reuben. It's like, *Oh!* My God!'

I laugh. 'Don't take this the wrong way,' I go, 'because I mean it as an actual compliment – you've become, like, so American. You just seem really at home here.'

She smiles, I suppose you'd say, warmly. 'The only thing I don't like about LA,' she goes, 'is that the water is – oh my God – *so* hard. Look, my hair's frizzy – and that's even *after* an hour with my GHD . . .'

I give her, like, a sympathetic look.

'That's why all of the stars are getting Evian filtered into their boilers. It said in *People* that Rhea Durham's doing it – even though she's denied it.'

I tell her I can't believe the size of the gaff they've ended up in. 'Are Pricewaterhouse actually paying for it?'

'No – it's, like, a weird one?' she goes. 'Bob Soto, who's, like, the head of the department that Cillian's been seconded to, his wife is, like, an attorney and it's one of her clients who owns it. They've gone on, like, a cruise for a year and they needed someone to just, like, house-sit? When we saw it, we were just like, Oh my God!'

I'm there, 'I'd say you were.'

'I can't believe you won't stay with us,' she goes. 'You've seen it, Ross – there's loads of room.'

I'm there, 'No, I'm Kool and the Gang in the Viceroy. Hey, did I tell you I'm in the exact same room where Christopher Moltisanti stayed in *The Sopranos*?'

'Oh my God,' she goes, 'that must be, like, *so* expensive.'

I'm there, 'Fock it – the old man's paying. The least he owes me when you think about it.'

It's at that point that I probably should mention Erika. But I don't – maybe I'm enjoying being around Sorcha too much. Instead, I ask her about work.

'Well, work-wise,' she goes, 'the last few months have been, like, a fact-finding mission for me? Even just walking around Melrose or Robertson, I've got – oh my God – *so* many ideas for the shop back home. Betsey Johnson's got, like, vertical TV screens playing actual catwalk footage? It's like, oh my God – why has no one in Ireland even *thought* about that? Except BTs, obviously.

'And I'm thinking of having, like, a seating area with huge pink couches – PVC, obviously, not leather. If people are relaxed, they *will* spend. Elodine told me that and she studied actual retail.

'And even just the way they talk to you in the shops, Ross. If they see you with, like, two or three items, they come over to you and go, "Do you want me to start a room for you?" And then they, like, compliment you? They're like, "Oh my God, that is *such* a good look for you!" I'm going to start saying *all* of those.'

Then she asks me what's been happening in *my* life. I'm there, 'Well, you know about the whole Andorra thing – a try against Ireland A, blahdy blahdy blah. Let's just say there's going to be a lot of teams all of a sudden interested in my services . . .'

Sorcha's phone beeps. Except it's not a phone – it's, like, a pink BlackBerry? I presume it's a text from Cillian – still bulling – but she reads it with, like, her mouth open, then tells me that members of the National Restaurant Association are furious with Kevin Federline for appearing in a commercial as a fast-food worker dreaming of becoming a rapper. They say it demeans low-wage restaurant workers.

Of course, I'm left just shaking my head.

'Oh,' she goes, 'it's this, like, celebrity alert service – Cillian got me a subscription for Christmas. You get, like, *all* the news and gossip, straight to your phone, as it happens. Even photographs. Oh my God, I *have* to show you the giraffe-print Escada halter that Jada Pinkett Smith wore to the New York Fashion Fête.'

Luckily, roysh, it doesn't come to that, because we're suddenly at the top of the queue. I order, like, a chilli cheese dog with, obviously, fries and I persuade Sorcha to have, like, a Patt Morrison Baja Veggie, even though she says she's trying to steer clear of guacamole.

We end up sitting in this little, I suppose, yord at the back of the place, at a little white plastic table, wolfing down what I would have to say is the most incredible hot dog I've ever tasted.

Sorcha mentions that she's going to buy Ayaan Hirsi Ali's autobiography again. 'I was only talking to Elodine the other night about her whole struggle?' she goes. 'And I thought, oh my God, I *have* to re-read it.'

I swat away a mosquito the size of a small bird, then I tell her it's great to see her. She smiles at me – like old times – and says it's great to see me, too.

The ugly munter – what is she, following me now?

She's all, 'What you're asking me, I think, is why do I write? And the answer to that is that I can't imagine *not* writing . . .'

I'm, like, shouting at the TV, going, 'You swamp donkey! You total focking mong!'

'I know this is going to sound, oh, impossibly celestial,' she's giving it, 'but sometimes it's as if my fingers are being directed – that I'm merely a cipher for this wonderful story that the universe has determined *must* be told.'

'*Karma Suits You*,' the dude interviewing her goes. 'Hey, what a crazy title – what's it about?'

'Well, it's the story of a fifty-something Irish woman who experiences a sexual reawakening – a re-blossoming, if you like – after going through the menopause. She abandons her old, rather repressed life *in* Ireland and comes to America, where she experiences this rebirth, which is where the idea of karma comes in. And of course she meets all these wonderful men – a fireman, obviously, a two-hundred-pound NBA star, even an elevator repairman – and has all these wonderfully erotic experiences, some of which she would have considered impossible without recourse to heavy pain medication . . .'

I'm, like, screaming now. 'You're a focking disgrace! You absolute focking manatee!'

'Of course, the full title,' the other interviewer – who's, like, a woman – goes, 'is *Karma Suits You – States of Ecstasy*. Because during the course of her year, she has – let's just say – *relations* with fifty men in fifty different states. And, controversially, fifty different positions. Can I just read out a line from one of my favourites, which is Alaska? This is the scene that ends with the kneeling lotus.

'He said he was a whale fisherman. She looked at him askance, studying his leathery face, his commanding, callused hands, his entire bearing, straight as a longboat. Her resistance melted like the polar ice cap. Soon, he was exploring her Inside Passage and she was groaning like an age-worn sled dog.'

The audience claps – they actually clap. 'You're a focking shambles!' I'm going.

Suddenly there's, like, a loud knock on the door, then it bursts open before I get a chance to even get out of the sack. There's all of a sudden a man stood at the foot of my bed – black, if the truth be told – and he's wearing, like, a uniform. At first, roysh, I think he's a cop, but then he says he's, like, hotel security.

'Sir,' he goes, 'we've had a complaint from one or two guests about a ruckus coming from this suite.'

'A ruckus?'

'A ruckus, Sir.'

I nod in the direction of the old Savalas. 'Well, can you actually blame me?'

He turns around, looks at the screen. '*Regis and Kelly*,' he goes. 'My wife never misses it. Though I gotta tell you, I *think* she preferred Kathie Lee . . .'

'I'm talking about *her*, the guest – focking so-called – they've got on . . .'

He sits on the end of the bed. 'She's kinda pretty,' he goes. 'She Irish?'

I'm like, 'Pretty? You've got to be shitting me – that's a double-bagger if ever I saw one.'

He's there, 'Got nice pins, too. What *you* got against this lady?'

'What I've got against her is that she *happens* to be my old dear.'

'Old what?'

'It's, like, our word for mother? And it's, like, how would you like to see *your* mother up on the wall there talking filth?'

'I wouldn't, I guess. But I gotta tell you, you gotta keep it down, my man. You in the Viceroy now – not the Y. You hearing me?'

I tell him I am.

'I'm Carl,' he goes.

A high-five in LA, I'm happy to say, is exactly the same as a high-five back home.

'No more ruckus – know what I'm saying?'

I'm there, 'Kool and the Gang, my friend. Kool *and* the Gang.'

Then he's suddenly gone.

My phone beeps – a text from, like, Sorcha: OMG ur mum is on live with regis n kelly! u must be omg SO proud.

'Because I think it's our duty,' the stupid hound's going, 'and I don't use that word lightly, *as* writers to challenge norms, be they sexual, be they . . . whatever.'

'Yeah,' this Kelly one's going, 'back in the, er, Emerald Isle . . .'

'The Old Sod,' Regis or whatever he's called goes.

'. . . you're considered something of an Irish Catherine Millet – would that be fair to say?'

16

'I think it would,' the old dear goes, 'insofar as we're both libertines. We both believe in free expression *in* a sexual context. *And* in all its forms, whether that's nihilism, sadomasochism, autoerotic asphyxiation . . .'

I can't actually listen to any more of this. I reach down, grab one of my Dubes off the floor and fock it straight at the TV. It bounces off, roysh, and I'm lying there thinking, it's a good job *I* don't wear John Lobb custom brogues, otherwise it would have probably cracked the . . .

The next thing, roysh – pretty unexpected, I have to say – the TV just, like, falls off the wall and there's what would have to be described as a loud explosion, we're talking sparks everywhere.

I'm like, 'Holy fock!'

I pick up the phone, dial zero for reception. I'm there, 'Listen, tell Carl not to bother his orse coming back up – everything's cool. By the way, I've pretty much broken the TV. Is that likely to show up on the Harry Hill?'

I was convinced that Sorcha was shitting me when I saw them first.

Stilettos for babies.

I asked her was it not, like, dangerous, but she said that girls eventually *have* to learn to wear designer heels and it's best if they stort young.

I *could* have pointed out that Chloe back home has been told she has to have both hips replaced, the result of a lifetime wearing designer heels, but it's, like, no – I'm actually over here to chill. So I said nothing while she put on Honor's little red patent pumps – '*so* like my *actual* Roger Viviers' – and warned me not to let her walk more than a few steps unassisted.

So we're sitting in, like, Bornes and Noble in Santa Monica – in the little Storbucks in there? – and it's nice, roysh, just the two of us, me and my daughter, spending some QT together, watching all the comings and goings.

Sorcha, I should mention, feels it's important for Honor to get a good grasp of conversational Spanish and Mandarin while she's still young. She said I wouldn't believe how important multi-ethnicity is over here. Every time someone passes our table, Honor's either like, '*Hola*,' or she's like, '*Ni hao*,' and the thing is, roysh, I haven't heard her say a word in actual English yet.

I'm there, trying to get her to say, 'Daddy,' going, 'Can you say, "Daddy"? "Daddy"! "Daddy"!'

'*Ni hao*,' she just goes. '*Ni hao ma*.'

She's also, by the way, trying desperately to get her hands on my grande triple shot *dulce de leche* mocha and I'm thinking, she's definitely my daughter. I end up giving her one or two little sips, thinking, you know, coffee can't be any worse for a baby than Toms that cut off the circulation in her feet.

So I'm sitting there, roysh, basically chilling, taking in the whole California experience, when all of a sudden there's a bird, we're talking one or two tables away – a ringer for Mandy Moore and that is *not* an exaggeration? – staring over, which is no big deal actually, because I *am* looking well at the moment and, as we all know, *every* bird is a sucker for a man with a baby.

'Oh my God!' she goes at the top of her voice. 'I *love* her!' which is always nice for a father to hear.

I'm there, 'Thanks. She's basically eighteen months old now – maybe a little bit more.'

It's only when she goes, 'She is such an inspiration to me,' that I realize that who she's *actually* talking about is Ayaan Hirsi Ali and the book I'm considering buying for Sorcha but am currently using as a coaster. 'Have you, like, read it?' she goes.

'Yeah,' I go, thinking on my feet as usual. 'Matter of fact,

I'm re-reading it? It's just I was talking to someone the other day about her whole, I suppose you'd have to say, struggle and I was thinking, Dude, you owe it to yourself to re-read it. And maybe re-read it again after that.'

She smiles at me. She's got teeth like Chiclets and she's interested in me – that much she's making pretty obvious. 'The bit where she's forcibly circumcised,' she goes, 'I was thinking, oh my God, if I could get my hands on those tribal elders . . .'

'Don't get me storted,' I go, then of course I haven't a clue what to say next – I don't know what the book's even about? – so I flip it over subtly and stort feeding her lines off the back cover.

'My own personal feeling,' I go, 'is that she has an open mind that has released itself from the old straitjacketed frame of reference of Right and Wrong. I mean, there's no doubt she is instinctively, deeply anti-authoritarian and – you'd have to say – unlikely to stick to straight ideological themes and shit? She will go on asking difficult questions. I could be wrong – that's just what I think.'

I thump the table then, just for effect.

No bird has ever looked at me the way she looks at me then – not even Sorcha on our wedding day. She wants me, and she wants me in a major way.

She goes, 'I know a guy who's hoping to turn her story into a Broadway musical. I would *so* love to play her.'

She sort of, like, indicates the chair beside me to ask if she can join me. I'm there, 'Yeah, coola boola,' because, like I told you, she's hot – and wearing half-nothing as well.

'I'm Sahara,' she goes, offering me her hand, the one that's *not* holding her frap?

I'm there, 'Sahara? What a beautiful name,' which it's not, of course – it's the name of a casino.

'It's actually Sarah?' she goes. 'But my agent thought it would help get me roles.'

I tell her I know a bird called Sophie who started spelling her name Seauphie as a way of, like, pissing off her old pair when they were getting divorced. It helps to get, like, a rapport going? Then I'm like, 'Hang on – did you say agent?'

'I'm an actress,' she goes.

I'm like, 'An actress?' showing an actual interest, which is something I'm going to stort doing more of. 'What are the chances! Well, without blowing my own trumpet here, I'm a pretty big deal myself back home.'

'Back home?' she goes. 'You mean you're not from California?'

I'm there, 'Er, my *accent*?'

She's like, 'You don't have an accent.'

'Are you shitting me?'

'No – where are you from?'

'I'm, like, Irish?'

'Oh my God, that is *so* random. I would never have known. So what are you, like, famous for in Ireland?'

'Well, not *just* Ireland, I could say. Have you ever heard of a certain game called rugby?'

'Rug . . .'

'Rugby?'

'I don't think so.'

I crack my hole laughing. 'Now I *know* you're shitting me.'

She has un-focking-believable Jakki Deggs, in fairness to her, smooth and tanned, and the way she's dangling her Havaiana on the end of her foot is doing it for me in a big-time way.

I'm there, 'Would it be rude of me to ask you for your number?'

She opens her mouth, only cracking on to be shocked. 'I'll

say this for you,' she goes, 'you're confident,' and I'm there, 'It *has* been said,' flirting my orse off majorly.

She's there, 'I bet it has. I only stopped by your table because I've just finished reading the same book,' playing the innocent, of course.

'You stopped by my table because you were attracted,' I go. 'You liked what you saw and you went for it – no one's judging you.'

She slaps me, sort of, like, playfully? You always know you're in when they do that. I'm there, 'So, what are doing Friday night?'

'What am I doing Friday night?' she goes, actually embarrassed. 'Oh my God, I can't believe I'm having this conversation. I'm having some of my girlfriends over. It's, like, my television debut? This thing I worked on . . . I don't know, do you want to come over?'

I'm there, 'Well, I've no other plans – plus I've broken the TV in my hotel room.'

I whip out my phone and she gives me her digits. She says it'll be me and, like, three girls there and I tell her I like those odds. She laughs. I put my hand on her knee, then she's suddenly serious again, fanning her face with her hand and saying *oh my God* over and over again, unable to believe her actual luck here.

But, like I said, think Mandy Moore.

I tell her I hoped she didn't get the wrong idea when she saw me with my daughter. 'Don't worry,' I go, 'I'm happily separated – on the way to being divorced. Yeah, *she's* with, like, a complete tosser now – he's, like, an auditor.'

Of course, I end up nearly falling off the chair when she turns around and goes, 'What daughter?'

I look beside me. My coffee has gone and, more importantly, so has Honor and I pretty much crap my board shorts. It's like, No! No! No!

The next thing, roysh, I'm literally running around the shop, calling her name at, like, the top of my voice, while at the same time kacking it – and who can blame me? I check, like, Crafts and Hobbies, Architecture, even Humanities and she's, like, nowhere to be seen.

On the outside, I'm trying to stay calm. I tell Sahara that she couldn't have gone far – she isn't walking that long. *And* she's in, like, high heels. But then I remember that she's had a coffee – the guts of a triple espresso – and I realize that she could be anywhere.

Then of course the guilt storts to kick in. I'm thinking about all the people down through the years who told me that this pretty face would eventually be my undoing and how they'd love to see me now, frantically running around Recommended, Judaism and Judaica and – this'll give you a laugh – Parenting, looking for my actual daughter, who wandered off while I was busy playing Mr Lover Lover.

Sahara, in fairness to her, keeps her head. She asks me for, like, a description, then says she'll tell security to lock down the store. 'If she's in here,' she goes, 'we'll find her – you go check outside.'

Outside? I hadn't even thought! I literally burst through the doors, out onto Third Street, and stort pegging it up the promenade like an actual lunatic. Every baby I see, I run, like, straight up to them, going, 'Honor!' and of course when it's not her, the parents are looking at me as if to say, 'Er, *weirdo*?'

It must be, like, half-a-mile up the promenade that I decide to give up, thinking, there's no way she could have got this actual far. That's when I notice this, like, ruck of people gathered around this crowd of buskers playing, like, salsa music. It's actually out of the corner of my eye that I *think* I spot a mop of blonde curls somewhere in the middle and I'm literally throwing people out of the way to get in there.

It's her! She's standing in front of the band, in her little red shoes, dancing away. And everyone's laughing and clapping, like they think she's part of the act?

'That's my daughter!' I go. 'That's my actual daughter!' and I sweep her up in my orms.

'Hey, Man, I was enjoying that,' someone shouts and then someone else goes, 'Asshole,' but I don't give a fock now that I've got her back, unhormed as well, although her body *is* sort of, like, twitching in my orms and she keeps, I don't know, clenching and unclenching her teeth.

'Is she okay?' this bird asks me. She's not that unlike Trista Rehn. 'Her eyes look kind of spacey.'

'Yeah, she's had a coffee,' I go, then she looks at me like I'm some kind of, I don't know, monster.

I carry her back up the street, promising to buy her all sorts of shit and grateful, I suppose, that she doesn't have the words yet to tell Sorcha what happened – certainly not in any language that her mother could understand.

Sahara – Sarah, whatever – is waiting for me at the door of Bornes and Noble. 'You found her!' she goes and then, 'Oh my God, she's *so* beautiful!'

I'm shaking my head going, 'If anything ever happened to her, I'd . . . well, I don't know what I'd do.'

She smiles, then leans forward and gives me the most unbelievable kiss on the lips, to the point where I'm suddenly feeling a bit spacey myself. 'You are *such* a sweet guy,' she goes. Then she hands me, like, a bag. 'I hope you don't mind – I bought that book *for* you?'

Sorcha asks me how Honor was yesterday and I tell her fine.

That's one of the good things about being a lady's man my entire life – I can lie without even thinking about it?

'It's just that it took me – oh my God – hours to get her to sleep last night,' she goes.

I pull a face like I'm trying to come up with, I don't know, the answer to a really hord crossword question? Then I shake my head. 'I don't know what that could have been.'

I'm just there, bouncing Honor up and down on my knee, going, 'I think it was just the excitement of seeing your Daddy again, wasn't it?'

'*Xing qi yi* . . .'

'Can you say, "Daddy"?'

'*Xing qi er, xing qi san* . . .'

Sorcha suddenly gets a text. She says that – oh my God – actress Julia Roberts and husband filmmaker Danny Moder are going to have a little brother or sister for Hazel and Phin. I just shrug. Then she goes, 'Oh my God, there's one about your mum, too,' and I have to admit, roysh, she suddenly has my attention. 'Oprah was spotted reading a copy of her book in The Rosebud in Chicago. Oh! My God! That is *such* a huge deal, Ross.'

I crack on not to be impressed. 'It's, like, who even *is* Oprah – I'm talking in the big scheme of things?'

She laughs and says that an endorsement from Oprah can turn a book into a million-seller overnight.

I shrug my shoulders. I'm like, 'The thing I don't understand is when did she even write it? She's only been in the States, like, a fortnight.'

'She wrote it when she was in, like, her twenties.'

'It's more of her usual porn.'

'It's *so* not, Ross. In fact, I was the one who told her to send it to an American publisher.'

'You?'

'About two years ago. I was the first one she ever let read it.'

She always was a crawler when it came to my old dear.

'She has this amazing line about Florida. *He exploded inside her like a first-phase rocket . . .*'

I suddenly cover Honor's ears. I'm there, 'Too much information, Sorcha! Too much information!'

She laughs, then takes Honor from me. She says that Cillian's late, meaning late home from work. I'm thinking that maybe now is the time to tell her about Erika. We're relaxing beside the pool with a couple of appletinis and I feel like I could say anything to her at this moment.

But I don't.

Instead, I end up talking about *him*. 'I think he feels threatened by me,' I go.

She's there, 'Cillian? Cillian has no reason to feel threatened by you,' except she says it a little bit *too* defensively?

I'm like, 'Some would disagree. What was all that shit the other night about his shoes? John focking Lobb.'

'Oh my God,' she goes, 'there's nothing wrong with wanting to look your best, Ross.'

'But he's an accountant.'

'Don't give me that – he happens to be a senior adviser in international risk assessment.'

'*What*ever! It's not just the shoes anyway. It's the gaff – he thought he was Puffy showing me around his crib. All he was short of saying was, "This is where the magic happens!" which, I reckon, would have been bullshit anyway.'

She looks at me, suddenly embarrassed, and I immediately know it's a touchy subject. 'What do you mean by that?' she goes.

I'm there, 'Well, I couldn't help but notice *Prison Break*, Season One, on the bedside locker. Boxsets in the bedroom are a definite sign of somebody who's not getting any.'

'That's none of your business,' she goes, pointing at me, which she only ever does when I've hit the nail on the head. 'You've no right to even talk to me about that side of my life. We're both free agents, can I just remind you? We've both moved on.'

Now it's my turn to laugh. I think she's just made it obvious that she still misses me in at least one deportment. 'All I'm saying,' I go, 'is that Cillian shouldn't feel under pressure with me here. He shouldn't feel like he has to compete with me.'

'Oh, believe me,' she goes, 'he doesn't.'

The next thing we hear, roysh, is a cor pulling up outside, except it's obviously not the focking Prius Nerdster that Cillian drove to work this morning – you can tell from the sound of the engine. We walk around to the front of the gaff and I end up actually laughing out loud when I see him – this dude who's supposedly *not* threatened by me? – getting out of a brand new, red Murciélago.

He's still wearing his Magee suit, bear in mind – focking D'Arcy's crowd.

Sorcha's jaw is practically on the ground and not in a good way. She's like, 'Cillian, where did you get this?'

He's there, 'I bought it.'

It's an unbelievable cor, in fairness – totally focking wasted on him. We're talking six-point-two litre engine, we're talking four-wheel drive, we're talking six-speed sequential automatic transmission. We're also talking three hundred Ks and possibly more. She goes, 'How much did you pay for this?'

He immediately looks at me. I pull a face that says, basically, rather you than me, mate, listening to that.

'Does it matter?' he goes. 'I got a loan.'

'A loan?'

He's there, 'Yeah. I'm earning unbelievable money, remember,' which is an attempted dig at me – except I've never been interested in earning money, only spending it.

'More to the point,' Sorcha goes, 'how fuel-efficient is it?'

I just, like, snigger, kiss Honor goodbye, then leave them to it.

'This particular table,' he goes, 'has been meticulously engineered *and* crafted. Solid oak construction. One-inch diamond-honed slate. These pockets – genuine leather, hand-tooled.'

I run my hand across the felt.

'Heirloom quality, Man. You play?'

I shrug. 'It was pretty much *all* I did in college,' I go. 'But it's actually a present for my son?'

'Well,' he goes, 'not only will your son enjoy it, so will his son, and his son after that. Don't let anybody tell you any different – pool tables are a very sophisticated piece of equipment. There's no MDF in this thing. You hear what I'm saying? Solid! Oak! That's why you got to pay that little bit more . . .'

'I don't care,' I go. 'It's not even me paying.'

My phone suddenly rings. It's like, speak of the devil. 'What do *you* want?' I go.

He's like, 'Where are you, Kicker?'

I'm there, 'Los Angeles – what's it to you?'

'Oh,' he goes. 'Well, I'm still in Andorra. It's just that, well, you left in a bit of a hurry.'

'Is there any chance you could stop babbling for five seconds?' I go. 'Is your credit cord still good – the one with the 1982 Triple Crown-winning team on it?'

'Actually, no,' he goes. 'I've just this minute discovered it's been stolen.'

I'm there, 'Well, *actually* it hasn't? *I* took it. So don't cancel it. You're about to become the proud owner of a state-of-the-ort pool table,' and I tip the nod to the shop dude, who immediately storts filling in the shipping documents, happy in his pants.

At the top of my voice, I'm like, 'I'm going to take the jukebox as well – the big Wurlitzer jobby,' and, then into the phone, I go, 'Seven focking grand – I presume you're good for it.'

Of course, he doesn't even *give* a shit. 'I *hope* it's vinyl,' he goes. 'Oh, even the mention of the word Wurlitzer brings me back, Ross, back to the old days. The Rainbow what's-it on O'Connell Street. "There's No Other Like My Baby". That was our song – Helen and I . . .'

Helen as in Erika's old dear.

I'm there, 'I don't actually *give* a fock? I bought, like, a jacuzzi an hour ago – are you not even curious as to why?'

'Well, I expect you felt your *old dad* owed you a present after the heroics at the Camp d'Esports del M.I. Consell General . . .'

'No, that's *not* it. Do you remember when I was kid, the bomb shelter we found at the bottom of the gorden?'

'Oh, yes – chap we bought the house from was absolutely convinced that Truman was going to drop the big one on China, unleashing hell and what-not.'

'Whatever. Do you remember saying to me we were going to turn it into a boys' room and then never actually doing it?'

'Well,' he goes, 'if I said it, I'm sure it would have been in the context of – wouldn't it be wonderful if . . .'

'Oh, but you were too busy with work, weren't you? Doing all the dodgy shit they eventually put you away for. So now *I'm* turning it into a boys' room – for me and *my* son.'

'What a wonderful idea,' he goes.

It's, like, impossible to hurt this focker. I try to come in from a different angle. 'By the way, when are you going to do something about that scabrous animal?'

'Your mother?' he goes. Isn't it funny how he immediately knows? 'Yes, I hear she's making something of a splash, inverted commas, stateside.'

'She was on TV yesterday, making a holy focking show of me.'

'Well, this is the book she wrote during her famous Paris years. She was only in her twenties, Ross. They say it's her *magnum opus* – pardon the French.'

I'm there, 'Why are you defending her? You're supposed to be getting divorced. Why can't you, like, hate each other?'

'Hate each other?'

'Yeah, like *normal* parents?'

'We were married for thirty years,' he goes, like *that's* any kind of excuse. 'Your mother and I will always be friends. We care about each other very much.'

'Well, I just think that's focked up, that's all.'

He doesn't even respond to that, just goes, 'Erika's gone back to Ireland . . .'

I'm there, 'Er, did I *ask* you about Erika?'

'I think after the initial euphoria, the anger's starting to kick in. Helen called me today – seems that Erika said some hurtful things to her.'

'I said, I don't remember asking about her,' and then I just hang up.

'I can't believe you're actually shopping with me,' Sorcha goes. She has to shout it over a seriously loud disco version of 'Can You Feel The Love Tonight?', which means we're obviously in Abercrombie. 'You used to hate shopping.'

I'm there, 'If you must know, I was shopping all yesterday

afternoon. I picked up, like, a jukebox, pool table, a few other bits and pieces for Ro.'

She looks at me like, well, like she did the night she first took advantage of me when I'd a few beers on board in the Wez. 'You are *so* a good father,' she goes. 'Anyone who says you're not is, like – oh my God – *so* wrong . . .'

Having said that, if she finds out I let Honor wander around Santa Monica on her Tobler for half an hour, she'll redecorate this shop with my focking intestines.

'I know,' I go. 'I think it's very much a case of, you know, give a dog a bad name . . .'

My focking eardrums are bursting in here.

A changing room finally comes free. I automatically follow Sorcha in and the funny thing is that neither of us actually considers it weird – as in, her stripping down to basically her bra and knickers in front of me?

The bird in charge of the changing rooms does, though – she knocks on the door and goes, 'It's only *one* person per changing room?' and I end up just going, 'Yeah – *what*ever!' to which there's *no* comeback, of course.

Sorcha's, like, examining her orse in the mirror. 'Do you think these jeans make my legs look thinner than my Citizens of Humanity ones?' she goes.

It's one of those questions where she already *knows* the answer she wants? So I make what I have to admit is a guess, 'Yes.'

'What about my Sevens?' she goes. 'Are *they* more slimming?'

I go, 'No,' solely on the basis that last time I said yes. It's like Junior Cert. foundation maths all over again.

She considers my answers while striking, I suppose, different poses in the mirror – one hand on her hip, one foot in front of the other, then pouting, whatever the fock difference that makes — and finally decides that she doesn't want them. So they come off again.

'You don't mind?' I go. 'As in, me staring at you pretty much naked?'

She's like, 'I *have* underwear on, Ross? And anyway, it's nothing you haven't seen before, right?'

She looks unbelievable. A Peter Pan's always suited her.

I'm there, 'I wonder would Cillian see it like that.'

She pulls her sea blue Tart Grace dress over her head and goes, 'Cillian would be fine with it. I'm sorry about the other night, by the way.'

I'm there, 'Is he keeping it? As in, the Lamborghini?'

'Well, he's bought it now. Or signed the finance papers. I think he's just very stressed with work at the moment.'

'I'm saying nothing,' I go. 'But I still think it's me.'

She laughs. 'Oh my God, Ross, he *knows* that you and I are more like Best Friends Forever these days?' and I'm thinking, yeah, you just keep telling yourself that lie, girl.

She steps into her Uggs, fixes her hair, then puts her sunglasses back on her head, and I open the changing-room door. The bird outside is bulling. She's a last word freak as well. 'Only *one* customer per changing room?' she goes, pointing at a sign on the wall.

You actually *should* have seen her face when I pretended to do up my fly.

On the way out of the shop, out of the corner of her mouth, Sorcha's going, 'I can't *actually* believe you did that!' but she's also smiling, as if to say, I can't actually control this dude — might as well just sit back and enjoy the show.

Back in the cor, she checks her texts and says that Lindsay Lohan was spotted dancing with Blink-182 drummer Travis Barker at a West Hollywood party two days after having her appendix out!

'My kind of bird,' I go.

'And Angelina has dropped the broadest hint yet that she might like to work with Billy Bob Thornton again one day . . .'

To which there's no real answer.

I tell her I'm storving. I'd eat the orse out of a roadkill raccoon. She says okay, we'll collect Honor from crèche, then she's going to bring me – her treat – to Ketchup, as in Ketchup from *The Hills*? As in, the place where Lauren and Heidi ran into each other for the first time after the big fight? And Spencer sent over a drink for Lauren and Jason, being – oh my God – *such* a wanker?

I have to say, Spencer's always been my kind of goy.

Ketchup turns out to be a pretty amazing spot. I order a pepper-seared Kobe with fries, Sorcha has a twenty-first-century cobb without the chicken, the bacon or the blue cheese – a grassbox, in other words – and Honor has a plate of sweet potato tater tots, which I'm pretty taken aback to see her eating with chopsticks – as in, her own personal set?

I can't even eat with chopsticks.

'I can't believe you have her eating with those things,' I go and Sorcha ends up nearly biting my head off. She tells me I don't live here, so I have no idea how important the whole diversity thing is. She goes. 'Poet, one of Honor's playdates, is actually part Asian-American, Ross.'

I'd forgotten how sexy she can be when she loses it. But I'm also thinking how *nice* this actually is? As in, the three of us sitting here, back together as, like, a family again.

I'm there, 'How would you feel if I told you I had a date tomorrow night?'

She looks all of a sudden serious. 'Oh,' she goes. 'I mean, that was quick. Can I ask who?'

'You're not jealous, are you?'

'No, it's just – you only arrived, what, three days ago.'

'I've always been a fast mover – *you* know that. And if you must know, she's an actress.'

'An actress? Oh my God, what's she been in?'

She's bulling – as in, seriously bulling.

'Well, it's early days yet. Obviously, we want to keep things below the rador for now.'

Honor all of a sudden storts crying, for no actual reason at all. Some people would say that's women for you. She's not only crying, roysh, she's pretty much screaming the roof off, to the point where Sorcha has to take her out of her baby chair and sort of, like, bounce her on her knee.

'Okay,' she goes, 'just answer me this, is it Jessica Stroup?'

'I can tell you it's definitely not Jessica Stroup.'

'Torrey DeVitto?'

'No, it's not Torrey DeVitto.'

'Hilarie Burton?'

'Whoa, enough with the guessing already!'

'I'm sorry,' she goes. 'But if it'd been any of those, I *would* have been jealous . . . Come on, Honor, what's wrong?'

She offers her everything from her bottle to her Dora the Explorer doll to a spicy tuna roll, but there's no calming her.

'You're saying you're *not* jealous?' I go.

She shrugs. 'You're a free agent,' she goes, then she stares into space, obviously surprised at how badly it's affecting her.

She stands up very suddenly and says she has to go to the restroom – and she actually uses that word. 'See if you can do anything with her,' she goes, plonking this bundle of basically noise in my lap. 'You know, she's been so irritable the last couple of days, which isn't like her at all.'

That gets me suddenly thinking. I follow Honor's line of vision and realize that, yeah, she's staring straight at my Americano. All she basically wants is a sip of my coffee. So when Sorcha hits the jacks, I check that no one's looking, then I hold the mug up to her lips. She immediately stops crying. She has, like, three or four sips – five at the very most – and she's suddenly happy like you wouldn't believe.

'Oh my God!' Sorcha goes, suddenly back from the can. 'What did you do?'

I'm there, 'I don't know. Maybe I've just got, like, a way with her.'

She's like, 'You certainly do. I am, like, *so* impressed. So what do you want to do – do you want to hit one or two more shops in the afternoon?'

I'm there, 'Hey, I'm easy like a Sunday morning.'

'I am *so* excited about my plans for the shop,' she goes. 'Oh my God, I'm going to blow Coast and Reiss out of the water with the dresses I'm going to be bringing in. We're talking Literature. We're talking Bailey. We're talking KLS. We're talking Cash Lords. And a simple question – why is no one in Ireland doing Antik and Taverniti jeans?'

On the spur of the moment – and this is totally unrehearsed – I decide that that's my cue to bring up, like, the whole Erika situation? It's only a matter of time before she rings her anyway.

'Speaking of antics,' I go, 'the major news back home involves Erika.'

'Erika?'

'Exactly.'

'As in, my best friend Erika?'

She definitely thinks I'm going to tell her I was, like, with her – as in, *with* with? – so this might even turn out to be a bit of a relief to her. 'Before you say it, it's not what you think,' I go. 'No, the thing is, it turns out – now *how* random is this? – that she's kind of, well, my sister . . .'

'Your sister?'

'Well, half-sister really. She found out that that dude Tim was never her old man . . .'

'Hang on, Ross. I can't take this in. Erika . . . is your sister?'

'Yeah, her old dear came clean. Told her that her old man was a goy she had, like, a fling with in the seventies, eighties, whatever . . .'

'Er, I know that, Ross? I talked to her at Christmas?'

'Well, the goy she had the fling with turns out to be my old man . . .'

'Oh! My God!

'Exactly – poor focking girl. How would you feel finding that out?'

Sorcha suddenly bursts into tears. 'Drive us home,' she goes without even looking at me. 'Now.'

'I thought you'd love the story,' I make the mistake of going. 'Especially with all those soaps you watch . . .'

She totally flips at that.

'She was, like, my Best *Best* Friend!' she practically screams at me.

I'm there, 'I dare say she still will be.'

'How *could* you, Ross?'

'What do you mean, how could *I*?'

'How could you do it?'

There's, like, silence in the restaurant. First Spencer and Heidi, now me and Sorcha – the drama never focking ends in this place.

I'm there, 'Er, this is one of those things that *isn't* my actual fault?'

'And you kept it to yourself this long?'

'Whoa,' I go, 'I only found out myself, like, four days ago.'

'Why didn't you say something the night you arrived?'

'Because I knew I had to get the timing right. And you *were* pretty keen for me to try those hot dogs. Which I thought were amazing, I don't know if I mentioned.'

Sorcha's shouting is drawing quite a lot of attention our way now. 'I never want to see you again,' she goes, standing up and pretty much snatching Honor out of my orms.

'Fair enough,' I go. 'Here, I'll give you a lift home.'

She's like, 'Actually, don't bother, Ross. We'll get a cab,' and then, just before she storms off, she takes one last look at me, narrows her eyes and goes, 'And whoever it is you're meeting tomorrow, she's welcome to you!'

Then she's suddenly gone, leaving me sitting there, picking my way through what's left of her salad, looking for something edible and at the same time thinking, that could have gone a *hell* of a lot worse.

I've spent, like, an hour walking up and down the beachfront in Santa Monica and I can honestly say I've seen more meat on a focking Barbie doll.

Los Angeles is one of those towns that could give even me a complex – that is, *if* I hadn't kept myself in such unbelievable shape.

This isn't me being big-headed, but I *am* looking the port, it has to be said, with the sunnies and the old pink apple crumble, which shows off my pecs really well.

A bird goes by me on rollerblades and ends up nearly snotting herself while checking me out. I end up just going, 'Drink it up, Baby – it's *full* of goodness,' though it's not in a sleazy way, because she actually loves it.

I sit down on a bench for a rest because the heat over here would actually wear you out. I whip out the Wolfe and dial the number. He answers on, like, the third ring.

I'm like, 'Christian, my man!'

'Ah, Ross,' he goes, obviously really delighted to hear from me. 'How the hell are you?'

I'm there, 'Not bad, Young Skywalker,' which he loves, of course. 'Although the question should be, *where* am I? Because I just so happen to be in a little town that goes by the name of . . . *Los* Angeles?'

'No way!' he goes.

I'm there, 'Yes way! You better believe it, Dude! It's happened! Just fancied a couple of weeks away – see a bit of Honor, possibly even Sorcha . . .'

'Oh, so you're staying in the mansion?'

'Not exactly. I'm in, like, a hotel. To be fair to her, Sorcha offered? But I don't want to cause trouble between her and that tosspot of hers.'

He's there, 'Yeah, *we* stayed with them. Cillian's an alright guy, Ross.'

'But he went to, like, Oatlands.'

'I know – but even so.'

I just laugh. 'Maybe. Whatever. I'm putting him under serious pressure, though. He's bought a Lamborghini.'

'A Lamborghini? Not the kind of thing you'd expect from an accountant, is it?'

'Obvious why, though, isn't it? His girlfriend's got the love of her life back sniffing around her. He's feeling threatened. Thinks he's got to prove his manhood.'

A bird walks by in literally just a bikini – a ringer for Hayden Panettiere. She has a good look – gagging for me.

'Hey, I read what happened in Andorra,' Christian goes. 'A try against Ireland A? That must have been . . .'

'Pandemonium – that's being honest.'

'Wow.'

'It was literally the closest thing to, like, Beatlemania that

I'll ever know. They were, like, carrying me around the pitch, pretty much shoulder-high, after the final whistle.'

'Really?'

'Big-time. It'll definitely go down in history as one of those moments – what were you doing the day when blahdy blah? Like the day – what was his name? – something Kennedy was shot?'

'Did it feel weird, though? You know, conspiring against your own country?'

'Well, we were ninety-something points down at the time. I don't think Michael Bradley's going to get the road for it. Oh, by the way – *I* did?'

'What?'

'Yeah, I got sacked.'

'Why?'

'Why do you think? Trying to dip the wick where it shouldn't have been dipped. In other words, the boss's wife. Still, you live and learn. Or at least that's the general idea. So what are *you* up to – do you fancy a boozy lunch?'

'What?'

'A boozy lunch. I'm in Santa Monica. I'll tell you what, you'd have some pole on you walking around over here, wouldn't you?'

He goes, 'Ross, we're in Marin County.'

I'm there, 'Oh. What would that cost you in a cab?'

'It's, like, a five-hour drive?'

'Whoa,' I go. 'It's a massive place, isn't it?' meaning the States.

'And obviously I can't just leave Lauren . . .'

'Oh, I forgot – she's about to drop, isn't she?'

'Yeah – and she's finding the last couple of weeks pretty tough-going.'

'It's going to be some year for you,' I go. 'Baby. Then work-wise obviously . . .'

I don't know if I mentioned that he's the project manager for the new *Star Wars*-themed casino in Las Vegas.

'Yeah, Mr Lucas loved my idea to style the helipad on the landing bay in the New Death Star. And to have, like, stormtroopers and royal guards escort the highrollers to the tables . . .'

I'm there, 'Oh, it's *Mr* focking Lucas, is it?'

It's great to hear my best friend in the actual world so excited about something.

'It's only six months to go, though. And there's, like, *so* much to do.'

'I'll tell you what,' I go, 'you stay where you are. *I'll* drive up to *you* – maybe next weekend . . .'

He's there, 'Er, cool.'

'Tell you everything that's happening. I haven't lost it, just in case you're wondering. I've got a sort of date tonight with an actress. Called – of all things – Sahara. She's invited me over to watch her TV debut with her and her mates. Planning to have my sweaty way with her, I don't need to tell you. The Rossmeister will never change, that much is guaranteed.'

In the background, I can suddenly hear Lauren asking him who's on the phone. He puts his hand over the mouthpiece, but I can still hear him go, 'It's Ross. He's *in* California. He wants to come up here . . .'

I don't hear what *she* says. Lauren, it has to be said, has always been very fond of me. 'Here, put me onto her,' I go. 'I'll tell her some of the shit I've been up to since I got here.'

Christian's like, 'She's, em, just going to have a lie-down,' and I'm there, 'Oh, cool – well, I'll see her next weekend, won't I? Say, Saturday?'

Who knocked Katherine Heigl into shape, Nia wants to know – like, she *has* to know? Corey says it was Harley Pasternak

– the man is, like, a God? Then Sahara says the Five Factor Diet is supposed to be *so* amazing.

Me, I'm sitting here like Jack focking Nicholson in the *Witches of Eastwick*, wrapping the old lips around a passion-fruit daiquiri, thinking even my critics back home would have to admit, on the basis of this, that my away form is every bit as incredible as my home form.

I'm here, what, less than a week? Fock knows what that is in hours, but here I am, in an unbelievable aportment on La Cienega Boulevard, wedged between Sahara, who wants me bad, and Corey, who's a banger for Odette Yustman, while Nia – if I *had* to compare her to someone, I'd have say Holly Madison – keeps giving me the old deep meaningfuls on the down-low, obviously thinking, I'll finish anything *they* don't.

And we're watching *Grey's Anatomy*, waiting to see Sahara's big TV debut, while milling our way through a table of food.

Corey says the hummus is – oh my God – *so* amazing and Sahara says she *wants* to put more wholegrain crackers out, but she's scared of, like, missing it?

'Is it going to be soon?' I go, getting a bit bored to be honest, and she's like, 'Yeah, it's coming up in, like, two minutes.'

I'm wondering is she going to be, like, a nurse. A corpse *would* be a bit of a let-down, it has to be said, though I suppose you've *got* to think in terms of what this could, like, lead to? I mean, I'm looking at her Wolfe Tone there on the table, thinking, *imagine* the focking numbers she's already got in there. The second she hits the shitter later, I'm going through it looking for Ellen Pompeo and Chyler Leigh. *And* Heigl, obviously.

Nia is giving me loads, by the way. She's all, 'So, Eye R Lind! That must be like, Oh! *My* God!'

'You'd be surprised,' I go. 'The circles *I* move in are pretty cool – pretty much the same as here, actually. The rest of the country's basically backward.'

From her reaction, I can tell she's pretty taken aback by my, I suppose, honesty. She thinks about what I've said for a few seconds, then suddenly smiles again and goes, 'So what do you think of WeHo girls?'

Of course I end up giving her a line that'd be, like, a trademark of mine back home? I'm there, 'I know what I like – and I *like* what I see,' which goes down unbelievably well.

'I still can't believe you're *all* actresses,' I go. Corey laughs at that, then tells me that *everyone* in this town is, like, an actor, actress – whatever! 'Not all of us have got major credits,' she goes, looking, you'd have to say, pretty proud of Sahara.

I'd say they definitely *would* if I put it to them?

All of a sudden, Sahara's shushing us, going, 'Here it comes! Here it comes!' and at first, I think it has to be a mistake, roysh, because it's not *Grey's Anatomy* anymore? It's, like, a commercial break and we're suddenly sitting there watching an ad for what turns out to be – and this is going to sound disgusting – a contraceptive coil.

I'm like, 'What the fock is this?'

It's like, 'Introducing Progestin-Plus – the new, no fuss contraceptive. Progestin-Plus is easy, dependable *and* reversible . . .'

'Is *that* you,' I go, 'rollerblading?'

Sahara's like, 'No, wait.'

'Progestin-Plus guarantees maximum safety *and* more bearable periods, offering *you* greater peace of mind . . .'

'That's not you bungee-jumping, is it?'

'No. *Ssshhh!*'

'So why not talk to your physician or healthcare provider about Progestin-Plus . . .'

'And that's obviously not you talking,' I go.

Corey goes, 'Ross, that's a man's voice.'

'That's why I said it obviously *wasn't* her?'

She's like, 'Oh my God, here it comes.'

We all automatically lean forward in our chairs.

A woman's voice – the fastest I've ever heard – goes, 'Must be fitted by a qualified medical practitioner. Candidates for Progestin-Plus are in a stable relationship and have no risk or history of ectopic pregnancy or pelvic inflammatory disease. Progestin-Plus does not protect against HIV or STDs. Ovarian cysts may occur and typically disappear. Complications may occur from placement. Accidental expulsion may result in loss of contraceptive cover. Missing periods or irregular bleeding is common in the first few months, followed by shorter, lighter periods.'

When it's finished, Nia and Corey give her, like, a round of applause. I *don't*, of course, because I'm seriously pissed off. I feel like I've been brought here under, I suppose you'd have to say, *false* pretences?

Corey's like, 'Oh my God, Sahara, this is only, like, the start for you?'

'Yeah, this time next year,' I go, 'it'll be rubber johnnies – you mork my words.'

But it's like they can't even hear me.

Nia's suddenly all Tyra Banks, clicking her fingers and flicking her head, going, 'You nailed it, Girlfriend!'

Then Sahara's old pair ring to congratulate her and Sahara tells them she thought about how she was going to do it for, like, *such* a long time and in the end decided to do it in exactly the same way as she did the disclaimer for Bank of America.

'If it ain't broke . . .' Nia goes.

This continues, it has to be said, for most of the next hour, until Corey eventually stands up and announces that she has, like, bikram yoga in the morning. Nia leaves as well, presumably not wanting to be a Klingon. On her way out the door, she tells me she hopes I'm proud of Sahara and I tell her of course I am – birds who can read fast don't come along every day.

I'm not a happy bunny, it has to be said, feeling like I've been taken for a mug here. But it's amazing how quick I am to let bygones be bygones when her friends are out the door and it's just me and her alone.

Not to put too fine a point on it, I'm all over her like I'm a diabetic and her tongue's sugar-coated.

She kicks off her flip-flops and drags me down onto the corpet. I yank up her structured Roland Mouret sheath – she told me what it was and how much it cost when she heard what she *thought* was a rip – then I'm suddenly showing her one or two tricks, which, judging from the oh-my-god tally, she definitely hasn't seen before.

Now this is going to sound weird, roysh, but despite all of this, I suppose you could call it, foreplay, it's pretty focking quiet south of El Paso. Which *never* happens to me. It might have been all the talk of pelvic inflammatory disease, not to mention stable relationships, but I'm suddenly limp as the proverbial bizkit.

Sahara *is* gagging for me so, all credit to her, she's pretty understanding in the circumstances. She suggests we take it through to the bedroom and just take our time. Which works a treat, as it happens. Five minutes of rolling around in the old Thomas Lees and she's suddenly taking the Lord's name again – this time at, like, the *top* of her voice?

At some point in the proceedings – I'd like to say halfway, but then I never make promises I can't keep – Sahara's face goes all serious and she's like, 'Fuck – what was that?'

I'm there, 'I didn't hear anything,' which I actually didn't?

But then, of course, I suddenly do. A man's voice going, 'I saw the TV! Congratulations!'

She says something then that always ends up nearly stopping my hort, no matter how many times I've heard it down through the years. 'Oh my God – it's my boyfriend.'

Of course, I'm out of that bed like the mattress is on fire and my orse is catching.

I'm going, 'Boyfriend? *Boyfriend?*'

She says he's supposed to be in Napa – as if that's *any* explanation.

'You never said you'd an actual boyfriend,' I go and she's there, 'Would it have mattered?' and I'm forced to admit – to myself obviously – that it never has in the past.

I'm telling you, if getting dressed running was an Olympic sport, Jockey Shorts would be banging the door down to sponsor me. I'm throwing on my clothes while she's rubbing her temples going, 'I need to think, I need to think, I need to think . . .'

However much time that's going to take, we actually don't have it? I jump into the old Dubes, then I reef open the window and look out. We're, like, two storeys up.

'I've got an idea,' she suddenly goes and, like a fool, I wait around to hear it.

'I'm really, really sorry,' she goes. 'You're, like, a great guy? But Trevion also happens to be my agent?'

I'm actually there thinking, Trevion? How random a name is that? when, all of a sudden, Sahara switches off the light on the nightstand, sending the room into total darkness, then storts screaming.

It all happens pretty quickly after that.

The next thing I hear is these big clumpy footsteps running across the landing, while at the top of her voice she storts going, 'Trevion! Trevion! I think there's someone in the room!'

The door flies open, the main light goes on and I'm

suddenly stood there staring at this enormous dude with biceps like focking basketballs. 'Who the fuck are you?' he goes, obviously surprised to see me.

I'm like, 'Okay, I kind of *know* how this looks?'

Sahara points at the open window. 'He must have climbed in,' she goes. 'Thank God you came home! I don't know *what* he was going to do to me.'

'Whoa, whoa, whoa,' I go, then I look at Trevion. 'I know it's no consolation to you, Dude, but this was an actual legitimate pull.'

Now I know fock-all about American sports, roysh, but I'd bet ten squids to your fifty that the thing that suddenly hit me across the side of the head and sent me falling against the wall was, like, a softball bat. My ears are suddenly ringing, but they're still working well enough to hear him tell Sahara to call the cops, which is when I realize that the time for, like, polite negotiation is over. The LA focking PD, I'm thinking, I've seen some of their work on YouTube.

I turn around and look at the drop to the ground. It's got to be, like, twenty feet, maybe more. But Trevion swings the bat at me again, this time missing my head, but taking, like, a huge chunk of plaster off the wall. I hop up onto the window-sill and, without even turning to Sahara to say goodbye, I jump two storeys to the street below.

2. On the shores of Lake Ewok

She's standing at the door of my hotel suite with a box of doughnuts and that smile that I never *could* resist? 'Peace offering!' she goes, waving them at me.

Of course, I'm not even that pissed off. But I'm still like, 'You were out of order – and we're talking bang.'

I let her in.

She goes, 'It's, like, oh my God, you have no idea how much of a shock that was to my system? But I totally over-reacted and I'm sorry.'

I tell her not to sweat it – it's LL Cool J.

'I've been trying to get her on her mobile,' she goes, as in Erika, 'but it's going straight to her voicemail.'

I'm there, 'I'd, er, leave her if I were you. I was talking to her – as in, yesterday? She said she doesn't want to talk to anyone. She mentioned needing space.'

'But she couldn't be including me in that. I'm, like, her Best Best Friend.'

'She said everyone.'

'But did she name me specifically?'

I just nod, which I suppose still counts as a lie. It's just I know that if the two of them get talking, *she'll* be on the next plane over and the next thing they'll be doing the whole sisters-in-law routine. I need time to get my head around this shit first.

I change the subject, tell her she looks well. She looks down and tells me it's a Brette Sandler sheer tunic and that *everyone's* going to be wearing them this year. And underneath she mentions that she's wearing an Ashley Paige bikini. I tell her I wouldn't mind checking it out, to see is it suitable for an establishment like this, and she laughs and tells me I'm *actually* dreaming.

'Anyway, get dressed,' she eventually goes, 'I'm taking you out for the day —*my* way of saying sorry.'

I grab a quick Jack Bauer, then we're suddenly on the freeway on the way to wherever it is we're going. We're in *his* old cor – the focking Prius – so I'm just sitting back, watching the sights. In the next lane, this – if I'm being honest – Alessandra Ambrosio lookalike in a Mercedes SLK Luxury Roadster gives me the serious once-over and from the look on her face, she's impressed.

'So,' Sorcha suddenly goes, possibly copping it, 'how was your date last night?' at the same time trying not to sound *too* interested.

I'm there, 'Not bad – I've *had* worse,' and she smiles and goes, 'Worse than a belt across the side of the head?'

She misses fock-all, in fairness to her. I touch my left temple. He could have killed me, the focking lunatic. She gives my hand a squeeze, to tell me she's only ripping the piss, and of course I end up *having* to laugh?

'So come on,' she goes then. 'Erika – tell me the story.'

I'm there, 'Not a huge amount to tell. Turns out my old man and her old dear were, like, childhood sweethorts . . .'

'Helen and Charles – oh my God, that's, like, *so* random.'

'Big-time. It's, like, who knows *what* the fock she saw in him.'

We end up stopped at lights. She goes, 'Your parents have had, like, *such* fascinating lives, haven't they?'

I'm there, 'Depends what you consider fascinating.'

'Like, I knew your mum was engaged before? Then that broke up and, well, she's told me loads about her Paris years. You know she had an affair with a bullfighter?'

'Yeah – and she ended up marrying a bullshitter.'

I'm actually pretty pleased with that.

She's there, 'Your dad, though – even though I've always got on, oh my God, *so* amazingly with him, he's still a bit of a mystery to me.'

'There's no mystery,' I go. 'Him and Helen were, like, boyfriend-girlfriend in, I don't know, the olden days, whatever you want to call them. She went to live in the States – probably to get away from him. Years later – as in *after* he married my old dear? – she came back and they ended up having a fling . . .'

'Oh! My God!'

'I know. Focking seedy. He's not exactly the Mr Nice Goy he cracks *on* to be? I've been saying that for years.'

'You know,' Sorcha goes, sort of, like, looking at me sideways, 'I can actually see the likeness between you and Erika now,' which I suppose – looks-wise –*is* a compliment.

The lights turn green again. I still can't believe I'm sitting in a Prius.

'How's *Cillian*?' I go, deliberately trying to make his name sound ridiculous. 'Are you letting him keep the Lamborghini?'

She doesn't answer. She just goes, 'He came home *so* drunk last night.'

I'm there, 'Drunk? The last I knew, he was a gin and tonic man – if you could call someone who drinks gin and tonic a man.'

'Well, last night it was beer. He went out with Josh and Kyle.'

'Who?'

'They're friends of his – they work in, like, Collateral Debt Obligations?'

'How has he got friends over here already?'

She's like, 'Well, they're both *from* California? But Josh went to the Smurfit School of Business,' which is where Cillian went. 'And Kyle is Josh's best friend.'

I actually laugh. 'Sad,' I go. 'So, what, he went out and got mullered? Who's he trying to be – me?'

'That's what I said to him. I said I've already had one unhappy marriage, Cillian – I don't *want* another one?' which I have to say hurts, although I don't let her know that.

Her BlackBerry beeps. She's like, 'Will you be an absolute sweethort and read that for me? It might be important.'

As it happens, it is.

'Cameron Diaz is reportedly angry with Jessica Biel for turning up at the Sundance Film Festival with Justin Timberlake,' I go, 'then going sunboarding with her former beau . . .'

'Oh! My God!'

'And Halle Berry wore a satin Monique Lhuillier dress with peacock feathers along with Terry de Havilland strappy sandals and glittery Chopard diamonds to some movie premiere.'

She repeats every word of this carefully, like she's memorizing it, then she nods, like she approves.

When Sorcha said she was taking me out for the day to apologize, what she meant was she was taking me to Kitson, the boutique on Robertson Bouvelard where she's already got – oh my God – *so* many ideas for her own shop.

So suddenly, roysh, instead of wrapping my face around a plate of wings and a couple of JDs, I'm standing there watching Sorcha go at the racks like a lion picking a wildebeest clean, my orms filling up with clothes that she's planning to try on.

'Robertson is *the* place to be,' she's going. 'That's why they're all here, Ross – Kitson, Curve, Lisa Kline. Because they know all the celebrities hang out here. Having Katie or

Halle or Reese photographed walking into your shop in, like, a supermarket tabloid is better than a two-page ad in *Vogue*. I read that in the *LA Times*. All the shops on this street, they're not so much retail outlets as, like, shrines to the major brands. That's why rents have gone up, like, five hundred per cent . . .'

A dude who works in the shop walks by and, at the top of his voice, goes, 'Whoa – you're working *three* summer trends there, girl! Baby blue, ruffles *and* a maxidress,' and Sorcha turns to me with a look of, like, awe on her face and says *that's* the kind of thing she wants to be able to say to customers.

'You want I start a room for you?'

She's like, 'That'd be amazing.'

Anyway, where all this is going is, I end up sitting in the little sofa area, flicking through magazines, looking at photographs of Faye Dunaway and thinking what a total and utter GILF she is, in fairness to her. The dude who's been helping Sorcha in the changing rooms wanders over and sits basically down beside me. 'Can I ask you,' he goes, totally out of the blue, 'are you, like, a footballer?'

I laugh.

'Near enough,' I go. 'I'm, like, a rugby player?'

I don't say *former* because that's the beauty of LA – you can be whoever you want?

'Rugby?' he goes.

I'm still trying to get my head around the fact that no one's heard of me over here.

'It's *like* American football?' I go. 'Except *we* don't go in for all the padding. Where I come from, that'd be considered majorly wussy.'

'So where *are* you from?'

He's actually a really nice goy.

'A place called Ireland?'

'Oyer Lund! Oh, that accent! So, this is, like, a personal question?' he goes, obviously checking out my biceps. 'But what do you bench-press?'

I'm there, 'I could tell you, but it'd probably make you sick.'

He seems pretty impressed by that, it has to be said. Which is nice because he's obviously in pretty good shape himself. He's there, 'So are you in, like, a gym?'

I'm there, 'Not over here. I *was* thinking of looking for one, though.'

'Oh! My God!' he goes. 'I am in *the* most amazing gym. You want to check it out sometime?'

I'm there, 'Dude, I'd love that,' because, like I said, roysh, he's pretty sound.

'Great. You want, we could get, like, a coffee later? I could show you my workout journal? I'm kind of a part-time personal trainer. I could give you some tips on your fitness goals.'

'Coola boola – that's what we say for, like, cool.'

'Okay, here's, like, my card? I finish at six? My name's Harvey?'

I'm there, 'Ross,' and we shake hands, which feels kind of weird? But I tell him I'll bell him later and I think nothing more of it.

Sorcha decides she wants none of the three hundred and seventy-five pieces of clothing she took into the changing room, though I notice that Harvey doesn't give her the filthies that *she* usually gives to customers who try on loads and buy fock-all.

On the way out the door, she tells me that she has, like, a treat for me. She's booked lunch for us at The Ivy.

So we tip over the road. I order the mesquite-grilled Cajun prime rib, she orders the lime shrimp salad, and we end up sitting there, eating and just shooting the shit. The place is, like, full of celebs and every so often, roysh, Sorcha will go, 'Peri Gilpin, six o'clock,' or 'Paul Sculfor, immediately behind you,' then tell me how she would – oh my God – *so* love to be famous herself.

She asks me how I'm liking LA and I tell her I'm actually loving it. I might even stay a few months. She tells me she loves the way they say, 'Those are lovely items,' when they're folding your shit and sticking it in the bag. She says she must remember to call things items. And the way they call you by your name when they're processing your credit cord. And the way they present you your receipt in a little cardboard folder with a chocolate – *always* fairtrade cocoa, by the way. 'It's, like, the customer over here is God?'

I tell her I thought that goy in that shop was really cool. 'Had a great chat with him,' I go. 'Seems big into his sport. I'm actually meeting him for a coffee later.'

'The guy in the shop?' she suddenly goes.

I'm like, 'Yeah.'

'The guy with the really good tan and the tight T-shirt?' 'Yeah.'

'And the BlackBerry like mine, except white?'

'Yeah, he's going to take me to this gym he goes to.'

She's there, 'After you have a coffee?' with a big smile on her boat.

I'm like, 'Yeah – what's the biggie, Babes?'

'What's the biggie? Ross, you're going on a date.'

'What?'

'You've agreed to go on a date with this guy.'

I'm there, 'It's hordly a date. It's, like, a mate thing – like I said, he's pretty keen to show me this gym of his. *And* his workout journal. But that's all there is to it.'

'Well, I wonder does he see it like that. It sounds to me like he was hitting on you.'

'Hitting on me? Do you think he's even . . . you know?'

'Are you honestly telling me you couldn't tell?'

'Well, no.'

'Ross, he wasn't even manbiguous. He was, like, *so* gay. Not that I've got a problem with that – as you *well* know, I've got, oh my God, loads of gay friends. Or I did in UCD.'

'Shit.'

'Ross, you've got to go and tell him.'

'Tell him what?'

'Tell him that he got the wrong end of the stick.'

I'm there, 'Nah, I just won't bother my orse ringing him – the usual.'

'Ross,' she goes, 'you will *not* do the usual. I don't want to be ashamed to go in there – it happens to be a shop I go into practically twice a week.'

'Sorcha, please do *not* make me do this.'

'You led this guy on . . .'

'I didn't lead him on!'

'Well, you must have done something for him to think you were interested.'

I'm there, 'It was you, with all your, *I have a Tracy Reese just like that one – but it's one of those dresses that has, like, hanger appeal . . .*'

'Ross!'

'*Anyone can pull off a silk Miu Miu – you just have to be confident in the way you accessorize* . . . He must have thought we were just friends.'

'We *are* just friends.'

'You know what I mean. He thought I was your gay friend.'

'For once in your life,' she goes, 'do the gentlemanly thing. Quick, before your apple transparent arrives.'

I don't believe it – she actually guilts me into it. I end up having to get up, roysh, and tip back across the road to the shop.

Harvey's down the back, checking himself out in the mirror and sort of, like, dancing – pretty well as it happens – to the Sound Bluntz version of 'Billie Jean'.

I suppose once you know, you stort to *see* the little signs?

This isn't me being big-headed, but his face lights up when he sees me. This is, like, a totally new experience for me – as in letting someone down gently. 'Okay, I just want to check,' I go. 'Are you – okay, I'm going to have to say the word – gay?'

He laughs.

'Ross,' he goes, really, I suppose, camping up his voice for my benefit, 'I'm as gay as *Mulholland Drive*!'

I'm there, 'So that's a yes, then. Okay, second question – you don't think that was, like, a date we arranged to go on, do you?'

I think I might have hurt his feelings. 'It was coffee,' he goes, shrugging his shoulders. 'What's the big deal?'

He's *not* actually hurt? He's taking it unbelievably well, in fairness to him.

'Because it's probably only fair to point out,' I go, 'that *I'm* actually straight?'

'You're straight?'

'Famously – believe me.'

'Okay, well, that's a surprise . . .'

'I don't know why it's a surprise,' I go. 'Was it because I was in here shopping with a bird?'

'It was lot of things?' he goes. 'I mean, you dress well.'

'Guilty.'

'You clearly look after your body.'

'Guilty again.'

'And your hair.'

'Three guilties – that's Blockbusters.'

He's there, 'My gaydar is usually pretty accurate. It's the first time I've ever been wrong.'

'Well, thank fock for that. No offence – that's what a lot of birds back home will be thinking . . .'

He goes, 'You're straight – but you're not narrow, right?'

I'm there, 'As in . . .'

'Well, you're not narrow-minded?' he goes.

I'm there, 'Of course I'm not.'

'So there's no big deal in us hanging out, right?'

One or two people in the shop are looking at us, listening in, including a bird who's a ringer for Ana Ivanović, which is why the conversation ends up turning weird. 'Er, exactly,' I go.

'It's just two guys getting a coffee, right?'

'I'm cool with that.'

'Are you sure?'

'You better believe I'm sure. We're going to *get* that coffee.'

'That'd be nice.'

'It's happening.'

'Good.'

'I've got your cord.'

'That's good too.'

'I'm going to put it in my wallet.'

'Okay.'

'You can count on it.'

'I will.'

'And I'll ring you. It'll be out of the blue. Bang! Coffee – tonight, tomorrow, whatever. I love my coffee.'

'Me too.'

'Be ready, then.'

'I'll look forward to it. *Have* a nice day.'

I hold my hand up.

'Oh, we're *high-fiving* now,' he goes, like he's never actually *done* it before?

So we high-five and I go, 'A focking coffee it is, then!'

Then I tip back over to Sorcha. My apple transparent has arrived and I tuck straight in. She asks me how it went and I tell her unbelievably well. 'I should be used to it by now,' I go, 'being desired by people in general. It's like, why should it *just* be women?'

'And you let him down easy?' she goes.

It's hord to talk with, like, a mouthful of apple. I'm there, 'We're still probably going to get a coffee. It's just he knows now that nothing's going to happen in the other deportment.'

Her face lights up like a pimped-up Hummer. 'Oh my God, Ross – you've got a bromance.'

I'm like, 'A what?'

She's there, 'A bromance! Like Brad and George! Like Ben and Matt! Ross has a bromance! Oh! My God!'

I'm like, '*What*ever,' but at the same time *I'm* even laughing.

Then she's suddenly serious. She digs her nails into my orm and goes, 'Kevin Sorbo – two tables over.'

My phone rings and of course I make the mistake of answering it. Of all people, it's Erika – crying, by the sounds of her.

'Ross,' she goes.

Bear in mind, roysh, that this girl has never been nice to me before. This thing has really taken her down a peg or two.

'What do *you* want?' I go.

She's there, 'I ended up having a huge row with my mum.'

I'm like, 'So I heard.'

'I called her a . . . Well, it doesn't matter what I called her. I'm staying in the Merrion.'

I actually nearly laugh. With most people, it'd be a mate's sofa. Or even the floor. With her, it has to be the Merrion. I'd say they'll be seeing a lot of her in Guilbaud's, crying into her, whatever, Cévennes onion and almond soup.

'Dad said you're in Los Angeles,' she goes.

Dad? He's *Dad* already?

I'm there, 'Yeah, what about it?'

She's like, 'Nothing,' but it's obvious, roysh, that she's looking for an invite. She asks me if I've told Sorcha yet and I tell her yeah.

'She left me one or two voice messages,' she goes. 'I wondered should I . . .'

'Do *not* ring her back,' I quickly go. 'And I'm saying that for your sake.'

'My sake? Why?'

'She's seriously pissed off with you. Yeah, in fact, she said your friendship was basically over.'

She's quiet for what seems like ages. 'But, Ross,' she goes, 'none of this is *my* fault.'

'Look, that's women for you,' I go. 'They don't need an excuse to do the shit they do. You should know that as well as anyone.'

'Maybe if I went over there . . .'

I'm like, 'Don't even think about it.'

She's there, 'I need to see you, Ross.'

I'm like, 'Why? Why do you need to see me?'

She goes, 'Because you're my brother. We need to, I don't know, get to know each other.'

She's had half her life to do that, but she was never interested. I'm there, 'Erika, I've got to go.'

Oh my God, *isn't* arugula great?

It's when I hear lines like that that I wonder will Sorcha

even *come* home. It's, like, everything she's ever wanted is here – as in the life she always dreamed of?

We're all sitting around the pool at the back of her big fock-off mansion and I'm looking at her, holding her basil punica with extra pomegranate syrup, laughing so hord at something Analyn said that her lips can't find the straw. She's got a tan, white teeth, even collarbones, which she always said were, oh my God, *impossible* for a girl to have in a country like Ireland.

And all these new friends. There's, like I said, Analyn and her also portner Mike – *she's* our age, *he's* at least fifty, maybe more, and he's just left his wife after twenty-two years and is having fertility treatment. There's Jenny, who's, like, Chinese – or *one* of those – an auctioneer whose specialty is Song and Yuan period Chinese porcelain. Her two kids are Poet, who's nearly three, and Tsunami, who's nearly two. There's Elodine and Steve, who've just given up their jobs to pursue their lifetime dream of running their own organic restaurant and whose daughter, Jagger, is playing with Honor in the little paddling pool. And there's Emmy, who works in Fred Segal but wants to get into acting – yeah, I'm sensing a pattern in this town – and who's got great tennis orms, like she could have *actually* gone to Loreto Foxrock.

They're all cool and what I really, really like about them is that they're interested in *me*. I mean, yeah, they're also talking about the evils of transfats, how much they all love Dave Eggers and how for-profit medicine is detroying the fabric of our society, but they're also asking me, you know, how I'm loving the States, then a bit about my rugby.

Mike says that Andorra sounds like a real case of David against Goliath, which is a story from, like, the Bible, and I probably don't need to tell you that Cillian is bulling about all this attention I'm getting. He's got his two mates there as well – the dudes that Sorcha was banging on about – as in, Josh and Kyle, who're basically just two random jocks. Kyle, who's supposed to have been a pretty good American footballer in college, is suddenly talking to Steve and Mike, explaining how Mortgage Company A can turn its income stream from its loans business into a lump sum by selling the rights to that cash flow to a Special Purpose Vehicle, which then places the money into trust. The trust then pays for the right to the mortgages by issuing bonds that receive the cash flow from the assets minus administrative costs.

Of course, I might as well be listening to Honor speaking Chinese or Spanish.

Josh, who all the birds think is a ringer for Ian Ziering – in other words, a grinning, blond idiot – says that you can increase your profits by slicing and dicing these asset-backed securities into tranches, which is what CDOs basically are.

Steve asks what kind of profits are we talking and Kyle says if he's interested, they should maybe meet up and he hands him his business cord. Mike asks if they're triple-A rated and Josh says yeah and Mike says his job must still be pretty stressful and Kyle holds up his can and says he always needs a few of these by the end of the week.

'Work hard, play hard,' he goes, then he turns around and high-fives Josh, and of course then Cillian has to get in on the act as well. I never saw him once high-five anyone in Ireland – it's just not the auditor way – and I suddenly realize that who he's trying to copy isn't me at all, it's these two tosspots.

'Cillian, I see you've storted to drink beer,' is all I go. 'A man's drink,' which he decides to ignore.

Elodine tells Sorcha that she brought her that Jubi catalogue and Sorcha says yeah, she's been wondering whether

Honor's crankiness lately is, like, an allergy thing? I tell her it's probably just, like, the terrible twos – even though she's not two yet – but then Elodine says that Jubi make towels and toddler robes using, like, water-based bleaches and safe dyes, which Sorcha seems to like the sound of more.

The conversation moves somehow onto, like, furniture and how amazing Crate and Barrel is, then Steve says that even though he really loves Crate and Barrel, there's no shame in Ikea and Elodine laughs and goes, 'We're beginning to sound like one of those – what do you call them? – dual income, zero orgasm couples you read about in *The New Yorker*!'

'Going back to the whole allergy thing,' Jenny goes, 'I want to get Poet and Tsunami a dog, but it's, like, *so* hard to find a good hypoallergenic breed. I thought maybe, like, a bichon frisé?'

Mike goes, 'Jed, my eldest son from my first marriage, we bought, like, a labrador for him? But his dander set off Jeff's allergic rhinitis. Our physician, who'd been our physician for years, suggested we try a soft-coated wheaten terrier. We did. Never! Had! A problem! They're a beautiful dog. And just great with kids . . .'

Emmy asks Elodine then how the restaurant plans are coming along and Elodine says that they're hoping to be open by, like, March, or April at the latest.

Then Steve goes, 'Hey, speaking of restaurants, has anyone got reservations yet for the Blue Orchid on Wilshire?' He says we've got to try this place, then Elodine says that you know you're in a good ethnic restaurant when there are, like, no white people in there, which at first I think might be racist, roysh, but then, when I see Jenny nodding, I realize isn't?

Steve's there, 'Their black pepper squid has to be tasted to be believed.'

'What about you, Ross?' Mike goes, again, including me in things. 'Do you cook?'

'Me?' I go. 'Sorcha will tell you, I use the smoke alarm as a timer,' and it would not be an exaggeration to say that everyone there just cracks their holes laughing. I'm thinking, it's weird, roysh, I'm actually even funnier over here than I am at home.

But Cillian has to, like, steal the attention back, of course. He's all, 'Hey, Steve, I met that personal shopper you recommended at Brooks Brothers,' with one eye on me and Steve's like, 'I hope he gave you the discount,' and Cillian's there, 'He looked after me – don't you worry,' and you'd swear the focker was actually from LA instead of, like, Cabinteely.

The next thing, roysh, we hear all this screaming. It's Jagger, basically bawling her eyes out. It turns out that Honor turned around, totally out of the blue, and pulled her hair, then belted her across the face. Honor's totally lost it, screaming like a mad thing. Cillian's about to go over to her, but I'm out of that chair like you wouldn't believe, thinking, er, *I'm* her father? You just happen to be the dude who moved in on her mother, getting her at a weak moment, Pricewaterhouse-who-gives-a-fock!

I pick her up in my orms, even though she's, like, soaking wet, and I'm, like, bouncing her up and down, making shite talk, the usual things you do with kids to try to calm them down.

'That's exactly what she's like,' Sorcha goes to Elodine. 'One minute she's fine, then she's, like, zero to possessed in, like, thirty seconds . . .'

'Are you using time-outs?' Analyn goes.

Sorcha's like, 'No, Cillian and I discussed it? But we decided against it.'

Cillian makes sure to have a good look at me, pretty much begging to be decked.

'I was going to say,' Analyn goes, 'most of the nurturing books that Mike and I have been reading think it's *not* a good idea. It's like, what if it doesn't work? What is your next option? A monster time-out?'

Sorcha's there, 'No, we've chosen the route of rewarding her with strong praise when she does the right thing, so as to positively reinforce good behaviour. But it's *so* difficult because my instinct right now is to tell her that what she did was very naughty.'

'You can't go using negatives,' Analyn goes, and even Steve and Elodine nod like they agree.

Sorcha's going, 'Honor, can you say, "*Lo siento*, Jagger. *Lo siento*,"' but Honor's still screaming and wriggling in my orms like a landed fish, so I tell Sorcha that I'm going to take her for a walk.

I bring her into the kitchen and have a mooch around. It's like the Storship focking Enterprise in there, she's got that many gadgets.

'Is this it?' I'm thinking.

It's not. It's a panini press.

'What about this?'

No, it's a waffle-maker.

'This must be it.'

Yes, it is. The De'Longhi Magnifica Cappuccino Maker – just the focking job. Honor immediately calms down when she sees it. It's like I've just produced a breast.

I'm going, 'Can you say "Daddy"? Can you say "Daddy", Honor?' but it's obvious that all she can think about is the coffee that's coming.

The machine turns out to be pretty simple to work. I grab one of the little espresso cups and I'm about to hit the button for a small one when I suddenly think, fock it, and I pour her a double instead. I blow on it to, like, cool it, because you have to be careful with kids, then, after looking over both shoulders, I put it up to her lips.

She honestly can't get it into her quick enough.

I grab a piece of kitchen roll, run it under the tap and wipe the little bit she spilled down the side of her mouth. Then I bring her back outside.

Would you believe me if I told you that the first words she says when we go outside are *Lo siento*?

Well, if you could see the reaction. Let's just say the words miracle and worker are bandied about like there's no *actual* tomorrow?

They're all mad, of course, to find out my secret and there's me – Patch focking Adams – going, 'I've *always* had a way with women,' which they all laugh at, even though it *is* actually true.

Cillian has to try and steal the limelight again, bringing up the whole subprime-mortgage-whatever-the-fock, basically showing off what he knows. He's all, 'You can criticize the lowering of lending criteria all you like. The fact is that without offering cheap money to lower-income families, the housing market – and obviously the building industry – would have stagnated,' and it's, like, who *gives* a fock?

After, like, an hour or so, people stort to drift off, making their excuses. Jenny says she's sorry to be such a loser face, but she has global dance aerobics at eight. Barneys – finally! – have the Lulu Guinness 1950s-style pleated tote that Emmy ordered, like, *forever* ago? And Steve and Elodine are spending the weekend in Dry Creek Valley, which is absolutely, *one hunnered* per cent, undiscovered Cabernet country.

But Steve also says that it was a real pleasure to meet me and

Mike says it was great talking to someone who understands sports and maybe we should take in a game while I'm here and Emmy says it was great to finally meet me and she hopes to see me again, which is all good.

So it's, like, major fan worship.

Cillian's mates barely even grunt at me, although it's not like I *give* a fock.

As they're saying goodbye, Sorcha tells Elodine and Analyn that she loves them, then they say it back, like they do in *The Hills*, although I think it's weird, roysh, because they've only known each other, like, a few weeks.

I'm thinking maybe I should hit the bricks as well, but Sorcha tells me I should stay a while, have another strawberry vice. Cillian has, like, work to do and it'll be nice to have a bit of company after she puts Honor down.

That, as it happens, takes, like, an hour and I'm thinking a single shot of espresso probably would have done her, especially that close to bedtime.

Sorcha eventually arrives back down and I can't help but notice that she's changed into something skimpier, which turns out to be an Ed Hardy tattoo-print bikini, which she's wearing with Girls Two Doors Down flip-flops, the exact same ones, Sorcha says, that Jessica Alba was wearing two weeks ago while shopping in Whole Foods on North Crescent.

'*You* were a big hit,' she goes, sucking a cherry on the end of a cocktail umbrella in a way that's really doing it for me. 'Especially with Emmy.'

I'm like, 'Emmy?'

'Puh-lease, Ross! She couldn't take her eyes off you.'

I'm there, 'And that bothers you?' playing it cool like Huggy.

'No,' she goes, obviously not wanting to give me the

pleasure. 'You're a free agent. She's actually a really, really nice girl. Be careful, though. I wouldn't trust her as far as I could throw her.'

'I'll, er, bear that in mind.'

'And tote bags? Hello? Oh my God, they went out with, like, Rachel Zoe. Tiny clutches are going to be in this year. Although, having said that, I'd always bring my Saskia leather tote if I was going to, like, an interview?'

I ask her if she fancies getting into the pool and she says yeah.

Of course, I famously can't swim, but Sorcha, in fairness, stays down the shallow end *with* me? She does, like, one or two widths, then stops and tells me I was amazing with Honor earlier. 'I think that *is* why she's finding it so difficult to settle at night,' she goes. 'Now that you're here, she just wants to be around you – oh my God – every waking minute.'

I'm there, 'I feel the same.'

She stares into the distance and says she never believed the human spirit was capable of loving the way she loves Honor and I'm thinking how much I love it when she says shit like that, even though I'm always meaning to make it my Google Mission later to find out is she getting her lines from, like, *Gilmore Girls* or one of those.

She looks unbelievable in the blue light thrown by the little spots along the side of the pool and I can see her nipples through the cotton of her bikini top.

I ask her how Cillian feels about us being out here alone. She doesn't answer, but there's, like, the tiniest hint of a smile on her lips, which I don't *think* I'm imagining?

'Cillian's actually a really, really nice guy,' she eventually goes. 'And he's good to me, which I *thought* you'd be pleased about.'

I'm there, 'I am. But why does he have to be so, I don't know, full of it? Full of talk. All that subprime mortgage ask-my-hole. I mean, it's not going to affect our lives, is it?'

She's like, 'Of course it isn't.'

I'm there, 'So why was he banging on about it, then?'

'I don't know,' she goes. 'You're suddenly over here and maybe you're right, maybe he does feel threatened by you. I've tried telling him that you're no threat.'

'Aren't I, though?'

'No. It's like I told Cillian – you and I have this amazing connection, even though it's just, like, friendship?'

I'm thinking, yeah? Well, *I've* a pole on me here you could hang a stars-and-stripes from.

'I just think you need to, like, bond,' she goes. 'Maybe if you went out together . . .'

'Er, no thanks.'

'What about tomorrow? He goes out every Saturday night with Josh and Kyle. Usually to, like, Big Wangs – you know, where Whitney had her first date with Jarett in Series Three?'

'You're pulling the piss! Josh and Kyle?'

'They're actual nice guys,' she goes. 'Anyway, it's not about them. This is about you and Cillian getting to know each other, which – if you're both going to be in my life – is something I would like to see happen.'

I get the impression that she's secretly loving playing us off each other.

I'm there, 'Anyway, I'm driving up to see Christian tomorrow.'

'Well, just agree *one* Saturday – if I mention it to him.'

I just, like, shrug my shoulders, not commiting myself either way.

'Hey,' I suddenly go, 'let's do the swan dive from *Dirty Dancing.*'

She's there, 'No!' going suddenly all shy on me.

I'm there, 'Come on!'

'No,' she goes, 'because we always end up nearly drowning,' which is true. It's happened a few times, roysh, that I've tried to hold her above my head, but the momentum of her jump always sent us both toppling into the water. Happened in Bali. Happened in Brook Lodge. Happened in practically every pool we've ever been in. In fairness, she'd a lot more weight on her in those days, probably because she was on the Jack and Jill, and I actually fancy my chances of being able to hold her now.

'Come on,' I go, 'Swayze and Gray — let's see can we rework that old magic.'

So she suddenly storts walking backwards in the water, smiling and shaking her head, like she can't believe she's *actually* about to do this.

I give her the line. 'Nobody puts Baby in the corner,' and she sort of, like, clenches her face, like a true Mountie about to take on *any* job. She runs through the water towards me and I'm sort of, like, studying her body, in much the same way that you weigh up the speed and trajectory of a pass in rugby before you receive it.

I reach out, roysh, and I grab her by the hips, just as she jumps into the air and my hands follow her upwards as she spreads her orms and it's immediately obvious that I've got the centre of gravity absolutely bang-on and I'm suddenly holding her above my head, her body, like, frozen in a perfect swan dive, so perfect, in fact, that it's a good ten seconds before she can even say anything.

'Oh my God! Oh my God! Oh my God!' she eventually goes, like we're having actual sex.

Then the next thing I hear is this, like, applause coming from up above us. I look up and I cop Cillian, out on the balcony, clapping – except, like, sarcastically?

'Very good!' he's just going. '*Very* good!'

It's arrived – the jukebox, the pool table, everything – and I've honestly *never* heard Ronan happier.

'You'd want to fooken see me,' he's going. 'I'm in the jacuzzi, with a doorty big cigar, watching *Scarface* on the plasma. What do you think of that?'

I'm like, 'Well, firstly, you shouldn't be smoking. Because a) it's bad for you and b) you're ten. And secondly, how the fock have you got signal down there?'

'Buckets of Blood put up a transmitter,' he goes. 'He's after doing all sorts, Rosser. I think he's really going to make a go of this going-straight lark. He did all the plumbing, electrics, surround-sound, the fooken lot. Here, he's even putting a ramp in – make it wheelchair-accessible for Bla.'

In other words Blathin, Ronan's girlfriend.

'He's after making shit of your ma's garden but.'

I laugh. 'I wouldn't worry about it, Ro. She's over here making a focking disgrace of the family name.'

'What's the story with your voice?' he goes.

I'm like 'Yeah, I'm using one of these hands-free speaker-phone jobs. I'm heading up to a place called Nicasio – here, I wouldn't have believed there's actual countryside in the States.'

'Mad.'

'I know. I'm heading up to see Christian and Lauren.'

'Here, when's he's casino opening?'

I'm there, 'We're talking, like, June, July? I can't wait for it as well.'

'Oh,' he goes, 'are you staying in America that long?'

He sounds disappointed, which is actually really nice to hear.

'I was *going* to,' I go. 'I can head back sooner if you want.'

'No, no,' he goes, suddenly playing the tough man. 'You've a lot of catching up to do over there – you're moostard.'

But then I'm suddenly thinking about *my* old man and how he basically never had time for me and I find myself going, 'I'll tell you what, Ro – how do you fancy coming over to Vegas for, like, Christian's opening night?'

He's there, 'Are you serious?'

'*As* a hort attack,' I go. 'What do you think?'

Now, I can't tell you how unbelievable it feels, roysh, to be bombing along some random Californian freeway in a big fock-off BMW 650 convertible, top down, sunnies on, wind in my hair, with my son on the phone telling me that I'm practically the best father who ever lived.

But – not for the first time in my life – what seems like *the* perfect moment is interrupted by the sound of a police siren.

There's suddenly a speedy in my rearview, signalling for me to pull over. Which I do. Because you're supposed to.

I'm like, 'Ro, hang just on a sec . . .'

The cop takes his time getting off his bike, just to make me sweat.

'Who is it?' Ronan goes.

I don't answer.

He approaches the cor from the passenger side. He takes off, like, his helmet. He doesn't look like the kind of dude who'd take shit from anyone, not like the cops at home.

'Sir,' he goes, 'let me see your licence and registration,' and I'm there, 'Fair enough,' deciding to play it straight. I open the dash and stort fluting around, looking for them.

'Who *is* it?' Ronan goes again.

'It's, em, a cop,' I go, looking at the dude as if to say, basically, sorry. I find my driving licence tucked into the rental agreement.

'Tell him to fook off, Rosser,' Ronan goes.

I watch the dude stare at the speaker, his eyes going wide.

'That's my, er, kid,' I go. 'He's a bit . . .' and I tap the side of my head with my finger.

I hand him all the shit. He studies the licence for what seems like ages. 'This you?' he eventually goes.

I'm suddenly shitting it. I tell him it is.

'JP Conroy?'

I'm there, 'The one and only!' but I can feel my hort *actually* quicken? You can do jail time for carrying fake ID over here.

'Smell the fooken bacon from here, I can,' Ronan goes.

I'm there, 'Ro, you're not exactly helping me here.'

The cop stares at me, then at the photograph, then at me again. 'Your nose doesn't match,' he goes.

I'm like, 'What?'

He's there, 'Your nose is, well, pretty enormous. But in the picture . . .'

'I actually broke it,' I end up having to tell him. 'Playing a certain game called rugby.'

'And you're from out of town?' the cop goes.

I'm there, 'Yeah – as in, Ireland?'

Which doesn't seem to impress him. I don't know why I thought it would.

'Let me see your international driving licence.'

I know straight away where that is – tucked into the inside of the sun visor. I hand it to him.

'I can't believe you're taking shit from him,' Ronan goes. 'A.C.A.B., Rosser. A.C.A.B.'

The cop stares at the speaker again for, like, ten seconds, maybe more, then he finally looks at the licence.

'Why does he call you Rosser?' he eventually goes and I end up nearly shitting myself.

'It's, em, a nickname,' I go.

'How does he get Rosser from JP Conroy?'

I can't even look the dude in the eye. It's, like, somehow he *knows*?

'It's, like, Gaelic?' I finally go. 'As in, the language? It's Gaelic for, em, Legend.'

He stares at me for, like, ages, then eventually hands me everything back.

'Well, *Legend* – you keep to the speed limit in future and you and your boy there will be hearing a lot less from us, you understand?'

I'm there, 'I do. I will. I swear.'

He gives me another long look, then walks back to his bike.

I sit there for, like, five minutes after he's gone, still trying to, like, compose myself.

'You were fooken bricking it,' Ronan goes. '*It's, like, Gaelic for, like, Legend?* Man, you wouldn't last pissing time in Pelican Bay.'

'Okay, young padwan,' Christian goes, 'you are now one of the priviliged few who can say they've set foot *inside* Skywalker Ranch . . .'

I'm a bit *whatever* about the whole thing, but I play along, roysh, so as not to hurt the focker's feelings.

'None of this is open to the public,' he goes. 'For *Star Wars* fans, this is *our* Area 51.'

I pull another interested face – I'd do it all day long for this dude – that's how much he means to me.

The next thing, roysh, he's handing me a piece of paper, which I take from him with all the, I suppose, wariness of a man who's been served injunctions ordering him to stay away from four debses.

'What the fock is this?' I go, after giving it the quick left to right.

He's there, 'It's a confidentiality agreement.'

'A confidentiality agreement? Er, saying *what* exactly?'

'Come on, Ross,' he goes, 'it's standard.'

I'm there, 'Not between goys who've been best friends since they were basically twelve.'

'It's just saying you won't reveal any secrets you might hear here today.'

'Dude, I'd be seriously hord-up for conversation if all I had to talk to people about was focking *Star Wars* . . .'

He looks around, obviously embarrassed by my voice echoing through the big entrance hall.

'Anyway,' I go, 'whatever happened to honour among Rock boys?'

He looks downwards, like even *he* can't believe what he's about to say. 'It's, er, not recognized over here.'

I *actually* lose it then. 'It's recognized *everywhere*!' I go. 'All over this focking planet, which we call basically Earth. Can I *remind* you of a certain story that Father Fehily used to tell us?'

'There's no need.'

'About being in, I don't know, Botswana or one of those? About being out in the bush and meeting this little pygmy dude?'

'Ross . . .'

'He asked Fehily where he was from and Fehily said a place called Dublin. The little focker had never heard of it. So he said it was in a country called basically Ireland. Again, he might as well have been talking about another planet. Then he mentioned that he went to a school called

Castlerock College. And the pygmy just went, "Ah! Rugby!"'

'Ross,' Christian goes, 'I think that story might have been apocryphal,' which, from the way he says it, obviously means the same thing as horseshit.

'I'll pretend I didn't hear that,' I go, pushing the confidentiality agreement into his chest. He takes it from me and I just, like, proceed with the tour. I tip into the room to my immediate right, where there's a humungous – and I *mean* humungous – Jabba the focking Hutt, as in the actual one they used in whatever movie. Big and slimy. I go, 'Looks like the photographs I've seen of my old dear after she had me.'

Christian laughs, but it's like it's a major effort? See, he's sulking now.

I'm there, 'So this was, like, a puppet, was it?'

'Er, yeah,' he goes, 'Took five people to operate it . . .'

'Cool – presumably that includes one in the tail . . .'

He nods. Big mopy face on him. I move on to the next room. Again, it's seriously impressive. We're talking full-size models of Boba Fett and Jar Jar Binks and all sorts of other shit I've never heard of.

'And you work *in* this actual building?' I go. 'I don't know how you get *any* work done with all these focking toys down here.'

I pull one of those laser swords down off the wall, switch it on, then stort swinging it at Christian, missing his nose by, like, an inch – on purpose, obviously.

'Ross,' he goes, 'I really would feel more comfortable if you just signed this. I mean, they are paranoid about this kind of shit . . .'

I'm there, 'Dude, where's George Lucas's actual office?'

He pulls a face, like he's telling me to keep my voice down. '*Mister* Lucas works upstairs,' he goes in this, like, hushed voice.

There's a fly buzzing around just in front of me. I hold the laser sword up, very focking steady, then – with a speed you wouldn't believe – I cut through the air with the thing, catching the fly straight in the mush.

I might actually *be* a Jedi. I should at least get it checked out.

'I'll tell you what,' I go, 'if you want, I can go up there and tell him to his face where he can stick his confidentiality agreement.'

He's there, 'Ross, I could lose my job.'

'Whoa! Who the fock is that?' I go, pegging it over to this big freaky-looking focker with – honestly – red eyes, a snake coming out of its head and a mouth like a box of smashed Denby.

'Bib Fortuna,' he goes, like he's in *no* mood to entertain me now.

I'm there, 'Oh, yeah, he's Jabba the Hutt's butler. Here, I've seen Oisinn with worse.'

This time he doesn't even smile.

It's at that exact point, roysh, that Lauren walks into the room. She's huge, roysh, and I don't mean as in fat. I mean as in pregnant. I'm straight over to her, giving her a pretty amazing hug, telling her how great it is to see her, hope she's looking after my little godson in there, blahdy blahdy blah.

I notice a certain, I don't know, unresponsiveness about her – *if* that's even a word. She's a bit, I suppose, rigid.

I ignore it, of course – nice to be nice – and go into, like, verbal diarrhoea mode about the drive up here, the size of the States and how this is place is basically fantasy land.

Somehow she knows about the issue with the confidentiality agreement. Either Christian, like, gestured to her in some way while I wasn't looking *or* she saw the thing in his hand, copped his miserable face and put, like, two and two together.

'Have you signed that?' she goes to me – her *first* words to me, remember.

One thing I've always been shit at is, like, gauging the right and wrong things to say in situations like this.

'You *know* me, Lauren,' I end up going. 'I'm a relatively straight shooter. And my attitude is, if someone comes up to me and says they don't respect the bond of trust that exists between two dudes who went to war together on the rugby field, then, frankly, I don't care *who* they are or *how* many movies they've made – they can pucker up and smooch my ample rump . . .'

The most unbelievable pain suddenly shoots through my body and for a minute I'm *actually* paralysed. Lauren has grabbed me by the knackers, so fast that I didn't even see her hand move. I can't even catch my breath.

I'm going, 'Lauren . . . plea . . . lego . . .'

With her other hand – the one that *isn't* wringing out my scrote like a dishrag – she takes the confidentiality agreement from Christian and hands it to me, then gives me a pen.

When I've signed it, roysh, with, like, a trembling hand, she finally gives me back my Charles de Gaulles.

Then Christian goes, 'Now – on with the show . . .'

This is the life.

We're sitting out on the front steps of Christian and Lauren's cabin, looking out over Lake Ewok, watching the sun disappear behind the giant Redwoods and the coals of the barbecue turn slowly white.

'I'm sorry about earlier,' I go. 'It was probably just me being Jack the Lad.'

He's cool with it, of course. He asks me if I'm okay and I remind him that I've had my beans ground many, many times over the years. They generally only hurt until the swelling goes down. I check over my shoulder.

'I thought she'd reached the stage where she could just about tolerate being in my company,' I go. 'I mean, what changed? I thought absence was supposed to make the hort grow fonder?'

He has a quick look over his shoulder as well – with a wife with a grip like that, he's probably learned the hord way? 'It's just . . . no, forget it.'

I'm there, 'How can I forget it after that? Come on, Christian – what the fock?'

'Well,' he goes, 'I told you, we've been down to see Sorcha once or twice. And, being pregnant, I suppose Lauren's especially sensitive to a mother's point of view at the moment. She's looking at little Honor there, growing up without her father. Just like *she* grew up with her own father coming and going . . .'

'Hennessy? Well, thank fock I'm nothing like him.'

'She thinks you are,' he goes. 'She sees you as, you know . . . cut from the same cloth.'

Which hurts, it has to be said. 'I hope you were defending me during all this.'

He's there, 'Of course I was. But it's hard, Ross. She keeps bringing up all this stuff. We had a huge row the other night after you rang. And she pointed out, you know . . . you slept with my mother.'

That stops me dead in my tracks. The subject hasn't come up for years and he's never just said it out like that.

'Hey, I explained that to you at the time,' I go. 'It takes two to tango.'

He's there, 'I know. But she also said . . .'

'What?'

'She said that you can't bear it when something good happens for me. You always have to ruin it. You're scared I'll make a success of my life and leave you behind. She thinks that's why you're over here.'

'I can't tell you how much that hurts,' I go. 'But I'm going to be generous to her and put it down to hormones.'

He hands me another can. I hold it up to my nuts, the cold soothing them. I change the subject. 'By the way, I'm putting *him* under major pressure, by the way – as in, Cillian?'

'Pressure? How?'

'Just by being on the scene.'

'Are you saying you still have feelings for Sorcha?' he goes, again getting straight to the point.

I can't tell you how good it feels to be shooting the shit with my best friend like this.

I'm there, 'I *do*. Except, I'm not sure anymore what those feelings actually *are*? I mean, don't get me wrong, if I thought there was a sniff of it, I'd be in there like swimwear. She's still a ringer for Jennie Garth. *And*, I suppose, my wife. But maybe it is going to be just friendship.'

'Do you think she still has feelings for you?'

'I'm not sure. And that's a tough thing for me to admit. I mean, not in the way that girls *usually* have feelings for me? *He's a bastard to women – but he makes my tummy all funny . . .*'

'So what, she wants you as her friend?' he goes.

'Worse. She wants me as her gay friend.'

He laughs.

I'm there, 'I'm actually serious. She has me going around clothes shops with her. *Do you think this emerald Abaeté is too like the ruffled Marchesa I already have?*'

'No!'

'I'm serious. *Do you think I could pull off a Herve Leger bandage dress as well as Audrina Patridge?*'

'She's probably just missing having a best female friend.'

'Well, I think she thinks I'm suddenly it. Some dude in Kitson actually hit on me.'

'What?'

'I shit you not. It's like, whoa, horsy, I'm *not* that kind of goy?'

'Exactly.'

'Actually, we're probably going to go for a coffee as it happens. But it's just to discuss the whole LA gym scene – nothing gay.'

I check on the barbie. Very little flame left. Could probably throw the old steaks on now. 'So what about you?' I go. 'How are you feeling about the whole fatherhood thing, blah blah blah?'

'Nervous,' he goes.

I'm like, 'Dude, you'll be great. You'd be shocked at how much of it comes naturally.'

But he's there, 'I'm worried,' and from his expression it's immediately obvious that he needs, like, a shoulder here. 'I mean, Lauren and I haven't exactly had great role models in that department, have we? I mean, Hennessy and Maeve are divorced. And God knows my parents have had their problems . . .'

Of which I was obviously one.

'It's, like, they're back together and everything? But everyone knows they're just flogging a dead horse . . . I think the only thing I've ever been scared of in life is bringing kids into the world, then focking their heads up by . . . becoming my old man.'

'That will not happen,' I go, mainly because his old man's a dick. 'Don't you even focking think that. You're going to be this amazing father – I genuinely feel that.'

He nods, roysh, like I've answered all his fears.

Then I decide to hit him with the big news. 'Okay,' I go, 'this is totally random. You know Erika? Of course you know Erika . . .'

Erika used to have a thing for him.

'It turns out she's my sister. Well, half.'

'Your sister? You mean . . .'

'My old man is her old man. You'd never think it to look at her, would you?'

He's genuinely struggling with it. He's there, 'I mean, that's like . . . whoa!'

'That's the understatement of the century,' I go. 'I mean, she'd found out that Tim wasn't her *actual* old man ages before. I think she was actually happy about that.'

'They never got on.'

'I know. Anyway, the *real* culprit was supposed have been some Greek shipping dude. Billionaire. Blah blah blah. That was the rumour.

'Anyway, there I am *in* Andorra, supposed to be having dinner with the old man after the match. He did an unbelievable job coaching the forwards, by the way, though I'd never say it to the focker's face. So we're sitting there and I happen to be talking about how much I'm missing Honor. Then *he* storts banging on about the special bond between a father and daughter. *Then* I notice there's, like, *three* places set at the table? I'm thinking, what's the Jack here? Next thing, I look up and Erika's there.'

'*That's* how you found out?' he goes.

I'm there, 'Big-time.'

'Jesus. And how are things between you – as in you and Erika?'

'I don't know,' I go. 'I skipped town, pretty much after finding out.'

'Have you called her.'

'Once. Well, she rang me. I can't face her, though.'

'But she's your sister.'

'Half.'

'Half-sister, then.'

'I know – that's the issue.'

'God, I never thought of that. I mean, you two . . .'

'Rode each other. Don't remind me.'

'Jesus. I mean, Luke and Leia, at least *they* only kissed . . .'

It's like, why does it always have to be *Star Wars*?

'The thing is,' I go, 'it's probably not incest if you don't *know* she's your sister?'

I poke at the coals with a bit of stick. After a good few beers, I'm suddenly getting all psychological.

'Can I tell you something honestly?' I go. 'Like, in loads and loads of ways, I *know* I'm a fock-up? I mean, Lauren's right – I had it all. Wife, home, daughter. Money, looks, body . . .'

'Well, she never mentioned those, Ross.'

'Dude, I'm paraphrasing. The point is, I threw it away. Except for the last three. But, I have to tell you – and this is something *you* should remember – forget the moo, forget the bod, forget the boat race, if it wasn't for my kids, I'd probably be one seriously unhappy dude right now.'

He gets what I'm saying. Has to be said, I've missed him. 'Would you like more,' he goes, 'as in, kids?'

I look down at the old knackers – mashed. 'I think more might be out of the question now!' I go, and the two of us crack our holes laughing and end up laughing for seriously ages.

Eventually, I tell him we should probably throw some carcass on this baby and he goes inside to get the steaks and Lauren. He's gone for, like, five minutes and I hear what I'm pretty sure are, like, raised voices. When he comes out he says that Lauren's gone to bed. She's got, like, a migraine?

I just nod, sort of, like, sadly and go, 'All the more for us, then.'

I wake up with that feeling of not knowing where the fock I am. The full-size bust of Darth Maul at the bottom of the bed reminds that I'm in Christian and Lauren's spare room. It turned out to be a late one. At some point the conversation moved on to his plans for the casino. It's going to have, like, its own currency – as in, Toydarian credits? It's also going to have, like, a full-size AT-AT, a virtual Pod Race with actual Pod Cors and a proper Rebo Band – men in costumes, obviously – playing in the nightclub.

I listened to, like, hours of this shit. We were pouring the JD into us all night – finished the entire bottle I brought with me. It was, like, six o'clock in the morning when Christian crawled off to bed, focking rubber. He never could handle spirits.

I realize, roysh, very suddenly, that the reason I'm awake is that my actual phone is ringing. I check caller ID and it's, like, Sorcha, probably ringing to tell me that lace is the sexiest fabric of the new season or that Ice Blue is going to be huge this year with Prada, Vuitton and Stella.

I answer it anyway.

She's crying.

'What's wrong?' I go.

'It's Honor,' she blurts out.

I'm there, 'Honor?' immediately throwing back the sheets. 'What's wrong with her?'

It's five minutes before I can get even a proper word out of her.

'I had to take her to see a behavioural psychologist this morning,' she goes.

'A what?' I'm there obviously going.

'Oh, Ross, she lost it the other night after you were here. Three o'clock in the morning, she was screaming the house down. Her eyes were going literally crazy . . .'

'Jesus.'

'She kept clenching and unclenching her jaw. I thought she was having a fit.'

'And she wasn't?'

'No, we took her to the emergency room and they just gave us a card for this, like I told you, behavioural psychologist. Ross, am I that bad a mother?'

'I wouldn't have thought so. I mean, what did this psychologist dude say?'

'He asked me – oh my God, I can hardly bring myself to say it, Ross . . .'

'What?'

'He asked me if I'd been caboosing her?'

'*Caboosing* her?'

'Yeah, it's when you give a positive comment, immediately followed by, like, a negative one? *You were a really good girl tonight – much better than you were yesterday.* How could *anyone* think me capable of that, Ross?'

'Er, I don't know.'

'Do I look like a monster?'

'Of course not. I hope Cillian decked the goy.'

'No,' she goes, 'he didn't come with me. We ended up getting in this – oh my God – *huge* fight last night. He tried to say that it was . . . that it was your being here that's unsettled her.'

'Whoa,' I go, 'I'm her *actual* father.'

'I know, but he says she's emotionally confused.'

'*He's* going to be emotionally confused when I'm done slapping him,' I go, throwing my legs out of the bed. 'I'm driving back . . .'

I throw on the old threads and take a wander around the gaff. Christian and Lauren are nowhere to be seen.

I step out onto the porch. It's another scorcher of a day. I think about picking up our empty cans from last night, but then I spot the pair of them in the distance, walking along the shore of Lake Ewok, holding actual hands.

I tip down.

'Christian, you dirty dog,' I shout from a distance. 'You were focked out of Irish college for the same thing!'

She is not a happy rabbit, from the way she's looking at me. The first thing she goes to me is, 'Why did you give him spirits?'

I'm like, 'Whoa, horsy. If he wants to drink JD, who am I to stop him? He's a big boy now – makes all his own decisions.'

I can feel Christian's pain, just looking at him. He's hanging, the poor focker.

She's there, 'What if I went into labour? He's in no state to drive me to the hospital.'

I don't even bother my orse arguing with her – there's no *point* when they lose it like that?

'Well,' I go, 'the good news from your point of view is that I'm going to have to head back to LA.'

'You mean now?' Christian goes. You can tell, roysh, that it hurts for him to even talk.

I'm there, 'Yeah. Sorcha rang. Bit of a problem with Honor.'

'Is she okay?' Lauren goes, suddenly all full of concern.

I'm like, 'Yeah, it's a weird one – she's been going a bit manic lately. Won't settle at night. Belting other kids. All sorts . . .'

'She's had a lot of upheaval in her life recently,' Lauren goes, which is a definite dig at me.

'Do you know what I'm thinking,' I go, 'as I'm talking to you here? I've been letting her have the odd coffee . . .'

Lauren's like, 'What?'

'Yeah, just the *odd* one. And she's absolutely mad for it. Like mother, like daughter. *You* know Sorcha. She's in and out of Storbucks like a homeless man with a bladder problem . . .'

'You've been giving an eighteen-month-old baby coffee?'

'Just baby ones. Usually espressos. Now the thing is – possibly me being paranoid here – I'm actually beginning to wonder if *that's* somehow the cause . . .'

Lauren loses it. Even Christian looks worried about what she might do. 'Of course it's the fucking cause,' she goes. 'You've got her addicted to caffeine . . .'

'Addicted?'

She looks like she wants to tear my towns clean off this time.

'You have to tell Sorcha,' she goes and the way she says it, it's not an actual suggestion.

I'm there, 'I will,' genuinely terrified. 'As in, I will if I have to.'

'What do you mean, if you *have* to?'

Christian's pulling faces at me, telling me to shut the fock up, quit while I'm ahead and whatever. But of course I'm stupid. I have to go, 'I was thinking I could always try to, like, wean her off?'

'Wean her off?'

'I don't know, Buckys do, like, chai teas, don't they? Maybe I could get her onto them. Bear in mind, I'm just thinking out loud here. Then onto decaf. Then eventually normal shit like Coke or whatever.'

'I don't believe it,' Lauren goes. 'I don't believe it,' and at first I'm thinking, as reactions go, this is a bit over the top. But then I realize that's it's *not* me she's going spare about? Because she can't catch her breath and her face is, like, full of panic. And I've seen that face before. I saw it with Sorcha. She's going into labour.

'It's coming,' she's suddenly going. 'My waters just broke. It's coming now!'

I look at Christian and the goy has just frozen – doesn't know what to do. He's not the only one either.

'Help me to the ground,' Lauren goes and we each grab an orm and we lower her down.

She's suddenly roaring at Christian. 'We went to classes for this,' she goes, pulling up her skirt, then whipping down her, well, I suppose, knickers. 'You're supposed to know what to do,' but the poor focker's gone. Too hungover to even know his own name.

I'm there, 'Come on, Dude, get your shit together,' because obviously I'm not going to be any use here.

Then all of a sudden I see his hand go up to his mouth and he turns away from us and the next we know he's bent in two, spewing his ring. The thing is, roysh, the second I hear it splashing on the ground, I feel my own guts do a somersault. Then the waft of puke and stale bourbon reaches my nostrils and I get that shorp taste in my mouth that you get when you know you're going to vom.

I literally can't keep it in. I'm like, 'Eeeuuuggghhh!!!' spitting chunks as well, and it's pretty much projectile?

'You useless fuckers!' Lauren's, like, roaring at the two of us, then she storts going, 'Help! Someone! Help!'

That's when a group of Ewoks suddenly comes running. Well, dwarves dressed up as Ewoks. The leader, who Christian later identifies as Chief Chirpa, takes total chorge of the situation. Turns out he did, like, three years in medical school?

He asks Lauren her name and she tells him.

Christian's like, 'Eeeuuuggghhh!!!' still spewing, except he's down on his knees this time, and that sets me off again. Chief Chirpa tells one of the crew – Logray – to get these two fucking jokers out of here, meaning us, and we're moved backwards to give them some space.

Wicket rings for an ambulance.

'Okay, Lauren,' Chief Chirpa goes, 'I want you to remember

that what's happening to you is *the* most natural thing in the world – so relax. Can you do that for me?'

She nods.

When Wicket gets off the phone, Chief Chirpa tells him to go up the other end and support Lauren's head, which he does. She actually looks quite comfortable. Like, I've never thought about it before, but I suppose an Ewok *is* just a big pillow.

'Slow breaths, Lauren,' Chief Chirpa is going. 'Remember, it's your breathing that's going to control the pain . . .'

I feel another sudden spasm. I'm like, 'Eeeuuugghhh!' and Christian hurls as well.

Chief Chirpa checks the, I suppose, relevant area – Ground Zero, if you want to call it that – and says that she's very dilated. Then he sends one of the baby Ewoks up to the gaff to get some disinfectant wipes for his hands.

'They're under the sink in the kitchen,' Christian manages to go before puking again.

'That's it,' Chief Chirpa's going, 'slow breaths. Remember, women's bodies have been doing this since forever . . . Now, can you time the contractions for me?'

'Eugh!'

Me this time. Dry-retching. Fock-all left in my stomach.

'Eeeuuugggghhh!!!'

Christian's keeps coming, though.

'Eeeuuugggghhh!!! Eeeuuugggghhh!!! Eeeuuugggghhh!!!'

The sound of an ambulance siren suddenly fills the air. The Ewoks all stort waving their orms to get the driver's attention and he ends up having to drive across a field to reach us.

To cut a long story short, the paramedics, or whatever you want to call them, load Lauren into the back of the ambulance, then they give Christian a sick bag and let him ride with her. I tell them I'll follow them in my cor.

'You stay the fuck away from us,' Lauren shouts and of course I don't know whether she means it or whether she's just upset.

So I end up going back to their gaff and stewing for, like, an hour or two, watching TV and drinking milk to try to, like, settle my stomach. Then I decide, fock it. My best friend's about to become, like, a father. I'm entitled to be there. So I grab my cor keys and the dude in the little security hut gives me directions to the hospital and I'm there in, like, five minutes flat.

I find the ward easily enough. The door's closed, roysh, but through it I can hear the most incredible sound I've ever heard. A baby crying. And the second most incredible. Christian crying.

I turn the handle and poke my head around the door. Lauren's out for the count and Christian's just sitting there with this little bundle in his orms, staring at it. I sort of, like, clear my throat to get his attention. He looks at me and tells me I wouldn't want to be here when Lauren wakes up. I tell him okay, I'll go, but first I want to know what it is.

He says it's a little boy.

I'm flying down the freeway, same drill as before, sounds on, wind in the old Tony Blair. I'm thinking about all sorts of shit – but mostly about Christian becoming a father – and the next thing, roysh, my face feels suddenly wet and I realize that I'm crying. The tears are flowing so thick and fast that I have to, like, pull into the hord shoulder.

I suppose it's, like, delayed shock, but I end up sitting there for, like, half an hour, just bawling my actual eyes out. Eventually, I get it together enough to ring Sorcha.

She answers by going, 'Oh! My! God!'

I'm there, 'You heard about Lauren, I take it.'

'Heard?' she goes. 'Ross, it's on the cover of *People Weekly*.'

I'm thinking, it only happened, like, an hour ago. News sure travels fast over here. 'The cover?' I go.

She's like, 'Yeah. It kills me to say it, but you did well.'

I'm there, 'Er, thanks,' wondering what the fock it says I did.

'I have to tell you,' she goes, 'when you said you were seeing an actress, I had *no* idea who it was,' and I suddenly realize that we're talking about two totally different Laurens here.

I'm there, 'Hang on a sec, Babes — *what* exactly is on the cover of this magazine?'

'A picture of you and Lauren Conrad,' she goes, 'leaving The Ivy together.'

3. My fifteen minutes

Lauren Conrad has had more than her fair share of heartache. Who remembers Stephen Colletti? Jason Wahler? Brody Jenner? But a buzz is building about the identity of the square-jawed, athletic hunk spotted sharing lunch with the reality star at The Ivy on January 19. So far, LC is remaining tight-lipped about her new mystery man – but from these photographs, there's no denying the love light is in their eyes.

'There's no doubt he's a ringer for me,' I'm going. 'I'm possibly a bit – I don't want to come across as arrogant – but *better*-looking?'

Sorcha's like, 'Ross, it *is* you. That's your pink Hollister T-shirt.'

Fellow diners said the pair chatted closely while they ate. Lauren is believed to have eaten crab cakes and her secret beau a mesquite-grilled Cajun prime rib . . .

'That's what you had the day *we* were there,' Sorcha goes, suddenly sounding – it must be said – pretty upset. 'I can't believe you even took her there – oh my God, that was, like, *our* place?'

I'm there, 'I didn't take her anywhere. He looks like me is all. Sorcha, I'm saying yes, it's uncanny. I'm saying yes, it's weird. But I think *I'd* know if I'd been out on a date with Lauren actual Conrad.'

I accidentally say this at, like, the top of my voice and practically the whole of In-N-Out Burger hears.

'Well, it's a bit of a coincidence, isn't it? You tell me you're seeing some actress, but you won't tell me who. The next thing the paparazzi get a photograph of you and LC leaving The Ivy together. It's like, *hello?*'

He's ruggedly handsome with a body that would no doubt drive even former lover Jenner insane with envy! But who is he? Bodyguard? Boyfriend? LC's reps aren't saying. In fact, they've denied that the stunning Hills star is crushing on any mystery man at the moment, obviously keen to keep the relationship out of the public eye for now. Even sources at MTV are sticking to the line that there is no upcoming storyline involving Lauren and any new flame.

However, there was no disguising the longing in their eyes as they parted – without getting all kissy for the cameras, LC returning to her famous silver BMW 3 Series, her new man disappearing in the opposite direction.

It suddenly hits me. 'Shit,' I go. 'That *was* the day I met you. That was when you sent me back to the shop to talk to Harvey.'

'Oh my God,' Sorcha goes, 'you *were* wearing your pink Hollister that day as well . . .'

'I must have been walking, like, two feet behind her.'

'Oh! My God! Did you not even *see* the cameras?'

'Like, I did? But you said they were always outside. Shit, so they obviously presumed we were together.'

Sorcha laughs. 'It could *only* happen to you,' she goes, seeing the funny side of it now.

'Yeah,' I go and then *I* laugh? 'I could be wrong, but it sounded to me like you might have been the tiniest bit jealous there.'

She tries to avoid the issue, of course. She picks up the magazine, turns immediately to the next page and says that Portia de Rossi was spotted buying a pair of Gravati loafers in Neiman Marcus. It must be getting serious between her and Ellen DeGeneres.

I finish my Double-Double, then wander up to the counter and order, like, another. 'I told you you'd love this place,' Sorcha goes. 'Britney eats here *all* the time . . . *Who* I'm really worried about, by the way.'

'Britney? As in Spears?'

'She's checked out of rehab in Antigua,' she goes, like they're friends or some shit? 'During a wild night at New York's One Little West 12, she danced in a bikini, Ross, before slipping outside with one of the club's dancers. The night before, she threw up in her car after partying too hard.'

'I think you might be reading too many of these magazines, Babes.'

'Well,' she goes, 'you better get *your* story straight for when they ring.'

I'm like, 'Ring? Who?'

She's there, 'Oh my God, Ross, the *press*? They're going to find out who you are.'

I tell her not to be ridiculous. LA's not even a rugby town, which is one of the things I love about it. I can get up to all my usual tricks but still remain unanimous? She accuses me of having – oh my God – *no* idea of the power of the media over here?

I stort horsing into my second burger and ask her how Honor is. She says she had another tantrum this afternoon – oh my God, her worst yet. 'You're not going to believe this,' she goes, 'but Cillian was pouring his coffee – and she was trying to get at it. As in, she was trying to take it out of his hand. She actually tried to bite him, Ross . . .'

'You're shitting me.'

'I'm not,' she goes. 'But anyway, we think we've finally gotten to the bottom of it – why she's been behaving the way she has been?'

For, like, a minute, my hort is beating like you wouldn't believe.

'This girl, Faris – her daughter Coco is in crèche with Honor – I bumped into her in Splendid Littles and I happened to mention it to her? And she was straight away there, "Oh my God, I know what that is!"'

I'm there, 'What? What is it?'

She's like, 'Well, she was saying that adults tend to be, like, *too* reactive during these little fits of temper? The way she put it was, the worst time to try to teach someone how to swim is when they're *actually* drowning. Wait until the situation calms down before you try to deal with it. Or better still – this is what she does with Coco and she's *so* good, Ross – hunker down to, like, *her* eye level, then hug her. And tell her exactly *why* you're hugging her? In other words, find *some* positive from the situation. It's like, "Oh my God, you got angry and yet you didn't bite anyone. You acted like – oh! my God! – *such* a good girl."'

Jesus Christ, Honor's going to end up shooting the focking crèche up if Sorcha keeps listening to horseshit like this.

I know at this point that I should tell her the truth. And I'm about to – or at least I'm considering the best way to break it to her – when all of a sudden her phone beeps. She reads the message and I'm expecting her to tell me that Nicole Richie's been spotted in vintage Missoni or Nick Lachey's been spotted, I don't know, picking his nose in Musso & Frank.

'The mystery of *Hills* star Lauren Conrad's new love has been solved,' she goes, reading it out. 'The five foot, ten inch hunk, first pictured with LC after a romantic lunch at The Ivy, has been revealed as Ross O'Carroll-Kelly, a 26-year-old socialite from Ireland. The son of chicklit phenomenon Fionnuala O'Carroll-Kelly, he has himself achieved some small measure of fame back home, as a player of a game called rugby (literally pronounced *rugg-bee*). "He's a gentleman," a former flame has revealed. "He's considerate – and not just in the bedroom. He'll always put the woman before himself."'

I stare into space. I'm in, like, total shock.

'That quote's definitely made up,' Sorcha goes. I tell her

thanks very much. 'You do realize,' she goes, 'that this is going to change everything?'

I drive back to Santa Monica, thinking mostly about how this thing is going to play out back home. I'm imagining especially Caroline Morohan's face. It's, like, er, Caroline, remember that dude who sent you over a slippery nipple in Renards, like, three Christmases ago and you sent it back, calling him, like, a loser? Er, you should have a look at this.

I'm actually having this conversation out loud as I swing the old beast into the valet parking area at, like, the front of the Viceroy and I end up having to brake hord to avoid hitting this, like, major crush of people outside. At first I presume it's for Jessica Alba and Cash Warren, who are supposed to be staying here, or even Michelle Trachtenberg, who I saw horsing into the scrambled tofu at the breakfast buffet this morning.

It's only when someone aims a camera lens at me through the window of the cor and storts flashing away like there's no actual tomorrow that I connect it with the whole Lauren Conrad thing.

Everything happens pretty quickly after that. Three or four of the valet dudes form, like, a human shield around me and we force our way through, like, a ruck of press people, all of them shouting questions at me, like, how did we meet, is it true that we're thinking of getting engaged and who am I wearing? In shock, I suppose, all I manage to say is, firstly, 'The story is total bullshit,' and secondly, 'American Eagle Outfitters,' before I'm bundled through the revolving doors into the, I suppose, calm of the hotel lobby.

I stand there, trying to catch my breath, then look back to see ten, maybe fifteen faces pressed up against the glass, flashes still going off and the questions still coming. Is it true I'm already married? Have I got Whitney and Audrina's stamp of approval yet? Am I aware that Solange Knowles said I looked kind of cute at a movie premiere in Westwood last night?

I'm in, like, a total daze. Obviously I've had fame before. I've lived with it most of my life – being, first, the rugby player that *everyone* thought was going to make it, then being the rugby player that nobody could believe *didn't* make it. But this? I've never experienced anything like it.

'Lot of people looking for you,' the duty manager walks up to me and goes, at the same time handing me, like, a big whack of messages. 'I've put them in order for you. Media – TV, then print – agents, corporations and companies, bars and restaurants, fans . . . Oh, Mary-Kate and Ashley called. But then they always do . . .'

I'm, I have to admit, totally overwhelmed.

I walk towards the lift – or, over here, I suppose *elevator*? – feeling literally dizzy. I hit the button for up, then stort reading through the names. MTV. CBS. Entertainment Channel! *Us Weekly*. Breitling. Cartier. Earnest Sewn. Oronoco Rum. The Boulevard Lounge. LAX Nightclub. Dan Tana's. Sushi on Ventura . . .

The – again – *elevator* arrives? I step into it, then hit the button for the top floor. Just as it's closing, I hear this voice go, 'Hold the doors!' and I spot this figure pegging it across the lobby towards me. I do that thing – we've *all* done it – where you *pretend* to reach for the button to open the doors, except you move so slowly you could be in outer focking space.

He still manages to get his foot between the doors before they fully close and they slide open again and I find myself looking into this dude's face.

I end up nearly shitting myself.

'Hello, again,' he just goes and I watch in, like, total terror as the doors close behind him.

Like a lot of jealous boyfriends I've had to flee from in

my time, Trevion turns out to be not quite as big as I remembered from the night I jumped out of his aportment window. In my imagination, he was six-foot-six with humungous biceps – now I'm pretty embarrassed to realize that he's actually an old man. It's, like, what the fock was Sahara thinking? The dude's well into his seventies for storters and he's small, we're talking five-foot-nothing, with hunched shoulders and huge ears and, like, grey hair, neatly ported, although *the* most noticeable thing about him is his face, which is just, like, covered in scors. It looks like someone corved a focking joint of beef on it.

He *is* pretty scary-looking – that much I remembered right. I immediately switch to, like, defence mode? 'Dude,' I go, 'if it's any consolation, *she* came onto *me*?' but he doesn't say shit, just reaches into his inside pocket for what I'm half expecting to be either a knife or a gun.

It's actually a business cord. 'Looks to me,' he goes, 'like you want help.'

I check it out. It's like, 'Trevion Warwick. Agent to the Stars', and then underneath it's like, 'It ain't show friends – it's show business', which I *know* is from *Jerry Maguire* because I've seen it, like, a million times.

I suddenly remember Sahara telling me that he was an agent. 'Five minutes of your time,' he goes. The lift goes ping. We've reached, like, the top floor. He goes, 'Believe me, fella, you need me more than I need you.'

I tell him okay.

When I walk into my suite, it's immediately obvious how much I've come up in the world. There's a bottle of champagne in an ice bucket on the table, compliments of the hotel.

'You gonna open that,' Trevion goes, 'or just stare at it?'

He's one of those permanently angry dudes – like Joe Pesci or one of that crew, except huskier?

99

'What do you know about fame?' he goes while I'm unscrewing the wire cap.

I'm like, 'Fame?'

He's there, 'Something wrong with your fucking ears?'

That pretty much sums up the vibe between us. 'I'd know a little?' I go. 'Like, I *had* it once before. I'd have been pretty well known in Ireland as, like, a rugby player. Then a rugby player who threw it all away . . .'

'Okay, here's how it's going to work, Big Talk. You're going to keep your sentences short. That's my oxygen you're wasting, too – you get me?'

'Er, yeah, whatever,' I go.

I pop the cork and fill two glasses.

'Me, I been fifty years in this racket,' he goes. 'If I learned one thing, it's this. Fame is like riding a bucking bronco. Oh sure, any schmo can climb up there. But when you get thrown on your ass is entirely up to the beast. Unless! Unless, my friend, you got someone on your side who can help you ride that animal. Make sure *when* you land – because land you will, Lover, that's as obvious as your fucking nose – you're gonna have a lot of money to cushion your fall. And girls. You like girls, right?'

I laugh. I'm there, 'Dude, where I come from, that's like asking Mo'Nique if she knows her way around the Dominos menu?'

'A comedian, huh? Well, get this, Funny Man, if I take you on – and right now that is a neon *if* big enough to light up Times Square – you will do what I tell you at all times.'

I'm actually more than a little bit terrified of him. 'Dude,' I go, 'to be honest, I'm not a hundred per cent sure I *need* an agent?'

He picks up my phone messages and waves them at me. 'Who's gonna return these calls? You?'

'I was thinking of, like, ignoring them – like you do with birds you don't want to see anymore?'

'You got fifty calls today, Fly Boy. You gonna have a hundred and fifty tomorrow. Three hundred the day after that . . .'

He walks over to the window. 'And that crowd down there – who's gonna manage their interest in you? Make sure they only know what you want them to know?'

I'm there, 'But it's all horseshit. I've never even *met* Lauren Conrad? I accidentally stepped into the photograph . . .'

'Who *gives* a fuck?' he goes. 'You're famous now.'

'But I don't want to end up as one of these people who're famous for being famous.'

'Well, what do you want to be famous for? You sing?'

'No.'

'Act?'

'No.'

'Ever do any modelling?'

'A lot of people would say I've got the body for it. I only lost out on the Magee job to a dude called Gordon D'Arcy.'

'Never heard of him.'

I laugh. I'm there, 'I can't wait to tell him that next time I see him. He'll flip the lid.'

'What I tell you about talking?' he goes, sort of, like, baring his teeth at me. It's like he's on the point of belting me.

'Sorry,' I go.

He stares at me for, like, ten seconds without saying a word, then he's like, 'You want to know about fame? Let me give you a flash here. Angelina Jolie's famous because she's got a perfectly symmetrical face. Alex Rodriguez is famous because his synapses are faster than ninety-nine-point-nine per cent of the human race. Both accidents of birth. You think that makes them any more deserving of fame than you?'

I'm there, 'I was just in the right place at the right time.'

'So was Neil Armstrong when they shot his fucking rocket at the moon. Fame is an illusion. That's right, Charlie. An illusion. You're lucky enough to have it happen to you, you don't question it. You suck on that little titty for as long as it's in front of you. You like tits, don't you? Women's tits?'

'Yeah.'

'You sure?'

'Big-time, believe me.'

'Anyways, here's the pitch, Kid. People are obsessed with celebrity lives. Jamie-Lynn Sigler partied the night away at Stride's summer solstice party in LA's Crown Bar. Jaime Pressly carried the crocodile Nuage Bag by Valentino at the CFDA awards. Mila Kunis wore a pair of Brian Atwood peep-toes to the Calvin Klein women's wear fashion show in New York. Who gives a fuck? Well, let me give you a little hint – half the population of this planet.'

'Including my wife,' I go. 'She gets, like, all that shit in text alerts.'

He's there, 'You're married? When the fuck were you going to tell me that, Screwball?'

'Well, we're actually separated?'

'You on good terms?'

'As in?'

'Would she sell you out to the papers? Say you liked dressing up as a lady, domestic pets in the bedroom, that kind of shit?'

'Definitely not.'

'You sure?'

'Yeah.'

'Okay. You stay away from her for now. I don't want you photographed with her – not until I've worked out how she fits into the story. You got kids?'

'Two. A daughter by her — she's here at the moment as well — then a son back in Ireland by another bird.'

'And Fyon Hoola O'Carroll-Kelly's your mother, right? The writer?'

'Unfortunately.'

'Hey, who's she got representing her?' he goes.

Suddenly, roysh, my nose is weirdly out of joint. 'Haven't a focking bog,' I go. 'And anyway, I thought we were talking about *me* here?'

'I'm just saying,' he goes, 'I seen her on TV. She got *real* star quality.'

I'm there, 'Well, what have I got, then?'

He knocks back his champagne in one gulp, then holds his glass out to be filled again.

He's there, 'The beauty of you is, no one in this town knows a damn thing about you. Means you're a blank canvas. You can be whoever we want you to be.'

He storts looking through my messages. 'Abercrombie?' he goes. 'No, no, no. You know what I think when I look at you? I think Turnbull & Asser. You got that buttoned-down, preppy shit going on . . . Gatorade? You got to be kidding me. You're doing Dr Pepper or you're doing no one. You're doing TAG Heuer. You're doing Blinde wraparounds. That's if you come with me . . .'

I'm there just staring at this obviously mad focker, with his big, ugly mess of a face, thinking, I don't even know anything about him, except that he's pretty handy with a softball bat.

'So I need an answer from you,' he goes. 'You *with* me, Flyboy?'

'No prizes for guessing why you're ringing,' I go.

Oisinn's there, 'Is it true?' and of course I'm sitting there with a big focking smile on my face. I'm about to go, 'Guilty!'

when he's suddenly there, 'Erika's your sister?' totally bursting my bubble.

I'd very nearly forgotten.

'That focking got around,' I go. 'Who told you?'

He's there, 'We're supposed to be arranging another Divorce Fair,' which is, like, a business they have together? 'This time in Cork. Except I haven't seen her since Christmas and she's not answering her phone. Then I run into her this afternoon coming out of Fallon & Byrne . . .'

I'm there, 'How did she look?'

'Sorry?'

'As in, did she look well?'

'I don't know – is it relevant?'

'Actually, no – forget I said it.'

'She just burst into tears,' he goes. 'I had to bring her back inside, get her a glass of wine. Shit the bed, it was twenty minutes before she could even talk to me.'

I'm like, 'And she obviously blabbed? About my old man being her old man?'

'Ross, she said you've turned your back on her.'

'I haven't exactly turned my back on her. I just told her, you know, I needed a bit of time to get my head around the fact.'

'She said even Sorcha doesn't want to know her.'

Shit. Talk about guilt-tripping someone.

'Yeah,' I go, 'she's not a happy bunny about the whole thing. In fact, she flipped.'

He's like, 'That doesn't sound like Sorcha.'

'My experience of women is you never know what they're going to do.'

'Ross, she's on her own over here. She's had a row with her old dear . . .'

'Dude, I'm dog-sick hearing about that row. And anyway, she's got her new so-called dad.'

'He's away.'

'Yeah, him and Hennessy are still trying to work out how to launder the money they stashed.'

'And she's getting a hard time of it, Ross. I mean, it's all over town. Of course, Chloe and Sophie and Amie with an ie are having a field day – saying this has finally cut her down to size.'

'Sorry, how is being my sister – half-sister – being cut down to size?'

'You know what they're like,' he goes. 'Ross, she's like a ghost wandering around the place. I rang her old dear. She's very worried about her. Would you not ask her to go over to you?'

'Bit difficult at the moment,' I go, then I try to kill the subject dead. 'Hey, did you hear the other major news?'

'Yeah,' he goes, 'Christian and Lauren had a little boy. I heard you disgraced yourself as well.'

'Well, yeah, that's true, but it's not what I'm talking about. Brace yourself for this – I'm scoring Lauren Conrad.'

He cracks on not to be impressed – possibly a little bit of jealousy involved?

'In fact,' I go, 'in the last twenty-four hours, I've become huge over here. I can't believe the news hasn't reached Ireland yet.'

'As in, Lauren Conrad from *The Hills*?' he goes.

'That's the one. She's gagging for me as well, although – you know me – I'm playing it cool. I've got myself an agent and all sorts of shit. There's talk of, like, a fragrance deal and all sorts of endorsements. Hey, if you see Drico or any of the goys around town, make sure and tell them – as in, really rub it in.'

He goes, 'Ross, just make sure and ring her, will you?' meaning Erika.

I'm there, 'I'd love to, Dude. But things are a little bit crazy at the moment.'

Sorcha rings me at, like, nine o'clock in the morning, asking if I want to come looking at dresses with her? She says she's thinking of doing Morphine Generation and Corey Lynn Calter and maybe even LaRok. Then she thought we might get lunch in Kokomo Café, which is the *actual* Peach Pit from *90210*? I tell her I can't.

'This isn't me being big-headed,' I go, 'but I've got bigger fish to fry. Trevion told me to stay in the room until he rings.'

She's there, 'Who's Trevion?' and I think, Of course – she doesn't know. It's mad how quickly my life's already changing?

I'm like, 'He's my agent,' and of course it's impossible *not* to say it in a fock-you kind of way?

She cracks on not to be impressed, obviously deciding that the way to handle the whole fame thing is to try to keep me grounded.

'We're having a movie night tonight,' she goes. I think I mentioned, they've got, like, an actual cinema in the gaff? 'Analyn and Mike are coming over. Elodine and Steve. And I think Josh and Kyle . . .'

'A movie night?' I go, thinking what a come-down that would be for me after the madness of the last twenty-four hours.

'Yeah, we're having, like, a foreign film season? All the 2007 Oscar nominees. Tonight it's *Pan's Labyrinth* . . .'

To be honest, I'd rather have all my skin peeled off, then roll in salt.

'I'm actually pretty busy tonight,' I go.

'Well, what about tomorrow? Promise you'll come for *Indigènes*.'

'Tomorrow's not good either,' I go. 'Bear in mind, there's going to be a lot of good shit happening for me. It looks like I'm going to be back in big-time demand.'

'Oh,' she goes, all disappointed. She's quiet then for a moment, then she goes, 'What about mornings? Do you want to come with me to Lisa Kline tomorrow? It's on, like, Robertson again? They do Madison Marcus, Karta, C&C California. Even Lorick.'

'The thing is,' I go, 'I'm going to have to level with you. Trevion's not sure how you fit into the picture yet.'

She's there, 'What?' and she says it like she's can't believe what she's just heard.

'I don't think he wants it out there that I have a wife, ex-wife, whatever you want to call it,' I go. 'It's the same shit they do with all the boy bands, isn't it?'

She all of a sudden flips. 'And has Trevion decided how your daughter fits into the picture yet?'

I'm there, 'Don't be like that, Babes. You've always said you wanted to be famous yourself. You of all people should be happy for me.'

'Well, as her father,' she goes, 'you *might* like to know that Honor bit a girl called Taylor in crèche today. *And* she drew blood.'

'Jesus!' I go. 'Who calls their kid Taylor?'

'Do you even care?' she goes. 'Do you actually care?' and I don't get a chance to answer, roysh, because she hangs straight up.

The timing couldn't be better either because it's at that exact moment that Trevion knocks on the door of my room. The first thing he does, roysh, is he tells me to look out the window, which is exactly what I do.

The press have all gone.

'There's, like, no one out there,' I go.

He's like, 'You want to know *why* there's no one out there? Because you're being *managed*! You got somebody controlling when these people get a piece of you and when they don't . . .'

Then he asks me if I know what day today is. I'm there, 'Is it, like, Thursday?'

'Yes, it's Thursday,' he goes. 'It's also the first of February. You know why that date's important?'

I'm there, 'To be honest, no.'

'Because it's Lauren Conrad's birthday. And *that* is why I'm paid the fucking greenbacks. To know this shit for you.'

'That *is* pretty impressive,' I go.

'You bet it is. You know where you're going tonight?'

'I don't know – is she having, like, a porty or some shit?'

'A party?' he goes, like he can't believe how *actually* stupid I am. 'You don't even know this broad.'

I'm there, 'Yeah, no, but if I'm *supposed* to be, like, her boyfriend? Won't it look a bit weird if I'm *not* there?'

'No. Because I put a story out there – you told LC you wanted to see other people.'

'As in, other birds?'

'That's right, Heartbreaker. So tonight, you're having dinner at Geoffrey's in Malibu. Valet parking. Food – sensational. You ever hear of Ptolemy Consuelos?'

That could be my date or it could be something off the menu. I decide to bluff it. I never know how to say no to people who are, like, permanently angry. I'm there, 'Big time,' except of course he sees straight through it.

'Ptolomy Consuelos is an up-and-coming actress,' he goes.

That is impressive.

'I have to say, I like your style,' I go. 'Being seen out with another bird on my *actual* bird's birthday. People are going to think I'm a player.'

He's there, 'You bet they're going to think you're a player.

Who *is* this kid? He doesn't do nothing, he ain't in movies, he ain't pretty. But here's the flash, fellas – he blows off Lauren Conrad! *On* her birthday! For who? Only the girl they're calling the next Vanessa Britting . . .'

He sits down on the sofa.

I don't know why – maybe I'm just, like, grateful for all the shit he's doing for me – but I suddenly get it into my head that I should maybe mention Sahara and possibly even apologize for what happened that night, even if just to clear the air.

'I just wanted to say about Sahara . . .' I go.

He's there, 'Forget about it.'

I'm like, 'No, no, I just want to say this to you. Just in case it's any consolation, she was all over me like a drunk driver the day I met her. That's why she had to, like, *pretend* I broke in? Out of guilt, I suppose.'

He's there, 'Will you just . . .' and for ten seconds it looks like he's about to go totally ape-shit. Then he suddenly looks sad.

'I knew you never broke in,' he goes.

I'm like, 'How?'

'Ah, I asked her, "Did he take anything?" She thinks for a bit, then she says, "The watch my mother gave me." I says, "The watch your mother gave you? The little shit-fuck." The next day, I takes her to Neiman Marcus on Wilshire. I says, "What kind of a watch was it?" She says it was a Storm Aphrodite – gold fucking plated.'

I'm there, 'Can I just say, I *didn't* actually take it?'

'The next day,' he goes, 'she says she's been checking through her shit and she noticed her Sondra Roberts mini chain-bag is missing. I'm still feeling sorry for her – cos of her ordeal. I give her my Amex, ring my friend in Bergdorf Goodman and tell him, "Look after her." She comes home six hours later . . .'

'Did she buy the bag?' I go. 'Just as a matter of interest.'

'Oh, she bought the bag,' he goes. 'She bought a lot of stuff. Once she got in the store she remembered that her Kara Ross earrings was *in* that bag. White quartz. Diamonds. Five fucking grand . . .'

'And I'm guessing you smelled a rat.'

'Sunglasses – Sama Eyewear. Two fucking grand. A Jennifer Fisher necklace. I don't know *how* much. I asked her and all she said was Kristin fucking Davis had one . . .'

'Dude,' I go, 'I hope you don't mind me saying this, but I think you're probably better off without her . . .'

He shrugs, then pulls a face. 'Ah, I know what you're thinking . . .'

I'm there, 'Go on, what?'

'Pretty girl, mid-twenties – what the fuck did that old guy think she wanted with him?'

That's exactly what I was thinking. With a face like that as well – it's like a map of the focking London Underground.

'She was a hooker when I met her,' he goes, staring into the distance. 'Can you believe that?'

I actually can.

'*With* an agency,' he goes. 'I mean, she wasn't turning tricks on Hollywood Boulevard or nothing. She was fucking classy.'

'*I* could see that.'

'Anyways, I had to go and fall for her – stoopit bastit. I mean, what'd I think she saw in me, huh? A 75-year-old man with a talent agency full of nobodies. And this face . . .'

I nod. I'm tempted to go, It's not your best quality, in fairness, but in the end I don't.

'This is what I got fighting for my country,' he goes.

I'm there, 'Were you in, like, the ormy and shit?'

'You ever hear of the Korean War?'

'Er, no. But that's not saying very much.'

'Well, I seen things would make your fucking teeth itch . . . Sahara, ah, she thought I was the man who was going to make all her dreams come true. Of course, I couldn't. I mean, she couldn't act for shit – all I could get her was that disclaimer work. Me, I never failed at anything in my life. You ever charge a machine-gun nest with a hole in your back so big your commanding officer can put his hand in and tickle your liver?'

'I'd have to be honest,' I go, 'and say no.'

'You ever hear the screams of a man burning to death in a tank?'

'No.'

'Ever carry your own brother across the thirty-eighth parallel – him bleeding like a stuck pig and begging you to put him out of his fucking misery?'

'Again, no.'

'*Again, no*,' he goes. 'That's right, Civilian . . . Well, I thought if I can do all that, then surely I can make this girl a star. But, Jesus, those disclaimers – used to take sixty, seventy takes to get them right. The studio used to say to me, "Act? She can't even say words on a fucking page?" But they're doing it for me as a favour. And all the time I'm stringing her along, telling her, "Just one more disclaimer, Cupcake – then it's the movies."

'But then suddenly she's got some producer hanging around her. Good-looking guy. You know the kind. Like you, you fuck – makes the scene. He's promised to make her the star in a musical. Filling her head with dreams.'

'Is this the one about – and this is going to sound racist – that African bird?'

He nods. '*Mutilation Nation*,' he goes. Then he smiles, sort of, like, sadly?

'So what else do I need to know about this bird I'm seeing tonight?' I go.

He's there, 'She used to date Kevin Cornish – was in a couple of episodes of *Dawson's Creek*. Never made it. *She's a real talent* – agent's a personal friend of mine. Wants to put her out there, get her known . . .'

'It all feels like a bit of a set-up. Like our old pairs have arranged, like, a date for us.'

'It's called a mutual convenience of wants,' he goes. 'And it's how this town works. Right now, you're Z list. You listen to me, you'll be D list inside six months.'

'That is pretty impressive.'

'You bet it is, Popeye. The car will pick you up at eight. There's gonna be press waiting for you outside the restaurant.'

'How do you know?'

'Because I fucking told them you're going to be there. You're going to be asked a lot of questions. Whatever you're asked, you keep your mouth shut!'

After Kevin, Ptolemy says, she really needed some time to herself? Which is why she hasn't, like, dated?

I wouldn't make any major claims for myself in the old intelligence department, but I'm beginning to feel like Einstein in this country. Or any of that crowd.

I checked out her MySpace page this afternoon in the hotel business centre and she lists one of her hobbies as tanning.

'It was like I needed to get back to *me*,' she's going. 'So right now I'm, like, one hundred and ten per cent focused on what's real. I just want to live my life and, like, *be*?'

This girl could fit her brains into her XOXO clutch without having to take out her lip balm or her iShuffle.

But one of the things I've always been amazing at is appearing genuinely interested in the shit that comes out of birds' mouths. And she *does* look like Gabrielle Reece, in fairness to her.

'The thing that really kills Kevin,' she goes, 'is that I've stayed really, really good friends with his sister? As in Bethlehem, who he still shares with? So, like, any time I call over to their condo, he's all, "You said you needed space, yet you're always here?" And, bear in mind, I was literally the only one who was there for Beth when her octoplasty went wrong. So last night? I turned around to Kevin and I was like, "Oh my God, I can't believe you're hating me for being a nice person," which is what he's doing when you *think* about it?'

I'm pulling all the right faces, of course, because there's, like, five or six cameras permanently pointed at us and Trevion made sure to position us in the window so they could get the best shots.

I ordered, by the way, the baked brie in puff pastry followed by the two-pound steamed marine lobster, but what actually arrived were the micro greens with walnut and tangerine vinaigrette, followed by the miso braised tofu. When I told the waiter that he'd focked up the order, he told me that Mr Warwick had – get this – *pre-ordered* for me.

Ptolemy shows not the slightest interest in any of this. She just continues playing with her cumin-dusted Ahi tuna and says she'd describe herself as spiritual but not *actually* religious, then asks me how she even got *onto* that?

'I don't know – you *were* talking about Maria Serra,' I go.

'Oh, yeah – Gwyneth's stylist . . .'

Her conversation's like one of those big long trains you see over here – no focking end to it. Our plates are eventually cleared away. I ask the waiter if I can see the dessert menu and he just, like, shakes his head. 'Sorry,' he goes.

So I make a move for my credit cord, but he tells me it's already been settled.

Ptolemy whips out her compact and checks her teeth for fock knows what – she hasn't eaten anything and her mouth has been Exit Only for the past hour. She says she can't decide if sushi mats are a good house-warming gift for her friend Rhiannon – the theatre festival coordinator she was telling me about?

Despite her horseshit conversation and the fact that she didn't look at me once tonight, I still have the inclination towards copulation. And even though she probably couldn't pick my face out of a book of mugshots, so actually does she.

We step outside and we're immediately blinded by flashes. The press are being held back behind a red rope, but the questions are coming thick and fast. They're asking me if I phoned Lauren for her birthday and Ptolemy if she's over Kevin Cornish and then both of us what we think of George W. Bush's decision to send an additional five thousand troops to Iraq.

We manage to get past them without saying a word, but at the same time looking really, really well? We get into the cor, then Ptolemy turns around to me and goes, 'How far is your hotel?' and I don't even bother my orse answering. It's, like, a ristorical question.

There's no need to paint you a picture of what went down back at the Viceroy. What I will say is that Ptolemy has more than a few surprises in her grab bag.

The following morning, I open my eyes to find her standing in front of the mirror, throwing her clothes on. She's got a waist like a focking matador, but she keeps checking it out from, like, different angles, then making, I suppose you'd have to say, disapproving noises. She's quiet this morning – wrecked, obviously, after the workout I put her through.

As I'm lying there in the sack, I notice her pop a couple of pills. When she hits the apple fritter, I have a root in her bag to find out what they are. It turns out they're, like, tan-optimizer capsules and I remember her MySpace page. She comes back and catches me with the packet in my hand, but she says fock-all except that Helena Christensen uses them.

I ask her does she have to head off, thinking I wouldn't mind another quick go, but she says she has Cardio Barre and I make the mistake of asking her should I get checked out now as well.

She actually laughs at me and I'm left thinking, er, *how* did it happen that I'm suddenly the brainless one?

She's gone about ten minutes, roysh, and I'm just drifting back into a nice, comfortable sleep when my mobile rings. It's Trevion. The first thing I do is tell him I owe him big-time. My entire life I've been looking for a girl who'll do the business without putting me through fifteen or twenty minutes of boreplay first.

I'm there, 'I'm beginning to love Hollywood.'

He's like, 'Well, Hollywood's beginning to love you. The *Star* website described you as one of LA's hottest young couples. *In Touch* said that Lauren Conrad is hopping mad, according to friends. And I have it on very good authority that *Us Weekly* is going to say that Ptolemy's tiered Bensoni top and whiskered Chip & Pepper jeans added depth to her petite frame.'

Which *is* all nice to hear. There's only one thing that's really bothering me. 'Do you mind me asking,' I go, 'what's with all this ordering my food *for* me? I've got to tell you, Dude, I love my lobster.'

He's there, 'You need to lose some weight.'

At first, roysh, I think I'm obviously not hearing right. I would have thought I was in pretty great shape. Ptolemy's hands were up and down my abs like she was playing the focking squeezebox.

'Whatever you say,' I go, 'although, I have to tell you, a lot of people out there would actually disagree with you.'

'A lot of people don't know shit,' he goes. 'If you're going to be famous, you're going to need to lose twenty pounds.'

'Twenty pounds?'

'Twenty pounds. And fast. You look soft in these photos. Next item of business – what are you doing today?'

I'm there, 'Em, I was hoping to spend a bit of time with my daughter? Sorcha's sort of, like, guilted me into it. She's got a strop on – she's never coped well with me being in the public eye.'

'Spending time with your kid – a nice touch. But keep this Sureeka – whatever she's called – out of the picture for now. Tonight, you got another date.'

'*Another* date?'

'That's right, Timberlake. Broad called Ginnifer. She's one of mine. Hoping to break into movies. She got thirty-six-inch breasts.'

It's like, thirty-six-inch breasts? End of conversation.

I hang up, roysh, then turn over and drift off to sleep again, thinking about how well I think I'm going to cope with fame the second time around. I'm thinking, this time, older, possibly even wiser, I'm more ready for it.

Of course, I have no idea how wrong it's possible for one man to be.

So I'm sitting outside Buckys on Hollywood Boulevard, wolfing down a couple of slices of their blueberry swirl cheesecake, with a firm grip on Honor this time. I decide to ring Christian, because I haven't actually spoken to the dude since the famous day.

He answers on the third ring. 'Well?' I go. 'Have you been reading the gossip magazines?'

He's like, 'What? Oh, it's you,' except, like, he whispers it?

In the background, roysh, I can hear Lauren go, 'Who is it?' and Christian's there, 'It's, er, George Lucas. The taun-tauns have arrived.'

'Oh,' she goes. 'Tell him I said thank you for the flowers. They're beautiful.'

He's there, 'Er, Lauren says thanks for the flowers, Mr Lucas.'

I'm like, 'She's obviously still pissed at me, is she?'

'Er, yes,' he goes. 'Listen, I better go. I'm in the middle of changing the little guy,' and he hangs up without me even getting a chance to ask how the little goy is or what they're even calling him.

'*Hen piao liang*,' Honor goes, so I give her another little sip of her espresso. And at the same time, I'm thinking, if Christian and Lauren's son turns out to be even half as happy as this little one, they'll be very lucky parents.

'I love coffee table books myself,' I go. 'They make you look smart without actually *having* to read?'

Ginnifer cracks her hole laughing, so I end up passing it off as a joke.

She's actually a major improvement on Ptolemy – even looks-wise, if you can believe that. She's so like Rachel Bilson, you'd actually do a double-take. Same eyes, same mouth, same reddy-brown hair. She used to be – get this – a volley-ball player and she has, like, a Pan American Games medal, albeit silver. My attitude would have always been – never bring runners-up to my table. But she's big-time hot.

And, like Trevion said, she's trying to break into acting. She's played, like, a nurse in *House*, a lifeguard in *One Tree Hill* and – even though she doesn't speak any language other than English – the head of a Trilingual Immersion Programme in an episode of *Gilmore Girls* that unfortunately never screened.

And, yeah, she's banging on about herself a bit, telling me that she had, like, a beehive for the Peabody Awards – like Katie Cassidy's? – and that it's easy to do, except you *have* to use a Mebco flipside comb. But she's also got a brain and she's really into hearing about *my* whole story?

I've actually got to talk to her about Ronan, who she says sounds hilarious, about Cillian, who she admits sounds like a total dick, and then a bit about why *I* think Ireland have no chance of winning the World Cup this year with Eddie O'Sullivan in charge.

She's literally one of those birds you can talk to about anything.

We're in, like, Capo in Santa Monica, where, again, Trevion seems to be God. Various waiters stop by and tell me to tell him they said hi. I suppose they all want to be famous, too.

It's, like, an amazing restaurant. Italian, which I love. It's rustic, yet elegant, according to Ginnifer, who especially loves the high-beamed ceilings. 'You seem to know your shit,' I go, 'in fairness to you.'

She says interior design is a passion of hers. I'm about to tell her that beautiful women are a passion of mine, but I think it might come across as, like, cheesy?

I'm just watching her, roysh, studying her menu in the candlelight, with the sound of the sea – I suppose – breaking on the beach and I've suddenly got a boner on me like a stickshift.

'Do you mind me saying,' I end up *having* to go, 'you're a serious ringer for Rachel Bilson – as in, you look like her?'

She looks up, obviously delighted. 'Rachel Bilson? She is, like, *so* pretty. I saw her, like, *two* weeks ago at a Clippers game!'

She's big-time happy with me. I just shrug and go, 'Well, it's out there now – just so you know.'

I order the meatballs, followed by the *pasta d'capo* with *quattro formaggi*. What ends up actually arriving is the organic Lyon artichoke, followed by the Dungeness crab risotto, though this time I don't bother saying anything.

Ginnifer asks me how I'm coping with the whole celebrity thing. I tell her unbelievably well, although bear in mind I've had, like, fame before, even though it was pretty much just Europe. This time, I tell her, I think I'm mature enough *not* to blow it?

'So what do you think of Trevion?' she goes.

I'm there, 'I don't know. He's one serious dude, isn't he?'

'Isn't that who you *want* on your side?'

'I suppose. But all that shit about men burning in tanks . . .'

She laughs. 'I guess he's seen a lot.'

'Especially judging from his face.'

Ginnifer shrugs. 'Well, he fought in, like, Korea.'

I'm there, 'I wouldn't know. I wouldn't be into, like, world affairs and shit? Then there's the whole weight thing as well.'

She laughs again – I think the word is knowingly?

'He's a control freak,' she goes. 'But being thin is, like, *so* important out here. Have you tried, like, diet pills?'

'No. I was thinking of maybe storting back in the gym. I met this goy who's gay, but he's also, like, a port-time personal trainer? I've been meaning to actually ring him.'

'Well, you still should try the pills,' she goes. 'Did you know, at any given time, you're carrying around as much as ten pounds in subcutaneous water retention?'

'Jesus.'

'For six months, I was just, like, chewing food, then spitting it out? Then I went on the pills. And look at me. I'm eating virtually full meals again.'

She knows her way around a plate of polenta, there's no doubt about that.

'I've gone from being anorexic to being orthorexic,' she goes, 'and I've never been happier.'

I tell her that's cool.

We get on, it has to be said, unbelievably well. I'm in top form as well. As in, somehow it comes up then that she's, like, Jewish? And I ask her about the holidays, which I've heard are pretty good. She laughs. She says she's not much of an observer but, as well as the Sabbath, work is forbidden on Rosh Hashanah, Yom Kippur, the first and second days of Sukkot, on Shemini Atzeret, Simchat Torah, Shavuot and the first, second, seventh and eighth days of Passover. I tell her if I ever *have* to get a job again, I'm definitely joining up. I'm like, 'I won't actually be *in* this week – yeah, it's *Castleknock*. I've got to, like, stay in bed all day playing, I don't know, *Grand Theft Auto Three*.'

She thinks I'm genuinely hilarious, in fairness to her, to the point where I'm thinking I could seriously fall for this girl.

Then I'm thinking about all the people who've tried to crack America and basically failed. Robbie Williams, blah blah blah. But look at me. Fame. Women. I presume somewhere down the line there'll be money. And it all fell in my lap.

I have to admit, inside, I'm giving myself big-time pats on the back.

Spirulean. Estrolean. Betalean.

There's, like, millions of the fockers and they all sound like either sexually transmitted diseases or Harry Potter's teachers.

Thermodynamx. Leptigen. Trimspa.

I reckon I've already dropped two waist sizes walking up and down the aisle of CVS.

Dermagain. Lipodec. Thyro Stak.

It's, like, how the fock are you supposed to know which one?

For instance, Hoodia contains *hoodia gordonii*, a succulent plant from the Kalahari desert, used for centuries by the San people to stave off hunger during their long and arduous hunting trips into the South African wild. But Dexatrim Max 20 is available in Strawberry, Kiwi *and* Mixed Berry.

But then there's also Sesathin. Accelis. Clenbutical. Hydroxycut. Lipe-Xen. Thermonex . . .

I'm on the point of actually giving up when my phone all of a sudden rings. It's Sorcha. She sounds seriously pissed off. Years of experience tell me that *I'm* somehow the reason?

Her opening line is, 'Have you *seen* the cover of *Us Weekly*?'

I tell her I'm actually in CVS.

'Oh, they'll have it there,' she goes. 'Go and focking get it!'

Now, when Sorcha swears, I always fear the worst. But nothing could prepare me for what I'm about to see.

The fockers must have used, like, a long lens to get a photograph of me sitting outside Buckys . . . holding a double espresso up to Honor's lips. The headline on the cover is like, 'Starshmuck!' which *is* pretty clever you'd have to say, but then underneath it's like, 'Book Queen Fionnuala Slams Son For Giving Baby Coffee!'

This would certainly explain the five missed calls from Trevion this morning. Sorcha's pretty much hysterical, going, 'I can't believe you've done this to me! Oh my God, I can't believe you've done this!'

I turn, as the cover suggests, to pages two and three and I skim through the story.

'Irish book sensation Fionnuala O'Carroll-Kelly has blasted her wildchild son for giving his baby daughter coffee. The bestselling author branded Ross an "idiot" after he was photo-graphed outside a Hollywood Starbucks feeding espresso to eighteen-month-old Honor, his daughter by his estranged wife. Asked how she believed former girlfriend Lauren Con-rad would react to the photographs, Fionnuala, who is due to arrive in LA this week for the latest leg of a coast-to-coast publicity tour, agreed that the *Hills* star would feel she had a lucky escape. "It was a stupid, irresponsible thing to do," she said during a publicity event at a Barnes & Noble in Boulder, Colorado. "He is very immature and has little or no common sense." Fionnuala looked stunning in a belted D&G dress with Neil Lane gems . . .'

I can't believe she's done this to me.

'I can't believe you've done this to me,' Sorcha goes.

I'm there, 'Okay, I admit it – I've been giving her the odd coffee.'

'*That's* why she's been like a demon,' she goes.

I'm like, 'Yeah. But I suppose another way to look at it is – thank God it's nothing more serious.'

She loses it then in a big-time way. 'I got a text alert half an hour ago to say that Oprah Winfrey has called for you to be jailed.'

I'm like, 'Jailed?'

'Jailed! For giving drugs to a minor.'

'Drugs? It was a coffee, Sorcha. It was the odd coffee. And Oprah Winfrey should mind her own focking business.'

Shit. There's more on pages four and five. It turns out that Lauren Conrad has strenuously denied that we were ever an item. In fact, she's denied ever even *meeting* me? A spokesman said that the day we were photographed together, she actually had lunch with pals Frankie Delgado and Doug Reinhardt and that I just happened to step into the photograph.

'I've got a newsflash for that girl,' I go. 'She's been with way bigger orseholes than me.'

Sorcha's like, 'Well, I've got a newsflash for you. I've spoken to my dad and I've spoken to Cillian and they're both of the view that I should get a court order to keep you away from us.'

I'm like, 'What? Sorcha, you can't do that!'

But she's just like, 'Congratulations, Ross – you're a *real* celebrity now.'

One of the people I feel sorriest for in all of this is, like, Ginnifer. The magazines all ran the photographs of us out together, except there wasn't a mention of the graphic frock by Alice + Olivia that showed off her enormous chesticles. The story was all about me and basically what an idiot I am?

The headline in *People* was 'Tweedle Dumb and Tweedle Double-D'.

I phone her the second it appears, portly to apologize, but also because I'm genuinely interested in, like, seeing her again? And, I admit it, getting in there.

Except she says that Trevion doesn't think it'd be good for her career to be seen with me. 'He thinks that Tweedle Dumb thing will stick,' she goes. 'And, let's be honest, it's not exactly Brangelina.'

Of course, I'm nothing if not persuasive, especially when it comes to the opposite sex. Twenty seconds later, I've talked her into coming out with me again – my treat, her favourite restaurant, which happens to be Le Petit Greek in Larchmont.

By the time our main courses arrive, we're actually laughing about what happened, if you can believe that. I'm telling her that Sorcha's never out of Buckys herself and that Honor actually took her first steps in the one in Dundrum Town Centre.

'But do you think Sorcha's going to accept her share of the blame?' I go. 'Er, I don't *think* so?'

By the time the Harry Hill arrives, she's telling me that I'm actually a really, really nice goy, which obviously I know, although it *is* nice to get the recognition, and when I suggest heading on for a drink, she's actually John B.

Which is how we end up in S Bar, on, like, Hollywood and Vine?

The place is hopping. I order a beer and Ginnifer has, like, a maple anjou and she asks me if I saw *Entertainment Tonight*. It turns out that Nicole Richie and Annette de la Renta have also called for me to be jailed. *And* Ozzy Osbourne.

I'm actually laughing about it now. Think of the drugs that focker took over the years – and he's criticizing me for giving a baby coffee?

'What's Trevion saying?' she goes. 'Has he told you how he's going to spin it?'

I'm there, 'To be honest, I've been ignoring his calls. I'm too scared to even listen to his voice messages.'

'Ross,' she goes, 'you've *got* to talk to him,' and then all of a sudden she stops, roysh, and screws up her face. 'Jesus! What is that smell?'

'I don't smell it,' I go.

'I got it in the restaurant earlier and I wondered whether it was the spanakopita . . .'

What I obviously can't tell her, of course, is that the smell is actually me. To cut a long story short, I couldn't make my mind up in the end which diet pills to buy. I had them whittled down to the ones with the night-time fat-burner, the ones that heat your body and help you lose it through, like, thermogenesis, and the ones that contain *the* most pivotal thermogenic agents internationally studied.

Then I thought, what the fock, and for the last couple of days I've been taking all three. The upshot of that is that I smell like a dead mouse rotting behind a skirting board and as I'm standing here I'm having to clench every muscle in my lower body to keep my orse shut.

Moussaka probably wasn't the smortest idea in the world either.

The next thing, roysh, Ginnifer spots a friend of hers from reiki and it's weird because it's at that exact moment that I spot, of all people, Cillian, up at the bor. I'm there, 'I'll tell you what, you go talk to your friend,' giving her the guns, but without taking my eyes off him, 'and I'll come looking for you later.'

It turns out that Cillian's with Josh and Kyle. Josh is telling some bullshit story that involves the line, 'We're being *raped* on these derivatives,' and you can tell he loves saying the word.

Cillian doesn't even realize it, but he's, like, ten seconds away from being decked. I'm there, 'Who the fock are you telling Sorcha to get a court order?' but he actually shushes me, roysh, without saying even hello first, then tells Josh to continue, which of course he needs no invitation to do. 'I told him, "Hang tough, Dude!" Which he did.'

Cillian's there, 'And?'

He just smiles, then just goes, 'Fourteen *fucking* million,' and makes, like, a whooping sound. Then he turns around and bumps chests with Kyle, then with Cillian, then with a fourth dude who's there – a big fat focker with greased-back hair – who turns out to be Bob Soto, as in Cillian's boss at PwC.

I'm just, like, staring at Cillian. He's still got his swipe card from work attached to his belt loop. No one ever got laid wearing a swipe card – Rossism number two hundred and twelve.

I'm there, 'I asked you a focking question.'

'Wait a minute,' this Bob Soto dude goes, sticking a big sausage finger pretty much in my face. 'Who the fuck is *this* guy?'

What I *should* do is grab his focking finger and snap it back – but I don't. It's nice to be nice.

'It's Sorcha's ex,' Kyle goes and he's got, like, a little smile playing on his lips.

'This is him?' Bob Soto goes. 'This is *the guy*?'

I'm there, 'Yeah, what the fock is it to you?' and he sort of, like, pats me on the back and goes, 'Nothing. Really,' like there's shit he *could* say, but he's not going to?

I turn back to Cillian. 'Of course, you're loving it,' I go. 'The whole Starbucks thing. It's your chance to get me off the scene. Well, I can tell you this for a fact – it's not going to work. Honor's my daughter and nothing can change that fact.'

'You ever heliski?' Josh suddenly goes.

It totally throws me. I'm like, 'What?'

'We're going heliskiing next weekend,' he goes. 'Up to the Bugaboos,' and then he holds his hand up for Kyle to give him the least deserved high-five I've ever focking seen.

'Oh, *I* ski,' I go, 'don't you worry about that.'

Josh is like, 'I thought rugby was your thing,' and Bob Soto's immediately there, 'Rugby? Isn't that the game George Bush played in college?' and it's obvious what he's doing – he's trying to make out that I'm automatically a dipshit as well.

I just point at Cillian and tell him that if he thinks I'm going to let an actuary come between me and my daughter and, I suppose, my wife as well, he's got another thing coming.

Then I wander back to Ginnifer. She's still talking to her

friend, who it turns out is called Suzette and who seems cool enough, even if she's not the best looks-wise. When Suzette heads for the shitter I bring up the subject that's been hanging around the edge of the conversation all night. I tell Ginnifer I like her dress. She says it's a Kate and Kass halter. I tell her I'd love to see how it matched the corpet in my penthouse back at the Viceroy.

'Nice,' she goes, smiling, obviously appreciating a goy who knows how to talk the talk. 'Unfortunately, I've got to check on Picasso, my pygmy cat?'

'Oh,' I go, thinking it's an excuse.

She smiles. 'What I'm saying is, why don't *we* go to mine?'

I don't need to be asked twice. She doesn't even stick around to say goodbye to Suzette. Five minutes later, we're in an Andy McNab on the way to Whitley Heights.

Now, I've had my share of beautiful women over the years – and a lot of other people's share as well – but I have to tell you, I've never been so gagging for someone in my entire life. Even though all we're *actually* doing is holding hands, I've a nightstick on me that could put manners on a G7 protest.

I'm also clenching my orse cheeks like my life depends on it.

I suppose I should know how this evening's going to end when I hop out of the cor and pay the driver and get a sudden savage cramp in the old Malcolm.

There's one in the post – that's as sure as my eyes are focking watering here. I consider trying to maybe squeeze it out before we go inside, but Ginnifer's standing right next to me.

She puts the key in the door and shows me in. The gaff is actually a really nice little house – I remember what she said about being into, like, interior design? – and I realize it would be, like, the height of disrespect to open my lunch in here.

'Have you got, like, a jacks?' I go. 'In other words, bathroom?'

thinking I could drop it in there, then open the window and sort of, like, waft it out?

She's there, 'You'll have to use the upstairs one. I've just got through painting the one down here.'

She points up the stairs. 'It's the door immediately in front of you.'

The door immediately in front of me. I'm staring up at it. All I've got to do is get to the other side of that and I'm suddenly free from pain. I take the steps two at a time. But of course, in all the excitement, I let my orse muscles relax halfway up and without warning a fart nearly rips my orse in half.

There are no words you can say in that situation.

But there's also no way to describe to you the shock I get when I turn around to see Ginnifer lying in what would have to be described as a crumpled heap at the bottom of the stairs.

'No!' I end up shouting. It's all very *The Young and the Restless*. 'No!' and I leg it downstairs to check, I suppose, if she's still alive.

As luck would have it, she is – she's still breathing, even though she's out of the game. I whip open the front door and the cab driver is just turning the cor around. I call out to him and I tell him not to move. Ten seconds later, I come out of the house, carrying Ginnifer in, like, a fireman's lift. I lie her down on the back seat and I sit there cradling her head the whole way to the hospital, going, 'Hang in there, Baby! Don't you dare die on me!'

The driver asks me what happened and I tell him it's a long story.

'What's that smell?' he goes.

I'm there, 'Just put your focking foot down, will you?'

When we get to the hospital, there's nothing *but* questions.

They put Ginnifer onto, like, a trolley and as they're wheeling her along they're going to me, 'Did she take something? Drugs, maybe?'

I'm there, 'No.'

'Alcohol?'

'One or two cocktails. Three at the most.'

'Is she pregnant?'

'All I know is not by me?'

'Is she a diabetic? Is she allergic to anything? Penicillin?'

I stop walking with them and I'm suddenly like, 'Enough with the questions already! I *know* what happened. I . . . I farted and knocked her out.'

It's, like, the entire focking hospital goes quiet, then suddenly bursts out laughing. Everywhere, roysh, people are repeating what I said, then Ginnifer's taken through a set of double doors that I'm not allowed to pass through, but I'm told she's in, like, the best possible hands.

I wander over to the waiting area. I ring Trevion, but he doesn't answer. It *is* the middle of the night. I leave him a voicemail saying sorry I haven't been in touch. I'm in, like, the emergency room of the Cedars-Sinai. Ginnifer's been taken in, blahdy blahdy blah.

Then I get chatting to this really cool homeless dude with cirrhosis and I end up spilling my guts out to him, a total stranger. 'She played, like, a nurse in *House*,' I'm going. 'I'm not sure if that's actual irony, but it certainly feels like it should be. Jesus, she had, like, her whole life in front of her . . .'

After maybe twenty minutes, half an hour of this, Trevion comes bursting through the doors into the emergency room. He totally flips, which I knew he would. 'What happened?' he wants to know.

I shake my head. 'I knocked her out cold with one of my farts.'

'What?'

'Hard and all as that is to believe. I'm rancid at the moment.'

'She's out cold?'

'Yeah.'

He shakes his head. 'She's fucking narcoleptic, you idiot.'

I'm like, 'She's what?'

'It's a sleeping disorder. I told you before you took her out the last day.'

He did mention something, now that I think about it. 'Oh. I thought narcoleptics were the ones who can't stop stealing shit.'

He looks mad enough to put me through the focking wall. 'What are you two doing out anyway?' he goes.

'We went out on, like, a date?'

'A date? I told her to stay away from you.'

'Look, I'm sure she tried. But I rang her up and asked her out, just to say sorry for, like, ruining her career as well as my own. I actually really like her.'

'Oh, you do?' he goes, cracking on that he's actually happy for us. 'Aw, ain't that something.'

'Yeah,' I go. 'And I *very* seldom get serious about birds . . .'

His expression suddenly changes. He goes, 'Life's a fucking party for you, huh? Big focking jamboree . . .'

'No.'

'You eat tonight?'

'What?'

'You take her for a meal?'

'Yeah, as it happens. Le Petit Greek.'

'What you have?' he goes, looking at my, I suppose, mid-riff. 'Tell me it was stuffed grape leaves.'

'To stort I had, like, hummus, but then also Greek meatballs because there wasn't a lot in it. If I'm being honest, I would have had some – probably most – of Ginnifer's feta salad as well,' and as I'm rhyming off all of this stuff, roysh, he's doing, like, calculations in his head, presumably working out the calories. 'For the main, I would have had moussaka, then one or two lamb kebabs, which I can never resist.'

Whatever bottom line he arrives at, he's not a happy camper. 'What are you, Elvis?' he goes.

I actually don't know what to say. I end up going, 'So who are the ones who can't stop stealing shit, then?'

'I don't *give* a fuck!' he goes, then marches over to the nurses' station. I hear him say Ginnifer's name, then the nurse mentions some shit about tests. 'She don't need no fucking tests,' he goes. 'She gets attacks of sleep. Mystery fucking over. Now go get her.'

He whips out his phone. He dials a number and the next thing he's going, 'Marty, it's Trev. Hey, I'm sorry for waking you. I got a story and it's all for fucking you, Bernstein . . . Yeah, that's it – you go *get* your fucking laptop . . .'

He puts his hand over the mouthpiece and tells me, totally out of the blue, that he doesn't *give* a shit about me anymore because today he signed a new star – a *real* star.

I'm there, 'Who?'

He just goes, 'Fyon Hoola O'Carroll-Kelly!'

Then he's back on the phone again. 'Yeah, Ginnifer Battles, you know her? *One Tree Hill. House.* You got it, Starsky! I'm here in the emergency room with her . . . Yeah, she nearly fucking died tonight. Choked on a Kalamata olive – can you believe that? Le Petit Greek . . . Larchmont, that's right . . . Hey, I'll find out . . .'

I'm beginning to think he was only ever using me to get to the old dear. It was probably him who told her to call me an idiot.

He turns to me. 'What was she wearing?'

I'm still in, like, shock, although I still manage to go, 'A red Kate and Kass halter dress.'

'You get that? Kate and Kass . . . Yeah, red . . .'

He turns to me again. 'Shoes?'

I shrug. 'It never came up.'

'Fornarina red heart peep-toe courts,' he goes, without skipping a beat. 'And the bag was a white Mulberry Alana . . . Friends said she's happy just to be alive – all that shit. Write it up . . .'

When he gets off the phone, I go, 'My old dear? How the fock did that come about?'

He's there, 'I picked up the phone. I said you got something, Kid, and I want to work with you.'

I'm there, 'So where does that leave me?'

He goes, 'All washed up, Starry Eyes. I couldn't even call you a has-been. You're a never-was.'

4. This is my comeback, girl

According to a poll on the internet, I'm the most hated man in America. Second in the world after Osama bin Laden and just ahead of Kim Jong-il, whose nuclear ambitions have apparently raised the spectre of annihilation for the planet. So I'm in the scratcher, roysh, shocked by this and, I'd have to say, even depressed.

I'm lying there also thinking, was that it? Was that really my moment of fame? I should have enjoyed it more, even for the seven days it lasted. I can suddenly understand why all these stars end up going focking bananas when no one's looking at them anymore.

I flick through the channels and find, like, an entertainment one, torturing myself I suppose. Because Amy Smart portied with fellow celebs Sandra Oh and Camilla Belle at the Foley + Carinna store opening in LA last night and even Sienna Miller was spotted enjoying herself in Foxtail looking fabulous in a Viktor & Rolf shirtdress with Sergio Rossi eel-skin pumps in blue.

I'm going, 'Enjoy it while it lasts, girls. Enjoy it while it lasts.'

Then, suddenly, up comes this photograph on Fox News that has my eyes out on actual stalks. It's a woman, roysh, totally naked, but painted from head to toe – including all of her various bits – in gold paint.

I'm actually lying there thinking it's one of the sexiest things I've ever seen when all of sudden I realize that it's *her* – as in the old dear? – and the old Malcolm does a quick lurch.

133

I have to turn up the sound.

'Now,' the newsreader dude goes, 'she's already the golden girl of women's fiction – now Fionnuala O'Carroll-Kelly is set to become the golden girl of marketing. The controversial writer – from *Ireland* – has been painted from head to toe in gold paint for a role in a commercial for Midas – a new brand of canned Prosecco. A warning to viewers that the following report contains *bodhrán* music . . .'

I don't focking believe it.

It comes on. It storts with, like, a picture of a leprechaun and – the dude's right – skiddly-eye music in the background. 'According to Irish mythology,' a bird's voice goes, 'the leprechaun is a type of male fairy who, many of the country's famously simple people will tell you, acts as a custodian for the pot of gold . . . contained at the end of *every* rainbow.

'Like the fabled creatures so beloved by Ireland's idiot people, Fionnuala O'Carroll-Kelly has shown that she, too, has the golden touch. *Karma Suits You – States of Ecstasy*, her steamy bodice-ripper about an Irish woman who experiences a sexual reawakening after coming to America, has topped the *New York Times* bestseller list for three weeks. And now Midas, a drinks company marketing a new brand of canned Prosecco, are banking on the fact that the stunningly attractive author . . . is worth her *weight* in gold.'

Then it switches to this dude with, like, a goatee? The caption says he's Richard Schor – Product, Promotion and Brand Executive, Midas. 'Fionnuala O'Carroll-Kelly is fresh, she's perky, she's effervescent,' he goes. 'But she also possesses a certain class and sophistication. The self-same qualities we associate with Midas Canned Prosecco. So in terms of matching a product *to* a star? This is what we would call a perfect strategic fit . . .'

'What he perhaps forgot to mention,' the report goes, 'is another quality they have in common – a great body . . .'

Whoosh. Up she comes on the screen, wearing half-nothing.

A focking bag of cement in a bikini. She's standing in what looks like an ort studio with all these, like, cameras and lights spread about the place and they're painting her – I shit you not – with, like, a paint gun?

'In the Irish language, Gay Lick, Fionnuala means, literally, white shoulders. Turning her into all-over gold was a job that took a total of six hours . . . *and* a lot of patience. First, they used a compressor gun loaded with liquid gold to give her body a first coat. A second and third were later added. Artists also used a special liquid gold leaf to colour her hair . . . while glitter varnish and eye shadow were painstakingly applied . . . to her nails and eyelids.

'Once the paint job was completed, Fionnuala had to remain deathly still – something that the highly driven author of three bestsellers back in her native Emerald Isle is unused to doing. And here – begorrah and be-to-hokey – are the results . . .'

They show her, like, fully painted, pulling various ridiculous poses in front of the camera.

'Fionnuala, who once posed naked for a Yummy Mummy calendar back in the Land of Saints and Scholars, was delighted with her new look, which is expected to adorn magazine spreads and billboards right across the country . . .'

They show her, like, afterwards – the focking whelk – with all the shit washed off her, going, 'Yes, it was wonderful fun. I've always said, *as* women, we should never be ashamed of our bodies – we *should* flaunt them more. Especially in later years. Like good Prosecco, they improve with age,' which was obviously totally rehearsed.

Then they show, like, one of the photographs of her in

all the muck again and the reporter goes, 'Midas will certainly be hoping that this Gay Lick Goddess helps them unlock the secret . . . *of* alchemy! Jess Cook, Fox News, *in* Santa Barbara.'

I straight away grab my phone. Trevion answers on, like, the third ring and I'm straight on the attack. 'I can't believe you let her do that. She's sick in the focking head. And *you're* taking advantage of that.'

'Hey,' he goes, 'quiet down, Tinkerbell – what do you want?'

'What do I want? What do you think? How would you like it if I painted *your* old dear and stuck her on TV?'

'She looked a million dollars up there.'

'She looked like she'd fallen off the top of a sumo wrestling trophy.'

'You know who I had on the phone today? Nous Model Management – mean anything to do you?'

I'm there, 'Not really.'

'Same crowd handles Paris fucking Hilton. Yeah, that's right, Smart Mouth. They're all over your mother. Offering her all kinds of work. I got Columbia on – can't wait to get her in the studio.'

'Studio?'

'They want her to make a record. Here in LA. Meanwhile, I can't move in my fucking office for all the shit that's getting sent to her. Shoes. Dresses. Bags. You like ladies' dresses?'

'No.'

'I think you do. I think they get you off.'

'They actually don't?'

'Yeah they do. My phone ain't stopped ringing. I got Marc Jacobs on one, Tony Burch on two, Zac Posen on three. They want to see her in their shit. I got a list of shows want her to cameo. *Ugly Betty. Desperate* fucking *Housewives.*

Everyone wants a piece of your mother and you want to know why?'

'Go on, enlighten me.'

'Cos *she* ain't you.'

'Exsqueeze me?'

'Hey, you heard it, Ladylove. She ain't you. She don't sit around getting fat and pissy. And remember this – she *done* something for *her* fame. Yours fell in your fucking lap and you still never knew which way was up.'

I'm there, 'Well, I would have thought in, like, a five-minute report there would have been *some* mention of the fact that her son happens to be Ross O'Carroll-Kelly.'

'Who?' he goes. 'Who's that? Never fucking heard of him. I got a newsflash for you, Friend – your mother's a star. You? You're nothing. You're last month's celebutard.'

You've no idea how actually hurtful that is to hear. 'Well,' I go, 'what if I told you I wanted to make, like, a comeback?'

He actually laughs.

I'm there, 'I'm serious. How do I get back up there again? I'm actually only realizing now how much I want all that shit – the clothes, the record deal, the whole blahdy blahdy blah.'

He tells me he's too busy with his real stars. I tell him I'll do anything he wants.

I've got, like, a roomful of people staring at me like I'm some kind of monster.

'You did *what*?'

And this from a dude called Snake, who's just admitted pimping out his wife for heroin.

'I gave my baby daughter a double espresso,' I go, shrugging my shoulders and trying to make it sound less of a big deal than it apparently is.

'You give me one good reason,' Bret, this sort of, like, trailer-trash dude, goes, 'why I shouldn't go over there and punch you into a twenty-year coma.'

Coke and gambling are Bret's bag. He sold his mother's gaff to pay off some bookie in Reno. She was still lying in her bed when they threw it out into the focking street.

'Bret,' Priscilla goes, 'one thing we don't dispense here is judgement – remember that?'

Bret takes a deep breath. 'It's just, you know, I got kids myself . . .'

Addiction Education was, like, Trevion's idea? He thought it might play well with the press, but I'll be lucky to get out of here with this pretty face intact.

This bird called Hazel (painkillers and surgery) says she recognizes my boat, then this Filipino bird called Dalisay (shoplifting and cybersex) says she saw me in a magazine. 'Giving that little girl coffee,' she goes. 'Laughing, real ugly,' and then all of a sudden Bret loses it again. 'You ever give my daughter anything,' he goes, jabbing his finger in my direction, 'be it a cappuccino, a macchiato, whatever – I will, *personally*, beat you unrecognizable with a fucking tyre iron. God fucking help me!'

'Let's control that anger,' Priscilla goes. 'Just visualize yourself back in that cell in Carson City and remember the breathing exercises we learned.'

Jesus Christ!

Priscilla turns to me then. 'Okay,' she goes, 'if we might take what I like to call a client-centred approach with you – what do you think was at the root of this behaviour?'

It's like being back in detention with the focking Jesuits – except there's no pulling the Senior Cup cord in here.

'Was it low self-esteem? Focal anxiety? Maybe simple insensitivity to the conventions of appropriate social behaviour?'

I'm there, 'I think it was simply the fact that she *wanted* coffee? If you knew her mother . . . Even though, I've noticed, she's become more of a tea person since she came to the States.'

'Piece of shit,' Hazel goes – meaning me – and I look around, roysh, at the other faces and I realize that I've got to get out of here. To be honest, roysh, the only reason I even came was so the paparazzi could get a shot of me on the way out.

According to Trevion, people love a comeback story. But this crowd aren't loving *my* story and I'm sensing that my life is in serious danger here.

Priscilla wants more, though. 'Tell me,' she goes, 'about some of your close, interpersonal relationships?'

Shrinks, I know from personal experience, are like lions or tigers or any of that crew – throw them the odd bone and they'll generally leave *you* the fock alone.

'My home situation is pretty focked,' I go, then I notice Bret and one or two of the other men straighten up in their chairs. I wouldn't say they're on my side yet, but they're definitely prepared to hear me out.

I'm there, 'My old man, for instance. He's a dickhead and I won't give him the pleasure of even talking about him. Except to say that he had, like, a daughter – in other words, Erika – who he kept a secret for, like, twenty-and-whatever years . . .'

This bird Jennie (compulsive disorders and crystal meth) goes, 'Man, that is fucked up!' and suddenly I feel like I'm in an episode of *Maury*.

I'm there, 'I've been trying to tell people what a dick he is for years, but no one listened. So Erika gets wind of this – that *he's* her actual old man – and she ends up not even hating his guts. She's even calling him Dad . . .'

'That's not right,' Bret agrees.

I stare into the distance. 'The thing is, this bird Erika — *before* I knew she was my sister, I hasten to add? — I would have, you know, once or twice . . .'

'Ain't no shame in that,' Bret goes.

I suspect there probably isn't wherever he comes from. It's not the kind of thing I want bandied around the Merrion Inn, though.

'If I'm being honest,' I go, 'I'd say she's possibly the most attractive girl I've ever laid eyes on.'

Hazel goes, 'Don't you go blaming yourself. It's *his* fault — your father.'

I'm there, 'In many ways, I wish he was in this room to hear you say that.'

Hazel's there, 'No wonder you gave your baby coffee — you ain't in your right mind.'

I'm there, 'Exactly. I wish my ex-wife could see it like that. She's banging on about court orders and all sorts.'

Suddenly, everyone in the room wants to share.

'My ex-wife's a bitch,' Bret goes.

'Mine's a prostitute,' Snake goes, 'slash exotic dancer.'

By the end of the meeting, roysh, they're all on my side. Bret even apologizes for earlier — the tyre iron, blahdy blahdy blah. He says he's been pretty wound-up since the police seized his fighting dogs.

I'm thinking, I've always had, like, a way with people. 'Anyway,' I go, standing up, 'you've heard enough of my tales of woe . . .'

'Your agent's right,' Harvey goes. 'You *could* do with losing some weight.'

This is us in Newsroom on Robertson, finally getting that coffee, although what I'm actually drinking is one of these Taiwanese Milk Teas that he's been banging on about — I suppose just to show him that I *am* open-minded, even though I think he's accepted that nothing's going to happen between us.

'It's weird,' I go, rubbing my hands up and down my body, 'because in Ireland, this would be considered pretty much ripped.'

He pulls a face as if to say, sorry to disappoint you. 'You've got, like, a little cellulite,' he goes. 'Don't take offence – two or three weeks, we can work it off you.'

I'm flicking through his training journal and I can't believe the sessions he's putting in. 'I have to tell you,' I go, 'I was pretty proud of what I was bench-pressing until I read this.'

He tells me that I have to decide, from the outset, what my fitness goals are and I tell him I want abs like focking grill morks.

'Well then,' he goes, 'let's get to work,' and the next thing we're tipping across the road to the gym.

This is, like, step two of Trevion's plan to, what he calls, refloat my career.

I start off with, like, twenty minutes on the treadmill, then a few weights. 'It's always a good idea to rotate muscle groups as you work out,' Harvey goes. 'Or alternate, if you can, between cardio and lifting? It gives your muscles more time to rest. *And* it keeps your routine from getting monotonous.'

I tell him I wish I'd had him with me in Andorra. There were one or two guys on the team could have done with a good fitness coach.

He holds my two legs while I do, like, a hundred sit-ups. I ask him how his weekend went – because there *is* that whole getting-to-know-each-other vibe?

'Mike and I got in, like, a huge fight,' he goes.

I stop mid sit-up and I'm like, 'Who's this Mike?' but not

in, like, a jealous way. Again, I'm more making conversation than anything.

Mike turns out to be some dude who's been dicking him around for a couple of years. He's married, roysh, but he's been stringing Harvey along with the promise that he's going to one day leave his wife for him. Except if you ask me, he's obviously not. A player always recognizes a player.

'He was supposedly leaving her in April last year,' he goes. 'Then again in September. Then again last week. But when it comes to it, there's always something. "She's having a hard time at work." "Her sister's not well." "Let me just get through Christmas with her." And all this time I believed his bullshit. He's never going to leave her.'

I shake my head, do another ten sit-ups, then stop and go, 'Dude, do you mind if I say something to you? You let people treat you like that, they're never going to respect you. Take it from someone who's been dicking birds around his entire life.'

He rolls his eyes. 'Ross, this is nothing I haven't heard before.'

'Well, I'm just saying, I'd imagine you could do better. You know, you're actually a good-looking goy . . .'

Even that doesn't cheer him up.

'Do you mind me asking,' I go, 'how old are you?'

He's there, 'Twenty,' which actually surprises me, roysh, because I thought he was maybe twenty-four, twenty-five. I think I actually laugh. 'Twenty?' I go. 'Why do you want to be settled down at twenty? Especially with someone dragging *his* baggage – what, a marriage break-up? Harvey, you're just a kid – you should be out there breaking horts, loving it, loving it, loving it.'

He smiles, in fairness to him.

I'm like, 'Twenty? If you only knew the craic you're going to have in the years ahead.'

He shrugs. 'It's just that Mike was my first relationship,' he goes.

I'm there, 'A goy of your age shouldn't even know that word. Okay, when I break up with someone, especially someone I like – my wife is just one example – I always ask myself one question: was I happy the day before I met her? So, like, were you happy the day before you met this Mike dude?'

'I guess.'

I give him the guns. 'Then you can be happy again.'

He laughs, finally, and tells me I have a good perspective on things.

I do another fifty sit-ups straight and end up putting in, it has to be said, an unbelievable session – the kind I haven't done since I was at school. Practically every muscle in my body is hurting at the end, which is all good.

Even Harvey has to high-five me, as if to say, you worked today – respect.

We grab a quick Jack Bauer – yeah, together. That's how much it *doesn't* actually bother me? I even borrow some of his Ein Gedi Organic Dead Sea Mineral body scrub.

As I'm towelling off, I check my phone and notice that I've got, like, fourteen missed calls from Sorcha.

I'm there, 'Uh-oh.'

Harvey's like, 'What's wrong?'

'Sorcha,' I go. 'You remember her from the shop?'

He's like, 'Yeah, she's, like, *so* pretty.'

'Well, she's talking about getting some kind of court order out against me.'

'A court order?'

'Ah, it's not as big a deal as it sounds. It's possibly even for the best. It was all getting a bit weird anyway.'

He storts rubbing moisturizer into his body. 'How was it weird?'

'I suppose the big thing is that she doesn't seem to want me anymore,' I go, checking myself out in the long mirror. 'Not in *that* way.'

'Did you tell me she's with someone else now?'

'See, that wouldn't have stopped her in the past. There were, like, loads of times when she tried to move on, but I always managed to get back in there. The thing is, I think this time she really *does* see us as just good friends?'

'But that's good, right?'

I'm there, 'Is it?' stepping into my boxers. 'I mean, you've seen us together. All she wants to do is bring me shopping and talk to me about celebrities and fashion. I mean, don't get me wrong, I don't mind the odd time her asking me – just for the sake of argument – do these black Balenciaga trousers go with this Stella McCortney tailored blazer? Or even just, do these Kasil jeans suit me? You know, I've no problem saying, actually, yeah, the adjustable side buttons help prevent gaping at the back, thereby presenting a longer, leaner leg . . .'

Harvey cracks his hole laughing. 'Yeah, I would say you've spent *way* too much time shopping together,' he goes.

Of course, then I have to laugh as well.

He goes, 'So who does she usually shop with back home?' and I feel instantly guilty.

'Her best friend,' I go, 'as in her best *best* friend would have to be a bird called Erika. They've been bezzy mates since they were, like, thirteen.'

He's there, 'Maybe she's just confused. She's got this new guy, then you're suddenly back on the scene and she's still trying to work out how you fit into her life. So she's trying to turn you into a surrogate for her best friend.'

'No,' I go, 'she's trying to turn me into one of these metro-sexuals. No offence.'

He looks at me like he hasn't a bog what I'm talking about. 'Er, none taken,' he goes.

I'm there, 'See, my whole line on metrosexuals is they're basically men *as* women would have created them. As in, they're sensitive to women's feelings, carry bags, remember birthdays, never piss in the sink. It took women basically thousands of years to fashion this ideal man – then they discovered they didn't actually fancy him?'

Harvey breaks his orse laughing and I mean *really* breaks his orse. He tells me I'm the funniest person he's ever met, which is a huge compliment, it has to be said.

I finish getting dressed, then I tell him I better see what Sorcha wants. From the second she answers, I can hear the panic in her voice. I'm there, 'Sorcha, what's wrong?' but she can barely get the words out.

'I drove up to Tarzana to see that shop – the one that does Susana Monaco, Sass & Bide and Thread Social,' she goes. 'And *some* Elizabeth and James. The one that you were *supposed* to come to with me . . .'

I'm there, 'Well, I didn't think we were even talking, what with the thing about the coffee, the court order, blahdy blahdy blah . . .'

'I heard all this shouting and I looked across the road and these – bastards! – were surrounding this hairdresser's. They have her trapped in there, Ross . . .'

I'm there, 'Sorcha, who?'

She's like, 'Britney.'

I'm like, 'Britney?'

Harvey even mouths the word, 'Britney?' his face full of concern.

Sorcha's there, 'I'm standing looking at her through this

hairdresser's window . . . Ross, she's shaving all her hair off.'

I'm there, 'Shaving her hair off?'

Harvey puts his hand over his mouth.

I'm like, 'Are you sure it's her, Babes?'

'I think *I'd* know what Britney Spears looks like,' she pretty much roars at me.

'Sorry,' I go. You have to when they're like that.

She's there, 'It's the paparazzi – they've driven her to this,' and then I hear her going, 'Leave her alone, you vultures! That's all you are! Actual vultures!' and it's obvious that Britney's not the only one who's lost it.

There's suddenly silence on the end of the phone for ten, maybe fifteen seconds, then suddenly the kind of scream I haven't heard from her since Saoirse Bannon pipped her for the Mount Anville Student of the Year award thanks to the casting vote of Sister Aquinata.

'Oh my God,' Sorcha goes, 'she's, like, totally bald . . .'

'She's totally bald,' I tell Harvey. He puts his head in his hands. There's a focking pair of them in it.

The next thing, roysh, Sorcha must try to push her way past Britney's security – you've got to say that for the Mounties, they're focking defiant – because I hear her go, 'Don't touch me! Do *not* touch me!' and I immediately feel sorry for whoever the poor focker is. 'I've been worried about Britney since she tripped and almost dropped Sean Preston coming out of New York's Ritz Carlton,' she's telling them.

The next thing, roysh, I can hear this noise go up and my guess is that Britney's coming out of the place.

'Britney,' I hear Sorcha shout, 'we share the same birthday!' which is actually news to me, then a few seconds later, 'I just want you to know that I'm thinking about you and praying that you get well.'

When she eventually talks to me again, it's only to tell me that Britney didn't even look at her. She's bawling her eyes out, going, 'She didn't even look at me, Ross – not even once.'

'They're back together,' Erika goes and I end up nearly dropping the phone.

I'm there, 'Who?' except obviously I already *know*?

'Charles and my mum,' she goes. 'They've picked up where they left off.'

I'm there, 'Picked up where they left off? What, thirty years ago? That's focked up.'

'Ross,' she goes, 'that's my mother and father you're talking about.'

'Er, *yeah*? But that's, like, ancient history. Back to-focking-gether! What are they, sixteen? Can I just ask, have you actually seen this?'

'No. I don't want to see *her*. Dad told me . . .'

Again with the *Dad*.

'He came to the hotel today,' she goes.

'I take it you're still in the Merrion. I wouldn't focking blame you.'

'He says he loves her and she loves him. He says they never stopped loving each other.'

'Never stopped?' I go. 'Oh, the things I'm going to throw at that focker next time I talk to him. I'm actually going to sit up all night tonight making a list . . .'

'Ross,' she goes, 'do you think it'd be okay to ring Sorcha now?'

I'm there, 'No way. The, er, shit she was saying about you yesterday. I was like, "Whoa, that girl used to be your actual friend." I think it'd do more horm than actual good.'

'Oh,' she goes. She sounds pretty devastated, in fairness to her.

'And the next time you're talking to *him*,' I go, 'is there any chance you could remind him that he's still married to *my* old dear? Just in case it's slipped his mind.'

'Donald Faison loves this place,' Trevion goes. 'Jennifer Morrison, too. Jennifer's here *all* the fucking time . . .'

He's talking about Republic, this pretty rocking steakhouse in West Hollywood, where the nosebag's supposed to be incredible. Except I wouldn't know. I'm having a plate of focking hedge-clippings – though Trevion's pork three-ways with truffle fries and cheddar mac *does* smell incredible, in fairness to it.

'I'm going to have to take out earthquake insurance on you,' he goes – actually *happy* with me for once?

I'm there, 'Really?'

He's like, 'You better believe it. One or two people already calling you the next Coe Lynn Farrell – how do you like that?'

I have to be honest with him. 'Where I come from,' I go, 'he'd be considered a bit of a knacker?'

I'm chopping away through *my* plate like Indiana focking Jones. 'Let me tell you something,' he goes, waving a piece of pork at me on the end of his fork, 'there ain't nothing plays like contrition. Addiction counselling was a masterstroke. Martha Stewart's on the TV this morning – says we ought to show compassion and understanding . . .'

'Wait a minute,' I go, 'are you saying that the public love me again?'

He laughs. 'No,' he goes, 'I ain't saying they love you. I'm saying they fucking hate you a lot less than they did last week.'

'I suppose that's something.'

'That internet petition, calling on the Government to put you in Guantánamo . . .'

'Guantánamo? Isn't that for, like, I don't know, terrorists and that whole crowd?'

'That's right, Carlos. But only three hundred new signatures yesterday. That's down from *seventeen* hundred the day before. Just to give you a little perspective here.'

I nod, *trying* to see the bright side. 'It's hordly hero-worship, though, is it?'

'Hey,' he goes, 'you ever spend sixteen days in a trench up to your fucking neck in rainwater?'

I'm there, 'No,' even though he already *knows* the answer?

'See, that's why you never learned patience. But you will, Pilgrim. You will.'

I'm sitting there, staring at the big, scaly head on him, thinking, seventy-five! Maybe I should I stort listening to him more. The shit he must have seen in his lifetime. And I suppose he is entitled to be a bit grumpy, with a face like a focking baseball glove.

'Anyways,' he goes, 'I got you some movie work.'

My mouth just drops open. I'm there, 'Movie work? Are you serious?'

'Did you hear me laugh?'

'Er, no.'

'It's a kiddies' movie,' he goes. 'American football.'

I'm there, 'Whoa. So what am I – like, the coach? Because I can definitely bring something to that role.'

'Slow down, Sinatra. They're looking for a body double. No one's going to see your fucking face. Let me ask you something – you say you can kick a ball, right?'

I actually laugh. 'Er, you could say that.'

'Well,' he goes, 'that's all you *got* to do – they want to film your feet kicking the ball through the posts. The director's

Chubby Waghorne – a personal friend of mine. And speaking of chubby . . .'

He sort of, like, looks me up and down.

I'm there, 'What?' genuinely meaning it.

'What are we going to do about you?' he goes. 'You're getting fatter?'

I'm like, 'Fatter? Dude, I put in an unbelievable session in the gym yesterday. Look at me, I'm living on plants and focking shrubs here.'

He's there, 'I want to see you walking Zuma Beach, hand in hand with Katharine McPhee, Elisabeth Rohm, Demi Lovato. *Friends say she's never been happier. Thinks she's found the one . . .*'

'That's exactly what I want.'

'You take *that* body onto any beach on this coast, you take my word for it, Big Guy, Greenpeace are gonna drag you in the fucking ocean . . .'

'That's horsh.'

'It's true.'

'But there's not a lot more I can do . . .'

He stares at my body and, with a cheese knife in his hand, draws imaginary cut marks on my chest and stomach. I tell him no way. No *focking* way.

'Bit of lipo.'

'No.'

'Abdominal sculpt.'

'I said no.'

'Everyone out here gets work, Friend.'

'There must be another way. Harvey, an actual gay friend of mine, was telling me there's, like, firming gels?'

He shakes his head. 'Kid, forget about firming gels.'

'But they tighten up the blood vessels to give your muscles a more toned appearance . . .'

'Will you forget about firming gels already?'

He practically roars it at me. Everyone in the restaurant stops talking and stares in our direction.

'Forget! About! Fucking! Firming gels!' he goes again, through gritted teeth this time.

He looks away, roysh, like he's disappointed with me. Then, totally out of the blue, he goes, 'You know your mother was photographed in Susie Cakes this morning – yeah, with Marcia Cross.'

It's like, holy fock! I've a thing for Marcia Cross – a major thing.

He's there, 'That's right, Kermit. They're friends now . . .'

I know what he's doing. He's very subtly letting me know that he has influence in this town.

'Matter of fact,' he goes, 'she's coming to Fyon Hoola's reading tomorrow night.'

'Reading?'

'Yeah, she's reading in Book Soup. Famous place on Sunset. Everyone's going to be there. Not only Marcia. Kim Cattrall. Diane Kruger. Ziyi Zhang . . .'

I'm there, 'It sounds like things are really happening for her.'

'You bet they are. Because she's prepared to do whatever it takes. *She's* had work, you know.'

I laugh. 'I know that. She's had her face lifted that many times, she's practically wearing her orse as a hat.'

'That's why she's fast becoming one of the biggest names in showbusiness . . .' he goes.

There's no doubt, he knows what buttons to press.

'And you,' he goes, 'will always be just her son.'

'Okay,' I hear myself suddenly go. 'I'll do it. Whatever it takes.'

His face is even uglier when he smiles. 'We're going to get you a beautiful body,' he goes. 'I'm going to take you to San

Sancilio. He's from Ecuador. He's a personal friend of mine. He's not a butcher . . . He *was* a butcher, but he ain't a butcher now. No, now he does plastic – best in the fucking business.'

She smiles at me through the screen door. 'Oh my God,' she goes, 'I was just about to have my dinner.'

She's got one of those, like, Weight Watchers meals in her hand, which presumably is about to go into the microwave.

'Low in calories, high in misery,' I go, which is, like, an old joke of ours.

She laughs, then she throws her orms around me and says she's sorry about the whole Britney thing. I tell her it's cool. It must have been hord for her to watch – as, like, a fan? Hopefully she'll get the treatment she needs now that she's hit rock-bottom.

'Speaking of which . . .' she goes. And she smiles, you'd have to say warmly. 'I heard.'

She's obviously talking about me going to addiction therapy. I give her the line that Trevion fed me about having to face up to my actions.

She's there, 'That's, like, oh my God, Ross – I am *so* impressed.'

I'm thinking, after all the shit we've been through together, we're always going to be in each other's lives – even if it does have to be just friends.

She tells me to come in, then leads me through the huge hallway down to the kitchen. I can't help but check her out. She looks incredible in this black-and-white-striped tank top, which I'm pretty sure is the Daftbird one she mentioned Victoria Beckham was wearing the other day coming out of Shizue Boutique.

I say fock-all, though.

She puts her Storvation Chicken in the microwave and asks me what I've been up to. I tell her I spent the day hanging out with Harvey.

She laughs.

'Oh, the big bromance,' she goes. 'What, did you get, like, a manny-peddy?'

She *is* only joking, I should point out.

I tell her it was nothing as gay as that. We actually went rollerblading on Venice Beach. Harvey was teaching me.

She says she got a text alert this morning to say I spent the day yesterday playing tennis with Lo Bosworth at the Pacific Palisades Center. It said we were later spotted sipping bellinis in Shutters in Santa Monica, then dancing the night away in Opera on Schrader Boulevard.

I tell her it's total horseshit and I presume Trevion put it out there. 'I'm back in his good books,' I go. 'He's even got me, like, a minor movie role for tomorrow.'

She says she'd have been surprised if it *was* true because Lo and Lauren Conrad are, like, Best Friends Forever, maybe even Best *Best* Friends Forever.

I think she forgets that the Lauren Conrad story was horseshit in the first place.

Honor is sitting in her little play-pen, playing with a toy that's, like, fair trade, made from fully sustainable materials and completely and utterly boring. She drops it the second she sees me and storts stamping her feet up and down, her little face lit up like Tallaght on Christmas Eve.

I look at Sorcha, I suppose for permission, and she just nods and smiles, the whole coffee business totally forgotten, and I pick Honor out of her pen and carry her over to the island.

Honor's all excited, going, '*Eee, arr, san, ssuh . . .*'

I ask Sorcha what's that she's saying and Sorcha says she's counting in Mandarin. '*Hen hao*, Honor,' she tells her. '*Hen hao*,' then she checks her dinner to see if it's hot enough and goes, 'I'm not sure Lo Bosworth even *plays* tennis? She's certainly never mentioned it on the show. Although I heard she gets her highlights done in Juan Juan – the same place as me . . .'

I'm going, 'Honor, can you say, "Daddy"? "Daddy"?' determined that I'm going to hear her say something in English before her second focking birthday.

She reaches out her little hand and makes a grab for Sorcha's copy of *Karma Suits You – States of Ecstasy*.

'Oh no you don't,' I go. 'Coffee was one thing – porn is a complete other,' and, in fairness to her, Sorcha sees the funny side of it.

I tell her I can't believe she's reading this muck. She definitely shouldn't leave it lying around.

'Oh my God,' she goes, 'it's definitely her best yet. Your mum is *such* an inspiration, Ross – to all women. Emmy's only met her, like, once and she's already thinking of going back to UCLA to do gender studies.'

'Emmy?' I go. 'With the tennis orms?'

She's there, 'Yeah, she was asking all about you, by the way. I told you she had a thing for you.'

'But when did *she* meet my old dear?'

'Well, you know she's *in* LA now?'

'I heard. *I've* no focking interest in seeing her.'

Sorcha blows on a forkful of chicken. 'Well, we all went out for dinner – me, Emmy, Analyn, Elodine, your mum. They're all, like, huge fans, Ross.'

'You've got to be shitting me . . .'

She puts it in her mouth. 'We went to, like, Cut, this – oh my God – *amazing* steakhouse in the Beverly Wilshire, where Tom and Katie go *all* the time. Then we went to, like, Kress.

Oh my God, your mum was, like, bopping away with the best of them.'

'Spare me.'

'She was wearing this amazing Galliano babydoll dress. It was, like, lace? And, oh my God, she totally pulled it off . . .'

I shrug as if to say, I don't actually *give* a fock?

'She glitzed it up with, like, Lorraine Schwartz crystals . . .'

I stort playing the bumble-bee game with Honor, where you pretend that the tip of your finger is, like, a bee and you get it to, like, land on her nose. She actually loves it.

Sorcha's there, 'And she paid for, like, everything – which I was *so* mad at her for.'

'Ah, let her,' I go. 'She can do with all the friends she can get – even *if* she has to buy them . . .'

Sorcha finishes her dinner and pushes the little corton away.

I ask her, just randomly, how she'd feel about me getting together with Emmy, but she doesn't answer. It's like she hasn't heard me? I immediately cop that there's something on her mind. I know her almost *too* well?

'Go on,' I go. 'Spill it.'

She sort of, like, smiles – but not in a happy way. 'It's nothing,' she goes.

I'm there, 'Sorcha,' and I put my hand on top of hers, 'we've known each other a long, long time – and I'd like to think we're still friends . . .'

She takes, like, a deep breath, then goes, 'It's Cillian.'

'Cillian?' I go. I can feel my fists immediately tighten.

'No, it's nothing bad,' she goes. 'I'm just, I don't know, worried about him . . . Since he came back from heliskiing, he's been . . . different.'

'Different, as in?'

'Well, the night he came back, I was sitting down to watch *Nip/Tuck*. He walked in, muted the TV and said he was getting rid of the Lamborghini.'

I laugh. 'I wondered how long it would take,' I go. 'I knew it was too much cor for a goy like him.'

'Then he started talking about the subprime mortgage crisis . . .'

'Again? Can he not let it go?'

'That's what *I* said. But he's, like, totally changed his tune, Ross. He kept saying that the world economy was on the verge of collapse . . .'

Even I have to laugh at that.

'He said that the irresponsible lending practices of the banks, as well as the trading of risky debt obligations on the financial markets, meant that the entire world economy was built on sand.'

'So? What's that got to do with any of us?'

She's there, 'I don't know.' She looks like she's about to burst into tears. 'But then he started asking me how many credit cards I had and how much I owed on them.'

'Whoa – that's out of order.'

'He said we were all in the throes of a consumer binge that simply can't be sustained . . .'

'*Bang* out of order.'

'And he didn't mean just me, Ross – he meant, like, the whole world?'

'Did he snot himself while he was heliskiing or something?'

She nods. 'He had, like, a fall? Josh and Kyle said he had, like, a minor concussion? The doctor told him to just sleep it off. He got up the next morning and that's when it started. He's already cancelled our joint MasterCard.'

I have to bite my tongue to stop myself from saying I told

you so. This is what happens when you get mixed up with financial services heads.

'It'll probably pass,' I go.

She's there, 'I hope so. I mean, he walked into Bob Soto's office yesterday morning and said we were eighteen months away from a global financial crisis as grave as the Great Depression. Can you imagine, Ross – he said that to the head of International Risk Assessment in PwC!'

She's quiet for maybe thirty seconds. Then she goes, 'You don't think he could be right, do you?'

I shake my head. 'I'm going to be honest with you,' I go. 'I think Bob Soto's a dick . . .'

'Don't say that. He's been – oh my God – *so* understanding.'

'I think Josh and Kyle are dicks as well. But this I will say for them – they seem pretty confident of their shit.'

'That's what *I* thought.'

'Look,' I go, 'I'll tell you my whole, I don't know, psychology about the whole financial thing. I know fock-all about the economy and blahdy blahdy blah. But sometimes, if I'm flicking through the channels and I end up on the news and I see all those dudes on Wall Street, I just think, well, *they* obviously know what they're doing. That's something else I don't need to know anything about.'

She smiles at me. 'I love talking to you,' she goes. 'You make everything alright.'

Then she gives me an amazing – even if it is just a – peck on the cheek.

She stands up and puts her corton in the bin. She takes Honor out of my orms and says it's time a certain little girl was in bed. 'Say *buenas noches* to your father,' she goes. 'Can you say *buenas noches*?'

After a little bit of coaxing, she finally gets her to say the words.

'*Buenas noches*,' I go, although I'd much prefer to be saying goodnight.

As she turns to bring her upstairs, Sorcha mentions that she's thinking of hosting a fundraiser for the Jolie-Pitt Foundation, and I know immediately that it's the old dear's evil influence.

I'm having, like, a late brekky in the Viceroy when I decide to ring Christian. From the second he answers, he sounds pretty hassled. 'I take it she has you doing the middle-of-the-night feeds?' I go. 'You're focking worse to do it.'

Of course, it's only then that he tells me that I'm on speakerphone and that *she's* in the cor with him.

I'm there, 'Hey, Lauren, that was an actual joke,' except of course nothing comes back.

I carry on making the effort, in fairness to me.

'So how is he?' I go. 'They're focking great at that age, aren't they?'

Christian's like, 'He's, er, fine, Ross.'

I'm there, 'What are you even calling him?' half expecting him to say, I don't know, Jar Jar or probably Chief focking Chirpa.

'Either Edward Thomas,' he goes, 'or Thomas Edward. They're our grandfathers' names.'

Then I hear *her* go, 'Just hang up, Christian.'

Except it'll take a hell of a lot more than a bird to come between me and my best mate.

I'm quickly like, 'So where are you two off to?' recycling and going again. 'Dirty weekend somewhere?'

He's there, 'We're actually driving to Vegas. We're going to just live there on-site until the casino actually opens. There's so much work to do and, well, none of it's in California anymore.'

I'm like, 'Yeah, you just keep pretending what you're doing is work.'

'Hang up,' I hear Lauren go again and Christian's like, 'Em, I better go,' but I'm there, 'Dude, before you go, I just want to tell you some of *my* shit? I've got a port in a movie, doing what I do best – in other words, kicking. I'm also getting, like, a body resculpt. Can you imagine how sick D'Arcy's going to be when he sees me? And the other big news is that Sorcha's not taking a court order out against me after all . . .'

The next thing, either he hangs up or she hangs up, but the line goes suddenly dead.

Teenage Kicks is a movie that Disney or one of that crowd are making about an American football team in a junior high school in, well, obviously, the States. The long and the short of it is that the kicker gets an intestinal parasite from some bad nigri – they're pretty focking sophisticated these American kids – and they end up drafting the school nerd onto the team. And of course, because of his knowledge of, like, geometry and astronomy and all that shit, he turns out to be the best kicker anyone's ever seen.

Which is why they're bringing in yours truly to do the actual real work.

Personally, I *would* have objections to the storyline – especially the idea that some little dweeb could come in and do what I do. It's a skill. And reading your schoolbooks has fock-all to do with it. Then again, it *is* my first break in movies, which is why I'm prepared to let it slide.

The filming is being done in some random high school in Beverly Hills, which has unbelievable facilities. It'd put Clongowes and Terenure to shame – if they didn't live in shame already.

So I'm there at, like, half-eight in the morning, big-time John

B. I pork the beast and ask this bird with a clipboard – who's nothing much to look at, in case you're wondering – where the actors are supposed to go. She directs me to this, like, trailer in the cor pork and I rock up, feeling – it has to be said – pretty pumped about the whole thing.

I walk in there, roysh, and I swear to God, I suddenly feel like Daddy focking Daycare. There's, like, six or seven kids in there, all of them four-foot-nothing, none of them much older than thirteen, maybe fourteen.

I'm there, 'How's it going?' but none of them answers – probably shy.

It actually reminds me of when I'd be asked to address the Junior Cup team at school – you've got to understand, a lot of these kids would be in, like, awe?

I give them the usual line I use to break the ice. 'You know who I am – and you know what I do,' and suddenly, roysh, this kid, who's obviously the geek in the movie – big Coca-Cola-bottle specs, the poor focker – stands up and goes, 'No – who *are* you?'

Believe it or not, he reminds me a bit of Fionn at that age. He even has, like, a turtleneck – his old dear obviously dresses him as well.

'Hey,' I go, 'I'm the guy who's here to make *you* look good.'

There's something about kids like that – I have to actually fight the urge to give him a dead leg and a wedgie.

The next thing, roysh, without saying another word, he whips out his mobile and he phones – get this – what turns out to be his agent? His opening line is, 'Why is there a fucking extra in my trailer?' and of course you can picture my face. I'm there going, 'Extra?'

He's like, 'Get him out of here now or I'm walking the fuck off this set,' then he just, like, hangs up.

It doesn't happen often, roysh, but I end up actually stuck for words.

That's the thing about American kids – they're a lot more arrogant than we ever were. It actually reminds me of the time we were over here on the old J1 for the summer and JP ended up getting a job in some toy shop in New York. Anyway, some spoiled little shit's ripping the focking stuffing out of, I don't know, a hippopotamus or one of that lot. Wouldn't stop, even when he was asked nicely. So JP has a sly look around – like he would have for the ref back in the day – then he belts the kid around the head, introducing him to the discipline of the ruck.

Saucepans are like that – if they sense weakness, they'll exploit it. So I let him know who's the focking daddy here. 'If you went to my school and you talked about me like that, your underpants would now be hanging from that focking lamp-post outside . . .'

He looks at me like a turd that just won't flush. 'Are you a fucking mental defective?' he goes.

All the other kids laugh. I don't believe it – I'm being bullied by the focking Disney Club.

I'm like, 'What?' in fairness to me, still a bit stuck for words.

He goes, 'You talk to me like you genuinely believe I'm interested in what you have to say.'

Violence against children is something I wouldn't believe in as a rule? But this kid's glasses *are* going up his hole.

'You know what I made on my last movie?' he goes. 'Three million big ones. You know what that means? Means I no longer have to talk to the help . . .'

'The help?'

'Now get the fuck out of here, before you're thrown out. On your fat ass . . .'

All the other kids crack their orses laughing again.

It's at that exact point, roysh, that the door of the trailer flies open and in walks this bouncer – bigger than any bouncer I've seen in a lifetime of being thrown out of nightclubs head-first. This focker could scratch Paul O'Connell's X5 and Paul O'Connell would have to stand there and go, 'Nice job.'

And he's black – I have to throw that in.

'What are *you* doing in here?' he goes, and, without even waiting for an answer, he's suddenly talking into his little mouthpiece, going, 'Yeah, I got him. An extra! Can you believe that?' and I have to say, roysh, I'm hurt by the way they keep saying that word.

'Out!' he goes. I don't need to be told twice. I don't even need to be told once. I'm on my way before he's even opened his Von Trapp. And I must look shaken up, roysh, because when we step outside, he asks me if I'm okay. I tell him I'm just not used to being abused like that, especially by a kid. I mean, if I spoke to my old man like that . . .

He laughs and says you get used to it. 'Child stars are the worst,' he goes. 'That's Danny Lintz.'

'Well, he's a little focker,' I go.

I realize, roysh, that I'm actually shaking and I get this sudden flashback to school, when I used to get the shit kicked out of me by Gary Gest and the odd time a teacher would come and rescue me.

'Nothing anyone can do,' the bouncer goy goes. 'You know what his movies gross? The studio loves him.'

Then he introduces himself. His name's Kobe and he's actually sound. In fact, he asks me am I the dude who gave his daughter a double espresso and, when I tell him yeah, he says it's cool the way I faced up to it. 'Too many people running away from their personal responsibilities,' he goes.

He brings me over to the extras' trailer, which is far focking shabbier than the actors' trailer, I can tell you that. But it doesn't matter, roysh, because I barely get a chance to put the American football clobber on before I get the call to say that I'm up.

I head over to the actual field and it's all set up. Everything I need. We're talking a set of goalposts, a bag of balls, then cameras set up at, like, various angles.

And there's obviously loads of people milling about as well. I spot this dude who I immediately presume is Chubby Waghorne. He's sitting in, like, a director's chair, smoking a cigar the size of, I don't know, Belgium – *if* Belgium's big – and I tip over and tell him I've one or two ideas about how we might do this thing.

He doesn't even look at me. He looks around and goes, 'Why is this guy talking to me?'

All of a sudden his assistant – who's a ringer for Gabrielle Union – puts her orm around me and ushers me away, telling me, politely but at the same firmly, that I'm here just to kick the ball and nothing else.

Which is *their* loss.

So they set up the shot. I'm told where to stand. All the cameras are in place and blahdy blahdy blah-blah.

Then someone shouts, 'Action!'

It's, like, a simple enough kick. Straight in front of the posts, we're talking thirty yords out – done it, like, a million times before. So I do my usual thing – the tried and trusted, four steps backwards, three to the side, rub my hand through my hair . . .

Before I even stort my run-up, I hear a voice go, 'Cut!'

It's Chubby. 'What's he fucking doing?' I hear him go. 'What *is* that?'

The assistant comes over and asks me what's with the steps to the side and the whole dance. I tell her it's called a routine. I'd be pretty famous for it back home.

'Well, can you *not* do it?' she goes. 'Chubby says it's spoiling the shot. Can you please just kick the ball through the posts?' making it sound like the easiest thing in the world.

I shrug. I'm there, 'I'll certainly give it a go,' never having done it that way.

So there I am, roysh, standing five or six steps behind the ball, limbering up to go again, when all of a sudden I hear *his* voice – Danny focking Lintz – go, 'This guy's a fucking clown, Chubby. What'd I say to you about working with clowns?'

Then another voice goes, 'And . . . action!'

Now I've faced hostile crowds before. I've taken penalties with practically the whole of Donnybrook whistling and booing me, like some focking pantomime villain, and I've still always taken the points. But this is different.

I don't *know* why?

I take, like, a normal run-up and hit the ball head-on. Whether it's, like, the weight of it, the camera lights or Danny Lintz's eyes on me, I manage to, like, shank it and it flies a good twenty yords wide of the posts.

'Fucking amateur hour!' I hear Danny go.

But Chubby, in fairness to him, goes, 'Okay, let's try it again.'

Which I do.

I use one or two visualization techniques to try to, like, block out what's happening around me?

Same thing.

I hit the ball dead-on and it wobbles like a shot duck, not only wide of the posts this time but short as well.

There's, like, total silence, except for the sound of Danny Lintz cracking his hole laughing. And that's when I realize – and it actually sends my blood cold – that he has exactly the same laugh as Gary Gest.

I can suddenly hear my own breathing. It's all, like, trembly? And people know there's something wrong. The assistant bird wanders over to me and tells me to just relax. She asks me if I need some water. Or even five minutes.

'It's actually the ball?' I go. 'It's basically heavier than what I'd be used to . . .'

She's like, 'Sure!' but she says it like she doesn't believe me.

My legs feel weak, like there's no actual blood in them?

I try it again.

Same result. *And*, of course, the laughter.

They move it forward ten yords. Same shit. Fourteen times I try it and fourteen times I miss the posts completely. 'Let's just do it with CGI,' Danny goes and that's when I end up totally losing it.

'I'd love to focking see you do better,' I go. He immediately takes it as, like, a challenge?

'Chubby,' he shouts, 'let me take a shot at this.'

So this is what happens. *I'm* told to step out of the picture, while *he* walks – like he owns the focking place – over to where I've been taking the shots from.

I watch him spot the ball in the cup.

I'm turning to the assistant one, going, 'It's actually a lot horder than it looks. It took me years to, like, perfect it.'

'And . . . action,' someone shouts.

The cameras roll.

The little focker runs at the ball, connects with it – even I have to admit – absolutely perfectly and sends it sailing straight between the two posts.

There's, like, cheers from everyone.

I turn to the assistant and tell her I wouldn't mind seeing it again. 'I'd actually have one or two criticisms of his technique.'

Danny – the little prick – turns around, points at me and goes, 'Get him *off* the fucking set! Now!'

No one says a word. No one even looks at me. It's like I'm dead to them? Kobe storts walking over in my general direction and I know to just leave.

As I'm walking past his chair, Chubby goes to me, out of the corner of his mouth, 'What can I say? Studio loves the little turd. Me, I go home and take it out on the wife.'

So I'm in the cor, still in a rage, when I pass the shop on Sunset and see the sign in the window. It's like, 'Book Soup presents . . . An Evening with Fionnuala O'Carroll-Kelly', and I suddenly remember what Chubby said. I'm thinking, it's about time this woman was taken down a peg or six – and preferably in front of an audience.

A bird stops me at the door, before I even get my foot into the place, and asks me if I've got, like, an invitation.

'My face is my invitation,' I go, because at first I think she has to be pulling my wire. It's like, who would come to an event like this except homeless people looking to get in out of the heat and, I don't know, the sick in the head.

But she *is* serious. She says it's invitation only. I tell her I'm Fionnuala O'Carroll-Kelly's son, though I also mention that I don't want the fact broadcast.

She stares hord at me, then opens her copy of *Karma Suits You – States of Ecstasy* and has a quick read of the old dear's biography on the inside of the, I suppose, dust cover?

She's there, 'There's no mention of a son here,' which is pretty hurtful, it has to be said.

'That's because she hates my guts and I hate hers,' I go. 'I'm embarrassed to be even related to the swamp monster,' and the bird looks at me like it's the weirdest thing in the world to say.

She's still Scooby Dubious, though, so I end up letting a roar at her. 'Do you honestly think I'd be interested in listening to a woman reading out her twisted sexual fantasies in public if I wasn't *actually* related to her?'

She obviously gets my point because she suddenly lets me in.

I wouldn't be into, like, bookshops – or even actual *books*? – but it *is* a pretty impressive shop, in fairness to it. We're talking floor-to-ceiling shelves – a dream of Sorcha's since she saw it in Ikea in Belfast – and books everywhere.

Again, if you're into that kind of shit.

The place – if you can believe this – is rammers, and it's not just her usual followers, in other words desperate, menopausal old trouts. There's, like, young girls – a lot of them serious lookers – one or two surfer-type dudes, a few stoners, then a lot of, I suppose the word is, *literary* types?

No sign of Marcia Cross, Kim Cattrall or any of that crew, though I do spot a bird who may or may not be Kirsten Bell – and then suddenly Sorcha, who's here with Emmy, the bird who's big-time into me, and Analyn, the one who's having, like, fertility treatment?

I take a couple of steps backwards and hide behind a stack of atlases, though I can still hear Emmy banging on about my old dear's graphic realism and Sorcha mention her linguistic daring.

The bird who wasn't going to let me in steps up to the mic – I'm beginning to think she looks a bit like Molly Sims – and a sudden, I suppose you'd have to call it, hush descends on the shop.

'Ladies and gentlemen,' she goes, 'Book Soup is honoured this evening to have, as its guest, a very special writer, but also a very special woman, who is taking the literary world by storm. Not for a long time has a woman written so graphically and yet so truthfully about female sexuality. *Karma Suits You – States of Ecstasy*, her debut novel on this side of the

Atlantic, calls to mind not just the writing of Catherine Millet but also earlier pioneers in the world of erotic literary fiction. Ladies and gentlemen, I'm proud to introduce you to . . . Fionnuala O'Carroll-Kelly . . .'

Everyone just claps – except me, obviously. I don't want to hear her bullshit.

She comes shuffling out from behind a set of bookshelves, like something out of the 'Thriller' video, botoxed to the point that she can't stop baring her teeth, dressed in some focking mother-of-the-bride outfit that makes her look like what she is – a landfill in a Michael Kors pant suit.

'Thank you,' she's giving it and the applause, if anything, gets louder. 'Thank you,' she goes, then she storts giving them the royal wave.

Some dude beside me actually wolf-whistles and I have to tell him to cop the fock on and he tells me I'm an asshole.

She opens her book on the sort of, like, podium thing and the noise suddenly dies down. She gets stuck straight in.

"'Petrol?" said the man in the service station, affecting a look of bewilderment.

"Gas!" Valerie snapped. "Or whatever you people call it," for she was certain he knew what she had meant. Why was it necessary to go through this tiresome catechism every time she stopped to fill up the Chevrolet? How many tourists drive the Cabrillo Highway every day? she wanted to ask him. Had he never met someone from out of town before?

But she didn't wish to engage him any longer than the exigencies of the transaction required. He was a nauseating animal – grossly overweight, his mean-spirited face crosshatched with stubble, and a sheen of sweat covering his body like a coat of cheap varnish.

She handed him a fifty-dollar bill and he turned to the till. His low-slung jeans revealed three inches of cleavage, which made her stomach heave.

She tried not to think about it.

Instead, she thought about the journey that had brought her to this point — the snaking road along the wave-lashed shore between San Francisco and Monterey, through the mist-shrouded pine groves to Carmel, then on again, along the dangerously precipitous road, to take in the vertiginous and deadly allure of the Big Sur . . .'

Everyone claps. Don't ask me why, roysh, because it's obviously shit. I spot Marcia Cross up the front, looking around. I catch her eye and pull a face as if to say, can you believe she gets away with this bollocks? But she ends up just looking away.

'The garage attendant turned and held out her change — a crisp, twenty-dollar bill. She stretched for it, but at the last moment he pulled it away.

"You give me that," she heard herself say. "You give me that money this instant!"

It sounded shrill, effete, like Claudette Colbert — though he was clearly no Clark Gable.

"Take it," he said, proffering the note a second time. With an ill feeling, she observed his sausage-like fingers and the dirt gathered under his nails. "Take your change," he repeated.

But again, as soon as she tried to, he pulled it away, then laughed cruelly.

She felt her heart quicken. "What do you want from me?" she said, her voice weak and skittery.

She felt his eyes trace the articulation of her breasts through her thin cotton camisole. Then he wiped his mouth with his open palm.'

'For fock's sake,' I shout from the back and one or two people, including Marcia Cross, turn around and shush me. *She* looks incredible, by the way, and I've a serious one on me.

'"She should have been repulsed by this. But the truth was she suddenly felt herself oddly aroused by his teasing.

"Please!" she said plaintively. "Give me my money."

"First," he said, still drinking her in, "you've got to tell me where a pretty thing like you is headed."

She looked away, then looked back at him, essaying a look of defiance. "If you must know," she said, "I'm on the way to Santa Barbara."

"Santa Barbara," he said, considering the words for a moment. "Santa Barbara. You want I take you to see the Redwoods?"

"The Redwoods?" she said. "But . . . I don't even know you."

"Just being hospitable," he said, putting a toothpick between his teeth. "You being from out of town and everything."

He held out the twenty-dollar note. He let her take it this time. He rolled up a newspaper and then, with an almost effortless flick of his wrist, swatted a mosquito into a dirt-begrimed window.

Valerie wanted this man. She didn't understand why, but she wanted him to fill her.'

'You're a focking disgrace to the animal kingdom!' I shout.

I notice Sorcha look around with a look of concern on her face and I take another step backwards to get out of her line of vision.

One of the staff comes over, puts his hand on my shoulder and tells me that if I shout anything else, he's going to have to ask me to leave.

I can't believe no one else is pissed off about this.

"'Yes," she said. "That would be very nice."

After thirty silent but tension-filled minutes in the car, Valerie found herself staring up at the God-like majesty of these natural superstructures.'

Another round of applause. Er, for *what* exactly?

"'Big," he whispered. She felt his hands seize her tiny waist and felt his breath in her ear, rank, like bad Gorgonzola. "Big . . . and firm!"

She no longer had mastery over her actions. She spun around, threw her arms around him and they wrestled each other to the ground.

Frenziedly, he kissed her face and neck, his stubble lisping cruelly off her cheek, his toothpick almost puncturing her windpipe. But she liked it. She liked the pain. Somehow it was as sweet as the Pinot Noir she'd had with lunch – the Wente Reliz Creek Reserve.

He pulled her camisole over her head, then explored the veritable Napa between her breasts. They writhed around on the forest floor, her nose taking in the bouquet of bougainvillea and body odour.

She opened his jeans and almost bucked with delight. For he, too, was a Big Sir.'

Jesus Christ, the dude beside me is playing pocket snooker. 'You focking filthbag!' I shout.

'*Ssshhh,*' comes the reply.

'*He tore off her light cotton skirt and panties and could suddenly feel his manhood hang between them like some throbbing Golden Gate Bridge – bold and graphic and a magnificent feat of engineering.*

She was naked now but for her espadrilles. He attempted to mount her with all the charm of the elephant bull seals she'd seen in Ana Nuevo State Park. But she stopped him and guided their bodies into the position she wanted to be taken from – the reverse cowgirl.'

'Dirtbag!' I go.

'Get him out of here,' someone shouts. It might even *be* Marcia Cross.

'*He made several blunt thrusts and she opened like the San Andreas fault. Suddenly they were thrashing nakedly among the bracts. Earth-quakes were going off inside her, her crustal plates rubbing bare and sending seismic shudders through her every synapse.'*

'You're a focking filth-monger!'

I'm suddenly grabbed from behind – it takes, like, two or three of them – but I'm dragged, kicking and screaming, towards the door, going, 'You're a focking shambles of a woman! A shambles!'

'Her pleasure came roaring like a giant kahuna breaking on a Pacific beach. He rode his own wave to the finish, then they lay there . . .'

I'm going, 'A sad sack of a woman. With a face like a bag of bent euros.'

'Dirty, naked and perspiring profusely, enjoying the post-coital moment . . .'

Sorcha must cop me because I hear her go, 'Ross? Ross!'

'For an hour they lay there in this Golden State.'

5. Ross, His Mother, His Wife and Her Lover

Degrees are fine, Fionn used to always say – but never, under any circumstances, trust a man who frames his diplomas.

Especially a doctor, he *could* add.

I'm having what they call a body assessment, standing stork naked in the consultation room, with San Sancilio poking and prodding me in various places, while constantly tutting and shaking his head, I suppose, disapprovingly?

He tells me to flex my stomach muscles, which I do. 'Meester Prune Belly,' he goes and he laughs, his little pencil moustache bobbing up and down, like he thinks he's focking hilarious.

He moves up my body. I wonder is that whiskey I can smell or, like, disinfectant?

He tells me to flex my pectorals and I tell him I already am. He nods in that just-as-I-suspected kind of way.

The next thing I hear is the door opening behind me, then Trevion's voice.

'Out of control,' he goes and somehow I know that he's reading the headline from a newspaper. 'Twelve hours in the life of an Irish hellraiser. Thrown off movie set after row with child star Danny Lintz. Verbally abuses author mother at public reading. Then falls down drunk in Area Nightclub.'

'Look, it's all true,' I go, bracing myself for a serious bollocking.

Instead, roysh, he just laughs. 'Kid,' he goes, 'I got to admit it, I got you all wrong. *All* wrong. I mean, here I been trying to turn you into the next Joey Fatone . . .'

There's something different about him. It's his clobber. Yeah, he's wearing, like, a jacket and tie. I've only ever seen him in, like, short-sleeved shirts before?

'You ain't no Joey Fatone,' he goes, 'and you ain't never gonna be neither. *This* is you!' and he waves the newspaper at me. 'An asshole! I forgot how much people love an asshole.'

'Well,' I go, 'that's very much what I would have been considered back in Ireland? I've always believed in, like, playing to your strengths?'

He's there, 'I got all sorts of people ringing today. I got MTV asking about you.'

'As in *actual* MTV?'

'That's right, Snowflake. You fucking betcha. They're excited. Might even want to do something with you. But I want you to forget about all that for a minute – I got a question for you. Now, you know I'm not normally a man who goes in for all that mushy shit, right?'

I'm like, 'Er, right,' wondering where this is going.

'You ever pull a Korean bayonet out of your own stomach?'

'No – it's on the list, though.'

'Laugh it up, Smart Mouth. What I'm saying is, when you look at that knife and you see, smeared all over it, the fucking shit you had for breakfast, it changes you. You never see the world through the same eyes again . . .'

I'm like, 'Er, *where* is all this going?'

He goes, 'What kind of flowers does your mother like?'

I laugh. The jacket and tie. Suddenly it all makes sense. 'Don't tell me you've fallen for her – you focking sap!'

'Hey, I just want to send her some flowers,' he goes, a bit *too* defensively?

I'm there, 'Dude, honestly – you do *not* want to go there. I swear to fock, two weeks and you'll be wishing you were back in Korea.'

'You won't tell me what flowers she likes?'

'All I'm saying is you can do way better than *her*...'

The thing is, roysh, I'm also thinking about him? Having him as her agent is one thing, but there's no way she'd be seen in public with him on her orm, especially with that face. Knowing her, she's probably got designs on Andy Garcia or one of that lot. If she burns Trevion, it could fock up my career before it gets even properly storted.

But he ends up just staring at me, roysh, until I eventually tell him that her favourite flowers are birds of paradise, knowing of course that she's allergic to them – they make shit of her sinuses.

He says good, twice, maybe three times, then he turns around to San Sancilio and asks him what he thinks. San nods and says he thinks he can do something with me, then he thanks Trevion for the Lakers tickets and Trevion says forget about it already. He goes, 'You're doing *this*, ain't you?' meaning my operation.

I'm like, 'Whoa back!' suddenly grabbing my clothes. 'He's doing it for Lakers tickets?'

'No,' Trevion goes, 'he's doing it for *great* Lakers tickets. Centre court, front fucking row, my friend. Anyways – San, talk him through what you're going to do,' then he whips out his mobile, dials directory enquiries and asks for the number of a florist in Beverly Hills.

So San storts rattling off all the shit he's going to do to me? First, he's going to slice me from hip to hip – or *heep* to *heep*, because he talks like focking Manuel out of *Fawlty Towers*. And as he says it, I can feel his felt-tip morker trace, like, a dotted line right across my waist. He's going to detach the skin from my abdominal wall, tighten the muscles and fascia using sutures and then remove the excess fat and skin.

I'm like, 'Er, I'm not sure I need to be hearing this?' suddenly feeling Moby again.

'Or do I suture the mooscles *efter* I remove the excess fet?' San goes. 'Ees one or other. I can check thees. I heff books – all sort of books. Then I wheel contour and shep your abdomeenal fet ped.'

I'm there, 'Actually, I'm having maybe second thoughts about the whole plastic surgery *thing*? I'm thinking possibly even a beer belly would be better for my reputation.'

He lifts up my orm and says he's going to make a small incision in either ormpit . . .

I'm there, 'You're going to, like, cut my ormpits open?'

Then he says he's going to, endoscopically, insert a silicone implant underneath the chest muscles on either side, using, again, sutures to hold them in place.

'Birds of paradise,' I can hear Trevion in the background going. 'A dozen. No, *two* dozen,' except it's weird, roysh, because his voice is all, I don't know, echoey? I feel my shoulders suddenly slump and my knees buckle.

San says he's going to slice open my calves and that's the last thing I remember. I was out of the game by the time the floor came rushing up at me and cracked me full in the face.

'Like, they're not actually Loubs? Even though they do look like them? They're actually Gunmetal courts. Red patent. Dita von Teese wore the exact same ones with a floor-length Malandrino to the premiere of *Little Miss Sunshine* in Malibu. Brittany Snow also wore them with super-bright Mischen and Bulgari jewels and totally nailed it.'

I don't know whether I'm asleep or awake.

'Anyway, they give me amazing toe cleavage – probably the best I've ever had?'

Where the fock even am I? Still in the surgery?

That's . . . Sorcha. Yeah, that *has* to be Sorcha – who else talks like that?

But who's she talking to?

Me?

'Oh my God, so many shops have donated items. You should see the Stella McCortney soft grey, scallop-tiered dress I got. We are going to raise so much money. I'm even hoping that one or two of the magazines are going to, like, cover it?'

I'm suddenly thinking all these questions. Have I *had* the operation? Did something go wrong? Have I been in, like, a coma? Has she been here at my bedside for years, trying to talk me out of it, like in loads of movies starring Sandra Bullock?

How even old am I?

No, I think. I can't have been out for long. Because *Little Miss Sunshine* is only just out and the Malandrino is obviously for the fashion show she's going to do for the Jolie-Pitt crowd.

So who *is* she talking to?

'Tasselled boots,' Sorcha's going. 'Paisley tunics. Patterned silk. Even Arabian carpet bags. Don't be surprised to see Moho make a comeback – if not this year, then next.'

'Oh,' another voice suddenly goes, 'very Marianne Faithfull.'

Who the fock is that?

I do a quick inventory of the old bod. My chest. My stomach. My calves. Nothing hurts. San obviously didn't touch me. So what's going on?

'Your earrings are amazing,' Sorcha goes.

And then I hear it. *Her* voice.

'Yes, they're Keselstein-Cord.'

My eyes just, like, shoot open. I'm like, 'What the fock are you doing here?'

'Oh, it's alive,' she has the actual cheek to go. 'Back in the land of the living.'

Sorcha's there, 'Hi, Ross. Don't worry – you just fainted and stuff?' but it's, like, *her* I'm just staring at. 'I asked you a question,' I go.

Sorcha clears her throat, then excuses herself. 'I'm going to get some tea,' she goes. 'They have orange pechoe here,' and the second she's gone, roysh, the old dear's like, 'I see you're just as pleasant as ever.'

I actually laugh at that. *And* shake my head. I'm there, 'Why couldn't you even stay in Ireland?'

'Ross,' she goes, 'I was in America long before you arrived.'

I notice, roysh, that her nose is running and she has to keep sniffing to keep the snot from running all over her face, which is hilarious. I'm there, 'Aw, you haven't picked up a cold, have you?'

She's like, 'No, it's my . . . my allergies.'

I laugh, just so she knows that the flowers were no accident. Then I go, 'Why couldn't you have stayed in New York?'

She's like, 'I'm doing a coast-to-coast publicity tour.'

'Oh, is that what you call it? Reading out your twisted filth in actual bookshops?'

'And what about you? Shouting at me like a common tramp – after everything we did to make sure you weren't raised in Sallynoggin. I couldn't even tell Garcelle Beauvais-Nilon that you were my son . . .'

'Garcelle who?'

'I said you were some crank I'd never set eyes on before.'

'Of course,' I go. 'Deny your own child. Because we're good at that in our family, aren't we?' She's suddenly all serious. She has no answer to that. 'I mean, there was the son I never knew I had. The sister I never knew I had. My guess is there's others. But don't tell me. I love these surprises.'

She looks at me with what I would have to describe as total

and utter contempt. 'Do you have *any* idea what it's like to lose your mind?' she goes.

I throw my eyes up to heaven. She's looking for sympathy now. It's no news to me that she's off her chops.

She's there, 'Have you thought about maybe showing some compassion?'

Her nose is running like a focking tap. I'm like, 'Compassion?'

'For the people involved.'

'Hand me my violin there, would you?'

'We're human, Ross – that's what you could never accept about your father and me. That's what you could never forgive.'

'Horseshit.'

'Yes. Imperfect people. And we made all the terrible, terrible mistakes that imperfect people make. But we tried to make the best of the mess we – all of us – created.'

'By letting Erika grow up thinking someone else was her old man? Yeah, *rul* nice of you. The thing is, I can't believe you actually stayed with him, even after you caught him dipping the wick . . .'

'Well, you're a fine one to talk about that,' she goes, staring at Sorcha's empty seat, *trying* to make a point? I decide to let her have her moment. But not for long.

'He's back with her,' I go. 'As in, Helen? I just thought I'd let you know that.'

But she already knows. I can't believe she already knows. Or that she doesn't seem to care. 'He loves her,' she goes. 'He's always loved her.'

'So why the fock did you stay together?'

'You don't know anything about the situation, Ross.'

'So explain it to me. Why don't you just . . . *explain* it to me?'

She doesn't say a word for ages. Eventually, roysh, she goes, 'I knew I got Charles on the rebound. We were *both* on the rebound. I'd been engaged myself . . .'

I'm there, 'Can I just say, I am actually stunned that there are that many desperate people in the world. But continue . . .'

'Your father and I met in Sandycove Tennis Club. It was the 1970s. And it was a terrible thing to be in your late twenties and on your own. For a woman anyway. We didn't love each other. But we liked each other and we had a lot in common. Tennis, for one thing. And maybe in our desperation we hoped that it was enough.'

'So, what, Helen came back from Canada, had a fling with *him*, got herself preggers . . .'

'It wasn't like that. I take my own share of the responsibility . . .' She dabs at her eyes. It's still her allergies. It's not tears, you can be sure of that.

I'm there, 'How?'

'I went through a couple of bad years. Almost lost my mind. My mother went loop the loop when she turned thirty and I was convinced I was going to go the same way. I drove him into Helen's arms . . .'

'You still haven't answered my question – why did he stay with you?'

'Because we had a six-month-old baby,' she goes, obviously trying to hang the whole thing on me. 'And we were married. And Helen was married, too. They were different times. Marriage was a life contract. It wasn't like switching phone networks.'

'So, what, it suited everyone to pretend it never happened?'

'I'm ashamed to say it, but yes. Your father and I decided to try to hold our marriage together. And I made his having no contact wth his daughter a precondition of taking him back. And I'm ashamed of that now. It was very, very wrong of me. But Helen had decided to go back to Canada. Tim said he'd raise Erika as his own. It suited everyone.'

'As long as no one ever found out the truth.'

'Yes.'

'It was the same with Ronan, wasn't it? Don't tell Ross he has a kid out there. Nah, just pay off his mother.'

'And that was wrong too . . .'

'Too focking right it was wrong.'

'You were *sixteen*. You were still a kid yourself. We did what we thought was right at the time.'

I sit up and take a good look at her. 'You sicken me,' I just go.

'I know,' she goes. 'But I'm hoping that one day you'll find it in your heart to forgive me. Just as you'll hope your children will forgive you for *your* awful, awful humanity . . .'

I'm thinking about Honor, whacked off her head on coffee, trying to horse that other kid's orm.

She goes, 'I'm hoping that one day you'll see that, on balance, given the problems we were presented with, we didn't do all that badly. I don't want us to go on hurting each other. I want us to be friends.'

Friends? She must have been at the vodka. 'You know, looking at you,' I go, 'I wouldn't blame the old man for going elsewhere for it.'

She smiles at me, roysh, but it's not a nice smile. It's, like, evil? 'And don't be jealous of my fame,' she goes. 'I *worked* for mine, remember?' which is about as low as you can possibly go.

'At least I didn't have to get half my orse fat injected into my lips,' is what I *should* say.

Except, like all the best lines, I didn't think of it until ages later.

*

So who, being honest, could put their hand on their hort and say they ever saw me in, like, a gay bor?

But I swear to God, roysh, there I am, sat with Harvey in Mother Lode in West Hollywood, the two of us drinking pink drinks with umbrellas and all sorts of accessories sticking out of them and playing a game that he calls P.S. Too? It basically involves watching men *and* women – because there *are* birds in there, don't you worry about that – and trying to decide who's had Plastic Surgery and who's, what Harvey calls, Factory.

So someone'll walk by, roysh, and I'll be there, 'Factory,' and he'll be like, 'You're kidding me, right? Those tits are, like, so P.S. Ross, they don't even match her arms!'

Then we end up getting busted. Some dude overhears us talking about him, walks over to us and goes, 'Wrong! I've had my ears done and a tattoo removed,' and he storts laughing, then we stort laughing and I can honestly say, roysh, it's the best craic I've had since I came to the States, and that includes all the birds I've scored.

'Hey, speaking of plastic surgery,' I end up going, 'I've decided *not* to go ahead with the whole body resculpt thing?'

He's there, 'Oh my God, why?'

They're all very dramatic, aren't they?

I'm there, 'Bottled it, in fairness. Went for the assessment and the dude storted drawing all over me, telling me all the shit he was going to do – rip this, peel that, chop the other. I ended up sort of, like, fainting?'

The dude just explodes – it's like it's the funniest thing he's ever heard? He's there, 'You fainted?'

Of course, I end up having to laugh as well.

'Yeah, I was out for, like, five or six hours. But I woke up and told Trevion, fock it, I'm going to keep doing the work in the gym – after that, the public are just going to have to take me as they find me.'

I ask the borman for two more pomegranate daiquiris.

Harvey goes, 'Good for you.'

I look around the bor. It has to be said, roysh, that if you walked in here off the street, you'd never know there was anything funny about it.

'This place is nothing at all like I expected,' I go.

Harvey rolls his eyes, which is another thing a lot of them do. 'Let me guess, you thought it would be, like, men in denim shorts, leather jackets and handlebar moustaches?'

I'm there, 'No,' even though that's exactly what I expected.

'I can bring you to one of those bars if you like,' he goes and I'm quickly there, 'No!' which he thinks is hilarious.

A dude walks by, bursting out of his shirt. 'Pectoral implants,' Harvey goes out of the side of his mouth, hordly even *needing* to look at him.

I'm there, 'Do you mind me asking you something? Like, when did you first know that you were . . . you know?'

'Do you mean *gay*, Ross?'

'Your word, but yeah.'

He takes, like, a sip of his drink. 'Thirteen?' he goes. 'Fourteen?'

I'm there, 'Wow,' really meaning it. 'See, the thing I'm always wondering is, how do you *actually* know?'

He's there, 'Well, with me, it was when I first started listening to my mother's Diana Ross CDs.'

'Really?'

'Ross, I'm joking?'

'Oh, sorry.'

'I don't know when or how I knew. I think I always just knew.'

I nod.

'Are you actually from, whatever, LA?'

'No,' he goes, 'but I'm from California? A town called

Barstow? It's in the Mojave desert, halfway between here and Vegas.'

'Sorry to, like, bombord you with questions,' I go, 'but I suppose I'm just curious. Like, did you *have* to come to LA, if you know what I mean?'

'Do you mean was I run out of town for being a homosexual?'

'Er, yeah.'

He laughs. I think he finds me one of the genuinely funniest people he's ever met.

'No,' he goes, 'I came to LA because Barstow didn't have much of a gay scene, that's all.'

I'm there, 'So what did your old pair say when you told them you were – exactly – gay?'

He doesn't answer, roysh, just stares at his drink. I'm thinking they must have taken it really badly and now I'm suddenly regretting bringing it up.

So I go, 'Do you mind me saying something to you, Harve?'

'No, what?'

'I really admire you. And that's not me being funny or anything? I've never met someone so, I don't know, comfortable in their own skin.'

He smiles at me and says thank you because, like, he *knows* I mean it?

It's at that exact point, roysh, that my phone rings. It's, like, a three-five-three number, so I answer it and it turns out to be Fionn, ringing from school. I don't know if I mentioned, but he's back working as, like, a teacher again?

'Ross,' he goes, 'I'm sorry to ring you so late at night.'

I'm there, 'Don't sweat it, Dude. At this precise moment in time, I'm sitting in – of all things – a *gay* bor, if that's okay to say. Would you believe me if I told you I've got – and you'll appreciate this more than anyone – a *gay* friend . . .'

I put my hand over the phone and go, 'Fionn's not *actually* gay? It's just a thing I've always slagged him about.'

Then I go back on the phone. I'm there, 'That's genuine, by the way – I have my first ever gay mate. And I'm completely cool with it, aren't I, Harve?'

'Except you keep mentioning it,' Harvey goes, 'like, every five minutes.'

'He's not one of the scary ones,' I go to Fionn. 'The ones where you'd always be thinking, if I was hammered, could I trust him?'

'Or trust yourself,' Harvey goes.

I'm there, 'Hear that Fionn? We're like Will and Jack here when we get going.'

Fionn's straight down to business. 'Is it true,' he goes, 'about Erika?'

I'm there, 'Depends – what have you heard?'

He's like, 'Ross, don't give me that. I met her in Dunne & Crescenzi tonight, eating on her own.'

I'm there, 'What was she wearing?'

He's like, 'What?'

I'm there, 'I mean, did she look well? Or healthy – did she look healthy?'

'Ross,' he goes, 'she looked like a broken woman.'

I'm there, 'Well, she's certainly playing the sympathy cord with you lot. And before you say it, I haven't turned my back on her. To be honest, it's, er, Sorcha – she's having serious trouble getting her head around the fact that Erika's suddenly my sister. As I said to Oisinn, give her time – she'll come around.'

'Have you told Ronan?' he goes.

The simple answer, of course, is no, but I end up getting in a bit of a strop with him? 'Sorry, how is this any of your beeswax?'

He's there, 'Well, I could say I'm asking you as Ronan's year head. I have an interest in his welfare. Or I could say that I'm asking you as a friend who actually cares about you.'

That hits me full in the chest. See, I never give the four-eyed focker the credit he deserves.

I'm there, 'Sorry, Dude – it's just been, you know, a bit mental even trying to get my own head around it.'

'Look,' Fionn goes, 'the story's already all over town. JP saw your old man and Erika's old dear coming out of the Bedroom Studio in Dalkey the other day.'

'That's *actually* revolting.'

'Whether it is or not, Ross, you should tell Ronan before someone else tells him.'

The dress code, she said in a text last night, was gorden party casual. I just threw on the usual chinos and Ralph, but when she cops me on the other side of the pool, horsing into a plate of zucchini custards with balsamic vinegar reduction, she checks me out, we're talking up and down, then mouths the words thank you.

Which is always nice to hear.

She doesn't look nervous, even though it's some turnout. There must be, like, two hundred people here, a load of them seriously rolling in it by the looks of them.

Of course, this is her in her element. I think she was born with a microphone in her hand.

'Hello and welcome,' she goes. 'And thank you for coming to what I hope will be the first annual Designer Clothes Auction (Including Vintage) in Aid of the Jolie-Pitt Foundation, which is one of the world's most – oh my God – amazing charities. Let me say at the beginning that fifty per cent of all monies raised today will go to the Maddox Jolie-Pitt organization, which is dedicated to eradicating extreme rural poverty, protecting natural resources and conserving wildlife by promoting sustainable rural economies that directly contribute to the health and vitality of communities, wildlife and forests . . .'

That gets an immediate round of applause. Did I mention that she looks amazing?

'The remainder will go towards helping children affected in various ways by the war in Iraq. Half will go to help military children through the Armed Services YMCA Operation Hero programme and half will go towards programmes that help Iraqi children sadly orphaned by the fighting.

'Obviously, Brad and Angelina can't be here today, but, as Angelina said herself in a recent interview with *O – The Oprah Magazine*, educational support programmes for the children of conflict are the best way to help communities heal . . .'

Everyone claps again.

'You know, she's even more beautiful than I remembered,' Harvey goes. 'She looks like Jennie Garth.'

I'm there, 'That's exactly what *I* used to think.'

I tell him that the nuns from that school of hers would be proud of her today. Public speaking was always one of her things.

The models stort coming out, except they're not so much models as all Sorcha's mates.

'Now, Barneys on Wilshire,' she's going, 'have donated this black, one-shoulder dress with bow detail by the fabulous Marc Jacobs. I think you'll all agree that Elodine totally pulls it off with this Touch Luxe silver scales jacket, Louboutin heels and – can we see the pin, Elodine? – a Lucite flower pin by Alexis Bittar, as seen in *Sex and the City*. And we're going to start the bidding for the entire ensemble at five thousand dollars . . .'

'And where's *he*?' Harvey goes.

I point over to the little group of them standing over by the actual buffet. Josh is throwing a bread roll like it's an American football and Kyle is running to catch it. I just shake my head. Aport from the fact that Sorcha paid good money to get this event catered, his throwing action is actually shit.

'Which one?' Harvey goes. 'Deion Sanders or Joe Montana?'

I'm there, 'Neither. The one sitting down. The pale, white, weedy-looking focker with the imitation Ray-Bans.'

He turns to me in, like, total shock. 'You lost *that* girl . . . to *him*?'

I'm there, 'I didn't lose her *to* him? Even though *he'd* like to think that. No, I was cheating on her left, right and centre. The nanny was the one I eventually swung for. Then he came in and hoovered up the pieces.'

'Now,' Sorcha goes, 'Kitson, one of my all-time favourite shops, on Robertson, have donated this ruffled Mulberry dress, which is stunning, I'm sure you'll all agree . . .'

I tell Harvey thanks, on Sorcha's behalf, and he just lifts his hand as if to say it's not a thing. 'Analyn is wearing it with these fabulous Alaïa pumps – lace-effect is going to be in this year – and an Orka Mesica friendship bracelet, as worn by Nicky Hilton, though in my opinion it would go equally well with simple flats, either Pierre Hardy or Rene Caovilla, and statement tights.'

Harvey gets up off his lounger.

'Where are you off to?' I go, but not in, like, a clingy way?

He's there, 'Are you kidding me? I've just mentioned the names of two sports people. I've clearly been spending too much time around you,' although, I should add, he *is* joking. Then he's like, 'It's a fashion show. Where do you think I'm going? To find cute gay guys.'

I laugh.

I'm just there, 'Good luck, Harve,' thinking how cool it

would be if he finally found someone nice – man *or* woman.

As he's walking away, roysh, I notice Cillian's crew staring over at me. Josh has his T-shirt rolled up, roysh, showing off his – I suppose – midriff and he's sort of, like, prancing around in, like, a gay way, basically ripping the piss out of Harvey. I actually feel like going over there and decking him. Kyle is laughing and sort of, like, slapping Cillian on the back, although he seems to be just sitting there, staring into space.

'The next lot,' Sorcha goes, 'is a soft grey, scallop-tiered dress by my favourite designer in the actual world – and that designer is none other than Stella McCortney . . .'

The model, in this case, is Emmy, as in Sorcha's friend? The one who, even Sorcha admitted, has a major thing for me. The opening bid is, like, two thousand doughnuts and my hand is, like, straight in the air, because, I have to admit, she looks amazing in it.

I've only got, like, one rival bidding against me and it's Bob Soto, as in Cillian's boss, the fat fock. He's over there with Josh and Kyle, then three or four dudes that Cillian obviously works with, because looking at them, I've seen more craic at an autopsy.

Bob goes to two and a half and I immediately say three and, of course, Emmy's little face lights up the second I up the ante. He puts his big fat sausage finger in the air to say three and a half. I give Emmy a sly smile, then I go to four.

I notice Josh and Kyle egging him on, telling him to blow me out of the water. He goes to four and a half, but I can tell from his whole body language that he knows – being in the business he's in – that the dress is worth nothing like that. And of course I'm like Harvey focking Norman here – I won't be beaten on price.

So the upshot is that he eventually drops out and I end up agreeing to pay basically six grandingtons for the dress, although that's *with* a pair of suede Manolos in electric-blue and a HK for Mouawad bracelet thrown in. Then I just lie back on my lounger, soak up the rays and wait for my prize.

A voice above me suddenly goes, 'Spending your money?'

I have to, like, shield my eyes from the sun. It's Trevion.

I forgot to mention, Disney still paid me for that movie.

I'm there, 'Actually, *yeah*, as it happens? What are you doing here?'

'I'm here with Fyon Hoola,' he goes. 'She's modelling.'

I'm there, 'Modelling? Modelling what?'

Sorcha's suddenly there, 'Kushcush have very kindly donated this stunning metallic silver monokini and it's being modelled by someone with whom I'm sure you're all very familiar – an amazing, amazing writer who I'm, oh my God, *so* fortunate to be able to call a friend, and no stranger to charity work herself, Fionnuala O'Carroll-Kelly!'

Out she focking struts, her big fat body bet into the focking thing. There's not only cheers, roysh, there's actual roars? It's, like, does anyone in this country have any taste?

Of course, I can't help myself. 'Someone stick an apple in its mouth and put it on the barbecue!' I shout.

Trevion doesn't even blink. He's just, like, staring at her. The poor focker's smitten.

'I should add that those amazing Jee Vice sunglasses are Fionnuala's own,' Sorcha goes, 'and not part of the bid.'

The old dear says something then – she *has* to be the centre of attention – Sorcha goes, 'Oh my God, thank you *so* much! Ladies and gentlemen, Fionnuala has very, very kindly agreed to throw in the glasses – and I think I'm right in saying that they're the same ones that Katherine Heigl was pictured wearing recently leaving the Christian Audigier Warehouse . . .'

I suddenly spot Emmy over at the ice-cream buffet. I get up, tell Trevion he's selling himself short – we're talking *way* short – then I tip over to her, giving her a big enthusiastic kiss on either cheek.

Of course, Bob Soto's taking all this in, totally bulling. If you can't hang with the big dogs, stay your puppy ass on the porch.

'Oh my God,' Emmy goes, 'I can't believe you paid all that money. And look, I'm eating sorbet in it! I should go and change.'

I'm there, 'Wait a minute – are you telling me *you* don't come with the dress?' which *sounds* corny but it's actually not, the way I say it. 'Dying kids or no dying kids, I'm afraid I'm going to have to ask for my money back.'

She's big into me and she's making it obvious, roysh, with the whole eye contact thing and then laughing at pretty much every line I throw at her. For instance, roysh, I tell her that tennis obviously suits her, judging from her body, then she asks me if I play and I tell her no, I'm not interested in games in which love means nothing. It's an old line, roysh, and one I've only ever known to work on Loreto Foxrock girls. But this is America – a whole new morket to crack. 'Oh my God,' she goes, her mouth wide open, 'that is *so* clever!' and what can I do, roysh, except shrug.

It's like, hey, I've got seven or eight lines just like that one.

Of course, you know the script. Twenty minutes later, we're in – funnily enough – the pumping house and we're up to our tonsils in each other. Emmy unbuttons my shirt, then we're suddenly rolling around on the filthy floor. She's keen, it has to be said – going at me like a dog with a focking chewtoy. We're pulling and ripping out of each other, neither of us giving a shit about the dress. If anything, roysh, knowing how much it cost actually adds an edge to proceedings?

Fifteen minutes later – or whatever – I finish up. We eventually get our breath back, then get to our feet and stort fixing ourselves, tucking ourselves in and whatever else. It's only then that Emmy mentions the dress. 'Oh my God!' she goes. 'Look at the state of me!'

I'm there, 'Who *gives* a fock?' feeling a bit Jay Z, if I'm being honest about it.

I'm looking down at the Manolos. The suede is, like, scuffed to bits and one of the heels has even broken off.

As for the dress, you wouldn't wash your focking car with it now. It's, like, shredded to pieces, especially around the orse, and covered in, like, dirt and oil and of course my mucky handprints. 'We shouldn't have done that,' she goes.

I'm there, 'Fock it, I'm, like, a celebrity now. Rock and roll! Blahdy blah!'

'It's not that,' she goes, 'It's just, Sorcha thinks you bought the dress for *her*.'

I could be wrong, roysh, but as she turns to leave, basically holding her various bits together, I think I notice the slightest trace of a smile on her face.

Much as I love women, I'll never fully understand them.

I make it back to the pool, roysh, in time to see Honor come out modelling a striped dress by Splendid Littles with Ryan Flex sandals by Pediped. It's the final lot of the day. Everyone's cheering, roysh, and she's loving being the centre of attention, going, '*Hola! Hola! Hola!*' and I'm thinking that I'm glad I didn't miss it – they're, like, the precious moments you can *never* get back?

My clothes are, like, filthy, so I end up hiding behind the hand-carved marble gazebo, trying to clean myself up, using a bottle of Club Soda and a piece of soft grey material that, in the throes of passion, I must have ripped from the dress.

That's where Sorcha eventually finds me.

The first thing she says is that she's been looking all over and I hide the piece of material in what would have to be described as a blizzard of movement. She doesn't even comment on the state of me and I immediately realize that she's upset. She throws her orms around me and, like, bursts into tears. I still suspect that this has something to do with Emmy and experience tells me to put one hand over my balls.

She eventually pulls away and goes, 'Steve and Elodine have gone home,' and I'm storting to relax, realizing that this might not be something *I've* actually done.

I'm there, 'What happened?'

She looks away. She says there was, like, a major fight. Everything was going *so* well until Cillian brought up the whole economy thing.

I shake my head. 'It's actually getting boring at this stage.'

'He said that the granting of mortgages to people who can't afford to pay them is going to set in chain a series of events that will drive the world economy to the point of collapse . . .'

I've just made shit of a six-grand dress. I don't want to be listening to this.

'He said the crash would be every bit as bad as 1929. Ross, what happened in 1929?'

I shake my head. 'Don't ask me. But I presume the rest of them weren't just standing there agreeing with him?'

'No,' she goes. 'Josh said that bad debts aren't necessarily a bad thing. He said it still makes sense to sign up riskier borrowers because, even with the increased rate of default, the ones who do pay will still generate greater profits for the banks and financial institutions than if the capital was lying there, like, unused?'

I'm there, 'See? That's that, then.'

'But Cillian said that assumed that the level of default can be predicted and managed. He said the good times would only last as long as the housing and employment markets remain buoyant and people with steady wages are able to service mortgages on properties that are steadily increasing in value. He said that a contracting economy, combined with a fall in house prices and the resetting of mortgage interest rates from the original teaser rates offered, would result in an increase in foreclosures that – because of the greed of people like Josh and Kyle – would set the whole edifice of Western capitalism crumbling.'

'Look, I'm not a fan of those two,' I go, 'but it sounds to me like Cillian was bang out of order there.'

'Well, can you *imagine* how Steve and Elodine felt? They gave Josh and Kyle money to invest, Ross. What if they lose their ethnic restaurant before it even opens?'

'That's not going to happen,' I go, liking the way my voice sounds.

'I've had their taster menu,' she goes, tears streaming from her eyes. 'Their pigori are amazing. What if . . .'

'I said, that is *not* going to happen.'

'But how can you be so sure? Cillian told them that those CDOs they invested in were essentially IOUs that one day someone was going to have to pay. Or *not*.'

'How can I be so sure?' I go. 'I'll tell you how. Because when it comes to shit like this – world affairs, blah blah blah – I always go with whoever makes the least sense to me. And when I hear Josh and Kyle banging on about the economy, I genuinely don't understand a word of it. I rest my case.'

That seems to put her mind at ease.

Unfortunately, it doesn't last long. All of a suddden, roysh, a voice storts coming over the, I supposed you'd call it, a PA?

'We were sold a dream of prosperity,' it's going, 'but it was all based on chronic indebtedness . . .'

Sorcha's hands go up to her face. 'That's Cillian!' she goes, then she immediately turns and runs in the direction of the gaff, with me haring along after her.

He's nowhere to be seen. People are standing around with their glasses of Pims and their canapés and totally bemused looks on their faces, while his voice continues to boom out. 'The simple fact is we have been living way beyond our means,' he's going.

People are turning to Sorcha, going, 'This is *not* what we came to hear,' and Sorcha, of course, is apologizing to everyone.

'Cillian!' she's shouting, looking around her. 'Cillian, where are you?'

'Yes, despite all the warnings signs, we continue to run up unsustainable levels of debt to feed the media-driven consumption frenzy and acquire the things we've been led to believe constitute success . . .'

People are storting to drift away now. One woman turns around to Sorcha and goes, 'I pay six thousand dollars for an Oscar de la Renta original with Le Silla Swarovski sandals, then I get a lecture?' and she walks off, not a happy bunny rabbit.

'Once, the US economy was the envy of the world,' he keeps going. 'It was based on the principles of enterprise, ingenuity and hard work. America built things – things it could be proud of, things that withstood the rigours of time. But not anymore. Now it builds nothing. Instead, it glorifies people who simply move money around the place and do so with increasing recklessness . . .'

Josh and Kyle come pegging it over, out of breath. They say he's somewhere inside the gaff, although with the size of the place, it could take, like, an hour to find him.

'When the crash comes – and come it will – we will remember these as the years when our insatiable appetite for consumer debt met the stop-at-nothing practices of our banks and financial institutions. We will be picking through the debris for generations to come. When I close my eyes, I see redundancies, insolvencies, bankruptcies and home repossessions . . .'

Sorcha has, like, tears running down her face. 'Please,' she's going, 'everyone stay.'

Even the old dear, who's holding Honor, is going, 'Everybody – it's just someone who's had too much to drink.'

Honor's going, '*Buenas noches*,' and at the same time clapping her hands. '*Buenas noches*.'

Nobody's thought about doing the obvious. But it's one of those moments – cometh the hour, blahdy blahdy blah. I go over to the PA system and just, like, rip the plug out of the wall. There's suddenly silence, roysh, but at that stage pretty much everyone has gone.

Harvey, who's standing talking to this blond dude in a yellow Hollister T-shirt, says well done to me, which *is* nice to hear.

Then Sorcha pretty much collapses on my shoulder, so upset she can barely get the words out to tell me that people have left without their seed packet favours. I stare at the gaff, with that lunatic somewhere inside, and I think seed packet favours are the least of her worries.

'Hey, Ronan, where are you?'

There's, like, shouting in the background. Someone's calling someone a fock-ass motherfocker and then that someone says, basically, fock you, you focking fock.

It sounds like he's in Dr Quirkey's.

But of course Ro has a Good Time Emporium of his own these days. 'We're watching *Casino*,' he goes. 'Here, Buckets – hit pause on that thing, will you?' and the shouting suddenly stops.

I'm like, 'Casino? You're already getting in the mood for Vegas, then.'

He goes, 'I'm after watching it eight times, amn't I, Buckets?'

'Eight times?' I go.

He's there, 'You wouldn't exist out here if it wasn't for me. Without me, personally, every motherfucker would have a piece of your Jew ass.'

'Maybe you should make this the *last* time you watch it?' I go, suddenly sounding like what I actually am, which is his father. 'Ro, I've got something I want to talk to you about. Don't worry, it's not bad. It's more . . . focked up. The thing is, you know Erika?'

He's there, 'Er, yeah.'

'Of course you do – you really like her, don't you?'

He's there, 'I love Erika,' and there's me forgetting how well they hit it off.

'Actually, that's probably going to make this a lot easier,' I go. 'The thing is, it turns out she's kind of your auntie?'

'Me auntie?'

'And it's *his* fault, in case you're trying to work it out – your focking hero.'

'Me grandda?'

'Exactly. He had a fling with her mother in the – whatever – old days. So the way it's set up now, she's, like, my sister?'

His reaction, I have to say, takes me by total surprise. 'That's great,' he goes, genuinely delighted.

I'm there, 'I mean, I know it's embarrassing – we're *some* family, aren't we?'

'It's great,' he goes. 'Here, get off the line, Rosser – I want to ring her.'

Talk about a conversation stopper. 'You ever read any Philip Roth?'

It's, like, where the fock does Trevion dig up these birds for me?

'*American Pastoral*?' she goes. '*Zuckerman Unbound*? Any of those?'

'No,' I go, not having a bog what she's talking about, but at the same time trying to *look* intelligent? Talking to birds is a bit like doing the oral Irish.

She's there, 'So who *have* you read?' actually wanting me to name books.

What I should say is, 'None – I'm still sexually active,' but I don't. Instead, I end up subtly changing the subject. 'Aisha,' I go, taking a whack of my appletini. 'That's a nice name – I presume it's after, like, the country?'

Birds named after countries *always* have chips on their shoulders. Birds named after months of the year have huge bazambas. Birds named after colours never wax their bikini lines.

'Country?' she goes. 'No, it's, like, the Stevie Wonder song? "Isn't She Lovely"?'

I shrug. In fairness, she *is* lovely, despite the attitude she's giving me. She actually looks a bit like Abbie Cornish.

We're in, like, Lola's in West Hollywood, this bor where they do, like, a hundred different martinis. Mine are all going straight to my head and I know deep down that I shouldn't be drinking them so fast.

Hindsight, blahdy blahdy blah.

Aisha asks me if I'll mind her bag – which is something I hate, by the way – because she's just spotted Maniche, who's *supposed* to be her sister's sobriety coach. Off she focks and, whatever, the two of them end up having what would have to be described as a heated exchange up at the bar which lasts, like, an hour?

Of course, bored off my tits – and this is going to *sound* bad? – I end up having a root through her Bottega Veneta knot clutch, looking for johnnies, if I'm being honest, because she's already mentioned that she has a kid and I don't want to end up paying vagimoney to a third bird for the rest of my actual life.

There's the usual shit in there – lotions, potions and mixed emotions. Then a picture of a little baby – presumably Coco, as in the daughter she's been banging on about? She looks about Honor's age. I wonder has *she* got any English yet?

But there's no zepps, roysh, although I do manage to find a packet of what are called Milktests. If you've never heard of them before, roysh, they're basically little breathalysers to tell birds who've had a few Bartons when it's safe to, like, breastfeed again?

I whip one out, open the little plastic package that it comes in, then give it a blow. The little strip changes colour and I check it against the code that comes with the instructions. It looks like Cardamom Yellow to me, which means I shouldn't breastfeed for, like, eight hours.

So what happens next is there's a crew at the next table, three or four dudes – jocks, roysh, but still sound – and they're all giving it, 'Hey, what's that thing you've got there?'

So I end up telling them and immediately, roysh, it's like I'm a God to these goys, in other words the biggest legend who ever lived? They ask me to come and join them, which I do, and of course then it's like, game on.

I throw the box of Milktests in the middle of the table and we order, like, a round of shots. They're all drinking Sambuca, so of course I end up going with that.

We knock our drinks back, as in skull them, then one of the dudes – he's a ringer for Zac Efron but it's *not* him? – blows a Tangerine, which is seriously impressive, in anyone's money. Don't feed for twelve hours! I'm second with a Pale Orange and the other three are all on Brilliant Saffron.

Of course, I love a focking challenge. I'm the guy who did the entire Alexander College Debs Committee – going through the cord, as we used to call it.

I order a tequila sunrise and also a baby Guinness, which gets a round of applause from the table. Even Zac Efron's giving me big-time respect. Straight down the Jeff Beck. Blow. Roars from, like, everyone. Cherry. Don't feed for sixteen hours!

The rest of them drop out. It's obvious this is, like, a two-horse race.

Zac Efron ups the ante. A gin rickey, then an Alabama slammer, which is, like, rocket fuel. I shake my head. No way. He knocks them back, one after the other, pulls a face like he might vom, but holds them down. Blows a Brilliant Vermilion. Do not feed for twenty-four hours!

I *have* to high-five him. No focking debates. Then I'm thinking that even though I'm in, like, another country, this is just like being back in Special Ks with the guys.

'I'll see you your gin rickey and your Alabama slammer,' I go, 'and I'll raise you . . . a zombie.'

There's suddenly what would have to be described as a collective intake of breath.

'You'll die!' Zac Efron goes. And he might be right. If I was a bird, my breast milk would already be, like, eighty-five per cent proof. The drinks arrive. My back teeth are focking floating. I grab the gin rickey – throw it down. I grab the Alabama slammer – throw it in on top of it. Then the zombie – get it into you, Cynthia.

Quick blow. Black! One of the goys is just, like, staring at the instructions. 'Oh my God!' he goes. 'Please consult your physician!'

Everyone just, like, cheers. Even Zac Efron makes, like, a sign with his hands as if to say, I'm out, dude, and the rest of them are going, 'Legend! Legend! Legend!'

I literally haven't experienced hero-worship like it since that day two months ago in Andorra.

All of a sudden, I happen to look up and who's standing over the table only Aisha, with a face on her like squashed cantaloupe. She snatches her bag, gathers up what's left of the Milktests and storms off.

The goys are all going, 'Man! You're in trouble,' and in normal circumstances I'd be like, 'Fock her – plenty more, blahdy blahdy blah,' but I actually fancy a shot at the title tonight.

See, birds with 'tudes have *always* done it for me?

So I say goodbye to the goys, then I chase after her. She's outside, trying to hail a Jo. 'One thing I'll never get tired of hearing,' I go, flicking my thumb in the direction of the bor, 'the applause of the crowd.'

She's *not* a happy plant-eating, burrowing mammal. 'There I am,' she goes, 'trying to talk sense into Maniche about her drinking, then I come back to find my date . . .'

She can't even finish her sentence. But she obviously wants me, roysh, because when a Jo finally pulls up, she gets in and leaves the door open for me.

It's only when I get in the back beside her that I realize how absolutely stupid drunk I am. And I say that just to let you know that anything that happened after that wasn't *my* basic fault?

We go to her gaff. Don't know where. Remember very little about it.

I do remember her yabbering away to the childminder in the kitchen, mostly about shite, while I was in the living room, like a good groundsman, testing the firmness of the sofa, the likely burn-factor of the corpet and – being a details man – the tensile strength of the coffee table.

It might have been all the waiting around, but I had a bat

in my chinos that could make Barry Bonds look like a Little Leaguer.

In she eventually comes, after letting out the childminder. Kicks off her Cesare Paciotti's and flicks off the light.

Of course, I'm straight out of my seat and all over her like an oil spill. She tastes of apple and boysenberry.

I'm actually unbuttoning my fly when she's suddenly there, 'Stop it! Wait!' and pushes me back onto the sofa.

'Let's take our time,' she goes. From somewhere she produces a box of matches and she walks around the room, lighting all these candles, which she has every-focking-where. 'Let's get the mood right,' she goes.

I crack on that I'm cool with it. She's obviously one of these I Have Needs Too freaks.

There must be, like, thirty or forty candles in the room and it takes a good ten minutes for her to light them all. But she does it without once taking her eyes off me and I have to say, roysh, it's seriously, I don't know, erotic looking at her boat race in the flickering light.

She crawls over to me on her hands and knees, a dirty big smile on her face. Then she hits me with it from out of nowhere.

'Do you like Satan?' she goes.

I'm like, 'Er . . . I'm pretty sure I misheard that. Lot of drink on board . . .'

'What do you think of Satan?' she goes again.

The last time I was asked a question like that was at Honor's christening, but that was cool because it was in, like, a church? But here I'm suddenly shitting myself and I can tell you, I'm sobering up fast.

'I'm not really sure I believe in messing around with that shit,' I end up going.

She's there, 'You'll give it a try, though – right?'

I'm there, 'Errr,' trying to think.

'Come on,' she goes. 'You'll love it. I promise.'

I'm there, 'But your daughter's in the next room.'

'She loves Satan.'

I try not to look too shocked, roysh, because inside my mind I'm suddenly planning my escape. 'Em, okay,' I go, playing it LL. 'I'll give it an old lash, then.'

Her eyes light up. 'Really?'

'As I always say, don't knock it until you've tried it.'

'Great,' she goes. Then she gets to her feet. 'I'll, em, go and get things started,' and she turns and heads for, like, the kitchen, presumably to get, I don't know, a crucifix or some shit?

The second she turns around, roysh, I'm up off the sofa like I don't know what and I pretty much launch myself at her. Now I've tackled some of the toughest in the business. Even Jerry Flannery will tell you that he's got, like, a permanent click in his hip from the time I held him up five metres from the line in a friendly years ago. But Aisha is surprisingly strong. I mean, yeah, she goes to ground pretty easily, as you'd expect, but she fights me back and manages to kick me full in the stomach, winding me for a few seconds.

She gets up, roysh, and tries to run, but I quickly ankle-tap her – the wily old pro – and she hits the deck again. Then it takes every bit of strength I have to drag her, biting and gouging, to this little cupboard beneath the stairs. I literally throw her in there and turn the key in the door.

She's going ballistic – and that's *not* an exaggeration? – calling me all sorts of names, some of which even *I've* never been called before.

'Well, what are *you*, then?' I'm going. 'You're a freak is what you are!'

'Let me out of here!' she's going, banging on the inside of the door.

I get out of there as fast as my legs can carry me. And it's maybe an hour later, when I'm back in the hotel, fixing myself a nightcap from the minibor, that I think about Coco, that poor little baby left alone in that actual house.

Because that's me. I'm an actual softie. I think about going back. Deep down, though, I know it's too dangerous. How long is that door going to hold her anyway? I decide that there's nothing else for it. When in doubt . . .

Trevion answers, sounding majorly cranky. It *is* four o'clock in the morning.

I'm there, 'Where the fock are you pulling these birds from?'

He's like, 'What?' obviously still only waking up.

I'm there, 'As in Aisha. I don't care who you owe favours to – I'm not dating any more lunatics.'

He's there, 'What are you talking about?'

'That bird – she's into, like, devil worship.'

He's there, 'Hey, slow down, Elmo. What are you talking about?'

I'm like, 'She kept banging on about Satan.'

'Satan?' he goes.

I'm there, 'Satan! She kept saying how she loved Satan.'

'Satan?' he goes. 'Are you sure she didn't mean seitan?'

I'm like, 'Satan – exactly.'

'No,' he goes, 'I mean *seitan*. With an ei.'

I'm there, 'Dude, Satan is Satan – no matter how you spin it.'

'*Seitan*,' he goes, 'is a kind of food.'

I suddenly feel my entire body freeze. It's one of those moments when you *know* you've focked up? You're just waiting to find out how.

I'm there, 'A food? What kind of food exactly?'

'Jesus, it's wheat gluten. Cooked. What the fuck does it

matter? Vegetarians eat it. Full of protein. Your wife had it at her party . . .'

I'm thinking . . . Actually, I don't know what I'm thinking. Oh fock definitely figures in the shuffle. 'No, no, no,' I go, 'she said she worshipped Satan.'

'Lot of girls do,' he goes. 'Especially if they want to keep the weight off.'

'She said she'd introduced all of her friends to it.'

'So?'

'She said it'd be Satan for breakfast, lunch and dinner if she had her way.'

'Are you done already?'

I'm there, 'Er, yeah,' at the same time thinking, Oh, fock!

'By the way, I need to talk to you,' he goes. 'You and Fyon Hoola.'

'Look, I don't want to be in the same room as that woman. What's it about anyway?'

'It's about fucking MTV, that's what. They want to meet you both. Tomorrow night. Chateau Marmont. Eight o'clock. You fucking be there, you hear me?'

I'm there, 'Er, okay.'

'Now let me get some sleep here.'

I'm like, 'Er, just before you go, Trevion. Back to the whole Aisha thing. Satan, blah blah blah. To cut a long story short, I locked her in a focking cupboard.'

He's there, 'You *what?*'

He does laugh, in fairness to him. Eventually.

'Which probably *is* out of order, looking back now. Is there any chance *you'd* swing by and let her out?'

I've honestly never heard her so down in the actual dumps. She says she's okay, but I've known her long enough to know when she's putting on, like, a brave face, even when it's over the phone.

'And how's *he*?' I go – not that I *give* a fock? Except that he *is* sharing a house with my wife and daughter.

She's there, 'Quiet. He hasn't got dressed for, like, three days.'

I'm like, 'Are you saying he hasn't even been to work?'

'Bob told him to take a couple of weeks off. He needs rest, Ross, but he's spending the entire time just reading. Constantly.'

I tell her that doesn't sound good, though she doesn't need me to point that out. 'Why don't you come and stay in my suite?' I go. 'And that's not me trying to get in there. It'd be separate beds.'

The thing is, roysh, I actually mean it?

'I really, really appreciate that,' she goes. 'But I can't just walk out on him, Ross. I think he's really unwell.'

'I'm just saying, the offer's there.'

She tells me that I'm – oh my God – *so* an amazing person and I'm actually feeling pretty good about myself until she mentions Erika.

'Ross,' she goes, 'can I say something to you? And please don't take this the wrong way because it has been, like, *so* great having you here? But . . . I really miss my best friend.'

I'm there, 'Give her time. I'm sure she'll ring you when she gets her shit together.'

'You know, I almost rang her today?' she goes. 'As in, I actually called up her number and hit dial? But then I changed my mind before she could answer.'

'I, er, wouldn't advise you make a habit of that. Like I said, she's pretty pissed off with you, for whatever reason.'

She sounds like she's out and about, by the way. I ask her where she is and she says she's in the cor, on the way to Emmy's.

I'm there, 'Emmy?'

'Yeah,' she goes. 'Oh my God, she's being *so* weird at the moment?'

I'm like, 'Weird, as in?'

She's there, 'Weird, as in she still hasn't given me my dress. She's not even returning my calls.'

I'm like, 'I, er, better go – I'm meeting Harvey for lunch.'

She goes, 'Oh my God, is it true that you and your mum are meeting some guy from, like, MTV tonight?'

I'm there, 'Er, yeah. I'm not exactly sure what it's about.'

'Oh my God, whatever it is, I would *so* love to be in it, Ross.'

I tell her I'll give her a shout later and tell her what it's about.

Harvey's sitting outside Café Midi with a couple of Tapioca Pearl milk teas. 'You certainly enjoyed yourself at the fundraiser,' I go. 'What was his name?'

He laughs. He's got that look about him. 'Hugo,' he goes, except he can't say it without smiling.

We've all been there.

'He's a good-looking goy,' I go, which is an amazing thing for me to admit. 'He better not come between our friendship.'

He laughs and says he won't. 'You look like you've something on your mind,' he goes.

I shake my head. 'Do you ever get the feeling,' I go, 'that there's a whole heap of trouble heading your way?'

They're already stuck into the Châteauneuf de Plonk, the two of them. She's rubbing her hand up and down her leg, like she does when she's mullered and making a disgrace of herself.

'Look at the focking state of you,' I go. 'If a fisherman pulled you out of the sea, he'd throw you back.'

She doesn't say anything. And neither does *he* – except, 'Sit down, Gracie. And keep your mouth shut. It's listening time.'

I was actually about to sit down anyway.

He's like, 'How would you like to star in your own reality TV show?'

I'm a bit taken aback. I'm there, 'Whoa! Are we talking like *The Hills*?'

He shakes his head. 'We're talking like *The Osbournes*,' he goes. 'Like I told you, I been talking to MTV. One or two executives. Personal friends of mine. Obviously, they know all about your mother . . .'

They automatically smile at each other. I think he's actually in love with her, the poor focker.

'They was there that night in Book Soup,' he goes. 'They wanted to know was you for real . . .'

I'm like, 'Was *I* for real?'

He's there, 'Shut up. Are you kidding me? I said. The way this kid speaks about his mother! The way his mother speaks about him!'

I turn to her, a bit hurt to be honest. 'What bad shit could you possibly say about me?' She just blanks me.

'So I starts telling this guy your whole situation. Your boyfriend . . .'

'He's not my boyfriend.'

'Your wife and kid. That crazy fuck they're living with. And just generally how stupid you are – giving coffee to the baby, taking that girl to the emergency room because you blew gas in her face, yada, yada, yada. Let me tell you, the guy nearly pops his hernia this morning laughing at the sei-tan story . . .'

I'm there, 'I'm glad to hear I amuse someone.'

He's like, 'Yes, you do, Chico. Yes, you do. Let me tell you, this guy says to me, we got to get this family on camera. This is *Newlyweds* meets *The Hills* meets *Hogan Knows Best . . .'*

From the general vibe of the conversation, I know that I'm basically Jessica Simpson.

'They want to give us Johnny Sarno,' he goes. 'One of the best directors in the business. Twenty-five years old. He's on his way here right now. And let me tell you, he's pumped about meeting the two of you.'

I look at the old dear, then back at him. 'Have shekels been mentioned? I presume they have.'

'They want to pay you guys — fourteen half-hour episodes — Two! Million! Big ones!'

'Two million?' I go. I've suddenly got my business hat on. 'Wait a minute, are we talking dollars?'

'No, we're talking Twinkies,' he goes. 'What do *you* think?'

'Okay, I just thought I'd check. They always say, don't they, that you *shouldn't* just rush in and accept the first offer? But, having thought about it, the answer is yes, I accept.'

'You *accept*? Well, hoo-fucking-ray for Jay Gatsby.'

The old dear laughs, loving seeing me under pressure.

The next thing I see, roysh, is this Chinesey-looking dude — and, again, that's not racist — walking towards us with his hand outstretched and his mouth open wide in a look of what would have to be called awe. Trevion wasn't bullshitting — he obviously *is* excited about meeting me?

I stand up, shake his hand and tell him that if MTV wants to follow me around while I do my shit — scoring birds, drinking for Ireland and roaring general abuse at that dog over there — then I've no problems taking their focking money.

I turn to the old dear. 'Are *you* up for it?'

You'd want to hear her. 'Television is one medium I've always been desperate to get into.'

'Yeah?' I go. 'That and medium dress.'

Johnny turns to Trevion with a big delighted smile on his boat – what I'm beginning to realize is his normal look.

'Isn't it great?' Trevion goes. 'That's how they talk to each other, all the time.'

Trevion calls over the waiter and asks for another bottle of wine.

'Couple of questions,' Johnny goes. He talks with, like, a normal American accent? Presumably he was born here? 'First, what are you going to do with this thing?' and I swear to God, roysh, he actually points at my nose.

'What's wrong with my nose?' I go, naturally enough.

Trevion gets in on the act then. He's there, 'It's huge is what's wrong with it.'

The old dear has the actual balls to laugh.

I'm there, 'I'm not going back to that San whatever-he's-called,' and then I turn to Johnny. 'Did *he* put you up to this?' meaning Trevion.

'No,' he goes, suddenly staring at the middle of my face, taking it in from, like, various different angles. 'I think it would be distracting, that's all – draw attention away from the action.'

I turn to the old dear. 'Are you not even going to stick up for your son?'

She just shrugs and turns her head away. 'You got your father's nose,' is all she goes.

Trevion's there, 'I'll ring San. We'll get you booked in for a new one tomorrow.'

'No.'

'It's just your nose.'

'I told you, I'm not letting that lunatic near me.'

Johnny goes, 'No nose, no deal,' leaving me with no choice.

Trevion laughs. 'Hey, cheer up,' he goes. 'When you're

really in the big time, you think anyone's going to take out their coke with that fucking thing in the room?'

'I don't do coke.'

'Well, you ain't gonna be offered any either. You're like an anteater there. So the nose goes – no vote. I'll ring San. He's done rhino a whole heap of times. He could do it in the morning.'

'This is going to be on, like, TV. So the whole world is going to know I had, like, a nose job?'

'We'll tell them it was medical. You broke it playing . . . what's that shit?'

'Rugby.'

'Yeah, whatever. An old injury – never healed properly.'

'We could film the operation for the show,' Johnny goes, looking delighted. 'Also,' he goes, 'we want to get you all living under one roof.'

Trevion's there, 'I was telling him, your wife's got that big house, right?'

I'm like, 'Yeah, but I'm not sure I could handle living with that focking Cillian.'

'Well, that's the deal,' Trevion goes. 'Take it or don't. *Ross, His Mother, His Wife and Her Lover . . .*'

I look at Johnny. 'Yeah, that's what we want to call it,' he goes.

Trevion's like, 'And that's what they want – the whole dysfunctional lot of you, under one roof.'

He gives the old dear a smile of apology.

I'm there, 'Well, I'll have to ask Sorcha first,' and the old dear's suddenly looking over my shoulder, going, 'No time like the present.'

I don't even get a chance to look around. Sorcha's suddenly stood in front of me, with a face like a dick in a bucket of Deep Heat. It's obvious that I'm in serious shit.

Without saying a word, she throws a glass of wine over me – *my* glass?

'That,' she goes, 'is for having sex with my friend at my party . . .'

Trevion turns to Johnny. He's there, 'See what I mean?' and Johnny's just, like, nodding his head, again looking like the cat that got the focking cream.

Sorcha picks up the old dear's glass. That goes over me as well. '*That* is for doing it in a dress that cost six thousand dollars . . .'

Then she makes a grab for Trevion's and I'm thinking, shit, what else *is* there?

'And that,' she goes, throwing it straight in my face, 'is for lying about Erika not wanting to talk to me.'

Like I've said time and time again about the Mounties, they're dogged.

Then she just bursts into tears.

The old dear stands up, puts her orm around her and gets her to sit down with us. 'Can we get some water over here?' she shouts to no one in particular.

Sorcha's like, 'Red tea, if they have it.'

'Red tea,' the old dear goes. 'And another bottle of wine,' then she sort of, like, strokes her hair and tells her that everything's going to be okay – which she's never done for me, can I just say?

Sorcha rears up at me again then. It's like the end of a focking horror movie – you never know when they're really done, do you?

'You *know* how I feel about Stella McCortney,' she goes.

She turns to the old dear for support. 'Anytime I have, like, a really difficult decision to make, I'm always there, WWSD? As in, What Would Stella Do?'

'Are you sure it's Stella?' I make the mistake of going. 'As in, are you sure it's not me being with someone else that's upset you?'

It's definitely *not* the wisest thing in the world to say?

She looks at me in, like, a suddenly nasty way and goes, 'I just thought you might like to know, Ross, that she's coming over.'

I'm there, 'Who?' presuming we're still talking about Stella.

She's there, 'Erika.'

My entire body just goes cold.

'I booked her a ticket,' she goes. 'She'll be here tomorrow.'

Johnny, of course, is totally confused. 'Who's Erika?' he goes, looking from me to Sorcha to Trevion.

It's the old dear who goes, 'Erika is Sorcha's best friend. Ross just found out that she's also his half-sister.'

Trevion smiles so wide you could fit that wine bottle in his mouth sideways. 'What'd I tell you?' he goes. 'They make the Manson family look like the fucking *Brady Bunch*.'

6. A brand new face for the boys on MTV

Pumped and all as Sorcha is about being on reality TV, I think that, on balance, I probably owe her an apology, which is why I call out to the gaff the following morning with a tub of Edy's Slow Churned Rich and Creamy Cheesecake Diva ice cream as, like, a peace offering – the small one, I *should* add, because she's already banging on about how the camera adds eight pounds.

It turns out I've just missed her. Cillian says she just left for the airport, which means that Erika's going to be here in a couple of hours. 'I wonder how she'll look,' I hear myself go. 'Not great hopefully – long flight, lot on her plate, blahdy blahdy blah . . .'

He looks like shit, I should mention. He's still in his pyjamas – *pyjamas*, by the way – with four or five days of beard growth and a hum coming off him that tells me he hasn't showered in that time either.

He doesn't even ask me in. He tries to talk to me at the door and I have to, like, push past him with my bags and remind him that I actually live here now?

Then I ask him, nice to be nice, if he's looking forward to being on TV and he laughs – again, *if* it was a word – dismissively. 'I've no intention of involving myself in that frivolous rubbish,' he goes. 'Obviously, I can't stop Sorcha . . .'

'No, you can't,' I go, checking out his weedy little auditor body and making sure he *sees* me checking it out as well.

'But I've told her my feelings, that our obsession with surface details – like clothes and superficial celebrity – is going to make it harder for us all to come down. Now is the time to start appreciating the things that *are* important.'

'Deodorant obviously isn't one in your book,' I go – and even *I* have to admit that it's one of my best ever lines. Then I'm bulling, of course, that the cameras weren't here to, like, witness it?

He shakes his head. 'You really have no idea of the storm that's coming, do you?'

I'm there, 'All I know is, I don't think those mates of yours would have been out of order decking you at the Maddox Jolie-Pitt fashion fundraiser.'

'Josh and Kyle?' he goes, then he laughs. He's there, 'The wizards of high finance!' Except you can tell he doesn't, like, mean it? 'The financial sector – people like those two – they used to be the servants of the economy and we let them become its master. But who's been looking after the interests of society?'

I hope he's not waiting for an answer from me.

'Our political leaders,' he goes, 'here, back home – have you ever noticed the way they behave around men with money? Like silly girls. They're so besotted, they forget whose job it is to govern whom . . .'

'Dude,' I go, 'I've actually got to be at the hospital in, like, ten minutes?'

'They gave spivs like Josh and Kyle what they wanted. Unfettered capital markets. The elevation of the City above all else. And what has it delivered? An economy entirely reliant on a financial sector engaging in riskier and riskier activities. We're all going to end up paying the price for their greed. And their arrogance.'

'Dude,' I make the mistake of going, 'why don't you say all that shit on camera?' and he's suddenly staring into space, lost in thought.

*

The thing is, roysh, I don't know how it can be that I could get to, like, twenty-seven years of age and no one – we're *talking* no one – has ever mentioned the size of the old Shiva, good, bad or indifferent.

But now even Harvey says it belongs on Mount Rushmore and of course I have to crack on then that I know what Mount Rushmore is.

'Okay, what about this one?' I go.

I'm standing side-on to the mirror, holding photographs of various noses up to my face. I've got to pick one and I haven't got long.

Harvey laughs. 'It's a bit, I don't know,' he goes, 'doughy.'

I'm like, 'Doughy?'

'It's, like, a boxer's nose,' he goes, shuffling through the deck. 'Hey, what about this one?' and he hands me one that for some reason makes me think of Reese Witherspoon. I hold it up to my face. He's there, 'That is *such* a good look for you.'

I'm like, 'Are you sure it's not a bit, I don't know, girlie?'

'But you *want* a pretty nose, right?'

'I suppose.'

He hands me another one to try.

I ask him how Hugo is and his face lights up. He says they're going horseback riding this weekend in the Santa Monica Mountains and I tell him I'm delighted for him, which I am, although – and this isn't jealousy – I'm just hoping he's still going to have time for me.

I'm there, 'Remember what I said, Dude, don't settle down too early. Learn a lesson from the master. Live your life.'

'Well,' he goes, 'I phoned Mike.'

'Phoned him? What did you do that for?'

'Just to tell him not to contact me. I've met someone and I'm, like, really happy.'

I've always wondered why people need to tell their exes that. Me, I just drop them like a three-foot putt. End of.

'This one makes me look like a focking Teletubby,' I go.

He laughs and shuffles through the deck again. At the same time, he's there, 'Hey, I can't wait to meet your sister.'

'Fock,' I go. 'I almost forgot *she* was coming.'

'But you're happy she's coming, right?'

I tell him it's complicated and he asks me how complicated.

I'm there, 'Well, before we were brother and sister, we actually had . . .'

'History?'

'Well, I was going to say intercourse – but history, yeah.'

His jaw just drops.

This one makes me look like the focking Grinch.

'You're the first person I've actually discussed this with,' I go, 'aport from my best friend. And a bunch of total strangers in addiction counselling.'

He's still in shock.

'In fairness,' I go. 'You've got to see this girl – even you'd be into her.'

'Even *me*?' he goes. He laughs. 'You mean *she* could be the one to cure me of this terrible affliction?'

'You know what I mean,' I go. 'And the whole reason I didn't want her coming over here is that I'm scared that my feelings for her won't have changed.'

'Hey, don't beat yourself up,' he goes, which is exactly what I need to hear, roysh, because I *can* be a bit hord on myself sometimes? 'You said it yourself – you didn't know she was your sister when you had . . . relations. Your feelings for her will resolve themselves – but not until you spend time around her.'

He's actually wise beyond his years, this dude.

I'm there, 'It's just, I don't want to end up feeling like some sexual deviant – even though we're only, like, *half-* brother and sister?'

'And cut!' Johnny Sarno goes, then he storts giving us, like, a round of applause with, like, the usual big smile on his face. The rest of the crew join in then. Apparently, we've, like, nailed the scene, although I'm not a hundred per cent happy with it.

'Johnny,' I go, 'I wouldn't mind reshooting that again. See, the whole thing about the nose job is it's *not* supposed to be for, like, cosmetic reasons? It's supposed to be because I'm having breathing difficulties from a kick in the boat I got back in the glory days . . .'

'We'll handle it in the editing suite,' he goes, without even looking at me.

I'm there, 'I think I'd prefer . . .' but he just, like, cuts me off.

'This isn't the movies,' he goes. 'We've got thirty minutes of television to film every week. We're already behind schedule,' and then he shouts, 'Can we get that doctor in here?'

Johnny tells me to put on my hospital gown and get into bed, which I automatically do.

I cop San – as in San Sancilio – standing just behind the camera, checking himself out in one of the monitors, like the crazy fock that he is.

'Okay,' Johnny shouts, 'you know how this works – same as before. No lines, no script and forget about the cameras. San, you walk in. Ross, you show him the nose you picked. San, you go through the procedure with him. Ross, you talk about maybe one or two concerns you have. San, you quote him some of those statistics you told me about success and failure rates . . .'

I'm like, 'Failure rates? Whoa back!'

'And . . . action!'

San walks in. 'Hello, Ross.'

It feels like a scene from, like, *Days of Our Lives*?

I'm there, 'Er, yeah, hi . . .'

'Haff you chosen a noss thet you would like?'

I hum and haw for a little bit, then I hand him the one that Harvey thought looked amazing on me. Out of the corner of my eye, I can see that Harvey's delighted.

'Aha!' San goes. 'Reese Weeterspun!'

'Is it, like, *actually* Reese Witherspoon's?'

'Yes! Thees wheel look ferry nice on your fess.'

'Well,' I go, throwing a sly look to the camera, 'it's not about how it looks – it's as long as I can breathe again. God, if I could get my hands on that Gonzaga number eight!'

'Stop talking to the camera!' Johnny shouts. 'San, continue.'

'Ferry goot,' he goes. 'First, I wheel giff to you a general anaesthetic, which means gutenight, yes? Sleeeepy byebyes. Then, I wheel cut you here, here and here. You feel nahthing. Then, I wheel chop away all of thees bone and cartilage . . .'

I'm there, 'Okay, I don't know if you remember what happened last time – best if you don't give me the details.'

He's there, 'Ferry goot. But I giff to you a noss like Elle Woods, yes? *Don't stomp your leetle last seesun Prada shoes at me, honey. Excuse me, thees are not last seesun shoes.* Clessic, clessic comedy, yes?'

'If you're into that kind of shit.'

'*It hess come to my attention thet the maintenance staff ees sweetching our toilet paypare from Charmeen to generic. All those who are opposed to chafing, please say aye.*'

He laughs like it's the funniest thing he's ever heard.

I'm there, 'Er, just getting back to the whole operation thing? Like I said, as long as I can actually breathe properly . . .'

'Yes,' he goes. 'And you wheel look ferry pretty. And do not be nerfous. I haff done thees many times. Many, many happy endings. But sometimes, I haff to say to you, if too much of the old noss is cut away, then the breedge wheel collapse and you wheel be deformed. Boo-hoo, ferry sad.'

'What?'

'Also, I say to you, if the teep of the noss is over-rotated, your nostreels wheel look like apeeg.'

'Apeeg?'

'Oink, oink, yes?'

'Jesus Christ!'

'No woman in the world like a men who look like apeeg, no?'

I'm suddenly having second thoughts again.

'For the stateestics, this happen in only eight per cent of my cases.'

I'm there, 'Eight per cent? Er, you know what? I think I'm going take two or three days to have another think about this.'

'You cannot,' he goes. 'Tomorrow I am – how to say? – deporteed.'

'Did you say deported?'

'Deporteed back to Ecuador. Say gutebye to Hollywood, say gutebye my bebby. Beely Joll. Ferry sad. Ferry sad to leave before I can fess my accusers on the Feetness to Precteese Committee.'

I'm like, 'Fitness to practice?' and I automatically throw back the sheets.

Trevion all of a sudden appears. 'Put him out!' he shouts. 'Put him out!' and two nurses appear out of nowhere, roysh, and hold me down while San grabs, like, a huge syringe, squeezes the air out of the top of it, then jabs it into my orm.

My eyes get suddenly heavy. The last thing I hear is Harvey go, 'Oh! My! God!' and Trevion go, 'Goodnight, Joycie!'

I'm like, 'Just don't make me look like . . .' and I'm out of the game before I can even *say* La Toya Jackson.

'Let me tell you,' Trevion goes, 'you're pretty as a fucking girl under them bandages.'

He's driving and I'm sitting in the passenger seat, still groggy. I'm there, 'I can't believe what you did.'

I'm in agony – and we're talking total agony.

'You're a total orsehole,' I go, because he got San to do the focking lot – the lipo, the abdominal resculpt, the pectoral implants, the new calves and the rhinoplasty, obviously.

'Yeah, you betcha,' he goes. 'Pretty as a fucking girl.'

I check myself out in the mirror on the back of the sun visor. I've got two humungous black eyes and I've been told I'm going to have to breathe through my mouth for the next week. I'm a family allowance book away from being an actual skobie.

'And, let me tell *you*,' he goes, 'poor San was *crying* at the airport this morning? Yeah, crying like a fucking baby. And it wasn't because the Feds escorted him onto the plane neither. No, no, no. They were tears of fucking happiness, my friend. That's right. Kept saying how pretty your nose was. I says to him, "What a way to go, San! What a way to go!"'

I shake my head, which even hurts. 'Giving someone plastic surgery against their will,' I go. 'I'm not surprised they deported him.'

'Well, it was more *extradited*,' he goes. 'Tomato, tomayto. But, hey, he wants pictures, the works. I got a hotmail address for his attorney.'

My nose, by the way, like my whole body, is totally bandaged up. 'So how long do I have to leave these on for?' I go, still majorly pissed off here.

'Three, four weeks minimum,' he goes. 'The nose, the longer the better. Less chance of collapse.'

'You're saying now there's a chance it's going to collapse?'

'Hey, there's always a chance. It's not a biggie. San says all we got to do is harvest some cartilage from your septum. Failing that, your fucking ear.'

'What?'

'Don't worry, he wrote it all out for me. There's a napkin there in the glove compartment.'

I whip out the napkin and just, like, stare at it. It's all, like, lines and squiggles. 'It's like focking cave drawings,' I go.

He laughs. 'Doctors and their writing, huh? And he *was* in handcuffs, remember.'

'You have got to be focking shitting me!'

'Hey, pipe down, McDreamy. Chances are we won't need it. I got other news. That sister of yours arrived yesterday morning . . .'

'Erika?'

He gives a sort of, like, long wolf-whistle.

I shake my head.

'She's a fucking beauty, ain't she?'

I'm there, 'Don't remind me.'

'A real beauty. And let me tell you, Johnny and the MTV boys are very happy. She got a great work ethic . . .'

Which is hilarious – she's hordly worked a day since she left school. Like the rest of us.

'She comes in, catches two, three hours sleep, then she and Sorcha, they go get a fucking hair soak together. They have lunch in the Spanish Kitchen, then they hit Barneys, shopping for shoes.'

'I've seen them two run *up* a down-escalator to get at focking shoes.'

'Well,' he goes, 'MTV got three fucking hours of footage – usable. Let me tell you, Johnny did some work on *Laguna* and the first season of *The Hills*. He says they're gonna be the new Heidi and LC.'

'I'm sure they'll be happy to hear that.'

'The kids are gonna love them. And that's to say nothing of your mother . . .'

I actually turn and look at him. I don't believe it, but I'm pretty sure I see that scar-laden, mangled face of his blush.

'Good idea,' I go. 'Say nothing.'

He shakes his head, roysh, like he's in awe of her, which of course he is. 'She got a record deal,' he goes.

I'm there, 'A record deal?'

'You fucking bet, a record deal.'

I actually laugh. 'Have you ever *heard* her sing?'

'She's got a beautiful voice. Anyways, they clean all that shit up in the studio. You think Beyoncé can sing?'

'I would have presumed she could, yeah.'

'Beyoncé sounds like two stevedores arguing over a prostitute.'

'Are you serious?'

'Yeah, it's all studio trickery. Anyway, what it is, is Columbia got their hands on some old Jeff Buckley recordings – they were in some schmo's attic. Or that's the *story*. Personally, I think they had them all along but they was never good enough to put out. Good tunes, though. "*Je N'en Connais Pas La Fin*". "Grapefruit Moon". "Please Please Please Let Me Get What I Want". All that shit. So what they want to do is clean them up and get your mother to sing every second verse . . .'

'You've got! To be pulling! My stick!'

'Fyon Hoola O'Carroll-Kelly sings a collection of heart-warming duets with the late but very great Jeff Buckley.'

'And you think *actual* people will buy that?'

'Hey,' he goes, 'people will eat shit if you put enough Splenda on it.'

'I doubt that,' I go. 'I seriously doubt that.'

He's quiet for minute and I know he's, like, building up to something – something I almost definitely *don't* want to hear?

'I think I've fallen in love with her,' he eventually goes.

I'm like, 'Spare me.'

'Sure,' he goes, 'go ahead and laugh. Let me tell *you* something, Chico, I ain't never felt nothing like this before. I thought I was done with all that, see. You spend six months in a prisoner-of-war camp, in the care of men with nothing to do all day except dream up new ways of torturing you, a certain light goes out in your fucking soul, you know what I'm saying?'

I'm there, 'Come back to me after you've known her a month.' Which he ignores.

'Seventy-five,' he goes, 'and I feel like I'm seventeen again . . .'

I think about the old man and Helen. I'm there, 'There's a lot of it about, believe me.'

So we pull into the driveway. Johnny Sarno's waiting outside for us. He opens the door for me, all smiles as usual. Various other people come running, including a make-up bird, who happens to be a ringer for Kim Raver. She's, like, poised with the powder brush.

'Do something to emphasize the bandaging,' Johnny goes.

I'm like, 'Emphasize? Do you not mean . . .' but she storts slapping me with the brush, roysh, before I can even think of the word unemphasize.

'Okay, your motivation for this scene,' Johnny goes, 'is that your sister has come over from Ireland. You haven't seen her since the night you found out she *was* your sister. So you're going to have all sorts of emotions – confusion, probably affection . . .'

He grabs me by the orm of my T-shirt and literally drags

me into the gaff, still smiling, through the hall and down to the door of the kitchen, which is closed. 'Now,' he goes, 'we've got cameras everywhere in there to make sure we capture the magical moment when you two finally come face to face. And don't worry if you fluff it first time – we can always go back and do it again.'

He opens the door, roysh, just wide enough to stick his head through. 'Yes, he's here,' I hear him go. 'Are we all set?'

Then he goes, 'You girls act like you're having just one of your everyday conversations,' and then he closes over the door again.

'And . . . *action*!' he shouts, then he sort of, like, indicates the door handle to me.

I'm actually kacking it. I don't know what her reaction's going to be. But I take, like, a deep breath, then I go in.

'Did you *see* the butler-inspired Zac Posen that Naomi Watts wore to the LA premiere of *The Painted Veil*?' Sorcha's going, and it has to be said she's a natural. I suppose she's wanted to be famous all her life.

They're both standing with their backs to me, at the Nespresso. 'It's like, when bad clothes happen to good people!'

'Hey,' I go.

They suddenly both turn around.

It's like, fock! Erika looks incredible – whatever a hair soak is. We both just stare at each other for what seems like forever? Then all of a sudden she comes chorging across the kitchen towards me, throws her orms around me and bursts into, basically, tears. The number of times I've seen her cry you could count twice on the fingers of one hand.

'Oh, Ross!' she keeps giving it. 'Oh, Ross!' and I realize then, roysh, that I'm actually crying, too.

'I'm sorry,' I end up going. 'I needed space. I just didn't know how to handle the whole situation.'

She smells of buttermilk and *Agent Provocateur*.

'We're *both* still in shock,' she goes. 'But you're my brother, Ross. And I'm your sister . . .'

I can feel the soft skin of her cheek against mine.

'I know,' I go, realizing at that exact moment . . .

. . . with total horror, I hope I don't *need* to add . . .

. . . that I've an oar on me that could row the whole focking lot of us to Hawaii.

'Half-sister,' I think about going, but in the end I don't, knowing that I have to act fast here. It's not only her who might notice – there's seven focking cameras in the room waiting to put this out to a worldwide audience of, like, hundreds of billions of people.

So I end up just looking her in the eye and going, 'I think what we probably both need is to sit down,' and I sort of, like, turn my body away from her – like I'm evading a tackle in rugby – and I plonk my orse down on one of Sorcha's high stools, thinking, no one ever notices you've a stiffy when you're sitting down.

She sits down on the stool beside me. My hand is on the black morble countertop and she lays hers on top of mine and sort of, like, strokes it with her thumb.

Which obviously *doesn't* help?

She goes, 'I'm looking forward to us getting to know each other.'

I look at Sorcha and notice that she's crying as well.

I've never known Erika to be anything other than a bitch. This whole scene is, like, too weird for words. 'You've only ever been a wagon to me,' I go, which must be true, roysh, because *she* even laughs?

She's there, 'Well, you've always made it difficult for people to like you,' which is possibly also true – though there's a lot *would* disagree.

'But this is a chance,' she goes, 'for us to start all over again. I always wanted a brother.'

I'm there, 'I suppose I always wanted a sister.'

'Okay, beautiful,' Johnny shouts. 'Now, move on. Sorcha, ask her about her mother.'

'By the way, Erika, how are things with, like, your mum?' Sorcha goes.

Erika shakes her head. 'I swear to God, Sorcha – I never, ever want to see her again.'

I'm pretty sure that Sorcha *knows* the full Jack by now, but she does a good job of cracking on *not* to? 'Oh my God,' she goes, with the full drama. Like an old pro. 'Why?'

I always forget she played Phoebe Meryll in the Rathmines and Rathgar Musical Society's production of *The Yeomen of the Guard* when she was only, like, fifteen.

I'm there, 'Why do you think? Imagine, after all those years, finding out that *he's* your old man. No offence, Erika, but what the fock was your mother thinking?'

She jumps straight to his defence, of course. 'Ross, he's doing his best to make up for lost time,' she goes. 'He really wants to be a father to me.'

'Well, that's going to be weird,' I go. 'Especially with them being back together, which I still can't believe, by the way. You know they were spotted coming out of the Bedroom Studio? Middle of Dalkey Main Street?'

Sorcha turns around to Erika and goes, 'Do you not think you're being a bit hard on *her*, though? Keeping it quiet required more than one person's silence, remember.'

'Look,' Erika goes, 'I'm entitled to be angry with her. You *know* how close I was to my mum, Sorcha.'

'That's why I'm saying it. You were like me and *my* mum? As in, Best *Best* Friends?'

'How could she keep something like that from me, then?

When I was a little girl, she always said to me, let's not have any secrets from each other.'

'There's secrets and there's secrets,' I go. 'But getting knocked up by my old man's not something you'd be shouting from the rooftops.'

'And cut!' Johnny shouts. 'Okay, Ross, I need you out of the kitchen. Girls, I want to reshoot the scene where you're waiting for him to arrive . . .'

I look at Erika. I'm like, 'It's good to see you.'

She smiles at me and squeezes my hand. 'It'll be easier to talk when it's not all . . . this,' she goes and she flicks her head in the direction of the studio lights, which have us all sweating focking bricks here.

'Sorcha, I loved the Naomi Watts line,' Johnny goes, studying his clipboard, 'but can you mention being happy with the Narciso Rodriguez black strappy sheath you bought earlier, because they've given us one for you to wear in a future scene . . .'

I jump down off the stool, totally forgetting that I'm still in, like, battle mode.

'And one of you,' he goes, 'I don't care which – say that you can't wait to check out Michael Katz on *Burton Way* . . .'

The next thing I hear is Erika go, 'Ross?' then Sorcha go, 'Oh! My God!' and they both put their hands up to their faces and I realize, roysh, that they're both staring at the enormous – and I *mean* enormous – bulge in my trousers.

He answers on the fourth ring. He's all, 'Hello,' and of course I'm not going to give him the pleasure of saying it back to him.

I'm just there, 'I hear you're back with Erika's old dear – as in *with* with?'

'Clearly nothing wrong with the transatlantic grapevine,' he goes, 'quote-unquote,' like he's not even ashamed of it.

I'm there, 'What are you, a focking teenager?'

He actually thinks it's funny. 'You know, I almost feel like I am. Helen here's got me trying all sorts of crazy things. Last night she took me to Eddie Rockers . . .'

'It's Eddie *Rockets*,' I go. 'And I can't believe you went there. I've been going there for focking years.'

'Then she has me listening to – what's her name, Helen? Oh, yes, Rhianna. Well, there's even talk of me getting one of these *iPods*. Have you ever heard the like of it, Ross?'

'Er, *no*? I focking haven't. Wait a minute – are you two in, like, bed there?'

'Of course,' he goes. 'It's after midnight. What time is it stateside?'

'Whoa back, horsy! You're in bed together?'

'Ross, we're in love.'

'You're not in love. *She's* desperate and *you* can't believe your luck that anyone would focking want you. And you're both making a show of yourselves. Have you no shame?'

He's there, 'What's wrong with your voice, Kicker?' trying to change the subject.

'What do you mean, what's wrong with my voice? I had a focking nose job.'

'A nose job? Why?'

'Er, maybe because I didn't want to grow old looking like you. *And* we're making a reality TV show, if you must know.'

'Oh,' he just goes and it's obvious he hasn't a focking clue what I'm talking about.

In the background, I can hear Helen telling him to ask me about Erika.

'Oh, yes,' he goes, 'you haven't heard from Erika, have you?'

I'm like, 'No – why would I have heard from her?'

'It's just, as you well know, she and her mother had words – words with a capital W. A lot of things said. Heat of the moment and so forth. But she's checked out of the Merrion and we're both worried about her . . .'

'Maybe she killed herself because she couldn't live with being related to you.'

'No, she hasn't done anything so drastic, thank God. No, I had a text from her yesterday, saying she's fine. She just won't tell us where she is.'

'Have you not thought that maybe she needs some space? No, because the two of you are too busy with your focking *High School Musical* routine.'

I tell him he's a disgrace and I hang up on him.

Harvey arrives back from the jacks – we're sitting outside Swinger's on Beverly, the sun beating down on our faces, the whole bit – and he catches, like, the tail-end of the conversation.

'Was that your *father*?' he goes, like he can't believe anyone could speak to their old man like that. I tell him not to worry, he's actually a penis. And he's used to it. If I was nice to him, it'd be too much of a shock to the system. He'd have a hort attack. Harvey *seems* to understand.

Our Ahi sandwiches arrive.

I ask him how the big romance is going. That's one of the other things I love about myself since I came out here – I've become, like, an amazing conversationalist? He tells me that Hugo's a yoga instructor and that the sex is amazing and at the top of my voice I'm going, 'TMI, Dude! TMI!'

He laughs, then he says it's not just the things they do together. They talk – as in really talk. And Hugo listens to him.

'I listen to you as well,' I hear myself go. I don't *know* why? But it's actually nice when he says he knows I listen.

'Mike never did,' he goes. 'He was, like, all about his Maserati and his time at Brown and how his wife was such a good person and if she wasn't, how come she ended up teaching children with special needs?'

I touch my bandaged nose, thinking I probably shouldn't spend too long outside. I don't want to end up with, like, tan lines on my face. 'So,' I go, 'have you had another think about this whole TV thing?'

See, he's changed his mind about appearing in *Ross, His Mother, His Wife and Her Lover* and now he won't sign the release form for the footage of the two of us in the hospital, where I'm trying on various noses. Which means, roysh, that MTV are going to have to either drop that entire scene or somehow splice Harvey out of it.

He says he's just not ready for something like this. Of course, if that's his decision, roysh, it'd be unfair to, like, push him.

'I'm disappointed,' I go. 'But I'll get over it.'

He looks suddenly sad. I'm wondering is he going to eat those potato chips.

'Look, can I tell you something?' he goes.

I'm there, 'Of course you can. Fock's sake, Harve.'

He takes, like, a deep breath. 'Remember before, when you asked how my parents took the news?'

'Yeah.'

I take a potato chip. Fock, my abs and pecs are sore today. 'They don't know, Ross. They don't know that I'm gay.'

I'm there, 'Fock! But the thing about reality TV is, you can be whoever you want to be. No one's saying you have to do gay shit. You can be in it as just some random mate of mine.'

He shakes his head. 'You don't understand,' he goes. 'They know nothing about my LA life.'

'Your LA life? What are you talking about?'

'Ross, when I'm here, I can be me. When I'm at home . . .'

'What?'

'I'm different. Look, I grew up in this macho family. I've got, like, five brothers. They tinker with cars. They like sports. You understand?'

'Er, I think so.'

'When I call home, I put on this, like, deep voice. I read the football pages so I can pretend to know what my father's talking about. They don't even know what I do here. They think I'm in college.'

I'm there, 'Dude, you have to tell them – take it from someone who always calls it like it is. With *my* old pair, I'm always thinking, you know, what if something happens to them and there ends up being things I haven't said to them? That's why you hear me offloading to my old man like that. I do it to *her* as well. You can't live with regrets.'

He doesn't say anything, roysh, except that I should maybe get in out of the sun – otherwise I'm going to end up with, like, a rhino tan.

Er, *remind* me again why we're here?

I'm actually talking about Whole Foods in Santa Monica, but Sorcha looks at me like I've just shed a load in one of her Roberto Cavallis.

'Because,' she goes, '*some* of us don't want to see our children poisoned by Agri-Business,' then she turns around to Erika and says that there's no point in even trying to talk to me because I've no even interest in, like, sustainability.

It's all for the benefit of the cameras, of course.

Erika gives me a little smile and sort of, like, rolls her eyes, as if to say, she's a bit focking much, isn't she? And it's amazing, roysh, because it's suddenly, like, brother and sister sharing an actual joke?

She looks amazing as well in, like, the Pencey mini and Alice + Olivia strappy top that I let her put on my credit cord this morning because her luggage is actually lost. I tell her I was talking to the old man earlier and she looks suddenly worried.

She's there, 'You didn't tell him I'm here, did you?' and I tell her no, there's no way in the world I'd do that. I'd rather let the focker sweat.

She takes Honor from me. I suppose she's, like, *her* auntie now as well.

We're in the artisan bread section, where Sorcha is, like, squeezing various loaves, testing them for what she calls *give*. 'Jackie Keller, the nutritionist who works with Ginnifer Goodwin, said somewhere that it's possible to *eat* a good proportion of your recommended daily water intake and artisan breads are, like, seventy-five per cent moisture?'

Me and Erika pull faces like we actually care.

Then we get back to, like, family matters. 'Erika, I know you hate your old dear,' I go. 'But can I make a case for you hating *him* just as much – possibly even more?'

She's there, 'Ross, Charles hasn't *been* in my life? The point is, *she* has? She had, like, twenty-seven years to tell me the truth – but that would have been, oh, too inconvenient for her.'

I'm there, 'Would you not think of even texting her? She's going to need all the support she can get if she's got herself mixed up with him again,' but there's, like, too much anger in her for her to see sense at the moment.

Sorcha pushes the trolley on. She says she saw Ashley Tisdale and Jared Murillo in here and that was, like, two weeks before she got a text alert to say they were even dating?

I grab a leaflet on the shop's policy regording genetically modified food and make, like, a paper airplane, which I then throw. I get unbelievable distance from it as well. Honor just, like, squeals with excitement and even Erika seems pretty impressed.

We head for the checkout and the bird – not the Rory Best, it has to be said – storts ringing our shit through. Organic vanilla ricemilk. Grain-fed chicken. Rennet- and rBST-free cheddar. Chewy Multivitamin Gummy Fruits. It's like, porty time at our place!

I stort packing all the shit into a biodegradable paper bag.

Sorcha picks up a copy of *Us Weekly* while she's waiting to hear the damage and mentions that waist-cinching dresses are going to be *so* in this year, although she'd almost literally kill for the tea-length vintage Ossie Clark that Keira Knightley wore to the Oscar nominee luncheon.

I'm actually putting the flaxseed oil in the bag when, for some reason, I happen to look up and, out of the corner of my eye, I notice the cover of *People* magazine. Or, more specifically, a photograph of me leaving Barney's Beanery two nights ago with a bird called Shelby Pienkowski, another of Trevion's up-and-coming actresses.

The headline is like, 'From No Job to Nose Job', and then underneath it's like, 'But Socialite O'Carroll-Kelly Keeps New Schnoz Under Wraps!'

My hands are, like, shaking with anger, to the point where I find it difficult to even turn to pages fourteen, fifteen, sixteen and seventeen, not to mention the 'Week to Forget For' feature on thirty-five, which I also made it into.

The main story's like, 'Celebrity wannabe Ross O'Carroll-Kelly has always had a nose for controversy. Remember giving espresso to a minor? Remember being thrown off the set of a Disney movie? Now, the wild child of literary sensation Fionnuala O'Carroll-Kelly is looking to reinvent himself – with a brand *new* nose!' and there's not a focking mention of me getting kicked in the face against Gonzaga.

'O'Carroll-Kelly (27) was spotted leaving a West Hollywood bar with promising actress Shelby Pienkowski (*One Tree Hill* pilot, *Angel* pilot, *My So-Called Life* pilot) late on Saturday night, sporting two black eyes and with his nose heavily strapped.'

Sorcha, who's, like, reading over my shoulder, goes, 'Oh my God, Ross, you are turning into *such* a male slut.'

I'm like, 'Sorcha, it's a set-up. Johnny Sarno just wanted a few shots of me out and about with some random bird, doing my thing. Give the public a taste of what I'm like.'

The story continues, 'The pair were later seen at nearby Coco de Ville, grabbing a table with *Hills* stars Audrina Partridge, Frankie Delgado and Doug Reinhardt,' which is total horseshit, by the way. 'Eventually, the group moved to the dancefloor, forming a circle and dancing to songs like Justin Timberlake's "Rock Your Body" and Madonna's "Holiday". "Ross looked a bit like Hannibal Lecter with all that strapping on his face," said one onlooker. "But he didn't seem self-conscious at all."

'Shelby wore a gold sequinned bubble mini dress by Jovani with Rene Caovilla sandals.

'A spokesman for the Irish lothario – who is separated from his wife Sorcha (meaning 'fair one') – refused to comment. However, a friend confirmed that he decided to have the surgery after years of jibes about his formerly wide and misshapen nose.'

I'm there, 'Bastard!'

'It's even rumoured that it was his monster schnozzle that came between him and former beau Lauren Conrad. What she'll think of the new one is anyone's guess. The friend said that Ross has been told to keep it under wraps for at least four weeks.'

I end up flipping the lid. I whip out my phone and ring

Trevion. 'You focker!' are the first words out of my mouth. 'You've stitched me up. Again.'

He's there, 'Hey, pipe down, Tin Strawn.'

'Coco de Ville?' I go. 'Frankie Delgado? This story's got your pawprints all over it, so don't even think about denying it.'

He's there, 'Hey, I'm keeping your name in the papers, aren't I? How about some gratitude?'

'Gratitude? The deal was we were going to say it was, like, a rugby injury.'

I get, like, a stabbing pain in my chest. I should stop shouting or I'll burst my stitches.

'You think anyone's interested,' he goes, 'in some sportsman-who-never-was, having an operation to help him breathe better? You know what people want?'

'What?'

'They want to know that the stars they see on TV are every bit as vain and unhappy with themselves as they are.'

'Oh, is that what you think?'

'Yes, it fucking is, Dorothy. People are going to tune in in their tens of millions to see you take them bandages off your nose. Now quit whining. I got news. Johnny's over the fucking moon with the footage he's got so far . . .'

I'm there, 'He's not going to use the bit where . . .'

He's like, 'The bit where you get an erection in your pants sitting next to your fucking sister? No. Even MTV's got standards. But the pilot's going out second Sunday in May . . .'

I'm like, 'Whoa!'

'Which means we got to keep working. You see that wife and that sister of yours, you tell them they're having breakfast in Viktor's tomorrow – just two broads having a girlie chat. As for you, your mother's in the recording studio eleven o'clock in the morning . . .'

'Mariah Carey,' I go. In other words, I'll be there.

'By the way,' he goes, 'I'm thinking about telling her how I feel.'

I laugh. I actually laugh.

'What,' he goes, 'you think I'm too old for her? Too ugly? Is it these scars?'

I'm just there, 'Look, just don't say I didn't warn you.'

I ring Christian, just to let him know that his best friend in the world is about to become a huge stor on MTV. It goes straight to his voicemail, so I leave a message telling him that I have news — we're talking major news — but he doesn't even ring me back.

'You like fah-ing terrapins?'

I turn around. There's a dude standing there with, like, long hair and big aviator shades. Must be 'Fah-ing' Ronnie Wheen — as in the dude who's producing this so-called record?

I'm there, 'I have to say I've never given them much thought,' then we end up both staring into this massive tank in the corner of the studio. They *are* pretty cool, I suppose – they've even got their own little Hollywood sign in there.

'They're my passion,' Ronnie goes. I probably should mention that he's, like, English? 'You wanna see my 'ouse – they're fah-ing everywhere. See this little fella, keeps eeself to eeself? That's Syd. You know his song, "Terrapin"? Course you do. Poor fah-ing Syd. Breaks my fah-ing 'eart to see him today. All that fah-ing talent . . .'

I obviously haven't a fah-ing bog what he's banging on about.

He's there, 'So this Finnhooler's your mum, eh?'

I'm like, 'Yeah – worse luck.'

'Nah,' he goes, 'she got a fah-ing great voice.'

I'm there, 'There must be something wrong with your ears, then. She sounds like a pensioner bending down for the TV remote.'

Ronnie shakes his head like he couldn't *actually* agree less? 'I've worked wiv the best and she's fah-ing up there. The uvver fing is, this idea's the perfect fah-ing synergy, in'it? They make a TV programme of 'er recording an owbum – the show promotes the fah-ing record and the record promotes the fah-ing show. Everyone's 'appy – way of the fah-ing future.'

I turn around to the console and I'm suddenly staring at the old dear through the window of the sound booth, thinking, What! The fock! Is she wearing?

This isn't horseshit, roysh, she's got on, like, a babydoll dress with leopardskin ballet flats and – sweet suffering fock – her hair up in a beehive, like Amy focking Winehouse. It would actually be hilarious if it wasn't so sad.

Trevion arrives with Johnny Sarno in tow. The way *he* reacts, you'd swear he just walked in to find Megan Fox sniffing his boxers.

'Look at you!' he goes, his big pumice-stone face going red. She gives him a little girlie wave through the glass – nothing for me, of course. Trevion turns around to Johnny. 'You give him his instructions yet?'

Johnny looks at me – everything seems to be funny to this dude – and goes, 'What we want from you is exactly what you did in Book Soup. Remember, you're going to be the Spencer Pratt character. So she's going to start singing and you need to go in there and start verbally haranguing her. Do you think you can do that?'

'Dude,' I go, 'this isn't even work for me.'

Trevion's there, 'We need to do it quickly, too. Then we're going to get you out of here, because your mother's got a record to record. We want to have it pressed and in the shops by the time this episode hits the screens.'

Jesus, what *does* she sound like, I'm thinking, going up through the scales – doh, ray, me, fah – like she actually *knows* what's she's doing?

'So . . . lah . . . tee . . . dohhh!' she's giving it, then she goes, 'Dohhh!' again, roysh, except she, like, holds it for ages, basically splitting everyone's ears.

Ronnie, Trevion, all the sound engineers, they're all suddenly clapping. I'm like, er, for *what* exactly?

She does a run-through for the first song, roysh, and it's, like, 'Grapefruit Moon'. You can hear The Late Jeff Buckley's voice sing the first, what they call, couplet, then the old dear comes in and *attempts* to sing the second, then they continue – I don't know – *alternating*, if that's the word?

Like, no disrespect to The Late Jeff Buckley – because it's not his fault? – but I can honestly say it's the most painful sound I've heard since a kid from Gerard's tried to tackle me in a Junior Cup match and, whatever way my studs caught him, he ended up with his nipple ripped clean off.

But everyone, roysh, we're talking inside *and* outside the booth, we're talking Ronnie and the engineering people, we're talking Trevion, we're talking Johnny and the MTV crew, they're all clapping and, like, nodding at each other, as if to say, a star is focking born.

She's in there suddenly going, 'Who do I need to sleep with to get a glass of water around here?' having the balls to actually play the diva. 'It must be a hundred and ten degrees in this room! My head feels like it's about to split!' obviously not a happy bunny.

Ronnie's there, 'I'm so fah-ing sorry, Finnhooler,' and she goes, 'Don't be *fah-ing* sorry – just *fah-ing* do something about it.'

'For the last time,' Ronnie shouts at no one in particular, 'it's a simple request – can we get a fah-ing glass of woater in there?'

'I'll get it,' I suddenly go, because I've had an idea – and as usual it's an absolute cracker. I pick up an empty glass, roysh, but instead of filling it from the jugs of water they've got lying around with, like, slices of lemon and orange in them, I have a quick look around and, when I'm sure no one's looking, I dip it into the terrapin tank, then pull it out, full to the top with dirty water.

This'll sort your focking voice out, I'm thinking.

I hand it to one of Ronnie's assistants and she immediately pulls a face. 'What the hell is this?' she goes because it's actually cloudy, to the point of being almost milky – probably all the shit and piss and whatever else is floating around in the top of the tank.

Of course, one of the things I was famous for on the rugby field was my quick decision-making. And that's something you don't just lose. 'I stuck two Alka-Seltzer in it,' I end up going. 'She said she'd a headache, didn't she?'

This seems to, like, satisfy the assistant bird. She goes into the recording booth and I watch her through the window explain it to the old dear, who doesn't look like she *gives* a fock one way or the other? She ends up just knocking the whole thing back in, like, two goes, then – and I know this is disgusting – she sort of, like, licks her teeth.

Johnny asks Ronnie if it's okay to send me in now and Ronnie says sure, but make it quick because they want to try to get, like, three tracks down today. Johnny turns around to me, roysh, and gives me my motivation for the scene – not that I need it. 'You've discovered you've got, like, a sister you never knew about,' he goes. 'And you're, like, mad at your mother? Now, the viewer will have already met you, remember, in the pilot. They've seen you get that done to your nose and they've seen you come face to face with Erika. But this is the first time, as far as *they* know, that you've confronted your mother. So make out like you're really angry with her.'

'Oh, don't worry,' I go, 'I was born for this role.'

Johnny shouts *action*, roysh, and I push the door of the booth. The old dear obviously doesn't know that we've storted shooting, roysh, because she's standing there telling Ronnie through the mic that she thinks her voice would be much better suited to dueting with someone like Eva Cassidy and can he find out if *she* left any tapes in her attic.

I automatically let rip.

I stort off, roysh, with a few old favourites – you might even call them timeless classics: 'You're so ugly, you could scare flies off a shit wagon. You've a face that would stop a sundial. You wouldn't get laid in a prison with a handful of pordons . . .'

She's just stands there with her Von Trapp open, which is hilarious.

'The last time I saw a mouth like that,' I go, 'it was trying to eat Jeff Goldblum.'

'Ross,' she eventually goes, 'I'm trying to make a record – I really don't have time for your obnoxiousness,' which is a pretty poor comeback, you'd have to say, given that she knew this was happening today.

I'm there, 'Who told you that dress fitted you anyway? You're coming out of it like a burst sofa. And eye make-up? At your age? Amy Winehouse? Amy focking Wino more like.'

'Ross!' she goes but I'm on, like, a roll now?

'And what the rest of them here are too scared to tell you is that you've a voice like a focked boiler . . .'

She's well used to me at this stage. What I haven't bargained for, of course, is that the abuse I'm giving her might prove too much for Trevion to take.

The next thing, roysh, the door flies open behind me and I turn around just in time to see him launching himself at me across the room. I don't have time to get out of the way, either. I have to just brace myself for the tackle.

He's going, 'Why, you little . . .'

I swear to fock, it's like getting hit by the focking Luas. I can't believe the dude's in his seventies. I feel all my organs sort of, like, jolt inside and I immediately hit the deck, my abs and pecs in absolute agony again. I'll be focking shocked if my stitches are still holding me together.

He's there, 'If I ever hear you speak . . .' and he's actually shaping up to hit me, roysh, on my brand new nose, when all of a sudden, out of the corner of his eye, he notices the old dear's hand suddenly go up to her mouth, like she's about to be Moby Dick. I notice, roysh, that her face is all of a sudden green and Trevion quickly forgets about me and asks *her* if *she's* alright.

She sits down, roysh, her face all worried, trying to catch her breath. It comes, roysh, like a focking tsunami. *I* even roll for cover.

'Eeeuuurrggghhh!' she all of a sudden goes, sending a wave of spew into the air – a big roller of organic tofu, watercress juice and whatever else she had for breakfast.

And riding on it, like some little crazy surfer dude, is little Syd.

Even Trevion, roysh, who as you know has seen quite a bit of shit in his day, is shocked. He looks like he might even puke his own ring up.

I crack my hole laughing, get up off the floor and then – as they say – take my leave of them all.

Outside, roysh, Ronnie and the others at the console are looking at the terrapin tank, then back at me, as if to say, surely you didn't . . .

Johnny is just, like, shaking his head. Ronnie says he's worked with the Stones, Zeppelin, the lot and he's never seen anyfing fah-ing like it.

'Welcome to my world,' I go.

Then I take a bow and fock off.

I can't remember if Sorcha said to try the red velvet or the vanilla cream, so what I end up doing is getting, like, two of each?

We're sitting outside Sprinkles in Beverly Hills, as in me and Erika – we're talking no cameras, we're talking just me and her, getting to know each other on our first brother-sister date. And it's actually really nice.

'I hated you,' she goes, applying gloss to her lips with a paintbrush in the mirror of her compact.

'Yeah,' I go, 'but you hated pretty much everyone.'

She sort of, like, smacks her lips together, then snaps the compact shut. 'That's true. But it was different with you. I despised you with a passion that frightened me.'

I actually laugh. 'Do you mind me commenting? A lot of birds have said that to me down through the years – the flip-side was that they were deeply in love with me.'

She shakes her head. 'Believe me, Ross, *I* wasn't in love with you.'

She's wearing the sky-blue Abaeté dress that Sorcha lent her with, like, XOXO flats and Jill Jacobson floral cuffs.

Okay, this is a weird thing to say about your sister, but she's always tanned well.

I'm there, 'Probably one of my favourite quotes that anyone ever said about me was that I'm like an electric fence. They *know* the dangers – but there's still a lot of silly cows who can't stay away. Jamie Heaslip said that, in fairness to him.'

She says that's why she always hated me. 'All those clever girls – beautiful, smart, independent girls. All you had to do was smile at them and they lost any modicum of respect they had for themselves. You set the women's movement back a century . . .'

I actually *like* the ring of that? It's the kind of shit I want on my gravestone.

I'm there, 'You're obviously including Sorcha in that.'

She breaks up a red velvet cupcake with the side of her fork, even though she looks like she's no intention of eating it. 'Sorcha most of all,' she goes. 'I mean, look at her. She's beautiful. She got enough points to study medicine if that's what she'd wanted. And her roles models are all these strong women . . .'

'Ayaan Hirsi blahdy-blah,' I go, pretty pleased with myself for actually remembering.

'But then I'd look at the way she acted around you and I'd think, where's your pride?'

If I'm being honest, I think that's the reason I always had a thing for Erika, aport from the obvious. She actually valued herself, which is, like, a major challenge for a goy.

Out of the blue, she tells me I have to taste her white chocolate mocha and she holds out the cup to me. I take it from her, roysh, just to be nice, but, just as I'm lifting it to my mouth, I notice that I'm about to drink from the exact spot where her lips have been and I know it's the exact spot because of the lip gloss on the rim.

'Go on,' she goes, 'you'll love it,' and of course I can't, like, turn the cup around because that'd be like saying she's got some, I don't know, disease. And I obviously can't wipe it because that'd be unbelievably rude, especially when we're getting on so well.

So what I end up doing is putting it straight up to my lips, roysh, and taking a sip and it tastes of not only coffee and white chocolate but strawberry as well.

She's there, 'Do you like it?' and I'm like, 'Fock, yeah,' and without having an actual sexual thought in my head, I suddenly realize that I'm, like, primed again.

'Go and get one,' she goes.

I'm like, 'What?'

She's there, 'A white chocolate mocha. Go in and get one.'

Of course, I'm in no position to stand up, especially in these board shorts. I crack on to look in the window of the shop. 'Nah,' I go, 'it's rammers in there.'

She turns fully around and looks in the window herself. 'Ross, there's only, like, two people in the queue. And I think they're together.'

'Yeah, no,' I go, 'I'll, er, stick with the Americano.'

She looks into my cup. 'But it's empty.'

I subtly change the subject. 'So what do you think of the whole Cillian thing?' I go. 'He wants to be port of the programme now. I know you're not a fan.'

'It's nothing personal,' she goes. 'I just don't think he makes her happy.'

I laugh. 'It's nice to see you sticking up for your *brother*,' and I actually emphasize the word brother, hoping the word reaches the south.

She's like, 'No, you didn't make her happy either, Ross.'

It's weird, roysh, but I've never known Erika to be this nice. It's like finding out that I'm her brother has changed her. She's chilled out to the point that you can actually talk to her.

'I hate to point out the obvious,' I go, 'but you weren't exactly a dream yourself.'

She shrugs her shoulders as if to say, you're right, in fairness to you.

I'm there, 'You had, like, a major chip on your shoulder. I thought it all had to do with the fact that your old man – or the man you *thought* was your old man – walked out on your old dear and that made you think all men were dicks. And especially me – being a major player and shit?'

'I don't hate Tim,' she goes. 'I mean, I did when I was sixteen. But now . . . Ross, he agreed to take on a child that his wife had fathered with another man. How *could* I hate him?'

I don't know the answer. I don't know that there *is* one? I always presumed he was an orsewipe.

'But I always felt different growing up,' she goes. 'And that wasn't Tim's fault. I mean, outwardly, we had the normal father-daughter relationship. But deep down, I always knew I was different.'

I'm there, 'Different as in?'

'I don't know. It's like something I understood on, like, an unconscious level? Even when he was being happy for me, I always detected a certain . . .'

'What?'

'A certain strain. Like the more he tried to be a father to me, the more his heart broke inside.'

'Is he still in, like, Canada?' I go.

She nods. 'I was thinking of maybe phoning him. To say thank you, which I never got a chance to do.'

She's quiet for a little while, then she goes, 'I called my mum a whore.'

I end up nearly choking on a piece of vanilla cream. 'Even I've never done that.'

Sitting there, she sort of, like, arches her back, then sweeps her hair back with her hands and uses her Dior Christal shades to hold it back. My eyes are sort of, like, tracing her shape through the fabric of her dress and at the same time I'm thinking, Jesus Christ! I belong in prison.

All of a sudden, I realize that she's staring straight at me. 'Oh my God,' she goes, her voice pretty much dripping with disgust, 'what way are you looking at me, Ross?'

I'm there, 'Errr . . .'

She's like, 'You're looking at me . . . the way you used to.'

'I know,' I end up having to go. 'It's hord to get used to *not* doing it, isn't it?'

'Not for me,' she goes. 'Not for me.'

I get, like, a text from Shelby, who's obviously John B on a second date. This ever happen to you? I've no interest obviously and I'm trying to kill the conversation dead with, like, short answers.

Wot r u up2 @ d wknd?

Chillin.

Interestin – want2 hang out 2gethr?

Wrecked.

Me2. ; -) Are u watchin tv?

Yeah.

Omg – same! Wot r u watchin? Im watchin americas next top modl! : -)

In ten years of using and abusing the opposite sex, it's one of the worst cases of replyarrhoea I've ever seen.

Harvey tells me there's a twenty-four-hour internet café next door and I tell him I'm sorry. 'Last word freak,' I go, shaking my head, then making a big show of putting the phone in my Davy Crocket.

'What's up?' he goes. He has to, like, shout over the music. 'You've hardly touched your mint julep,' and he's right. We're in the Velvet Margarita, but I might as well be somewhere else.

'Come on,' he goes and I end up following him off the dancefloor, back to where we left our drinks. 'Well, that answers the question once and for all,' he goes. 'Only a straight man could dance that badly.'

I'm there, 'Sorry, Dude. I'm still a bit sore from the op. And the head's not in it either.'

'So what's up?'

I end up pretty much spilling my guts to him. 'It's the whole Erika thing. Exactly what I was scared of. I mean, I only have to look at her and straight away I'm . . .'

I end up looking over both shoulders.

'*Aroused* would have to be the word.'

He says she *is* attractive – she looks like Denise Richards looked five years ago.

I'm there, 'Dude, she's my sister! It's, like, I met her for a coffee the other day – it was, like, half an hour before I could stand up afterwards.'

'Because you were . . .'

'Exactly. She's even noticed.'

In fairness, roysh, he does look suddenly sympathetic. He takes a sip of his kir royale.

'I mean, I'm pretty well known as a filthbag,' I go. 'I always will be, I like to think. But even *I* know that's beyond the beyonds.'

He shakes his head from side to side. 'It doesn't make you a deviant,' he tries to go.

I'm there, 'Fancying my own sister? Dude, I'm a pair of wellies and a headage grant away from being an Irish farmer.'

'Look, don't worry about it. Like I said to you before, in time your feelings for her will redefine themselves. You just have to be patient.'

I'm there, 'Dude, that's easy for you to say. You don't have, like, TV cameras pointing at you pretty much twenty-four hours a day.'

He pulls a face, like he suddenly knows where I'm coming from?

'Okay,' he goes. 'I've got an idea. Have you ever heard of tantric celibacy?'

'Er, no.'

'Well, I told you that Hugo's, like, a yogi, didn't I?'

'Yeah. And?'

'Well, he says that using meditation, it's possible to completely turn off your sex drive. Do you want to go see him?'

I tell him I'll try it. At this stage, I'll try anything.

7. A dream is a wish your heart makes

After the disaster of her fashion show in aid of the whole Jolie-Pitt thing, Sorcha decided to get back on the charity horse by organizing a Lunch for Life, with the intention of raising awareness of something – although she never quite got around to deciding what?

She *has* been busy – shopping with Erika, lunching with Erika, confiding in Erika what a total and utter lunatic she's currently going out with, while sitting in the sun outside various coffee shops.

Johnny Sarno says American kids are going to love them. He says they're Lauren and Heidi except with more intellectual depth. *And* a baby who's got thirty or forty words in Chinese and Spanish – 'key demographics' – and none in actual English.

Sorcha and Erika have really gotten into it as well. All birds from South Dublin want to be famous, but they did, like, media presentation skills as port of transition year in Mount Anville and I've heard Johnny comment more than once on their actual screen presence.

Anyway, cause or no cause, the Lunch for Life goes ahead, except they're calling it a First of May Barbecue. Johnny loves getting all of us together because he knows that sporks always fly.

I take an eggplant and zucchini kebab off the barbie and listen to Analyn – who's finally pregnant – telling Steve and Elodine that she got, oh my God, *the* ugliest bread box for a house-warming gift two years ago, even though it was, like, Williams-Sonoma and contemporary. But she and Mike decided to put it away with the intention of one day, like, regifting it? Anyway, her friend Judith was having her Coming Out porty, so she put the wrapping paper back on it and gave it to her, totally not realizing, of course, that it was Judith who gave it to her in the first place.

Erika is wearing a Norma Kamali ruched halter that I can practically see down every time she bends down to give Honor a charred vegetable. I notice Josh nudging Kyle and nodding in her direction and even Bob Soto's copping an eyeful, although he's being a bit cleverer about it, being the head of international risk assessment at PwC and everything.

I ask her would she not put, like, a cordigan on and I realize how immediately weird that possibly sounds coming from, like, her brother. I get a look from her, so I end up having to go, 'I'm thinking it might get suddenly cold.'

Except, of course, that it's, like, a hundred and ten degrees today.

'Or you might burn,' I go. 'Either/or.'

Sorcha comes out of the gaff, carrying a tray of lean turkey mince burgers, looking, it has to be said, more than a little bit down. I notice she's wearing the exact same storfish necklace as Lauren Conrad. I *could* rip the piss, but I don't. Instead, I ask her what's wrong, doing the whole caring husband bit.

'It's Cillian,' she goes. 'He's cooped up in that study. He won't come out.'

I'm there, 'I'm not surprised. I can't believe you invited those two dicks.'

She's like, 'Josh and Kyle have been *so* good, Ross. You know, if it wasn't *for* them, I might have even started to *believe* some of the things that Cillian's been saying . . .'

There's suddenly silence.

She reaches for me and hugs me with the orm that isn't

carrying the turkey mince burgers. I hold her for a few seconds, then she suddenly pulls away and sort of, like, studies my face, her eyes full of fear. 'Ross,' she goes, 'he says that TV shows like the one *we're* making have changed the world's consumption patterns and persuaded people that they can have whatever they want now and pay for it later.'

I give her my best concerned look. I'm there, 'That's crazy talk.'

'He also says the banks are lending out more money than they have in their care to people who can't afford to pay it back. He says that when the extent of it becomes apparent, it's going to send panic spreading like a bacillus through the world financial markets and that everyone – even our kind – are going to pay the price.'

'He doesn't deserve you,' I go. 'He really doesn't,' then I pull her close to me again and hold her even tighter this time.

'Beautiful!' Johnny shouts. 'Ross, I want you to stare into the distance, all glassy-eyed. I got Colin Hay singing an acoustic version of Metallica's "Nothing Else Matters" to fade out the scene,' so I do what he tells me and, like, thirty seconds later, he shouts, 'Cut!'

He says we're going to film my old dear's arrival next. He gets everyone to sit around the patio area on, like, sun loungers.

I pick Honor up – '*mucho gusto en conocerte*', she's giving it – and I wander over to the barbecue.

Johnny goes, 'You've all seen *The Hills*. We're going to film you sitting around making everyday conversation, then at some point – we're not going to tell you when exactly because it's got to look spontaneous – Fionnuala is going to walk in. And I want you to ask her all about her new record.'

He shouts, 'Action,' and Sorcha turns immediately to

Analyn and says that Quaker chic is going to be huge this year – we're talking puritanical hair, scraped back obviously, and lacy knee-length tea dresses with a peplum . . .

The old dear eventually arrives, *with* Trevion, and you'd swear it was Whitney focking Houston the way they're, like, fawning all over her – *if* that's the actual word.

Elodine tells her that her dress is stunning and the old dear says that it's BCBG, then Sorcha says she – oh! my God! – loved the updo she had in the studio. 'We saw the footage of your first day of recording,' she goes. 'Oh, my God, *so* Amy Winehouse.'

Which is exactly what the old dear wants to hear, of course.

The rest of them are all over her, asking her how the record is coming along. I drop a lean turkey mince burger onto the barbecue and there's, like, a sudden sizzle.

A few of them look around and there's, like, an immediate tension in the air. You can hear people thinking, uh-oh, it looks like it's going to be game on here.

Trevion fetches her a glass of champagne. She can't go ten seconds without a drink, the lush.

She takes, like, a sip from it. I can't help but notice his orm around her waist and how free and easy she is with it. I'm suddenly thinking, whoa, has something happened here? And if so, when the fock?

I play it cool, though.

'You know, that always makes me laugh,' I go and you can see everyone pretty much freeze. I'm holding Honor in one orm, while flipping the burgers with the other. 'You know when they say they found a load of recordings by this focker or that focker in some other focker's attic? Then you listen to them when they come out and you realize there's a reason why they were in the focking attic in the first place.'

Everyone's suddenly quiet, obviously not wanting to come out and laugh in her actual face. *They* might all think she's a stor – I know what she *actually* is?

Sorcha knows the routine well enough to come in and try to rescue her. She changes the subject, telling Analyn that Erika bought the new deerskin Prada yesterday and it's – oh my God – *total* orm-candy.

I suppose that's why my eyes actually drift to Erika. She's rubbing suncream on her upper orms and chest, while I'm – and I know this is going to *sound* bad? – watching her top tens wobble up and down like two puppies drowning in a sack.

I hear someone suddenly laugh and it turns out to be Josh. 'Are you checking out your sister?' he goes, in front of pretty much everyone, the dick.

Of course I have to go, 'Checking her out? Er, *no*?'

'He was,' he goes, turning around to everyone, and bear in mind, roysh, that the cameras are still rolling. 'He was staring at her chest!'

There's, like, total silence and they're all just staring at me. There's maybe one or two who sort of, like, screw up their faces and say how totally gross that is.

Even Erika's looking at me with, like, total disgust on her face, even when I go, 'I swear, I wasn't.'

Kyle gets in on the act then. 'Look at him!' he goes. 'He's salivating!'

I *can* feel wet on my chin.

'Er, I *happen* to be cooking turkey burgers?' I go. Then I'm like, 'Erika, I swear!' but she tells me to shut up.

One or two others, including Mike and Steve, who I thought I got on pretty well with, literally turn their seats around so they've got, like, their backs to me.

Sorcha walks over to me, shaking her head sadly, takes Honor out of my orms and walks slowly back to the gaff.

I notice, roysh, the slightest hint of a smile on the old dear's face. 'Oh, you're loving this,' I go, 'aren't you?' but she doesn't even answer.

And that, as they say in showbusiness, would have been a wrap – if it wasn't for the sudden sound, sixty seconds later, of Sorcha's screams coming from the gaff.

Now, a lot has been written over the years – and not all of it by me – about my turn of pace over the first ten yords. Let me just say that everyone makes a run for the house – the screams would have to be described as, like, blood-curdling? – but I get there first, followed by the cameraman, who keeps filming, then Johnny, who keeps smiling, and then Trevion, who's surprisingly fast on his feet for a man of his age.

I follow the screams through the house, through the kitchen, into the hall and towards the study, thinking if *he's* hurt her, I can guarantee he'll never use a calculator again.

I reach the study. The door is closed, roysh, but I push it and I have to say that I'm not actually *ready* for the sight that greets me?

I actually stop – my jaw pretty much on the floor.

The rest of them, arriving behind me, are the same. 'Sweet Jesus!' Trevion even goes.

Bob Soto puts his hand over his mouth and has to actually turn away.

There, lying on the floor in the middle of the room, is a focking mountain of money. One point six million dollars to be exact – the proceeds from the sale of a gaff in Terenure that Cillian's granny left him – in neat bundles of tens.

Johnny's turning around to the cameraman, going, 'Tell me you're getting this! Tell me you're getting it!' which the dude *is*, of course – it's focking dynamite.

Once the initial shock has worn off, it's either Josh or Kyle who goes, 'Cillian – what the fuck?' speaking for us all.

He's there, 'We can't trust the banks anymore,' like it's the most natural thing in the world to say?

I look at Sorcha and I ask her if she's okay. She just nods. Honor – I should add – is sitting on top of this mountain of money, going, '*Me llamo Honor. Me llamo Honor.*'

'You know,' Cillian goes, 'when I was younger, being invited in to see the bank manager was like being told by the hospital that they'd found a shadow on your X-ray. You were terrified – he was, at best, a figure of cold probity. Grey. My dad was one.'

'No surprise there,' I go, which he ignores.

'Then the banks were suddenly permitted to lend out more money than they had on deposit and all that changed. The TV ads . . .'

He laughs.

'Bank managers were suddenly smiling men in shirt-sleeves who were happy to see you. You could tell them lies – "I need money for train-tracks. It's all cash – cha-ching!" – and they'd still give it to you. Jesus, there's an ad back home where an *actor* gets a loan . . .'

'What exactly is your point?' I go, worried that this bit is going to make pretty boring TV.

He says that it's thanks to their cavalier attitude towards risk-taking and a fall in the quality of risk assessment that lending institutions are running far too high loans-to-deposits ratios. He says they've loaded up on investments backed by subprime mortgages and we don't yet know the extent to which they're exposed.

'Very little,' Josh goes.

Cillian says he begs to differ. I look down and notice he's not even wearing his John Lobbs anymore. He says the housing market here is already deflating and people are defaulting on their mortgages in huge numbers. Then he goes, 'Those subprime CDOs are loaded with toxic waste . . .'

He lost me back with the actor who got the loan. But I notice Steve turn to Elodine at the mention of CDOs, with a look of sudden fear on his face. This is what caused the borney at the Jolie-Pitt do. Kyle cops it as well. 'Steve, don't listen to him,' he suddenly goes to them. 'I told you before, he doesn't know what he's talking about.'

Cillian says that when the morkets realize it, all hell is going to break loose, roysh, because no one will be able to tell which CDOs are good and which are, like, bad? He says it's like when you discover a single cow with CJD – you've got to take every bit of beef off the shelves.

I haven't a bog what he's talking about, although the big fear is that he sounds like he does. But then Josh weighs in. He asks Cillian does he even know what he's saying. He's there, 'You think a few people in a trailer park in Warren, Michigan, defaulting on their home repayments is going to set in train a series of events that will bring the entire world economy to its knees?'

He laughs. Then everyone laughs, I suppose suddenly relaxing when they hear it put like that.

'Someone just deck him,' I make sure to go.

This is, like, a major thing for me. I want to put that out there, just so Hugo knows that it's not a case of me not being *able* to get it? In Ireland, I tell him, I'd be considered the ultimate players' player.

He seems pretty shocked by that. He goes, 'This is something you're, like, proud of?'

I'm there, 'Who *wouldn't* be? It'd be a well-known fact back home that I can have any girl I want, and that's not me being big-headed.'

But he's like, 'That *is* you being big-headed. Sex is ego. What I hope to teach you is that your use of it to satisfy

your sense of yourself is blocking your connection to your inner life.'

It has to be said, roysh, even though he talks a lot of shit, Harvey's actually done well for himself here. Hugo's a good-looking goy, if that's your thing – blond, stocky, smiley face. If you had to say he looked like anyone, you'd say Owen Wilson.

He's sitting cross-legged on the mat of this gym he uses and he sort of, like, indicates for me to do the same, which I do.

Most of the people who come to him for instruction, he says, *are* sexually active, often overactive. But more and more people are choosing abstinence to deepen the spiritual side of their relationships, to redirect their sexual energy into friendship or even to devote their attention to their studies.

'Harvey was telling me you gave up sex for, like, two years,' I go.

He just, like, shrugs. 'For me,' he goes, 'sex became a perfunctory thing, a routine duty – superficial and meaningless.'

'Same,' I go. 'But I wouldn't consider that, like, a bad thing?'

Aport from my marriage breaking up, obviously, though I don't mention that.

He's there, 'That's because you haven't tried celibacy. Periods of denial can enhance our awareness of the erotic impulse and heighten our enjoyment of the act.'

'Me,' I go, 'I just want to stop fancying my sister. I mean, do you *do* that kind of thing?'

He laughs. 'I think we can manage that,' he goes, then he tells me to close my eyes and turn my palms upwards.

He's there, 'The yogi believe that too much sex diminishes our union with life's nourishing harmonies. Our need for sex can be rendered vestigial through sensual and supersensual fulfilment. Okay, let's start off with some breathing exercises to get you relaxed. I want you to take a deep breath, hold it for six seconds, then release it.'

We used to do shit like this at school before big games. I do a good few of them and I think he's even surprised at how quickly I pick it up, even though it *is* only, like, breathing.

'Tantric yoga is a system of rituals, exercises and philosophical teachings that have evolved over the course of our two-and-a-half-thousand-year search for a more profound feeling and awareness. Ross, you are going to become an expert in the arts of feeling and concentration.'

'Coola boola.'

'Yogi can focus their minds on a particular feeling or problem for hours on end, picking away its layers until they achieve a true understanding of it. What we're going to do, while you're coming here, is use exercises based on yoga, kundalini and chakra meditation to help you understand the nature of your genital urges. And to recognize how, like all addictions, they're blocking your way to achieving true spiritual fulfilment.'

I'm there, 'Er, I *think* there's been an actual mix-up. It's not *all* women I want to stop wanting – just my sister?'

'Ross,' he goes, 'this is true enlightenment. It's not *à la carte*. Now, close your eyes,' which I do. 'And trust me . . .'

This isn't me blowing my own trumpet here, but *I* turn out to be the star of the pilot of *Ross, His Mother, His Wife and Her Lover*. MTV put on, like, a private screening for us in the little movie theatre in the gaff – this is, like, the morning of the day it went out on TV? – and all I can think is, 'Okay, they've already *had* a little taster – but wait'll the American public get a proper look at me, as in the *real* me?'

I'll give you a quick run-through of what's in store for them. It kicks off with Sorcha and Erika sitting having lunch. The caption says it's Cobras & Matadors on Hollywood Boulevard and obviously they are going for the whole Lauren and Heidi vibe, which I suppose *is* a proven winner. Plates of tapas on the table in front of them, basically untouched, and Sorcha banging on about Courtney Cox and how she believes you shouldn't, like, overload your hair with product, that some-times a blast of cold water in the shower will make it shine better than anything.

Then they get down to the nitty-gritty – in other words, me. Sorcha asks Erika if she's, like, nervous about seeing me again and Erika says she is, but she's also, like, excited? Sorcha tells her that I haven't actually changed, then she fills her in on my antics at the fundraiser – I suppose giving the viewer a little flavour of what they're in for. Sorcha mentions that Emmy has – oh my God – *the* worst bingo wings ever, despite doing, like, two hours of power pilates a day, then she smiles and tells Erika that she's *so* excited that they're, like, related now, at least until the divorce comes through. Then they go their separate ways – or pretend to – with Sorcha going, 'I love you' and Erika going, 'I love you' back.

The next scene – hilarious – is the old dear standing on Venice Beach, roysh, watching them put up this humungous poster for Midas – her in her focking raw, painted gold. And again she's doing the whole stor thing, asking various flun-kies if they think the picture does justice to her clavicles.

You can imagine me, roysh, sitting there, watching this. I shout, 'That poster'll keep people out of the water better than any shork!' and I end up getting shushed by Erika beside me and Trevion in front, even though you can see that pretty much everyone's gagging to laugh.

Then it's, like, showtime – me in Fred Segal, trying on

T-shirts – but not in, like, the changing room. I'm doing it in the middle of the actual store and you can see the two shop-girls, who I've got minding Honor for me, checking me out in a serious way. This is obviously *before* the operation?

As an introduction to me and my whole *thing*, it really works, roysh, because the viewers already know the danger signs of getting mixed up with me from Sorcha's conversation with Erika, but now with the way these two are checking me out, the public is getting to see exactly *why* so many birds are prepared to ignore those warnings.

The next scene is Cillian in the gorden, sitting in the swingchair with Honor, telling her that the economies of the developed world have downgraded manufacturing as a means of wealth creation and become almost wholly reliant on a financial sector that sees speculation and risk-taking as its *raison d'être*. He says that the great political project of the early years of the twenty-first century was selling people a dream of an expanding home- and share-owning middle class, where people could exist off the income from multiple rental properties, giving them time and money to consume more. Then he says that people bought a lifestyle dream that they believed was prosperity and that millions of people are going to pay for it with their jobs, their homes and their pensions.

I stand up and throw my half-full Coca-Cola cup at him and it hits him – *thwock!* – on the back of the head. 'Don't you be filling my daughter's head with that shite,' I go, but Sorcha turns around in her seat and tells me to leave him alone, then I see her put her orm around him and say something – presumably soothing? – in his ear.

The next scene is, like, Sorcha and Erika in the kitchen, shooting the shit about some floor-length Versace that Han Ye-Seul wore to some charity benefit or other in Pepperdine

University. Then Sorcha mentions that I'm getting, like, a nose job – not a word about it being an old rugby injury. In fact, Erika even says that she's glad that she got her mother's nose and not her old man's, like I did.

Everyone in the cinema cracks up laughing – it's like, yeah, *whatever*.

Then it's back to me again. You see me in, like, the hospital waiting room, checking out the different noses to see which one suits me best. Harvey has been, like, spliced out of the scene, which *was* his choice, I suppose.

It comes as news to me that I actually died twice during the surgery – as in, my hort literally stopped? – and that two scrub nurses had to twice go up to the roof of the hospital, first to talk San Sancilio out of focking himself off, then second to talk him into putting some kind of feature over the gaping hole he'd left in my face.

It's all very *Grey's Anatomy*.

I'm just about to tap Trevion on the shoulder, roysh, to ask him if that actually happened or if it was all set up for the cameras, when it suddenly flicks to the next scene and it's, like, him and the old dear, sitting in an office in Columbia Records, negotiating her so-called record deal. And *she's* full of it, of course, demanding this, that and the other – the water *has* to be San Pellegrino and it has to be, like, a certain temperature.

But to be honest, roysh, it's more the caption that grabs my attention because it's like, 'Trevion Warwick, agent and boyfriend', and I'm thinking, I don't believe it – she's leading him on, the poor focker.

I'm sure she's only dying for me to say something, though, which is why I don't.

The next scene is, like, me and Erika, face to face in the kitchen that day, the deep meaningfuls, blahdy blah, then the final credits roll and it's, like, Greg Laswell singing an acoustic version of Madonna's 'Beautiful Stranger' while the two of us just, like, stare into each other's eyes and – I'm happy to say – you can't see that I've got a horn on me.

At the end, roysh, they show a preview of, like, next week's show, which is basically me giving my old dear dog's abuse while she's trying to sing. I actually forgot that I called her a truffle-hunter – it was just one of those moments of, like, pure inspiration, some would say genius.

We all give ourselves a major round of applause, then we head down to the kitchen, where Sorcha's prepared some canapés – chicken and chickpea satay skewers, prawns wrapped in courgette strips, then duck and spiced nectarine miniature bruschettas, which are all my old dear's recipes, by the way. She's *such* a lick-orse.

So we're all standing around – the cast and crew. I notice Sorcha piling food onto a plate for Cillian, who wants to eat his in the study – sitting with his money.

I'm holding Honor in one orm and I'm milling into the chicken with the other and I'm going, 'Honor, can you say, "Daddy"?'

But she's just going, '*¿Me trae helado, por favor?*'

Then, for some reason, she wants to go to her grandmother, so I hand her to the old dear, then take my nosebag outside and sit eating it in the sun. A couple of minutes later, Trevion comes out and sits down on the step beside me. He says that MTV focking love the scene in the recording studio – one of the senior executives even said I was a bigger orsehole than Spencer and Justin Bobby combined – and they want more of the same. He says Joni Mitchell's playing at the Hollywood Bowl next week and they've managed to secure the old dear a guest slot singing a duet with her. Johnny Sarno wants me there, hurling abuse at her from the audience.

I'm there, 'As long as you think you can handle it this time.'

I look at him, checking out his face. The focker looks like he's been bobbing for apples in a deep fat fryer. 'I got to admit,' he goes, 'when I hear you talking to her the way you do, all I want to do is rip your fucking head off . . .'

I nod like I understand. 'I saw the caption,' I go. 'You're together now? Congratulations. Although from Sahara to her – that's some comedown.'

He just stares off into the night. 'I seen bad things in my life. Man's inhumanity to man. I been tortured in a thousand different ways. When I hear about waterboarding, I laugh – waterboarding would have been a fucking holiday for me. It hardens your heart, I can tell you, to the point where you think you can never truly feel again . . .'

'Let me guess,' I go. 'Then you met my old dear and all that changed?'

He goes, 'You betcha, Swayze.'

Being honest, I've never heard of Joni Mitchell, although the Hollywood Bowl *is* rammers in fairness, we're talking fifteen thousand people paying up to two hundred snots apiece to hear her sing a collection of her favourite songs, along with – get this – her *friends*.

I only laugh, roysh, because you already know who one of her mates suddenly is.

It's an unbelievable evening – must be still, I don't know, eighty, ninety degrees out, even though it's after nine o'clock – and the bag of rotten fruit that I've got between my knees is actually starting to hum, and we're talking seriously hum here.

Beside me, Johnny tells me to try to recapture, if I can, the same intensity of feeling as that day in the recording studio. I tell him it won't be a problem.

Out she eventually comes – not the old dear, I'm talking Joni Mitchell – and the crowd goes ballistic, even though, if I'm being honest, it wouldn't be *my* kind of music? Her voice is a bit, I don't know, miserable, like one of those whalesong CDs that Sorcha used to listen to when she was up the spout.

Anyway, she tells the audience how wonderful it is to be here, blahdy blah, and how she's going to be singing – like I told you – some of the songs that have inspired her, from way back to the time she was busking on the streets of Toronto exactly forty years ago. Yeah, whatever.

That even gets a round of applause. See, it's that kind of crowd – easy to please, which should suit the old dear.

She says she's going to be joined in this celebration by some of her dearest, dearest friends and I end up turning to the couple beside me – we're sitting in sort of, like, pens? – and going, 'You *know* who one of those friends is, don't you?' but they just blank me.

I've a bit of a wait ahead of me, as it happens.

First up is, like, Carol King and the two of them end up singing 'I Feel the Earth Move' and 'Sweet Seasons' together, followed by – apparently – 'Smackwater Jack' and you can see everyone, like, really getting into it? Then it's, like, her and Carly Simon giving it 'Will You Still Love Me Tomorrow?' and 'You're So Vain', which makes me laugh, roysh, because that was Sorcha's breaking-up song for me when I finished with her once – I have to admit – two days before her Leaving.

Then it's, like, Faith Hill, who I *have* heard of, and they end up singing 'Where You Lead', then some other song I've never heard of.

Then, finally, Joni goes, 'My next guest is someone who, in the very short time that I've known her, has inspired me greatly and reminded me that art, ultimately, is about confession. She is a wonderful writer. She is an extraordinary singer. But most of all . . . she's a woman.'

That actually gets a massive round of applause by itself.

'Ladies and gentlemen,' she goes, 'Fionnuala! O'Carroll! Kelly!'

The audience, I'm ashamed to say, goes absolutely ballistic. The next thing, *she* appears, the focking plumpa lumpa. They've got this, like, trapdoor at the back of the stage and the guests come up through it – presumably there's, like, a lift underneath it?

She walks to the front, waving, and airkisses Joni twice on each cheek. My phone beeps – a text from Sorcha, who's sitting with Erika in the front row. It's like, 'Omg she luks AMAZING – thats d ruffled moschino i told her to get insted of d catherine malandrino 1! U must b SO proud ☺.'

I send her one back, just going, 'Proud? She looks like she should be sweeping the stage.'

But then the singing storts. '(You Make Me Feel Like) A Natural Woman'. What else? She focking slaughters it. And that's me being, I don't know, objective. I mean, Joni holds *her* end up, but the old dear sounds like a brick in a focking tumble dryer.

'Okay,' Johnny goes beside me, 'we're rolling here – whenever *you're* ready.'

I stick my hand in the bag and whip out what I'm pretty sure is a mango. Gerry Thornley, who's one of the few people in the world who's ever seen me take a lineout throw, actually wrote in the *Irish Times* once that I could even do a job for Leinster as a hooker, if it came to it. And it's Gerry – obviously a legend to me – that I actually think about when I shout, 'Get off the focking stage!' and launch that mango in her direction. It goes *ppphhhttt*, flying through the air and lands, splat, right at her feet, exploding everywhere and splashing her, I don't know, Sergio Rossis.

Suddenly, roysh, there's, like, literally hundreds of people turning around in their seats, squinting into the sun, trying to see where it came from, and the one or two who *know* where it came from tell me I'm an asshole.

Of course, I'm thinking, fock it, I lived with that – and worse – for most of my rugby career and I never let it put me off my game. So I reach into the bag again and pull out, this time, a honeydew melon, big and heavy and dripping like a focked fridge.

'You suck!' I shout this time.

And, again, I launch it, straight and on target, and the old dear has to actually step out of the way to avoid having her focking head taken off by it.

Again, it just explodes all over the stage and I turn around and look at Johnny, who gives me the thumbs-up, as if to say, yeah, he got it on film.

The old dear finishes up and gets – unbelievably – a standing ovation, while I continue giving her dog's. And it's at that exact point that I sense the mood of the crowd stort to turn. There's a lot of people suddenly turning around in their seats, telling me exactly what I am, then more and more stort to suddenly recognize who I am.

It's all, 'Hey, that's her son.'

And then, 'It's that jerk off the TV with the bandage on his nose!'

And even, 'Fucking a-hole gave coffee to a baby.'

I've always been pretty good, roysh, at gauging the public mood, which is how I'm already up out of my seat when I notice this humungous focker, three or four pens in front of me, with a shaved head, pretty much bursting out of just a leather waistcoat, turn to his wife and go, 'I'm going to go beat the shit out of this guy,' except he says it, like, casually, like you'd say, I'm just going to go get a hot dog.

Then he storts making his way out of the row and up the steps towards me. Again, it's my turn of speed that would have impressed most neutrals there. I leave him standing and eating my dust. But there's a lot of people who get suddenly brave when they see me running for my life. They're, like, kicking me in the orse as I leg it past and throwing shit from their picnic baskets at me. A piece of Stromboli hits me smack in the face and an entire rotisserie chicken misses my head by, like, inches.

'Fucking a-hole!' they're all shouting. And then, 'Show your mother some goddamn respect!'

There's actually a herd of people chasing me, but thankfully, roysh, I just so happen to have what they don't have – in other words, a backstage pass. I head for the VIP area and stort flashing my laminate at the bouncers – four of them, standing shoulder to shoulder – from, like, forty yords away. They sort of, like, part at the last minute to let me by, then – suddenly safe – I turn around and watch them hold back the angry mob, who are shouting all sorts of abuse in my general direction, like I'm the biggest orsehole on TV and how if it was, like, *Big Brother*, or even *Dancing with the Stars*, I'd have been voted off the show after week one.

I'm standing there, picking bits of avocado and meatloaf out of my hair, suddenly seeing the funny side of it now. I just laugh, give them the famous finger, then I turn around and go look for *her*, just to rub it in, I suppose.

It turns out she's in, like, her dressing room? Her and Trevion are having a moment. I can hear him telling her she was sensational. And – get this – they're, like, kissing, as in kissing on the mouth?

'Did I keep my composure,' she's going, 'when the first piece of fruit struck?'

'Hey,' *he* goes, 'you didn't miss a note. Did you hear that crowd? They loved you.'

'He's lying,' I go, sticking my head around the door.

She's in his orms. It's like, puke!

He looks at me like he *actually* wants to kill me.

'Remember, Trevion, it was acting,' I go, with a big smirk on my face. I still owe him big-time for letting that lunatic loose on my body. 'It was all just for the cameras,' and of course he can do nothing.

She doesn't even look at me.

'Come on,' he goes to her, like he thinks it'll bother me, 'LeAnn Rimes can't wait to meet you.'

I end up hanging around backstage, roysh, drinking a beer, not knowing at that point that the evening is about to get even focking better. I find myself standing, roysh, directly under the stage and I'm watching the live feed from what's happening above me on this little monitor. There's, like, a kid singing with Joni now and they're doing, like, a medley of songs from all children's movies?

It's, like, 'A Whole New World'. 'Can You Feel The Love Tonight?' All that muck.

All of a sudden, roysh, I realize there's something about this kid that's, I don't know, familiar? Then suddenly it hits me.

It's Danny Lintz.

I barely recognize him without the Coca-Cola-bottle lenses. He's got, like, a little tux on as well and his hair has been Brylcreemed to one side. But it's him. I'd recognize that face anywhere. I think to myself, okay, let's see how big you are without the rest of the Barney kids to back you up.

I look over both shoulders. There's no one else around,

although I still haven't made my mind up yet what I'm actually going to do.

The last song they do together is 'A Dream is a Wish Your Heart Makes' and it finishes with what I'm pretty sure is called a crescendo, then yet another standing ovation and the crowd going basically ballistic.

I'm watching on the monitor as Joni gives him a hug, then goes, 'Ladies and gentlemen – Danny Lintz,' and he takes the applause of the crowd – the little prick – with his orms outstretched, walking backwards.

Backwards . . .

Backwards towards the trapdoor . . .

Any of the greats who've played the game will tell you that in the split-second before you get an intercept, you know firstly exactly what's going to happen and secondly exactly what you're going to do.

That's what this is like.

My eyes immediately turn to the right and I cop this massive hydraulic machine thing, directly under the trapdoor, which I know straight away is the lift that takes people up and down through the stage.

Without taking my eyes off the screen, I kick away the two blocks that are holding the wheels in place.

I know that timing is everything here.

So I'm looking at him, holding out his orms, nodding and smiling and mouthing the words, 'Thank you!' the little focker that he is.

He's walking backwards, backwards, backwards . . . Until his foot reaches back to step onto the platform behind him.

That's when I suddenly throw my shoulder against the machine and roll it out of the way.

The next thing I hear is, 'Aaarrrggghhh!' as Danny Lintz

comes hurtling through the focking ceiling and hits the floor beside me with a pretty much splat.

All of a sudden, people come running, people with clip-boards, people with headphones, people with walkie-talkies, going, 'There's been an accident! There's been an accident!'

I lean over him, roysh, pretending to be checking on him. He looks seriously dazed, but he looks at my face and, even allowing for the bandages, I see, like, a flicker of recognition in his eyes.

'No one,' I go, 'and I mean *no one* – focks with Ross O'Carroll-Kelly.'

It's some question.

'When you meet a girl for the first time, what goes through your mind?'

I'm about to say that it depends what she looks like. But that'd be a lie. 'I usually think, I wonder what she'd look like naked,' I go. 'And that's me being honest. Either that or, how do I *get* her naked? I'd be considered a major player back home.'

I have to say, roysh, it should feel weird talking about this shit in, like, a yoga pose, but it actually doesn't?

'So sex *is* about ego for you,' Hugo goes. 'It's about domination.'

'Can be,' I go. 'I mean, I wouldn't be, like, *anti* it?'

'And this girl you talked about the last day . . .'

'Erika, yeah.'

'What is it about her that you find so attractive?'

'*Found* so attractive,' I go. 'I'd prefer to talk about it as in, like, past history? Because I saw her yesterday and, well, it might have been that last session we did here, but I honestly had very little interest in her – as in, I think I'd have actually said no, even if I was offered it on a plate.'

He doesn't say anything, but I can tell he's thinking that this is, like, major progress.

'But to answer your question,' I go, 'the big thing with Erika – aport from looks, amazing body, the whole bit – was that she always had zero interest in me. She never fell for my bullshit – one of the very few, believe me.'

He's there, 'So, again, I would suggest to you that your interest in this girl was in establishing physical primacy over her. And what I want you to do now – similar to the last day – is to try to think about your sexuality as being something other than a need to subjugate others for the gratification of your ego. Can you do that?'

I only picked up, like, half of what he said, but I tell him I'll give it a shot.

'Okay,' he goes, 'again like the last day, I want you to think of your sexual desire as an energy. And I'd like you to realize how much of your energy is taken up by what is simply a desire to vanquish, to satisfy your basest need. Okay, I want you to think about someone else – anyone else – who you find desirable.'

'Melissa Joan Hart,' I go. 'I was actually already thinking about Melissa Joan Hart.'

He laughs. He's there, 'Okay, this desire, this hankering, this longing you have for Melissa Joan Hart, you feel this energy in your . . .'

I'm there, 'Em, I suppose in my . . .'

He actually says genitals at exactly the same time as I'm saying balls.

'Okay, I want you to think about that energy as something physical. A giant ball of something. Can you do that?'

I'm there, 'Yeah, big-time.'

'Okay, take some time to do it. Think about every aspect of that ball. What does it look like? What colour is it? How much does it weigh?'

'To be honest,' I go, 'I'm actually imagining a chicken stock cube – except, like, a massive one?'

'That's perfect. But using the techniques we learned the last day, examine it, pick it apart, understand it . . .'

Which is what I do. It's, like, a good fifteen minutes before he says another word. I even wonder has he, like, nodded off.

'Now,' he eventually goes, 'I want you to imagine this chicken stock cube beginning to dissolve . . . Feel it fizz . . . Now imagine it slowly dissipating . . . Slowly . . . Slowly . . . Watch it just . . . melt away . . .'

He gives me a good ten minutes to do that.

'Now, imagine those pieces – those pieces of energy, remember – dissolving into your bloodstream. And this blood, filled with energy, is being carried . . . being carried . . . being carried . . . *away* from your genital area . . . and around your body . . . that thick, energy-rich blood . . . feeding oxygen into your muscles . . . giving you life . . . feel it in your muscles . . . Can you feel that tingle?'

I actually can. It's like an actual thing.

'And then it continues its flow into your brain. Feel that beautiful, energy-rich blood nourishing your mind . . . Now feel it working its way down your brain stem and into your backbone . . . *Feel* that blissful radiance in the seven spinal locations we covered in our first session . . .'

I feel un-focking-believable.

'Can you feel it, Ross?'

'Yeah,' I go.

'Can you feel it?'

'Big-time.'

'Don't be afraid. Imagine the distinctive tonality of each and every one of those seven chakra. Feel it, Ross. Feel the passion pulsing up and down your spine. Feel it – the primordial wonder and indescribable fulfilment . . . building up . . . into an orgasm . . . of consciousness . . .'

Trevion rings me and asks me if I'm watching CNN, which I tell him is possibly the most ridiculous question I've ever been asked.

'Well, put it on,' he goes, which is exactly what I do.

There's, like, a newsreader bird – a ringer for Mary Elizabeth Winstead – and behind her is a picture of, like, Cillian, looking like the tosser that he is.

'Now,' she goes, 'it started out as a reality TV show about a Coe Lyn Farrell wannabe, his famous mother and their dysfunctional extended family. But the star of MTV's *Ross, His Mother, His Wife and Her Lover* has turned out to be an Irish risk assessor who is predicting doom – for the world economy. This report by Sam Green . . .'

The next thing, roysh, *his* face fills the screen. It's, like, a clip from last night's show. Cillian's there, 'Irresponsible lending practices, reckless speculation and investment in toxic securities mean the world economy is in its most precarious position since 1929 . . .'

This Sam Green dude goes, 'This is 28-year-old Cillian Mongey, the modern-day Cassandra who has caused minor panic among depositors and investors by forecasting a return to the days of the Great Depression. On last night's show, he told a startled friend, "The Big One is coming."'

The next thing, roysh, they show some bank manager dude going, 'We've had customers arriving at this branch this morning with – lidderully – wheelbarrows, looking for their life savings, on account of what they heard on TV last night. I can assure those people that what he's saying is purely for entertainment purposes – and it's not supposed to be taken seriously.'

'Or isn't it?' Sam Green goes. 'Mongey certainly seems to believe what he's saying. On last night's episode of *Ross, His Mother, His Wife and Her Lover*, he claimed that the globalization of finance, the financialization of most developed economies, the abandonment of controls to curb speculation and the complacency brought about by years of low inflationary growth had helped place a ticking timebomb underneath the US and world markets . . .'

The next shot is of Cillian going, 'I'm not just talking about redundancies and foreclosures. I'm talking about bank runs. I'm talking about middle-class people queuing up for food parcels.'

Sam Green's there, 'MTV confirmed that their switchboard was jammed after last night's broadcast with viewers asking, "Is this guy for real?"'

They've got some other random suit going, 'The fact is, he's not for real. I think he's right in some of the things he said, for instance, criticizing the predatory lending practices of the subprime sector – coming into the living rooms of the unemployed or the part-time employed, by running ads on daytime television. That's why subprime *is* in trouble today. But to suggest that it would have a contagion effect on the world economy, or that it might challenge the collective might of financial giants like Goldman Sachs or Bear Stearns or Merrill Lynch or Citicorp, is – quite frankly – fantasy.'

Then it's like, 'Sam Green. CNN. Wall Street.'

When they go back to the newsreader, she's actually laughing. 'Cillian Mongey,' she goes. 'What a wacky guy!'

The trick with my old man is to put him on the back foot straight away. Don't let him get *too* palsy-walsy? So the second he answers, I go, 'You need to throw a muzzle and lead on that wife of yours – and you preferably need to do it now.'

But, of course, it's like I haven't even spoken.

'Hello, Kicker!' he goes, then I hear him turn to, presumably, Helen and go, 'It's young shape-a-m'lad! Ringing from across the proverbial pond! Line as clear as a bell!'

I'm there, 'What do you think this is – the 1920s?'

He's there, 'It's funny that you should ring. Helen and I have some wonderful news.'

I'm like, 'Spare me, will you?'

'If I was to say to you, "*Majorero, Chabichou du Poitou, Queso Ibores, Caprino Noccetto* and *Pouligny-Saint-Pierre*," what would you say?'

'I'd say you should lay off the focking brandy,' I go, although what I reckon they really are is, like, cheeses? They certainly *sound* like cheeses. And *caprino*, I would imagine, comes from *capra*, the Italian word for goat?

'If your answer was, "Aren't they all types of cheese, Old Scout? Specifically, goat's?" then, Ross, you now would be the proud recipient of a Corrrrrrect!'

'I *did* know, as it happens. Weird as that sounds.'

'Well, let me assure you, I'm here swotting up on my *Cabri Ariégeoises* and my Harbourne Blues. Helen and I are considering opening up a cheesemonger's, Ross.'

'What?'

'Yes! In the Merrion Shopping Centre! In point of fact, two doors down from Sorcha's mum's shop! What do you thnk of that?'

'A focking cheesemonger's?'

'One of our crazy teenage dreams – we talked about it when we were back in college, didn't we, Helen?'

'A cheesemonger's? What about your actual marriage?'

'Ross,' he goes, 'your mother and I are separated, very happily as it happens.'

'Oh,' I go, except sarcastically? 'So it doesn't bother you

that she has a new boyfriend? Oh, yeah, you heard me right. I saw them getting off with each other the other night.'

'Well, I'm very happy to hear it,' he goes and it's not even bullshit. 'I should think it's only right that a wonderful woman like your mother has someone special with whom to share her extraordinary success.'

'I can't believe how well you're taking it,' I go. 'You need to grow up. All of you. You're all carrying on like a bunch of kids.'

He's there, 'I won't deny it, Ross. These last few weeks, I've felt like one of these, inverted commas, teenagers, all over again. God, I feel so full of life.'

'You all need to get your act together,' I go. 'And fast. I mean, did you end up *getting* an iPod in the end?'

He's like, 'Oh, yes. Picked it up in one of these famous Sony Centres last weekend.'

I'm like, 'Thirty gigs or sixty?'

He's there, 'Sixty.'

'You make me want to puke,' I go. 'Well, actually, as it happens, *I've* got news for *you* as well. Brace yourself for a bit of a shock – Erika *is* over here. She's been here all along. She just doesn't want to talk to you, probably because you're behaving like a couple of focking saddos.'

Then, roysh – and I know how random this is going to sound? – it suddenly pops into my head that De Moivre's Theorem says that $(\cos x + i\sin x)n = \cos(nx) + i\sin(nx)$.

Hilarious.

The Entertainment Channel says that Disney have had to postpone filming on *Teenage Kicks* because thirteen-year-old star Danny Lintz fractured his ankle in a fall backstage at the Hollywood Bowl last weekend. The even funnier bit is that his representatives have denied that the accident was a result of him taking alcohol along with his depression medication. The delay is expected to cost the studio up to five million dollars.

Hugo has this saying, which I'm really storting to believe in now, that the universe has a way of evening things out. Another way to put that would be payback sucks, my friend!

I find Sorcha and Erika having coffee outside Lulu's, except I can't just rock on up to them because the cameras are there, filming them having one of their blah conversations – a Philip Lim high-waisted pencil skirt with a nice tight tank would be *so* the right thing to wear if you were going for a job interview in, like, fashion.

It's, like, ten minutes before Johnny tells me I can join them. I tip over and they're all, 'Hey, Ross,' but I just look at Erika and I'm like, 'By the way, the latest on my old man and your old dear? I thought you *might* like to know that they're opening a focking cheesemonger's now. In, like, the Merrion Shopping Centre?'

'I know,' Erika goes.

I pull up a pew beside them. I'm there, 'Who told you?'

She's wearing the Erdem pleated floral dress that I let Sorcha put on my credit cord because hers was, like, maxed out and she's still waiting for, like, her new one to be approved. She looks really well in it, but I stort thinking about that chicken stock cube and – it's actually like a miracle – suddenly I've no basic interest in her.

Sorcha goes, 'Her mum rang the house this morning, Ross,' then she sort of, like, stares me down. 'We're trying to work out how she knew she was here.'

Of course I stort taking a sudden interest in the menu. 'Okay,' I'm going, 'what's good in this place?'

She's there, 'Did you have anything to do with it, Ross?'

I give her the old wounded look. 'I can't believe you'd even ask me that.'

'*Duirt sé len a athair go raibh tu anseo,*' Sorcha suddenly goes. This is a thing they do whenever they want to say shit without me understanding. They either use big words or they talk to each other in Irish. *Duirt sé len a athair go raibh tu anseo* means, he told his old man that you were here.

'*Ceapann tu?*' Erika goes, in other words, do you think?

'*Oh! Mo! Dhia!*' Sorcha goes. '*Feach ar a aghaidh. Ta fhois agam nuair a bfhuil sé ag insint breaga. Bhi me posta leis ar feadh dha bhliann,*' in other words, I know when he's lying – I was married to the dude for, like, two years.

'Okay,' I hear myself go. '*Duirt mé leis. An bhfuil sibh sasta anois?*'

I swear to God, roysh, I'm as much in shock as they are. 'You don't know any Irish,' Sorcha goes.

I'm there, 'I know. At least I didn't *think* I did?'

'Ross, you got, like, an N.G. in your Leaving.'

'Er, you don't have to remind me, Sorcha. I got an N.G. in everything in my Leaving.'

'*An tuigeann tu anois?*'

'Do I understand what you're saying now? Yeah, *tigim.*'

'Oh! My! God!'

'What happened?' Erika goes.

I'm there, 'I don't actually *know?* There's a lot of weird shit happening with my mind. It's, like, yesterday, when I was talking to Dick Features, I suddenly knew this Italian word.'

'Did you even *do* Italian?' Sorcha goes.

'No. But I went to, like, three or four grinds in the Institute on Friday nights and that was only because I fancied a bird in the class.'

'Melanie Ryan?' Sorcha goes and I suddenly realize that I've opened up old wounds. 'As in, Loreto on the Green?'

'Er, *we* were on a break,' I go.

She's there, 'I know when you're talking about, Ross, and we were certainly *not* on a break?'

I'm suddenly rescued from this line of questioning by these two random birds, who tip over just to say that they – oh! my God! – loved the first episode of the show and that Sorcha and Erika have both got *such* an amazing fashion sense and blahdy blahdy blah blah. Sorcha especially looks delighted. I suppose it's what she's wanted her entire life – the fame thing? Then one of the birds turns to me and tells me I'm an asshole the way I speak to my mother and that I look like a freak with all that bandaging on my nose.

I give her the finger, then get up from the table and find a quiet corner of the street to make a phonecall.

He answers straight away. I'm there, 'Hugo, it's Ross.'

He's like, 'Hey, Ross,' and blahdy blahdy blah.

I'm there, 'Dude, I need to talk to you.'

'Sure,' he goes. 'How's celibate life treating you?'

I'm like, 'That's *exactly* what I want to talk to you about. It's like I suddenly *know* loads of shit?'

'You *know* loads of shit? What does that mean?'

He genuinely hasn't a bog.

'I'm talking different ports of the world. I'm talking Irish, as in the language – I'm pretty much fluent in that. All this other shit keeps popping into my head at, like, random times. For instance, right this second, when I close my eyes, I can see a diagram of the human ear with all the ports labelled. Hammer. Anvil. Stirrup. Tympanum. Cochlea. Eustachian tube. I mean, how wrong is that?'

He laughs.

'It's not funny,' I go. 'It's like I've gone to bed and woken up in a bad movie. One with Hilary Duff or a young Lindsay Lohan in it.'

He's there, 'This is what can often happen when we free up our consciousness, Ross. When we leave aside our most base instincts, things that have lodged in the knolls and dells of our memories blow free again. Often things we knew but didn't think we knew. It's exciting, right?'

I'm like, 'Exciting?'

'Sure,' he goes. 'Suddenly having all this knowledge?'

'To be fair,' I go. 'I can't say that I'm altogether comfortable with it?'

I ring Christian's phone, but it's, like, a bird who answers. She's like, 'Hello, Christian's phone.'

It's not Lauren either. It's a bird with, like, an American accent? And my first reaction is obviously, go on, you dirty dog.

Then I'm thinking, er, Christian? A cheater? I don't think so. Even though a lot of birds do go off Posh & Becks straight after having a kid.

'Who's this?' I go.

She's like, 'This is Martha – Christian's PA.'

I'm there, 'Well, Christian's PA, any chance I could speak to the man himself?'

I might be celibate, but I haven't lost my famous gift of the gab.

She goes, 'He can't really talk right now. Can I take *your* name?'

'It's Ross O'Carroll-Kelly – in other words, his best friend?'

'Well, he's got a meeting with Mr Lucas in, like, ten minutes. He's busy prepping.'

I laugh. 'Just say the name to him and I guarantee he'll want to talk to me.'

I hear her turn around and go, 'Ross O'Carroll-Kelly,'

except she says it like it's a question? Like she doesn't believe that he actually knows me?

'Oh,' Christian goes – I shit you not – as in, oh no! He's there, 'Can you tell him I'm busy.'

Of course there's no need to – I got the message loud and clear.

We're sitting outside Toast on West Third and I'm telling Harvey how well the whole tantric celibacy thing is going and how even the sight of Camila Alves in my bed with her legs in the air couldn't put storch in my collar.

And how I've suddenly ended up with all this useless shit in my head, like the five tropisms in plants, which are photo, geo, hydro, thigmo and chemo. Of course, I'm too busy banging on to notice that he hasn't even touched his Garden Scramblette.

'Dude, what's the Jack?' I go. 'You're, like, miles away.'

He sort of, like, fidgets with his Kanye West shutter shades, then just blurts it out. 'I slept with Mike,' he goes.

I can't actually help myself. I'm just like, 'Whoa! *Bad* move, my friend.'

He goes, 'It was, like, the night of his birthday?'

I'm there, 'No excuse,' and that's not me acting all high and mighty just because I happen to be off it at the moment.

'He came over and he was all, "I just want to spend this night with the one I love." And I fell for it. Like I always fall for it.'

'And let me guess what happened. He got what he wanted, then he went back to *her*. I bet he didn't even stay the night. Dude, what about Hugo?'

'Look,' he goes, 'you can't make me loathe myself any more than I already do,' and he's probably right. Even in the few months I've known him, I've never seen him so upset.

I'm there, 'Dude, can I say something to you?'

'Not if it's about how nobody's going to respect me until I learn to respect myself. I watch *Oprah*, too, you know.'

He hasn't touched his Berry Berry Frappe either.

'It doesn't have to be *Oprah*,' I go. 'It's actually true. And I say that as someone who's been treating girls like shit since I was, like, fifteen years of age. The ones with low self-esteem, I went through them like tapas. Twenty minutes later, I knew I'd *had* them – just don't ask me to remember what the fock they looked like.'

'So what are you saying?' he goes. He actually seems a bit pissed off with me.

'What I *think* I'm saying is that maybe it's time to tell your old pair that you're, you know . . . gay.'

He all of a sudden stands up. 'No,' he goes, 'I've got to tell Hugo what happened.'

I'm there, 'Er, I don't think that's the actual way to go. What he doesn't know can't hurt him. My policy has always been, even if they come up with evidence, deny, deny, deny . . .'

He slams, like, a twenty down on the table for the breakfast, then tells me he's not interested in my advice, which hurts. I have to say it hurts.

Then off he goes.

I'm actually reaching over for his Garden Scramblette when someone behind me calls me a stupid fock. I already *know* it's going to be one of those days when I can do nothing right? It turns out it's Trevion and he is *not* a contented temporary tent dweller.

He goes, 'I just had a reporter on the phone,' which I immediately know means trouble. 'You forgot to tell me about tantric celibacy, huh?'

I'm there, 'Tantric celibacy?' like it's the first time I've ever heard the words.

'That's right, Grasshopper. And you better tell me the fucking truth.'

I'm not going to be able to bluff my way out of this one. 'Okay,' I go, 'it's true – I *have* been doing tantric celibacy.'

He sits down opposite me and checks out Harvey's untouched breakfast. 'What is that – a vegetarian omelette? What kind of trouble are you in?'

'None.'

'I'm your agent,' he goes. 'It's my fucking business to know.'

I'm there, 'Look, the omelette's not even mine. And the tantric thing – it's because I wanted to do my sister. And that's all there is to it, I swear.'

He shakes his head at me. 'You can't keep secrets from me.'

I'm there, 'Dude, I didn't want half the world knowing I was a sexual pervert. Which they're probably going to now, if the papers are on the case.'

He's there, 'You're lucky you got me in your fucking corner. You forget it sometimes . . .'

'What did you tell them?'

'I told them you was a sex addict and you was in treatment.'

A sex addict? Actually, that's going to play unbelievably well back home.

'You got to have it, thirteen, fourteen, fifteen times a day, I told them. Became a problem. Lines of fucking women. It was like throwing live mice to a python.'

I tell him I don't know how to thank him, but he tells me not to go blowing him yet. 'Have you any idea how pissed MTV are at you?'

'MTV?' I go.

'That's right, Heffner. They're paying you for access to

every intimate detail of your life. And you keep this from them? That you're a fucking freak?'

'I'd hordly say freak.'

'You want to bone your sister, you're a freak in my book. Anyway, now they want to get you on camera – the tantric shit – doing whatever it is you do, you sick fuck.'

8. An inconvenient truth

'You're all *over* the papers here,' Oisinn goes and he means Dublin. '*Irish Family New Stars of US Reality TV Show*. I don't believe it.'

I'm there, 'You better believe it, Dude. Go on, give me a little taste of what's being said. It's probably all true.'

'They've been described as the family that even the Sopranos would regard as the neighbours from hell,' he goes. 'But the day-to-day happenings in the lives of well-known Dublin family the O'Carroll-Kellys are currently gripping the American public.

'This is the focking *Sunday Indo*, Ross!'

I'm there, 'Go on, give me more, though.'

'*Ross, His Mother, His Wife and Her Lover* is a brand new reality TV show that centres on the life of South Dublin-born chicklit phenomenon Fionnuala O'Carroll-Kelly as she sets out to conquer both the US book and music charts against the backdrop of her extended family's disintegration. Fionnuala, the estranged wife of disgraced businessman and politician Charles O'Carroll-Kelly, is currently recording an album of duets with The Late Jeff Buckley . . .'

I'm there, 'Blah blah focking blah – is there anything about me in there?'

'Hang on,' he goes. 'Her son, well-known Dublin socialite Ross, a former rugby hopeful who failed to make the expected breakthrough . . .'

'Unnecessary,' I go, 'but continue.'

'. . . is featured, heavily bandaged after recent rhinoplasty, attempting to derail his mother's career by subjecting her to various public humiliations, while also attempting to build bridges with his recently discovered sister, Erika Joseph, and his own estranged wife, the glamorous, Killiney-born boutique owner, Sorcha Lalor.'

'Nothing about me coaching the Andorra team that scored a try against Ireland?'

'You mean Ireland A?' he makes sure to go. 'Er, no. It *does* mention that you're having treatment for a sex addiction, though . . .'

'Well, that's something, I suppose.'

'The character proving the most popular with US audiences, however, is Cillian Mongey, Sorcha's current boyfriend, a risk assessor whose apocalyptic predictions about the future of the world economy have spawned the catchphrase, "The Big One is coming!"'

'That's what happens when you get involved with accountant types,' I go. 'It's, like, they *try* to be cool? But they can only pull it off for so long.'

'Even former US Federal Reserve Chairman Alan Greenspan made a reference to the show this week, saying, "The Big One certainly isn't coming," insisting that bubbles could not affect the overall health of the economy and that the subprime mortgage problem would be contained.

'Mongey's most recent outburst, when he told his boss that the coming economic storm would spell the end of Western capitalism as we know it, was third-most watched item on YouTube last week, with more than one million hits.'

'You're probably wondering about the whole sex addiction thing,' I go. 'The thing is, I'm doing, like, tantric celibacy?'

He's there, 'Tantric celibacy?' and you can tell he's immediately worried.

I'm like, 'Yeah. I haven't had my rock and roll in, like, four weeks now. I've barely even had, like, a sexual thought? And it doesn't even bother me.'

'Let me see can I get a handle on this. You're in LA. You're famous. You're surrounded by beautiful women. And you're celibate? What the fock, Dude?'

'It's actually great,' I go. 'I've honestly never had so much energy. There are one or two weird side-effects, though.'

'Side-effects? What are we talking?'

I'm there, 'A moraine is any glacially formed accumulation of unconsolidated glacial debris occurring in currently glaciated or formerly glaciated regions, for example areas acted upon by a past Ice Age.'

He's like, 'Shit! The bed!'

'It's focking crazy stuff, Oisinn. This is what I'm telling you – I'm suddenly remembering all sorts of shit that I apparently learned at school, obviously without realizing.'

He laughs.

'Cytoplasm,' I go, 'aqueous solution of salts with dissolved proteins and enzymes, provides a liquid medium for enzymes and a suspension for cell organelles . . .'

'That's pretty impressive. If it's true, of course.'

'You want more? When two expressions in x (or any other variable) are equal to one another for all values of x, we can equate the coefficients of the same powers of x in the two expressions . . .'

'But what does any of it even mean?'

'I still don't know. It's like I've been given these special, I don't know, call them super-powers if you want, except I haven't been told yet what they're for, what my mission is, blahdy blahdy blah.'

'I'd say if you sat the Leaving again tomorrow . . .' he goes.

I'm there, 'Exactly – it'd be a whole other story. And don't rule it out, either. Hey, by the way, *you're* coming over, aren't you? For Christian's opening night?'

'Yeah, I think so.'

'Vegas, baby! Hit those casinos in a major way, huh?'

'Er, yeah.'

'You, me, JP, Christian, even Fionn – the old crew back together again.'

He's quiet for second, then he goes, 'Ross, can I talk to you about something?'

I'm like, 'Dude, we won a Leinster Schools Senior Cup together – if you can't talk to me, who can you talk to?'

He's quiet again. 'Doesn't matter,' he eventually goes. 'I'll tell you another time.'

The first thing that hits me when I swing the beast into the driveway is the shock of seeing the place in, like, total dorkness? When I walk through the door, I have to actually feel for the switch, but when I flick it, nothing happens.

'Hello?' I go.

Nobody answers.

I feel my way along the wall to the main, I suppose, living room. I press down on the handle, but it's locked. Then, as my eyes stort to adjust, I suddenly notice it, strung across the door – a strip of scene-of-crime tape.

I wander around the hall. Pretty much every door downstairs has the exact same tape across it and they're all locked, too.

I can hear, like, raised voices coming from the kitchen, so that's where I head.

Sorcha is sitting at the island, next to Honor, who's cutting pictures out of her Victoria's Secret Pink Collegiate Collection catalogue. '*Hola!*' she goes with a big smile when she sees me.

I'm there, 'Hello! Honor, can you say, hello – or even hello, Daddy?'

Cillian's pacing the floor, reading what I guess are Sorcha's credit cord bills. The cameras are in there as well – Johnny and the whole MTV crew. 'What's the Jackanory?' I go.

They barely even look at me. The tension is unbelievable.

'Van Cleef & Arpels, Rodeo Drive,' Cillian's going. 'Two thousand dollars . . .'

Sorcha's there, 'That's the vintage necklace that I already *told* you about? You even agreed it'd go amazing with my Thierry Mugler white chiffon dress.'

'Matthew Campbell Laurenza . . .'

'And they're those bangles – we've already *had* this conversation?'

'Two thousand, one hundred dollars . . .'

'Yes! *And* I told you Rihanna wears them. And I'm pretty sure Anna Faris.'

I think Sorcha's storting to see what an actual loser he is? 'One hundred and twenty dollars in Williams-Sonoma?' he goes.

'That was for the ravioli crimpers. Oh, so suddenly you *don't* want me to start making my own pasta?'

He's a fool even arguing with her. This is the girl who represented Iraq at the Model UN and, as anyone who was there will tell you, made an amazing case for gassing the Kurds.

I suppose it's the sight of Honor sitting there in her My Heart Belongs To Daddy romper suit, but I decide to remind him exactly who is the real man of this house.

'I asked you a question,' I end up going. 'And I didn't get an answer. So I'm going to spell it out for you again – what is the story here?'

'Ross, it's none of your business,' he has the actual balls to go. 'Stay out of it.'

I'm there, 'Hey, that's my daughter over there. And that is my, technically, still wife. So I would say it's, er, *plenty* my business?'

'He's threatening to cut up my credit cords,' Sorcha goes.

I look at him. He has no idea how out of order he is. He's there, 'Sorcha, you have seven cards . . .'

I notice that he has them in his other hand.

'But I've reached the limit on most of them,' she goes, not unreasonably. 'So they're useless.'

He's like, 'But eventually you're going to have to pay these bills. What are you going to do, take out a second mortgage?'

'Don't give me that,' she goes. 'It's *called* a house equity withdrawal, Cillian – you're the one who's *supposed* to work in finance,' which puts him big-time in his place.

'And all the focking doors locked,' I go. 'What's that about?'

He's like, 'Have you any idea how much it costs to run a house of this size? In terms of electricity, lighting, air-conditioning . . .'

'What are you,' I go, 'Eddie Hobbs, all of a sudden?'

Sorcha's there, 'He wants us all to live in four rooms, Ross. He's even locked my walk-in wardrobe.'

I'm there, 'Four rooms?'

'Us in one,' he goes, meaning presumably him, Sorcha and Honor. 'Your mother and Trevion in one, then you and Erika in the other. The kitchen will be a common area.'

I'm there, 'Me and Erika in the same room? Er, we're focking *related* in case it's slipped your mind?'

Then I turn around to him and I'm like, 'Give me the keys,' trying to sound as patient as I possibly can with the focker.

He actually blanks me. He turns to Sorcha and goes, 'Love Quotes – three hundred dollars?'

Sorcha's there, 'Oh! My God! They're those *scarves*, Cillian.

Er, embroidered with inspirational quotes from people like Gandhi and Mitch Alborn?'

I'm thinking, scorves? Fock, I used one as a tea towel. I say nothing, though.

'Sorcha,' he goes, 'sooner or later, we're all going to have to start adjusting to a new economic reality. We're going to have to start asking ourselves, not, "Do I want this?" but, "Do I need it?"'

I actually laugh at that.

'I'm sorry,' he goes, 'but I'm going to have to do this,' and he goes to take the scissors out of Honor's hand, the plan being obviously to cut up the cords.

I end up just exploding.

I launch myself at him, roysh, and obviously having never played rugby – or *any* focking sport – he goes down pretty easily, knocking over a stool and sending a bottle of Fuze Slenderize in strawberry melon smashing to the floor.

Sorcha, of course, screams and then that sets Honor off crying.

If I'm being honest, I'd have to admit that this is about more than just Sorcha's credit cords or 'Do I need this?' This is, like, months, possibly even years, of tension basically built up.

'Stop it!' Sorcha's going. 'Stop it!'

I'm, like, lying on top of him, roysh, and he's putting up a bit of a fight in fairness to him, kicking his legs, then making a grab for my nose, which is dirty – anyone who sees it later on TV will have to admit that.

I've got, like, my fist cocked and with my other hand I'm trying to hold him still, roysh, just to get in, like, one serious punch. The camera moves in for a close-up.

I'm like, 'Dude you've had this coming – from way before you even *went* heliskiing . . .'

I'm just about to pull the trigger, roysh, when all of a sudden I feel the most almighty focking crack across the back of my head. I'm, I suppose you'd say, temporarily stunned and Cillian – oh, yeah, big strong man now – manages to roll me off him onto the floor.

I look up to see Sorcha standing over me with one of her Viktor & Rolf ballet flats in her hand. 'You know how I feel about violence,' she goes, tears streaming down her face. '*Non-violence is the law of our species, as violence is the law of the brute.*'

Yeah, that's the one I dried the breakfast dishes with.

She helps *Cillian* to his feet, if you can believe that. She asks him if he's okay and he says he thinks so.

I'm like, 'What the fock, Sorcha?'

She goes, 'Is that what you want your daughter growing up seeing, Ross? Her father brawling on the floor like a . . . I won't even say the word.'

The word she won't say is knacker.

'I can't believe you're taking *his* side,' I go. 'I was the one who was about to say that those scorves sounded kind of cool. But you know what? You can forget about that now.'

The camera comes in close for a better shot of my boat. 'Turn that focking thing off,' I go. 'This better not go out on TV.'

I ask him if he's even *been* to school this week.

'Ah, I've been showing me face,' he goes. 'We're doing summer tests at the moment.'

Shit, I forgot. I'm like, 'So what did you have today?' letting him know that I'm on his case, like any father would.

He's there, 'History. Ah, all about the Celts, so it was.'

'The Celts?' I go. 'You mean the race whose culture developed back in the Late Bronze Age, who went on to inhabit much of Europe and Asia Minor in pre-Roman times and who came to Ireland in approximately 700 BC?'

'Er, yeah,' he goes, literally unable to believe what he's just heard. 'And then a bit about Brian Boru.'

I'm there, 'Which Brian Boru would be that be? The fearsome warrior who became High King of Ireland in the tenth and eleventh centuries, who drove the Vikings out of Ireland but was killed by a retreating Norseman at the Battle of Clontorf?'

There's, like, silence on the other end. 'Are you reading that, Rosser?'

I laugh. 'Actually, no.'

'You fooken are,' he goes, 'you doorty-looken doort boord. You've Wikipedia there on yisser phone.'

I'm there, 'Ro, I'm honest to God just sitting outside a café called Toast, eating a short stack with bacon. It's all shit from school that's suddenly in my, I suppose, brain. Don't worry, though, I don't know what any of it means. Anyway, you heard about us all being on TV over here, did you?'

'Me ma said there was a bit in the paper . . .'

'Well, it's all true. We're pretty much stors. And you're going to be as well when you get over here,' and as I'm saying it, roysh, I'm thinking, wait'll they get a load of this kid over here. They're going to love him.

'Word of warning,' he goes. 'I'm going to be having one of me wurdled famous schemes going down.'

I'm there, 'That's great, Ro,' pretty much humouring him. 'What kind of scheme are we talking?'

He's there, 'Roulette, Rosser. I'm after been telling Buckets of Blood here about it.'

'Hey, say hello to Buckets for me, will you?'

'See, people think it's random, Rosser — what number's going to come up. But it's not. If you can measure the speed of the ball, then take into account the friction and drag of the wheel, it's possible to predict the precise number into which the ball is most likely to land.'

Of course, I'm left there going, 'Errr, cool. Anyway, tell your old dear to book the flight. I think the easiest route is, like, Dublin–JFK, then JFK–Vegas. She has my credit cord details.'

'Ah, I'd have luven to see LA,' he goes. 'I says to Bla the utter night, says I, "One day I'll bring you shopping on Rodeo Drive." Be like that *Pretty Woman*, Rosser.'

I'm there, 'Yeah, I can just picture you going, "We're going to be spending an obscene amount of money in here," then slapping your Credit Union book down on the counter.'

He cracks his hole laughing, in fairness to him.

I ask him if he's sure he's okay taking the flight by himself and he says he's moostard. Then I tell him good luck with the rest of the exams and we say our goodbyes, except he doesn't actually hang up, as in he *thinks* he has? But he obviously hasn't hit the button properly.

So I hear him tell Buckets my line about the Credit Union and he's laughing, roysh, as in laughing so much he's actually losing it. 'Can you believe that?' he's going. 'He's a funny fooker, isn't he?'

Sorcha has nothing to wear, although *her* idea of nothing to wear is different from, I'd imagine, most people's?

After long and careful negotiations that lasted well into the early hours of this morning, Cillian agreed to let her into her walk-in wardrobe for, like, twenty minutes to grab anything she really needed. She took Erika in with her and they went through that room like, I don't know, me through the Orts block in UCD.

So now, roysh, her new room looks like the Prada Epicentre

after a focking earthquake. But being a glass-half-empty kind of girl, all she can think about are the things she had to leave behind. Her L'Wren Scott cocktail dress. Her Juicy striped cardigan and her City of Others jeans. Her berry-coloured Gucci with statement collar. Her Vuitton monogrammed patchwork bag and her Vuitton Multipli-cité tote. Her brocade Valentino frock. Her stormy grey Alberta Ferretti that Claudia Schiffer was spotted wearing in Locanda Veneta. Her vintage Bottega Vaneta sunglasses with intrecciato detailing.

She says she begged – oh my God, *begged!* – Cillian to let her back in, if even just to get her Sharkah Chakra organic cotton trousers, but he was like, 'Sorcha, you've got to do something about your obsession with material things,' which she's obviously taken personally, because she storts reminding me of all the shit she's done for charity in her life?

I'm there, 'Where is he anyway?'

She goes, 'He's in our room, writing a letter to George W. Bush.'

You can imagine my reaction. I actually laugh. 'As in . . .'

'Yes,' she goes, 'the President?' like she's actually defending him.

Honor smiles at me from her high-chair. She's definitely her daddy's girl. I break her off a bit of my Butterfinger, but Sorcha notices and ends up just, like, snatching it out of her hand.

I'm there, 'Oh, so that's a drug now as well, is it?'

She's there, 'We don't give her chocolate. That's why we *have* the carob,' and I end up having to point out that the carob tastes like shit, which it does, and I shake my head, roysh, thinking that between her and Cillian, there's actually a pair of them in it.

I head for my room, which is no longer just my room, of course. Johnny and the cameraman follow me. MTV, I should say, love the new living arrangements. Fewer rooms means it's easier to keep an eye on us, seven-eleven.

I lie on my bed. Ten seconds later, Erika comes out of the Jack Bauer, dripping wet, with just, like, a towel around her.

'I still can't believe we're living like this,' she goes, dragging a comb through her wet hair.

I'm lying there, thinking, 'Chicken stock cube, chicken stock cube . . .' but at the same time, I also slip under the duvet, just in case.

She's there, 'What is she still doing with this guy?' which is nice for me to hear.

'Don't ask me,' I go. 'If you remember, I *never* understood what she saw in him.'

She whips open her underwear drawer, then lays out various bras and I suppose knickers on the bed, trying to decide which to wear.

'I'm a cathedral,' I'm thinking, which is another line Hugo taught me, 'housing a single spork of divinity.'

She eventually chooses a matching pair – nice ones as well.

'He's sick in the head,' I go. 'You know he's writing to George Bush now – as in George *W*. Bush?'

With the bath towel still around her, she steps into her knickers, one leg, then the other. Then she sits on the side of her bed and checks herself out in the full-length mirror, paying – I can't help but notice – close attention to her skin.

'We're going to have to keep a close eye on her,' Erika goes, then she smiles at me and it's an amazing moment, roysh, because it's the first time I've felt like we're a proper brother and sister.

She rubs the cream up and down her orms, then into her long, I suppose, slender neck.

I tell her that's what happens when you get involved with an actual psycho.

'Good afternoon, Hook, Lyon and Sinker – JP Conroy speaking . . .'

I laugh.

'Dude,' I go, 'I never thought I'd hear those words in that exact order again.'

He's like, 'Hey, Ross!' genuinely delighted to hear from me. 'I presumed you'd forgotten about us. I hear you're a big star now.'

I'm there, 'Don't you worry about me, JP. I'll never forget my roots,' meaning Foxrock obviously. Sallynoggin's long gone. 'So you're back selling gaffs for your old man – how's that working out?'

'Ah, it's not like the old days,' he goes, getting all nostalgic on me. '*Mountmellick – A Dublin Suburb with a Country Prefix . . .*'

I laugh. 'I'll never forget that court case,' I go. 'I still can't believe you convinced the jury. They were the glory days, though – anything went.'

'It's different now.'

'Different, as in?'

'Well, it's definitely slowed down. Ah, the rate they were throwing apartments up, it was always going to happen. Supply outstrippng demand . . .'

I'm there, 'Hey, by the way, listen to this – acetylcholines are chemical messengers that pass an impulse from the synaptic knob of one neuron to the dendrite of another across a synapse . . .'

'Wow!' he goes. 'What does it even mean?'

I'm there, 'Haven't a clue. I've just storted to remember loads of shit from school. At the moment, it's just a good porty piece. And speaking of porties, you're coming over, aren't you?'

'Yeah,' he goes. 'Two weeks. How's Christian?'

I'm there, 'You're asking the wrong *buachaill*. I can't even get him on the Wolfe.'

He goes, 'He must be up the walls.'

I'm like, 'Yeah, he must be – if he can't find time in his busy schedule to talk to his best friend.'

He seems to take my point. 'By the way,' he goes, sounding kind of, like, wary? 'Have you heard from Oisinn?'

I'm there, 'Er, yeah, I spoke to him the other day?'

'How did he sound to you?'

'Well, now that you mention it, like he had something on his mind.'

'No one's really seen him for a couple of months. Some-one said he's playing a lot of online poker. I met his old dear in Terroirs – she said he's practically nocturnal.'

I'm there, 'Fock! I wonder is Vegas a good idea for him?'

'You should do it in my black Miu Mius,' Sorcha goes. 'They're high heels, but – oh! my God! – they're *so* comfortable, they could actually *be* flats?'

She's talking about the California High-Heel-A-Thon, which is a, basically, race they have in Santa Monica every year for, like, charity – this year it's to provide a Sony Vaio for children in developing countries.

Well, *more* than one, you'd hope.

But they basically invite all celebrities to do it, roysh, and the biggest laugh is that they're obviously so hord up for people, they've had to ask the old dear.

Erika tells her she's certainly in good company this year. Sally Jesse Raphael and Kelly Ripa have both said yes. I have to say, I'm storting to think I much preferred Erika when she was an actual bitch?

'Okay,' Cillian goes, 'what do you think of this?'

This being his letter to that dude, what's-his-name. He's, like, pacing the kitchen, giving it, *'Dear Mr President,'* even though no one's *actually* listening?

'I am an Irish-born auditor working on secondment with Price-waterhouseCoopers in the area of international risk assessment. I hope you will permit me just a few minutes of your time to point out a few observations – or inconvenient truths – that will help you see why I believe that the world is on the verge of an economic catastrophe . . .'

Erika goes on flicking through her magazine. Sorcha says there's, like, an amazing Hale Bob dress in there – 'the next page, no the page after' – and that she loves busy prints because you can wear them with, like, minimal accessories?

'The growth of Western economies has, it should be obvious to everyone, become overly reliant on speculation and not reliant enough on production. Over the course of the past thirty years, we have seen the financialization of the world's major economies happening hand in hand with their de-industrialization. Since the fall of Commun-ism, the political consensus has been that the free movement of capital, free trade, deregulated labour markets and low taxation will deliver stability to the world economy. It is my contention that they have left it more vulnerable to collapse than at any time since the Great Depression . . .'

Erika says that Matthew McConaughey and Camila Alves have put a conservatory onto the back of their Malibu home using lime putty and *no* tropical hardwoods. Sorcha says that an amazing name for a clothing label would be Ethical Elegance.

'Unfettered capital markets were supposed to deliver lower interest rates and inflation, as well as increased employment and productivity. Instead, the slow erosion of any contol over the activities of the financial sector has allowed it to engage in increasingly risky activities. Alongside this, a largely media-inspired cultural shift in attitudes towards consum-

erism and credit has allowed this sector to sell hundreds of millions of people into a lifetime of indebtedness for things they don't need and can't afford . . .'

That's a dig at Sorcha – and she knows it. 'Cillian,' she goes, 'oh my God, can you not just read it to yourself?' then she actually looks at me for back-up. I honestly feel like giving her the old *Judge Judy* line – 'Hey, you picked him!'

'The strength of the US economy is built on the principle that rising house prices support increased borrowing, which supports economic growth, which pushes up house prices. The circulation is maintained as long as people keep borrowing money against the cost of ever-increasing assets. But it can't go on indefinitely. Eventually, even a chain letter runs out of subscribers. Soon, the US economy – and then the entire world economy – will arrive at that point . . .'

Sorcha asks the old dear where Trevion is today and the old dear says she doesn't know. 'He's being very secretive,' she goes.

Sorcha's there, 'I have to say, Fionnuala, you're *actually* glowing these days?' and the old dear just blushes. Then Sorcha's like, 'Oh my God, you *looove* him,' like a focking sixteen-year-old would say to her mate.

The old dear laughs. 'Yes,' she goes. 'I do, Sorcha. I really do. I'd never have imagined I could feel like this again.'

'But he's focking ancient,' I hear myself go. 'I'm still trying to work out what your actual angle is.'

'When it happens,' Cillian goes, *'there will be devastation and it will stretch far beyond Lower Manhattan. Markets will fail, but so, too, will banks. Financial titans will go to the wall. Tens of millions of people, not only here, but all over the world, will lose their jobs, their homes, their pensions . . .'*

Sorcha says she would – oh my God – *kill* for a set of those CC Skye bangles that LC wears – they're, like, crystal-studded?

And they make yours orms look – oh my God – *so* thin? Hilary Duff wears them as well.

'PST!' Erika suddenly goes, which is a thing they do. Means Poppy Seed Teeth. Sorcha sort of, like, licks her front teeth, then wipes them with a napkin and Erika goes, 'Gone.'

'The effects will be so cataclysmic that the financial elite who demanded that the markets be freed of the cold hand of the state will become socialists overnight. Leading bankers and CEOs, who took a market view of rewards and seven-figure bonuses, while scarcely concealing their disdain for Government, will come looking for public money to bail them out . . .'

Erika mentions that florals are, like, everywhere this year.

'Not back home,' the old dear goes. 'Charles was saying they're having a terrible summer – rain every day.'

'Who are you,' I automatically go, 'Evelyn Cusack? Why the fock were *you* talking to him anyway?'

'He phoned me,' she goes. 'A couple of times this week, if you must know.'

I'm there, 'Oh, *very* cosy. I'm sure Helen won't be happy to hear that. *Or* your new boyfriend. Even though I think it's only fair that I tell them.'

She just blanks me and reaches for, like, Erika's hand. 'I spoke to your mum as well,' she goes. 'She's very worried about you too, Darling.'

Erika says fock-all, but her eyes fill up.

'What are you, all focking mates?' I hear myself go. 'She's *his* other woman. The reason you're actually *getting* divorced. Can you not behave like normal people for once in your lives?'

Sorcha's giving me serious filthies across the table, although *she* just blanks me again.

'Yours sincerely, Cillian Mongey.'

Erika sort of, like, shakes her head. She's there, 'I can't

forgive her,' and in this really gentle voice, the one she'd use to talk to me when I was, like, a kid, the old dear goes, 'You just take some time. I told them both that *I'd* mind you – is that okay?'

Erika just, like, nods, like she knows if she opened her mouth, she couldn't trust herself *not* to burst into tears? Then the two of them just, I don't know, *spontaneously* hug each other, if there's such a thing. Sorcha looks at me with this really happy smile on her face.

'Oh my God, Fionnuala, you're, like, a mother to all of us over here!' which for some reason makes me want to puke.

She's all delighted with herself, of course. You can see her secretly thinking, that'll look great on the old Liza Minnelli.

'What does everyone think?' Cillian goes. 'Of the letter?' but no one even answers him.

I get up, roysh, and walk over to the knife block. I check that no one's looking, then I grab the big bread knife, with the really, like, jaggedy edge? I hold it sort of, like, upside-down, so my orm is hiding the blade. I check again that they're not looking. Then I slip out of the room.

Johnny and the cameraman follow me. See, they know who the real stor of the show is.

I find Sorcha's Miu Mius easily enough. I'm thinking, it's a good thing Cillian's gone mental, otherwise there'd be, like, three or four hundred pairs of shoes to look through. As it is, roysh, there's only, like, fifteen or sixteen. There's actually two pairs of Miu Mius? But I decided it has to be the black patent leather ones, roysh, because I know my wife and there's no focking way she'd let anyone run in her coral satin ones on a dusty running track.

I pick up the left one, sit down on the edge of the bed and, using the bread knife, stort sawing off the heel. As I'm doing it, roysh, I'm thinking there are birds in the world who would probably tear my orms off for what I'm doing here.

It only takes, like, ten seconds to saw it completely off. It's an unbelievable knife, like one of those ones you see advertised on TV that come with, like, a pen that writes in outer space.

'Fock,' I suddenly go. 'How am I going to stick this back on?'

I look up and Johnny's smiling, holding out a tube of what turns out to be superglue. I'm there, 'How the fock did you . . .'

'I'm in television,' he goes. 'I read your mind three plays back.'

I don't believe it. I mean, it was bound to happen, but at the same time I still *don't* believe it?

The Big One is coming T-shirts.

I get asked to, like, autograph one in the California Pizza Kitchen on La Cienega, where I'm having a spot of lunch with Harvey. This dude comes over and says, oh my God, he's *such* a huge fan of the show and then, roysh, while I'm signing his T-shirt, he's there, 'And well done for being such a bastard to your mother – she totally deserves it,' which is a nice thing for him to say.

'The one where you made her drink that terrapin,' he goes. 'Oh my God, that was, like, *so* awesome. And that name you called her in the last show . . .'

'A plump-monkey?'

'No.'

'An offal-guzzler?'

'No.'

'The Blubbernaut?'

'Yeah, the Blubbernaut. Oh my God, that was, like, *so* cool.

See, I hate my mother, too. I called her up after the show and I was like, "You know what I've always wanted to say to you? You're a fucking blubbernaut! And you ruined my life, you bitch!" Oh my God, you are *so* my hero.'

I'm there, 'Er, that's cool,' and then there's that awkward moment, roysh, where neither of us really has anything else to say to the other. 'So, em, okay,' he goes, 'it was lovely to meet you. And thanks for the autograph,' and I'm there, 'It's not a thing,' and he focks off.

I turn to Harvey. 'People – and by that I mean the general public – can be really nice, can't they?'

He's there, 'I don't know,' but what he really means is he doesn't actually *give* a fock?

I did warn him to keep his mouth shut, but of course he had to tell Hugo about Mike. Surprise, surprise, he ended up getting dumped like a focked cooker.

'I was the one who told you to keep your mouth shut,' I go. 'Remember? *Deny, deny, deny?*' but it doesn't make him feel any better.

He just stares into space and goes, 'Why do I always sabotage my own happiness?'

'Hey, that's you just feeling sorry for yourself,' I go, trying to buck him up a bit. 'Dude, you're twenty years old. I wish I could help you see how little anything really matters when you're young. It's all ahead of you, Harve. Sure a lot of hortache – but, on the plus side, a lot of horts to break . . .'

I reach over and grab one of his Cabo Crab Cakes. I just think, if he's not going to eat them . . .

'It's, like, whenever something good happens,' he goes, 'I have to go and totally fuck it up.'

I'm there, 'Dude, I did a bit of psychology, philosophy, whatever you want to call it, with this, I suppose, shrink in Andorra? From the little I know, I reckon you're – what did you say, sabotaging? – your happiness because deep down you're not fully happy.'

'Not this again.'

'Yes, this again. And you're not going to be happy until you tell your family.'

'I told you, Ross, I can't.'

'Dude, when you think about it, it's nothing to be ashamed of, especially in this day and age – the internet, blahdy blahdy blah.'

'I can't!' he pretty much shouts at me. One or two people look up from their lunches. 'Look, Ross, I'm not brave like you.'

I'm there, 'Brave? You're pulling my chain here, aren't you? You tell me you're not brave. Look at you. You come to LA and you live the way you want to live. You don't think that takes guts? See if that was me? If I was gay? I'd never come out. I wouldn't have the actual guts.'

He nods like he understands, but then he stands up. He's there, 'I've got to go.'

I stand up to go as well.

I hand the waiter fifty snots without even asking for the Jack and Jill – er, sorry, Cillian, does it *sound* like the economy's in trouble? – and I follow Harvey to the door.

Just as he's about to open it, roysh, he suddenly spins around with a look of, like, total horror on his face. 'Oh, no!' he goes.

I'm there, 'What?'

'There's, like, photographers outside?'

I'm like, 'So? It's me they probably want – I'm well used to it by now, believe me.'

'But *I* can't have my photograph taken,' he goes. 'Not like this,' and he looks down at, presumably, his Yohji premium jeans and Ralph Lauren down-stuffed leather vest.

'Tell you what,' I go, 'you stay here until they've gone. I'll bell you later,' and I give him the guns, then turn and go out to face the, I suppose, media scrum?

'When are we going to see your new nose?' a voice goes, the second I step outside. I stop and I'm there, 'All in good time,' even though I know it's going to be, like, next week. It's good to keep them guessing.

'Do you think Katie Holmes has lost too much weight and are you concerned about her appearance recently?'

'I honestly think it's just the way she's dressing?' I go, a master at handling these kinds of questions by now. 'My wife-slash-ex-wife says that bright-coloured blouses draw eyes to a slim upper half. Whereas if you look at Katie's legs, they're actually a bit chunky – she could possibly even do with losing a bit.'

They're, like, hanging on every word.

'Ross,' someone else – a man's voice, probably a reporter – goes, 'who's the mystery man you were having lunch with?'

I'm there, 'No mystery there – he's, like, a friend of mine, who'd prefer to remain unanimous.'

It's the next question that actually knocks me sideways. 'Ross, are you gay?' and he's out with it, just like that.

I'm there, 'Gay?'

'Yeah, would you like to comment on rumours that you're gay?'

I'm like, 'Rumours? What rumours?'

'Why are you being so defensive?'

I'm there, 'Er, because it's not *actually* true?' I go. 'I'm as straight as an arrow. I'm so into birds, I had to become celibate.'

'You *could* just be compensating,' the same voice goes.

I end up totally losing it then. I'm there, 'Get it into your focking heads, I'm into strictly women. Too *much* into them, my ex would tell you if you asked her . . .'

It's at that exact point, roysh, that I hear the door open and close behind me. The paparazzi are suddenly clicking like crazy and pointing their cameras at Harvey, who's coming out of the restaurant behind me, shielding his, I suppose you'd have to say, identity with, like, a pizza menu?

I'm the only one who can see his actual face and I can tell straight away that he's not happy.

It's only then that I realize the shit I've just been saying.

'Quite a vigorous denial,' he goes, practically spitting the words at me.

I'm there, 'But I'm *not* one – you know that.'

He's like, '*Dude, when you think about it, it's nothing to be ashamed of,*' basically throwing my words back at me. '*Especially in this day and age – the internet, blahdy blahdy blah,*' and the worst thing is, roysh, that he says it in, like, a real Irish accent, which I don't actually have?

Actually, no – that's not the worst thing. The worst thing is that I was there, telling him that life'll be so much easier when he tells his old pair – and this is how I react when someone thinks I might possibly be gay when I'm not *even*?

He walks off down La Cienega, still holding the menu tight to his face, photographers scurrying all around him. He stops once and turns back just to tell me that he never wants to see me again.

News certainly travels fast in this town – although I suppose that's the idea of, like, text alerts?

'Oh my God!' Sorcha suddenly goes. And straight away, from the way she says it, I know that it's about me.

I'm there, 'Go on, let's hear it.'

'Well, firstly, Paris Hilton is out of jail and was spotted in Don Antonio's looking classic in a monochrome bandeau,' she goes. 'But secondly . . . Ross O'Carroll-Kelly denies gay rumours after tiff on street with mystery friend. And I have to warn you, Ross, that friend is in, like, inverted commas?'

'Shit!'

'Was that Harvey?' Erika goes.

I'm there, 'Yeah. It's, like, they asked me *was* I? And I was like, "No." Then *he* ends up getting in a blob strop with me.'

Sorcha's like, 'Why did you deny you were gay?'

'Er, because I'm *not*?' I go.

She's like, 'Oh my God, what about his feelings, though?'

I'm there, 'Sorry, is it a crime to suddenly *not* be gay?'

'No,' Erika goes, 'but *how* did you deny it?'

Listening to the two of them is like having all the shit that goes with being married but in, like, surround-sound?

'Did you just say no, or did you freak, like it was some kind of disease you were being asked about?'

I end up just turning the other way. '*What* is the Jack with this race?' I go. 'It was supposed to stort, like, an hour ago?'

I can hear the two of them laughing at me behind my back. Sorcha even turns around to Honor and goes, 'Isn't your daddy a silly thing?'

'Welcome, ladies and gentlemen,' the announcer dude finally goes over the public address system, 'to the Santa Monica Track Club, here *in* Santa Monica, to what has happily become an annual event – the California High-Heel-A-Thon. Before we get proceedings under way with what promises to be a very exciting race, we might like to pause for a moment to remember what today is really about and that's providing laptop computers to people in the developing world who otherwise might never get to own one. Imagine, if you can, ladies and gentlemen, a world without e-mail or even MP3s . . .

'Okay, now to our runners. And I want to hear you really big it up for them because they are the real heroes of today.

317

In lane one, wearing a stunning pair of Kurt Geiger snake-skin platform courts, *from* the hit TV show *The Biggest Loser*, ladies and gentlemen, Alison Sweeney . . .'

There's, like, a big cheer and she sort of, like, waves to the crowd, like a good pro. Yes, is the answer, by the way – in a focking hortbeat.

'In lane two, an actress I'm sure you're all familiar with. Wearing a classic red slingback by Yves Saint Laurent, her sponsor for today, the star of both *Days of Our Lives* and *Melrose Place*, it's the beautiful Lisa Rinna . . .'

Another roar. There's no sign of Sally Jesse *or* the other one, by the way.

'In lane three, you all know her, I'm sure, as the man-eating Edie Britt from TV's *Desperate Housewives*,' and there's, like, one or two boos from the crowd, although it's all in good spirits, it has to be said. 'Wearing a stunning pair of Tony Burch wedge sandals, it's actress Nicolette Sheridan!'

Sorcha turns to Erika and goes, 'Tony Burch?' and she says it like she's suddenly worried.

'In lane four, standing in, at the eleventh hour – and we're very grateful – for Kelly Ripa, who unfortunately couldn't be here, wearing nude Louboutin peep-toes, it's socialite and . . . sorry, I thought there was something else down here, no, *just* socialite, Tinsley Mortimer.'

There's, like, another cheer.

'And in lane five, what can be said about this woman that hasn't already been said . . .'

I'm there, at the top of my voice, 'I'll write you a focking list!' and various people in the crowd turn around and shush me, then they look at my T-shirt and shake their heads, I suppose you'd have to say, disapprovingly?

Sorcha and Erika had them made and they're, like, plain white, roysh, with, 'Go, FO'CK!' on them.

Of course, after half an hour of nagging from the two of them, I put mine on, but then I went and wrote the word 'Yourself' underneath, which *is* funny, you'd have to admit.

'Acclaimed author, singer and the undoubted star of MTV's *Ross, His Mother, His Wife and Her Lover*, ladies and gentlemen, wearing classic Miu Miu patent heels, let's give a good old-fashioned – let me see can I say this right – *caid milla failty* to the beautiful Irish *coleen*, Fionnuala O'Carroll-Kelly!'

She ends up getting the biggest cheer of any of them. This country's taste is seriously up its hole.

Her face suddenly comes up on the huge screen they've got and I'm staring at her big, all of a sudden bee-stung lips and it's like, *who* gets botoxed before something like this? She looks like a focking monkey with hot tea in its mouth.

The race, I probably should say, is a straight hundred-metre dash, the length of the running track. But before it actually storts, roysh, there ends up being a major borney over whether Nicolette Sheridan's wedge sandals are a technical breach of the rules. Alison Sweeney and Lisa Rinna are of the strong opinion that, even though they're high, they're not actual heels? Tinsley Mortimer – while accepting that they meet the minimum four-inch height requirement – argues that she was told stilettos and that wedges give Nicolette an unfair advantage over the rest of the, I don't know, grid.

While this argument is raging, I should point out, the old dear is staying out of it, with Trevion in her ear, telling her to concentrate on her own race and no doubt bulling her up as well. She's doing all these supposed stretching exercises, though take it from someone who played sport at the highest level, she hasn't a bog what she's doing.

After, like, five full minutes of arguing, the judges decide that wedge sandals, while possibly against the spirit of the rules, do not represent a material breach and Nicolette Sheridan should be allowed to race.

Then, at last, it's, like, game time.

Trevion kisses the old dear on the lips and I watch her mouth the words I love you, then he says it back to her, like the saps that they are.

'Take your mark,' the announcer suddenly goes. He's like, 'Set . . .' and then, after a few seconds, there's a bang and they're away. *She's* first out of the blocks – *has* to be the centre of attention, of course – and she straight away puts a good five yords between her and Alison Sweeney in second, with Tinsley Mortimer a close third and the other two – it has to be said – nowhere

After all the hassle, Nicolette Sheridan looks immediately out of the race after a strap opens, one of her sandals goes flying and she ends up having to go back to, like, put it on again. 'Oh my God,' Sorcha says excitely. 'I was going to say that when the others were trying to get her to change into those Zanottis. Wedge sandals are really light, but – oh my God – they *always* open when you try to run in them.'

The old dear's, like, ten yords ahead and moving like a focking train. Sorcha's like, 'I can see now where you got it from, Ross,' and what she obviously means is my turn of pace, roysh, but there's no way I'm going to let her associate me with her.

'I'd beat her running constipated,' I make sure to go.

Erika's going, 'Come on, Fionnuala! Come on, Fionnuala!' like the kind of knicker-wetting girls she absolutely hated at school, then she's at Honor, telling her to cheer for her grandmother.

Honor just goes, '*Hen hao! Hen hao! Hen hao!*' leaving it open as to who she's actually up *for* here?

The old dear stretches her legs and suddenly she's, like, fifteen yords ahead. I'm standing there thinking, superglue or no superglue, there's no way it can hold that shoe together for much longer, espcially given *her* weight.

By the time she reaches the fifty-metre mork, she's already dropped Tinsley Mortimer and, in fairness to her, Alison Sweeney is the only one making an actual race out of it. But even she's way behind now.

'They're actually *my* Miu Mius,' Sorcha is telling people in the crowd, obviously excited. 'They *are* actual high-heels? But they *feel* like flats.'

Nicolette Sheridan loses a sandal again, the other one this time, and all the women in the crowd exchange what would have to be described as knowing looks.

The old dear is, like, twenty yords from the line and the crowd is going ballistic. 'Go on!' they're giving it. 'Go on!'

Ten yords from the line, I'm thinking, why didn't I use, like, ordinary glue?

Then it happens. And, I have to say, it takes even me by surprise.

What I see first is her orms sort of, like, flailing, if that's the word? They certainly go up in the air and her body sort of, like, lists to the left, to use the old *Titanic*, I suppose, terminology. She runs on another few steps, roysh, but then her ankle just buckles and she goes down like focking Tupac, literally inches from the line.

I can even see the heel on the track, snapped off, about five metres behind where she's suddenly lying, holding her left ankle and moaning, looking for sympathy basically.

Sorcha screams, though I imagine more for her shoes than for my old dear. Erika looks pretty upset as well.

What happens next, I like to think, is a lesson in what basically separates life's biggest winners from life's biggest losers.

Alison Sweeney's hands go up to her face and she runs immediately over to where the old dear's writhing around, to see if she's okay. Tinsley Mortimer and Lisa Rinna forget about the race as well and go to check on her, their faces full of concern.

Nicolette Sheridan, possibly thinking, 'Okay, what would Edie Britt do in this situation?' sees her chance and makes a bolt for the finish line, literally hurdling over the old dear, who fell into her lane, before dipping over the line.

The crowd, it has to be said, are not happy rabbits. In fact, I'm the only one who's actually cheering, obviously having been a bit of a villain myself back in my Senior Cup days. I'm wolf-whistling her and everything as she whips off her Tony Burch wedge sandals and holds them up over her head, basically taunting the crowd with them.

I'm actually gesturing for her to throw them to me when Sorcha goes, 'Ross!' and she says it in a way that means, go and see if your mother's okay?

I throw my eyes up to heaven, then tip over. She's fine, of course. She's got plenty of attention, as in Trevion's, like, cradling her head, telling her there's an ambulance on its way, even though she's already said it's only a sprain, and the others are all cooing over her as well.

Then Sorcha and Erika arrive and stort giving her all the sympathy she's looking for.

I end up getting into a bit of a row with this bird who expresses the opinion that the race should be declared void, since everybody knows that Fionnuala is the *real* winner, and I point out, reasonably, that that's not what the record books will show.

It's just as she's calling me a jerk that it happens.

Trevion goes, 'I was going to do this tonight, Fyon Hoola. I was going to take you out to dinner, somewhere real nice –

Ortolan – have the sommelier bring your favourite champagne . . . But you know what? Here's as good a place as any.'

He reaches into his inside pocket and whips out this little black box. Of course, he doesn't even need to open it for me to know what it is. He goes, 'I got a hunk of ice here, Fyon Hoola, says I want to spend the rest of my life with you.'

I'm there, 'Trevion, don't be a focking dope.'

It's a six-carat canary focking diamond.

Sorcha goes, 'Oh! My God!' In fact, everyone goes, 'Oh! My God!' now that I think about it.

He's like, 'What do you say? Will you marry me?'

She stares at *me*, roysh, while she thinks about it, then she turns to him and she goes, 'Yes,' like what she's *actually* being offered is a look at the focking dessert menu. 'I rather think I will.'

9. The dreaming days when the mess was made

I leave a message on Harvey's phone. I'm not sure if the word is, like, garbled? But I tell him that I'm about to get all the bandaging off and that it feels, I don't know, weird him not being here to see the new bod, but especially the new nose, seeing as he was the one who picked it.

I don't go as far as to say that I miss him, blahdy blahdy blah, although that *is* the general vibe?

The nurse sticks her head around the door and asks me if I'm ready yet. I carry on staring at my phone and she goes, 'You know, it's *been* two hours – I don't think she's coming.'

I'm like, '*He*,' and she's there, 'Oh,' and I'm about to tell her that I don't mean it in, you know, *that* way. But I don't.

I stand up. Deep down, I know she's right. I follow her into the little room.

'What I can do,' she goes, 'is just cut the Band-Aids holding the bandages to your face and body, then leave you on your own.'

I'm there, 'Why?'

'A lot of people who have procedures like to see the results in their own time,' and it's only then, roysh, that I realize how *actually* nervous I am?

I whip off my T-shirt anyway and she takes, like, a scissors and cuts the plasters on one side, then sort of, like, smiles at me, as if to say, this is the moment of truth. She looks a bit like America Ferrera looks in *real* life?

'Take your time,' she goes, then she disappears out of the room. I turn around, looking for a mirror. There's one across the room – above, like, a washbasin? – and I tip over to it and stare hord at my reflection. I'm thinking, I could literally look like anything under here.

I'm thinking, okay, here goes.

I grab the corner of the bandage stuck to my upper chest and I close my eyes and give it, like, a shorp tug. It takes off pretty much all of my chest hair.

'Aaaggghhh!' I end up going.

Without opening my eyes, I grab the corner of the bandage covering my pecs and rip it off in the same way, quick and shorp. Then I take, like, a couple of steps backwards and open my eyes.

My jaw pretty much hits the floor. I'm a focking Adonis – and that's not, like, an exaggeration?

Being honest, roysh, I've never looked in the mirror and *not* liked what I've seen? But this is, like, different. I can't actually take my eyes off myself.

Fair focks to San Sancilio – you could zest lemons on my abs and my pecs are like actual tits.

Then I'm looking at my face, thinking, okay, the old Shiva Rose is next. I'm suddenly kacking it again. My face is my fortune, after all, and I'm thinking, what if it's a mess, a real focking chewed toffee of an effort? Would I have to go looking for San Sancilio? Where even *is* Ecuador? And would the VHI even cover me there – if it's, like, Plan E Options?

Then it comes into my head that, as usual, I'm probably *over*-thinking here? I decide to just be brave. The quicker you do it, the better, a bit like ripping off a . . .

I close my eyes, grip the bandage by one corner and just pull. Then, very slowly, I open my eyes again. And I'm left suddenly staring at San's handiwork.

I'm thinking, Fock! *What* has he done to me?

It's magnificent – and that's not a word I'd ever use.

It's possibly the most perfect nose I've ever seen. It makes me look a good twenty per cent better-looking, if you can believe that's even possible. I'm trying to be objective here, but I'm quite honestly one of the best-looking men I've ever seen, although, really, I'd have to leave that for others to say.

Even twenty minutes later, roysh, when I'm heading back to the gaff, I end up nearly hitting a concrete bollard on the freeway because I keep looking at *it* instead of the actual road in front of me. I've got, like, the rearview turned towards me and I can't stop checking it out. Or touching it either.

Those who said that I couldn't get any better-looking have been proven well and truly wrong and naturally I'm thinking, maybe I'll give the old tantric a miss tonight, hit Les Deux instead, or maybe even Goa – have me some non-committal fun. It's literally ages since I've had any. I've got balls like focking planets here and, as I'm pulling into the driveway, it randomly pops into my head that gaseous exchange in plants occurs through pores in the leaves called stomata, the size of which are controlled by guard cells. They open wide in day-light when CO_2 is required for photosynthesis.

I go into the gaff and through the kitchen door I can hear Sorcha mention that Lindsay Lohan has admitted that she's not happy with her weight after her skimpy Shoshanna bikini revealed a much fuller figure at a party at the DKNY Beach House last week.

In my head I'm thinking, yeah? You think *that's* news? Wait'll you get a load of my boat.

I push the door and go in. Sorcha is sitting at the island, flicking through a magazine. The old dear is hobbling around on – get this – crutches, looking for sympathy, like it's some-thing *worse* than a sprain?

They both look up, roysh, at exactly the same time. I go, 'Ta-dahhh!' like a focking magician doing a trick.

I have to say, roysh, I'm not ready for the reaction that I get? Sorcha screams, roysh, and it's a scream that pretty much bursts my eardrums, as in, '*Aaaggghhhh!*'

She looks, it has to be said, terrified, though it's her next line that really throws me. She's there, 'Who *are* you? How did you get in here?'

I look at the old dear, then back at her. I'm there, 'What are you talking about – it's me!'

She goes, 'Just take whatever you want. Don't hurt us. I have a nearly-two-year-old baby.'

I'm there, 'Er, I *know* you've a nearly-two-year-old baby?' and I look at the old dear and I can see that she knows exactly who I am. She goes, 'Don't worry, Sorcha, it's only . . .' but then she stops and I watch her eyes look suddenly over my shoulder.

'It's . . .'

I'm there, 'Go on, tell her . . .'

But then this, like, evil look crosses her face. 'It's some kind of sex fiend,' she shouts. 'Do it, Erika!' and I immediately turn, roysh, to find myself staring not at Erika but down the nozzle of a spray can.

The next thing I hear is, like, a fizzing sound, then I feel the most unbelievable pain in my eyes and I'm straight away blind. I fall to the floor and then they suddenly set upon me – Erika with one of her XOXOs, Sorcha with a rolled-up copy of *Us Weekly*.

I'm lying there going, 'Not the face! Not the face!' and of course it's only when I say that that they realize it's actually me.

Sorcha says that if she was getting married again, it would definitely be, like, a green wedding? As in, all the invites would be on, like, recycled paper, the dress would be made of organic cotton, the food would be sourced locally and, instead of gifts, guests would be asked to donate money to, like, dolphin charities?

Of course, I'm barely even listening to her. I'm just, like, staring at the old dear, going, 'Unbelievable! *Un*-focking-believable!' and what I mean by that is that she spent the morning shopping for a wedding dress, even though she's already married?

And all for the cameras, if you ask me.

She blanks me and asks Erika what she's going to have and Erika says either the *salmone arrostito* or the *zuppa di pesce* and I'm left just shaking my head.

Sorcha says her favourite is definitely the Badgely Mischka – I should point out, we've moved back to dresses now – and the old dear asks whether it made her hips look big, fishing for a compliment.

I tell her that her hips would look big in a focking circus tent.

The next thing, roysh, my eyes suddenly sting. I ask how long does it take for mace to clear and Sorcha says she doesn't know, but she's sure it's karma for what I did to my mum.

'Okay, *ssshhh*!' Erika suddenly goes and she's shushing me because Trevion has suddenly arrived and he's not supposed to *know* anything about the dress before the big day?

We're in Il Cielo, in case you care, on Burton Way.

He leans down and the old dear kisses him.

He's there, 'So, did you get a dress?'

Sorcha's like, 'Yes, she did. And don't ask any questions about it, Trevion. It's bad luck to know.'

I'm not sure if that's true. I knew fock-all about her dress before *our* wedding and we were in trouble before the bisque arrived.

I'm there, 'Er, is nobody else going to point out the obvious here? You can't *get* married, not while you're still married to the old man. So what's the point in even buying a dress? It could be, like, years before you're divorced. And God knows what size you'll be by then.'

Sorcha's there, 'Ross!'

Trevion looks at me like he wants to pull my legs off and beat me to death with them, and he probably would if there weren't witnesses. *She* still orders the *scialatielli*, I notice.

Then she goes, 'There's nothing to say we can't have a non-legal ceremony to demonstrate our commitment to one another.'

And she's serious.

I'm there, 'When? Where? What are you talking about?'

'Vegas,' *he* goes.

'Vegas? As in *Las* Vegas?'

'That's right, Ginger. You got a problem with that?'

'When are we talking?'

'Next weekend.'

I end up just laughing. It's, like, I *have* to? 'Let me guess,' I go. 'It just so happens to be the exact same day as Christian's casino is opening?'

No one answers.

I laugh again. 'This is all Johnny Sarno's idea, isn't it? Ross is going to Vegas anyway. Why not set up, like, a sham wedding for his old dear while he's there – see how he reacts. Can I just say, I wonder what the old man's going to think of it?'

She goes, 'Well, why don't you ask him? He's coming.'

I'm there, 'You invited him?'

Erika looks suddenly worried.

The old dear goes, 'Don't worry, Darling, he's coming on his own.'

Erika just nods, but at the same time she looks kind of sad?

Sorcha's phone suddenly rings. It must be serious, roysh, because she gets up and walks away from the table to take it.

'So what do MTV want?' I go, looking at Trevion. 'Me standing at the back of the church objecting?'

The old dear's like, 'I don't remember telling you that you were invited, Ross.'

I'm there, 'Oh, I'll be there – one way or the other. It'll be worth it just to watch you hobbling up the aisle on your focked ankle.'

Sorcha arrives back. She's got a look of, like, total shock on her face. 'That was . . . Bob Soto,' she goes. She looks like she's not going to be able to get the words out. 'Cillian . . .'

I watch Erika make a grab for her hand.

'Cillian's . . . been sacked,' she finally goes, which comes as no great surprise, although the rest of them crack on that it *does*?

'Bob has been – oh my God – *so* understanding – giving him time off so Cillian could get his head straight. But he said last night's show was, like, the last straw? That stuff about the major banks and corporations looking for money from the public purse – he said it was Communist talk. He said he could tolerate most things in life – but not Communism . . .'

'Some of us fought wars against those bastids,' Trevion goes, suddenly angry. 'I died a hundred fucking times fighting them.'

The old dear puts, like, a consoling orm around him.

Sorcha goes, 'Bob said they've revoked his work visa,' and I'm like, 'So what are you going to do?' and she's there, 'I don't know,' except that, deep down, I think she actually *does*?

What ends up happening is this. We forget about the meal. The old dear and Trevion offer to collect Honor from the crèche and the three of us – we're talking me, Sorcha and Erika – drive back to the gaff.

There's, like, total silence in the cor? It's like we all know what's coming. I'm tempted to point out that I was the one who said it wouldn't work, but for once in my life I keep the old Von Trapp shut.

He's home as well. The Prius is in the driveway. I automatically laugh. I never thought about it before, roysh, but its emissions are no better than the latest generation of small diesel cor, which cost half the price and are probably cooler to be seen in.

In a weird way, I think, I'm actually looking forward to this?

Johnny Sarno's already there ahead of us. God, he's good.

'Are you sure you want us there with you?' Erika goes, and Sorcha's like, 'I really don't want to be left on my own with him,' and with the shit he's been coming out with lately, you couldn't really *blame* her?

He's in their bedroom, believe it or not, packing.

'Sorcha,' he goes, 'I've been trying to get you on the phone.'

She's there, 'I already know, Cillian. Bob Soto rang.'

He cops me and Erika standing either side of her, roysh, and it's like he immediately knows?

You can see him still not wanting to believe it, though.

'We've got to go home,' he goes. 'But it's not the end of the world. I can put the message out just as effectively from home. I was thinking of setting up my own blog . . .'

I actually laugh out loud. A blog? It's almost, like, *too* funny?

He looks at the camera nervously.

'You need to start packing,' he goes. 'There's a flight at eight o'clock tonight.'

Sorcha's there, 'Cillian, I'm not going.'

This he again tries to ignore. He walks over to her, holds her by both shoulders and stares deep into her eyes. 'I'm especially worried about Ireland,' he goes. 'It's too reliant on a lot of shaky things continuing to support each other . . .'

She's there, 'Cillian, please . . .' and suddenly the tears stort to flow from, like, her eyes?

He's there, 'Our own economic growth has been sustained by high levels of consumption, which is dependent on high levels of borrowing, which is dependent on continuously increasing property values. But as soon as something happens to that market . . .'

'You're not listening!' Sorcha goes.

He suddenly stops.

She's there, 'Cillian, I don't know what's gotten into you. Or what you're mixed up in. But I don't want any part of it . . .'

'Don't tell me you're staying?'

'I'm happy here.'

'What,' he goes, 'appearing on some brain-dead TV programme that celebrates superficiality?'

I say fock-all. My attitude is, he's doing a good enough job hanging himself.

'I'm over here,' she goes in that real matter-of-fact way, '*trying* to come up with new ideas for my shop.'

He's there, 'Does it bother you that in two or three years time, you might not even have a shop? That Grafton Street could end up being a commercial wasteland?'

She shuts her eyes really tightly and shakes her head. The tears keep coming, though. 'I can't believe you'd say that to me,' she goes.

I take a step forward then. 'You'd, er, want to be hitting the road pretty soon,' I go, 'if you're going to make that flight. You're not in the Lamborghini anymore, remember?'

He's bulling, of course.

I hold out my hand and go, 'Keys?' meaning the keys to all the other rooms. Because the second he's gone, we're back living in a mansion again.

He tells me they're downstairs on the kitchen table.

He looks at Sorcha, obviously trying to come in from a different angle. 'What about Honor?' he goes. 'Will you say goodbye to her for me?'

I'm there, 'We'll do better than that. We'll say *adios*.'

He just nods. He's an auditor – he knows the bottom line. 'Well, goodbye,' he goes.

And then, suddenly, he's gone.

Sorcha literally collapses into Erika's orms, crying like I haven't seen her cry since . . . well, since *I* broke her hort. I'm so glad that Erika's here for her.

I wander over to the wardrobe to see has he left anything behind. There, sitting at the bottom, on their own, are his John Lobb custom brogues.

I sit on the side of the bed and try them on. They're, like, a perfect fit.

I'm driving home from tantric celibacy when, totally out of the blue, the poem 'Exposure' by Wilfred Owen pops into my head. I'm just thinking how it's structured in eight stanzas of equal length, each of which concludes with a short, emphatic statement or question that emphasizes the utter futility of war. The tone of the poem is depressing and negative. The language of the poem is bleak and Owen uses linguistic devices such as sibilance to help create an atmosphere of tension.

I haven't a clue what it means, of course – *or* what I'm supposed to do with it? But it's while I'm contemplating it that I decide to give Christian another try.

'Who?' the bird on the other end of the line goes. I'm talking about Martha, as in Christian's PA?

I'm there, 'Ross! O'Carroll! Kelly! The same Ross O'Carroll-Kelly who rang yesterday. And three times last week.'

'He didn't return your call?' she goes.

I'm there, 'No.'

She's like, 'He *has* been busy. Can I take your cell?'

I'm there, 'He *has* my, as you call it, cell. We've been mates since we were pretty much kids.'

'I'm sure, if he thought it was important, he would have called you. Just give me the cell again . . .'

And I do.

Like a fool, I do.

She's putting a brave boat on it. See, that's the Mountie way. *In te confido*, which literally means, 'Whatever!'

We're sitting in Mr Chow in Beverly Hills. Hilary Duff's never out of the place apparently. *And* Usher.

It's nice to get away from the cameras, just the three of us. Honor's eating her steamed dumplings, going, '*Eee, arr, sahn, ssuh, woo, liu, chi, bah, jeou, sher* . . .'

Still fock-all English. I'm thinking, at least when she goes back to Ireland, she'll be able to ask for directions in petrol stations.

Sorcha's BlackBerry beeps. Kate Bosworth was spotted arriving at the OmniPeace Charity Party in a dramatic Zac Posen with Yossi Harari bangles, although you can tell that Sorcha's hort's not really in it?

A waiter stops by, hears Honor babbling away and he goes, '*Ni hao ma?*' and Honor's like, '*Hen hao, xie xie,*' and the next thing, roysh, the two of them are having this pretty much conversation.

I'm just sitting there totally, I don't know, mesmerized if that's the word?

Sorcha barely even raises a smile. I feel like I should

suddenly say something, so I remind her that she's still a beautiful, intelligent girl – great face, amazing body – and without actually using the words 'fish in the sea', I tell her that one day she's going to meet someone who actually deserves her.

'You mean *you*?' she goes.

The funny thing is, I don't mean me at all. But I nod anyway. I'm happy to be her punchbag if it's a punchbag she needs right now. I owe her at least that.

I watch her give up on her crunchy snow pea sprouts, then for some reason my eyes sort of, like, stray over her left shoulder and I see a familiar face sitting three tables behind us.

At first, roysh, I'm thinking, no, it couldn't possibly be . . .

I keep watching her, just to be a hundred per cent sure.

'Sorcha,' I eventually go. 'Stella McCortney's sitting behind you.'

The colour immediately drains from her face. She's like, 'What?'

I'm there, 'Stella *actual* McCortney. She's having lunch just there – obviously tofu or some shit.'

Sorcha looks suddenly sad. 'Ross, this isn't like the time you rang me up pretending to be Maya Angelou saying thank you for the poem I sent her?'

'No, I swear.'

'Or the time you told me you saw Jane Goodall on TV giving cigarettes to a monkey?'

'Look, I apologized for that as well. I'm telling you, it's *the* Stella McCortney. Left hammer.'

She does that thing that birds do when they *think* they're being subtle? She pretends she's spotted a bit of, I don't know, lint on the shoulder of her See by Chloé T-shirt and as she's, like, sweeping it off with her hand, she has a quick look back.

She goes into what would have to be described as shock

then – as in, she turns back around to me with both hands up to her face and she's having palpitations. She's literally struggling to breathe. I'm telling her to calm down, that she's just another, I suppose, human being, though that's like saying that Brian O'Driscoll is just another rugby player or that Paris Hilton likes engagement presents.

'Drink some water,' I go, which she does. Then I reach across and put my hand on top of hers. I'm there, 'Be aware of your breathing,' passing on some of my yoga, I suppose you'd call it, wisdom?

'In . . . and out . . . in . . . and out . . .'

I get her calm again, roysh, then I go, 'We're going to go and focking talk to her.'

She shakes her head.

I'm there, 'Yes . . .'

'Ross, I wouldn't know what to say.'

She storts getting worked up again.

I'm there, 'You'll think of something.'

'I could tell her that she was *so* right about jumpsuits,' she goes. 'Halston, Marc Jacobs, Preen – they're all doing them this autumn. Or, no – I could tell her that I've got, like, *all* of her CARE range – even the Purifying Foaming Cleanser and the 5 Benefits Moisturizing Fluid?'

I'm there, 'Why don't you stort by saying hello? Then just be yourself, Sorcha. She'll focking love you – everyone does.'

I stand up. 'Look, I'm done with my food,' I go.

I pick Honor up, hold her in one orm, then I take Sorcha's hand and she stands up as well. I watch her take a deep breath. Then I go, 'Ready?' and she sort of, like, nods, then breathes out.

We tip over. Stella's on her Tobler. As we approach the table, I can feel Sorcha's hand tighten in mine.

338

It has to be said, roysh, that Stella is an absolute cracker. I always *thought* she was in photographs? But in real life, I have to tell you, she's even better.

Sorcha's there, 'Excuse me,' and Stella looks up.

'Oh, hello,' Stella goes, unbelievably friendly.

'My name's Sorcha and I'm from, like, Ireland? And I just want to say that you are my – oh my God – *total* inspiration.'

'What a lovely thing to say,' Stella goes.

Even though she hears it probably fifty times a day, she acts like it's the first time anyone's ever said it to her, which is a mork of, like, true class. She's even inspiring me and I've only just met the bird.

Then she's like, 'And what a beautiful baby,' and she stands up.

Sorcha goes, 'This is Honor. Honor, this is Stella McCortney.'

'*Ni hao ma,*' Honor goes.

Stella's, like, stroking Honor's cheek, going, 'How old is she?' and Sorcha's there, 'Nearly two,' and Stella goes, 'Oh, so she's putting sentences together?' and I'm there, 'None that you'd actually understand – she could probably talk you through the menu, though.'

She laughs, even though she probably doesn't really get the gag. 'And you're Sorcha's husband?' she goes, offering me her hand.

I'm about to go, 'Used to be,' but Sorcha gets in before me and goes, 'Yes, this is Ross,' which is nice, because she didn't *have* to say it?

Stella's there, 'Well, won't you sit down? I was about to have tea,' and of course Sorcha's face lights up like a skobie on the last Luas to Belgord.

'Sorcha,' I go, 'I'm going to take Honor out. She's getting a bit restless,' which is horseshit, of course. I just know that, given my form, I'd end up saying something to totally fock it up for her.

I make the shape of a phone with my hand and I go, 'Give me a ring and I'll come and get you,' and the look she gives, it'd almost make you want to be a nice goy all the time?

One of the things that's always been said about me is that I look really, really well with a tan. Which is why, at this moment in time, I'm out on the patio, catching a few rays before Vegas, where they're going to film, like, the series finale of *Ross, His Mother, His Wife and Her Lover.*

I'm reading an orticle about myself in *Weekly OK!* – some vegetarian shower are up in orms about the 'Real Women Eat Meat' T-shirt I was wearing in last week's episode and I'm praying that Stella didn't see it – otherwise the internship that she's promised Sorcha could be out the focking window.

I can hear voices coming from the kitchen – Erika and my old dear having the DMCs. The old dear's going, 'I know what Ross thinks. He thinks I'm doing it for the benefit of the cameras. For the publicity. But it's not, Erika. I'm so in love. I know he's old and I don't know how many years he has left. But somehow that makes our time together all the more precious.'

I actually feel like puking again.

She gives a little girly giggle. 'He's so self-conscious about his face . . . I've told him a hundred times that it doesn't matter to me. And it really doesn't. I've always been more interested in what lies beneath. My first boyfriend, Conor, he was a frightful-looking thing. Still is – I saw him on television not so long ago, at Leopardstown. And as for your father . . .'

She lets it just hang there.

Erika's there, 'I suppose that's *one* thing I should be grateful to her for – unlike Ross, I got my mum's looks, not his.'

They both laugh, then eventually the old dear goes, 'It was *my* fault, you know.'

Erika's like, 'What?'

'You being brought up thinking someone else was your father . . .'

'It was *her* fault, Fionnuala. She was my mother.'

'She would have done the right thing – and your father would have done the right thing – had I not given him that ultimatum. I was convinced I was losing my mind. I *did* lose it . . .'

'It's still not your fault,' Erika goes.

The old dear's there, 'I'm going to tell you a story. And this'll be my last word on the subject. But I had no relationship with my mother. She went insane when I was, well . . . not long after I was born . . .'

'I'm sorry . . .'

'It's okay. My father used to take me to see her every Sunday in what we used to call Mummy's House. It was a – oh, God forgive me – a bloody nuthouse. And we'd sit there for a couple of hours talking to this woman and I'd wonder why she never talked back. Why she never even seemed to see us . . .'

I realize that she's crying.

'I still go, from time to time,' she goes.

Erika's there, 'She's still alive?'

'Well – *if* that's what you consider alive. I go there and I sit opposite her and most of the time I don't even say anything. We just sit looking at each other. I don't know what I'm waiting for. Just some flicker of recognition, I suppose. Crazy, I know. But I would give up everything I have, Erika – everything! – just for one conversation with her. Just to say, 'Hello, Mum,' and have her say, 'Hello, Fionnuala,' and then to tell her that, in spite of everything, it all worked out in the end, because look at me – I'm happy . . .'

341

I can hear Erika crying, too.

'If you live to be my age,' the old dear goes, 'I can assure you, Darling, you're going to have lots and lots of regrets. Just make sure, if it's at all possible, that they're regrets you can live with . . .'

That's the thing about my old dear. If you let her, she could actually have you feeling sorry for her?

'The good news,' I go, 'is that *he's* gone,' meaning Cillian.

Ro knows who I'm talking about – he's a smort kid.

'Don't un I know,' he goes. 'He's home – he's after being in all the papers, saying all sorts. The wurdled's gonna end, according to him. They're calling him Dr Doom.'

I laugh. They're unbelievably quick the way they come up with these names.

'Well,' I go, 'she's a lot happier without him, I can tell you that. The other major news is that your, I suppose, grand-mother is getting married – you'll be here for that.'

'Maddied?' he goes. 'Is she not still maddied to me grannda?'

I'm there, 'She is. It's actually just a sham wedding? They're only doing it for the cameras. Anyway, did your old dear book your ticket?'

'She did, yeah.'

'So what day are you arriving?'

'Er, Toorsday – seven in the night.'

'Cool – what's the flight number.'

'It's, er, EI EIO.'

I write it down.

He's there, 'Anyway, Rosser, I'd better go,' and he quickly hangs up.

At that exact point, roysh, a bird walks past – she's kind of, like, a cross between Kristin Cavallari and Adrienne Bailon – and she checks my boat out in a serious way.

'I'm Ross,' I automatically go. 'You clearly like what you see.'

She just laughs and goes, 'Your nose is bleeding.'

I'm like, 'It's what?' and I put my finger up to it and it ends up being red. I'm there, 'What the fock?'

She goes, '*Eeewww!*' and turns her head away and I'm there thinking, I wonder is that supposed to happen?

So I finally find him, sitting outside Newsroom, where we had our first – okay, if you want to call it that – *date*, drinking another one of his famous Taiwanese milk teas. I have nothing rehearsed, but I've always been good in, like, situations, especially when it comes to talking my way out of them.

I sit down opposite him and I go, 'Okay, I focked up in a major way. And I just want to say, you know, sorry, blahdy blahdy blah. I'd have to say, in my defence, I'm not used to having gay friends. I was probably just a bit, I don't know, homophobic, if you want to call it that. So, basically, sorry – and it's not often I say that . . .'

He sort of, like, screws up his face and goes, 'Ross? Ross, is that you?'

Which throws me a bit. I'm there, 'Er, yeah.'

'Oh my God,' he goes, 'your *nose*!' and he grabs me by the shoulder and sort of, like, turns me to the side, to see it from *another* angle? 'It's . . .'

I laugh. I totally forgot that he hasn't, like, seen it yet. I'm there, 'Go on, what?'

'It's . . . *stunning*,' he goes.

I think that's one of the things I've really missed about Harve – the way he's always bigging me up?

'You want to check out the bod?' I go. He smiles. I grab his hand and place it on my left pec, then guide it slowly across my chest and down my washboard stomach. 'Oh! My! God!'

he goes. I think he really appreciates that there's no way I'd do that if I was really ashamed to have him as, like, a mate. 'You are *so* ripped!'

I'm there, 'Thanks.'

'Your eyes are still quite bloodshot,' he goes.

I'm there, 'Yeah, no, don't worry about that – that's where Erika sprayed me with mace.'

'She sprayed you with mace?'

'Yeah, she thought I was going to hop her. Hop them all – Sorcha and my old dear included.'

He looks at me, sort of, like, worried?

'So am I forgiven?' I go and he just smiles, being obviously a sucker for a pretty face, and I order a Taiwanese milk tea, just to show him it's still the same old me.

I'm like, 'The point I was trying to make just there – to break it down for you and blahdy blah – was that I do want you as a friend. And fock what the press think.'

He's obviously delighted. 'I *was* going to call you,' he goes, acting all bashful. 'I've been doing a lot of thinking as well . . .'

I never said I'd been doing a *lot* of thinking, but I let it go.

For some reason, roysh, I look down and I notice the bags at his feet. He's there, 'I mean, who am I to lecture you about your attitudes when I haven't properly faced up to who *I* am?'

I'm suddenly speechless.

'I'm going to go see my parents,' he goes.

I'm like, 'Whoa! Are you absolutely sure about this?' suddenly feeling guilty for having, like, pushed him. 'I mean, are you not scared?'

'Yeah, I'm scared,' he goes. 'But since when has that been an excuse for not doing something?'

I shake my head. See, he thinks he's learned a lot from me – it's actually the other way around?

'If they love me,' he goes, 'they'll accept it. Either way, I can't go on living a lie.'

I'm there, 'You tinkering with cors? Doing the voice?'

'Exactly. It's, like, *so* exhausting.'

He asks me how Sorcha is and I tell him not bad, considering everything. 'You know she gave *him* the road?'

He's like, 'Cillian? I saw last week's show. That letter to George Bush was, like, so funny.'

I'm there, 'Yeah – but only up to a point. I'm glad he's gone, though. There's no way someone like him was going to keep her happy, especially with me there putting pressure on him.'

'Is she upset?'

'Let's just say she's getting over it. Stella McCortney's offered her a job.'

He laughs like he can't actually believe it. 'Stella?' he keeps going. '*The* Stella?'

'Yeah, we met her in a restaurant and they just hit it off. Well, you know Sorcha. People just fall in love with her. Then she had, like, a formal interview. So you can imagine, we were up at, like, five in the morning. All the drama. Should should wear her Issa "Lucky" day dress with a Ritmo watch or her Express tunic dress with Kara Ross cuffs and her Anya Hindmarch clutch . . .'

'Which did she choose in the end?' he goes, sitting forward, genuinely interested.

I'm like, 'Neither. She actually wore a navy cap-sleeve dress by Burberry with her petrol-blue Robert Sanderson pump heels . . .'

'That is *such* a good look for her! Will you tell her I said that was *such* a good look for her?'

I'm like, of course – it's the least I can do.

I tell him I'm driving to Vegas this afternoon. I can't wait to see Ro. He asks me if I'm coming back to LA again. I tell him I don't really know my plans yet, but deep down I think we both realize that this is goodbye.

I'm actually a lot sadder than I thought I'd be, although I try to put, like, a brave face on it? 'The thing is,' I go, 'I'm not sure if it's ever *really* goodbye these days, when it's all Facebook, texting, blahdy blahdy blah.'

He smiles. He knows this is my whole macho act, just as *I* know how absolutely hopeless I am at keeping in touch.

I feel, like, a sudden heaviness in my chest and I'm suddenly taking a huge interest in an oil stain on the tablecloth, going, 'That's not going to come out easily.'

Then I look up and notice that Harvey is bawling his eyes out and I realize that's it's alright for me to cry, too.

We end up just throwing our orms around each other, then after hugging for maybe twenty – at the very most thirty seconds – he pulls back, looks me straight in the eye and tells me that he loves me. And I think, fock it, and I tell him – you know what? – I love him, too.

And then I leave him where I first found him – on Robertson Boulevard, looking great.

Father Fehily used to tell us that some friendships are for a particular time. He used to say, is a butterfly any less beautiful if it lives for only one day?

I stort the cor and pretty soon he's just a speck in my rearview. Then I'm back on the road, the tears flowing freely now and me wiping them away with, like, the palm of my hand.

It's maybe the tenth time I've heard the story, but, to be honest, she could tell me a hundred times more if she wants. It's a long time since I've seen her this happy.

'I told her all about my shop back home and she asked me about my plans for it. I was like, "Oh my God, I've thought of *so* many over here, I can't *actually* decide? But I definitely want to do Tracy Reese, Anna Sui, Pedro Garcia, Kooba, Tibi, Chaiken, Gryphon and CC Skye. Oh, and Rich & Skinny. I can't believe that no one in Ireland is *doing* Rich & Skinny."

'And she was like, "But what do you really want to do?" and I was thinking, like I always do, WWSD? Is she talking about Charlotte Ronson? Or Rag & Bone? Or something totally outside of the box, like Tolani scarves, because no one's doing those either? Then she goes, "In your heart, Sorcha," and – oh my God – it was like she *knew*, Ross. It was like she could see into my soul.'

I'm there, 'Cool.'

It's, like, one o'clock and I'm going to have to be heading off soon if I'm going to meet Ronan off that flight. We're sitting on the edge of the pool, with our legs dangling in the water. I'm holding Honor and she's chatting away in her usual gibberish. Erika's inside, on the phone, finally talking to her old dear – they've been on for, like, three hours, which has to be good. *My* old dear and Trevion are having lunch in Il Sole with Johnny and a few of the other MTV heads, planning this shambles of a wedding.

'So tell me again,' I go, 'what happened next?' even though I *know*.

'I just started telling her about my dream – which I'd told absolutely no one about before – to start up my own clothing line that allows you to *dress* thin and yet *be* healthy? Blazers that skim the hips, jeans with low back pockets to lift your bum and thicker heels that de-emphasize the ankles.

'Oh my God, I was on fire, Ross. I started coming out with all this stuff. Jewelled necklines take centre-stage away from less-than-toned mid-sections. Open peep-toe sandals elongate and slim the lower half of the body. Even something as simple as a portrait collar and belt can transform uneven proportions into an hourglass figure . . .'

She suddenly stops, looking, I don't know, embarrassed by her excitement. Or maybe she's waiting for me to burst her bubble.

I tell her I think it's a great idea.

She's there, 'Really?'

I'm like, 'Yeah.'

'It's just that, for girls, weight is *so* connected to self-esteem. But there are ways of dressing ten pounds lighter without *actually* starving yourself?'

Deep down, I know she's thinking about Aoife. I doubt she ever stops thinking about her.

We're both quiet then and it's nice. 'Can I say something to you?' she eventually goes.

I'm there, 'Yeah.'

'When you and I broke up, I really thought it was the end of everything. I never thought I'd end up with *the* most amazing friend in the world.'

And it's incredible, roysh, because I tell her I *thought* the reason I originally came to LA was to try to, like, win her back. Now I know it wasn't. I came here just to try to make things right. She reaches for my hand and she tells me that I have.

Then she goes, 'Why don't you give Honor some of that?'

See, I'm eating, like, a Payday? 'But it's actual chocolate,' I go.

She smiles. 'I'm sure it won't do her any harm.'

I break her off a piece and I'm there, 'Look, Honor – chocolate,' and she goes at it like a focking sailor on shore-leave.

The next I hear is the sound of someone making their way down from the gaff. I sort of, like, *half* turn around?

It's Erika. 'Hey,' she goes.

She kicks off her flip-flops and sits down beside us, her feet in the pool.

We're both like, 'Hey,' then Sorcha asks her if everything's okay.

Erika just nods.

I look at her, roysh, and it's amazing because for the very first time I can honestly say that she does nothing for me. No yoga, no tricks. I just don't fancy her, even though she *does* have incredible legs.

'They're both coming over,' she goes. 'I'm going to meet them in Vegas – Charles *and* Mum.'

In other words, Helen and Dick Features. She's smiling – she seems to be happy. I tell her that's great, although I don't let her know my true feelings, of course.

She asks me when I'm leaving and I tell her now. She says she can't wait to see Ro and she's not the only one. It's, like, there's already a buzz, just around the fact that he's coming.

I stand up and tell them I'd better get going. I hand Honor to Sorcha, then I give them each – I suppose you could call them the three women in my life – a hug and a peck on each cheek and I tell them I'll see them in a couple of days.

I'm, like, ten feet away from the house when I hear Honor go, 'Chocolate, Daddy! Chocolate!'

I turn back and smile. It might be the happiest I've ever been.

Ronan's not on flight EI EIO. In fact, there *is* no flight EI EIO.

I'm standing in the arrivals hall of McCarron airport and I'm scanning the board, thinking maybe he just got the number orseways, still prepared to give him the benefit of the doubt, the little focker. But there's nothing coming in from New York at 7.00 p.m. and I suddenly know how all those birds I've scored on holidays must feel when they find out there's no 1 Main Street, Dublin.

I whip out my phone and ring his number. He answers – he has the *actual* balls to answer – and all I can hear in the background is, like, *beep beep beep* and then *ding aling aling* and of course there's no even *need* to ask him where he is? Except I do ask, because I'm his father.

'I'm in a little carpet joint Downtown,' he goes, as casual as that. 'Here, there's a fella here, Rosser – I'm after been watching him. He's betting lavender chips – five hundred large – and he always guesses right. Do you think he's part of the skim?'

I'm there, 'I don't know. I don't even know what you're talking about. What *I* want to know is, why aren't you at the airport?'

'Ah, I got in a bit early,' he goes.

I'm there, 'How early?'

'Depends – would you count today as a full day?'

'Ronan!'

'Alright, keep your knickers on. Three days.'

'Three *days*?'

'But that *is* counting today as a full day.'

'You've been in Vegas for three days? A ten-year-old boy? On his own?'

'Ah,' he goes, 'you're never on yisser own in this town. No, what happened was, I wanted to get the lie of the land before you got here,' and then I hear him suddenly shout – I don't know at who – 'Hey, what kind of bull feathers is this? I said two-fifty large!'

I'm there, 'Are you gambling? Tell me you're not gambling.'

'Don't sweat it, Rosser,' he goes, 'Luck's running against the house tonight.'

I'm there, 'Running against the house?' and I'm thinking, this is Tina, letting him watch whatever the fock he wants on TV and hang around with criminal types three times his age.

'Ro,' I go, 'get the fock out of there now. And I mean it,' and he's suddenly quiet. He knows when I'm being serious, in fairness to him. I'm there, 'Go to the hotel and wait for me there.'

'I'll tell you what,' he goes, 'I'm just going to stick me head into Caesars on the way back up. Meet me there. I'll be mooching around,' and then he just hangs up on me.

I'm straight back to the cor lot and you can imagine how actually pissed off I am. The traffic on the Strip is murder and it takes me, like, an hour to get there and, of course, the whole way I'm thinking, if they find a kid on the gaming floor, they'll call the cops.

I swing up outside, practically throw the keys at the valet and peg it in.

Caesars is humungous. There must be, like, five thousand people in there, milling around, literally all human life, we're talking rich-looking dudes in ten-grand suits, we're talking fat mums and dads with their fat kids, we're talking stunning-looking birds wearing half-nothing, a fair few of them giving me the elevator eyes, although I don't give them anything back, which shows you how worried I am.

The place smells of tequila, *Issey Miyake* and sweat and I'm being deafened by the sound of polyphonic music and bells and whistles and, every ten seconds or so, someone some-where cheers and I run to where the noise is coming from, thinking – from past experience – that he's bound to be at the centre of it, but this time he never is.

I'm trying his number, but it's going straight to message-minder, which means it's off.

I head for the area where the machines are, remembering

how much he used to love those ones with the moving floors that you stuck a coin in and tried to send, like, an avalanche of money into the chute. He was forever kicking those. I couldn't tell you how many times I've had the call from the lads in Quirkey's telling me to come and pick him up.

He's not there. It's mostly elderly women, sitting on high stools, feeding coins into machines and hitting buttons without even looking at the screen.

Then I remember him on the phone, banging about the ball and wheel, so I head for the roulette tables.

I see a man in a stetson dropping chips all over the grid — he must have every focking number on the wheel covered. The last time I saw a man in a stetson was in Lidl in Arklow. His wife checks me out in a major way and sips her margarita, imagining — I can always tell — that the straw is actually me.

I push on. Again, no interest.

I head for the craps tables. Ro's always had, like, a thing for dice and he carries around a lucky one that Martin 'The Viper' Foley's supposed to have had in his pocket when he survived the third attempt on his life — or maybe even fourth.

There's, like, no sign of him there either, just mostly gangs of goys — a lot of stag porties, I'd imagine — shouting and generally giving it loads.

I'm actually on the point of giving up when I finally cop him. He's leaning against a pillar, staring at these four dudes playing blackjack, roysh, and at the same time he's, like, chatting to himself, except it's like he's making, I don't know, calculations in his head.

I morch straight over to him, roysh, grab him by the shoulder and sort of, like, spin him around, obviously catching him by surprise. 'What the fock do you think you're doing?' I go.

He looks at me like I'm the TV licence inspector he's been brought up to fear.

He's there, 'Who the fook are you?' and I realize all of a sudden that he genuinely *doesn't* know?

But I don't get a chance to explain about my nose. Because the next thing I know, something hits me square in the chest, the wind is taken out of me and I'm all of a sudden on the deck, flat on my face, with what feels like the entire Munster pack on top of me.

It's like the entire casino is suddenly quiet and I don't know whether it's because everyone's watching or because I'm dead.

Then I think I can't be dead – because of the pain. My orms are pinned behind my back and someone's applying pressure to them and it feels like they're going to, like, snap off. And I can't even beg for mercy, roysh, because I haven't a focking breath.

I'm lying there, if I'm being honest, waiting to feel the bones just break.

'Hang on a second,' I hear Ronan suddenly go. 'Ah, sure, it's Rosser – here, let him up, Man,' and the next thing I know, my orms are suddenly released and I'm lifted – *literally* lifted – back to my feet.

I turn around, roysh, still dizzy, and there, standing next to Ro, is this humungous focker, who's as wide as he is tall – and he must be six-foot-eight – his body so ripped that his suit looks like a focking lagging jacket. He's like something out of *The Sopranos*. He's got dork, greased-back hair and a face as ugly as Darndale and twice as dangerous.

He's late forties, early fifties maybe, but he could give Martin Johnson a wedgie and make the focker say thanks.

Ronan's laughing. He's there, 'What happened to your nose, Rosser?'

I touch it, just to double-check it's still there. I'm there, 'Never mind that – who's this guy?'

The rest of the casino goes back to its own business again.

'This is Big Juice,' Ronan goes.

I'm there, 'Big Juice? Er, I think I'm going to need *more* than that?'

Big Juice sticks out his hand. 'Anthony Trombino,' he goes.

My hand just, like, disappears into his.

'He's a minder,' Ronan goes. 'You can rent them. Three hundred snots a day. Nudger and Gull got him for me as a surprise.'

I'm wondering will he ever have friends with *actual* names?

'I *should* be pissed off,' I go, then I look at Big Juice. 'But at least someone's been looking after him. Thanks.'

He's there, 'Hey, forget about it,' except he says it like it's one long word, the way they say it on TV.

Ronan goes, 'Here, watch this, Rosser,' and he points at me and goes, 'Hey, Big Juice, this fella here's wising off at me, so he is.'

Big Juice looks at me, roysh, straight in the eye and goes, 'I'm going to ask you nicely, Sir – step away or I will feed you your *fucking* teeth . . .'

My body literally shivers.

Ronan laughs. 'He's the fooken business, isn't he, Rosser?'

I'm there, 'Er, yeah, he's the business.'

'He's grandda was Joey Trombino – had points in every casino with a fooken horse book. And he's da was Jake Trombino. He was a fooken button man for Lefty Rosenthal . . .'

I'm there, 'I have to say, I'm pretty sure I'd have ridden the tackle had I seen it coming,' and Big Juice just nods. He says he's sure I would, which *is* nice of him.

'He knew them all,' Ronan goes. 'Benny Siegel, Meyer Lansky, Frank Costello, all them boys . . . What was the other fella?'

'Lucky Luciano,' Big Juice goes.

'Lucky Luciano! Ah, he's some fooken stories as well. Here, tell Rosser about Mad Sam Spilotro . . .'

'It's late,' I go, cutting him off. 'It's late – and it's been, well, a long day for me . . .'

'Point taken,' Ronan goes. 'You go get yourself some shut-eye, Rosser. Me and Big Juice are going to take the party on to Private Eyes, a little club I know.'

I'm there, 'Private Eyes, my hole – you're coming with me,' and he sort of, like, rolls his eyes at Big Juice and says it was woorth a try, in anyhow.

'I'll see you tomorrow,' Big Juice goes, then he turns to me and says, provided that's okay. 'I been paid up to the end of the week,' he goes.

I look at Ronan's little face and of course I *can't* say no? I'm there, 'Er, cool, yeah.'

'Moostard,' Ronan goes.

As we're walking away, roysh, Big Juice grabs my orm – he can put his entire hand around my bicep and still his fingers touch – and he tells me that that's one smart kid I got. I tell him I know – that's what frightens me.

Ten minutes later, we're in the cor – just me and Ro – out on the Strip, heading for the *Star Wars* Casino, where Ronan tells me he's already checked in.

'Big Juice!' I can't help but go, shaking my head.

We've got the top down. It's, like, a muggy night.

'He's the business, isn't he, Rosser?' Ronan goes.

I'm there, 'Yes, he's the business.'

'You'd know not to fook with him, wouldn't you? See, in my line of work, it pays to advertise.'

I'm there, 'Only you,' and I laugh – I suppose at, like, the good of it?

He laughs as well. 'He fooken floored you but, didn't you, Rosser?'

'Yeah,' I end up having to go.

'Like a sack of fooken spuds.'

He's suddenly serious. 'You're not going to tell me ma, are you?'

'So she thinks you've been here with me the whole time?'

'Er, yeah.'

I think Tina's the only person in the world he's *actually* scared of?

'I'll tell you what,' I go. 'I won't tell her *if* you promise not to pull a stunt like that again. I worry about you, Ro.'

'Ah, I'm wide, Rosser.'

'I know you're wide. And I know you're, like, way more intelligent than me, even though you're only, like, ten. It doesn't mean I don't still worry about you.'

'Okay.'

'Honestly, I don't care what you get up to – just don't leave me in the dork. There's been too many secrets in our family.'

'Okay.'

The next thing, roysh, we're stopped at a red light at the junction of The Strip and Flamingo Road. I'm looking at the fountains of the Bellagio, the ones you see on, like, *Ocean's Eleven*?

There's, like, a gang of heads on the corner and they're mostly – and I don't know if this is racist – but black. Two or three of them stort walking over towards the car and – again, this is racist – I'm suddenly kacking it.

I'm thinking, will I just nail the accelerator here?

It's only when they come closer that I realize they're basic-ally handing out concessions for, like, clubs and then, like, escort services as well? They've got this way of, like, holding the cords between two fingers and flicking them with a thumbnail, so they make, like, a *ffftt, ffftt* sound and they're also going, 'Girls! Girls! You want girls?'

One of them goes to hand me a cord, roysh, and I'm just about to go, 'Sorry – black or not – I'm actually here with my son?' when he suddenly turns around and goes, 'Hey, Ronan – *what's de stareee*?' and offers him the high-five.

Ronan goes, 'Alright, boys?' and then he sort of, like, flicks his head at me, presumably to say, 'Get out of here – I'm with the oul' fella.'

The light turns green and I step on the accelerator. There's a squeal from my tyres and the three – again – black dudes jump back in fright.

Of course, I'm left shaking my head again, but this time not in a good way?

'Ah, they just know me from walking up and down The Strip,' Ronan goes, as I'm pulling into the casino cor pork.

I'm there, 'Ro, forget what I said about secrets. There's shit I don't actually *want* to know?'

10. Vegas, Baby

I tend to do a lot of my – I suppose you'd have to call it – deep thinking while I'm shaving. So there I am, roysh, staring into the mirror, and it's suddenly going through my head how much I've missed the goys and how much I'm looking forward to hanging out with them again. They flew in last night and I'm trying to work out how long it's been since I last saw them. We're talking November to the end of June – you do the maths.

Ronan's outside the door, telling me that the Nevada Gaming Commission are on his case – or, more specifically, busting his balls, over what he calls his 'associations'.

'Oh, no,' I go, 'not again,' because sometimes you've got to just, like, play along? It can be good sometimes for kids to have an imagination.

'Piece-of-shit motherfuckers,' he goes, 'saw me having breakfast with Solly Abrams and Santo Trafficante! At the Dunes! Ah, you know how that goes.'

'So that's, like, a bad thing, is it?' I shout out to him.

'What have you got, rocks in your head? Everyone knows they're wiseguys.'

'Of course – I forgot.'

I finish up and wipe the rest of the foam off my face.

'I wouldn't mind,' Ronan goes, 'but I'm the one trying to keep the fucken peace out here. Phil Profaci's gone kill-crazy. You know Blowtorch Phil?'

'I know the face,' I go. 'I've never heard the name.'

'Well, he's *supposed* to be the outfit's outside man here –

shouldn't be *on* the floor. Anyway, two nights ago, he has a bad night at the craps table. You know Abie Zwillman? Best fucken stickman *on* The Strip. Abie's been with me for thirty years. Phil breaks his fucken arm, then tells Johnny Guzak, the pit boss, to tear up his marker or he'll melt his fucken face – I'm talking about a marker for twenty large here . . .'

I slap on the old Kiehls.

'Then, he hits the bar,' Ronan goes, 'gets all liquored up, comes back, busts his way into the soft count room and walks out with a caseful of big ones . . .'

And the old *Gaultier* the Sequel.

'So anyway, they've decided to take him out. Giuseppe Bonnaro and Tony the Ant are flying in. He gets a shave every morning in the barber shop at the Silver Slipper. Phil's sweet on one of the broads there – ah, she's up in the paints age-wise, but she still knows a few tricks . . .'

I step out of the bathroom. I'm there, 'Can I just ask, Ro – we *are* just bantering here, aren't we?' because it *does* always pay to check with him.

'Course we are,' he goes. 'Ah, it's just I been listening to Big Juice and he's stories. I'm telling you, the fellas over here, Rosser, back in the day, thee'd put the boys back home in the fooken ha'penny place.'

I'm actually pulling on my green Apple Crumble, roysh, which is maybe why I stort to feel suddenly patriotic? And it's weird, roysh, because I'm the one suddenly *defending* Ireland? 'What about The Genoddle?' I go. 'The Penguin? The Monk?'

It's actually the mention of The Monk that gets him. He stares into the distance and smiles. It's nice to see he's still a major fan.

'Here,' he goes then, 'I need to talk to you about this wrinkle I'm after coming up with.'

I don't know what a wrinkle is, but it doesn't sound *very*

legal? I check my phone. I've got, like, a text from JP. They're actually out on The Strip. He's like, 'Hav u seen this thng?' presumably meaning the *Star Wars* Casino and I suddenly realize that I haven't. We came in the back way last night and, because Ro already had the key, we went straight up to the room in the lift – or elevator, if you want to call it that.

I turn around to Ro and I'm like, 'The goys are outside – why don't you tell me while we're walking?' which is exactly what he ends up doing.

'See, I'm after been examining traditional algorithms and equations which describe various kinds of wheels and spindles,' he's going. 'For example,

$$V^2 = \frac{Wrad^2}{k\,(4C + md^2)}$$

which is a cracking little equation for figuring out the speed of the wheels of a train . . .'

We pick Big Juice up in the lobby. It's, like, mayhem down there – loads of *Star Wars* characters milling around. I spot three or four Jar Jar Binkses serving drinks, although I'm pretty sure they're called Gungans.

Ronan's still going. 'Using a Markov chain – a stachostic model describing a sequence of possible events in which the probability of each event depends only on the state attained in the previous event – it's possible to predict, with great accuracy, what a ball will eventually do, based on the first few seconds of the spin . . .'

I hear Big Juice tell him that it's the best scam he's heard since Tony 'Big Tuna' Collovati took the Hacienda for seven-hundred-and-fifty large and I'm thinking, I'll definitely have to ring Nudger and Gull to tell them that, whatever they paid, they really got their money's worth with this dude.

They're waiting in front of the place – we're talking Oisinn,

JP and Fionn – and of course, you can imagine the banter. What, after having not seen each other for, I don't know, however many months?

We're *all* on fire.

Of course, straight away they stort on my nose. At first they don't recognize me and then, when I finally convince them that it's *actually* me, they stort giving it loads.

'I thought it was Tiny Winky,' JP, for instance, goes. 'I didn't know whether to say hello or eh-oh!' although I *do* end up hitting them back with one or two cracking one-liners of my own, don't you worry about that.

Then it's, like, high-fives and hugs and introductions. I tell Big Juice that these three, plus the dude we're about to meet inside, are my, basically, *capos*, which I'm pretty proud of, it has to be said.

Fionn looks well. Three months' summer holidays – why the fock wouldn't he? 'So what do you think of it?' *he's* the one who goes.

I realize I haven't even looked at it yet, so I spin around and I swear to God, roysh, I end up nearly crapping my pants. The building is in the shape of Dorth Vader's head – well, head *and* shoulders – and it's honestly the most impressive thing I've ever seen.

I look around me and there's, like, hundreds of people standing around, staring at it in total awe and I feel like telling every single one of them that my best friend actually built it. Well, project-managed it.

I think I speak for all of us when I say we're all just, like, shaking our heads as we stort walking towards the thing. 'Imagine trying to get planning permission for something like this back home,' Oisinn goes.

JP's there, 'Ross's old man probably could – with some of *his* contacts,' and everyone laughs and I end up having to point out that *his* old man sold most of the gaffs that my old man built – which means he basically put him through focking school.

JP says he didn't *mean* anything by it? See, the thing is, roysh, I'm my old man's biggest critic, but what I really hate to hear is people having a go at him when he's not here to defend himself, the stupid dickhead.

Fionn puts his orm around my shoulder and tells me that I'm probably just nervous for Christian, as we all are.

The doors into the casino bit are Vader's actual mouth. We walk through them into the main reception area and I don't know about the others but I am just blown away. There's this life-size Rancor in the, I think it's called, like, an atrium? – must be, like, a hundred feet high – reaching right up to the ceiling, which is black with, like, stors painted on it?

We tip over to the security desk, where a Sandtrooper asks us if he can help us. I'm there, 'We're actually here to see Christian? As in Christian Forde?' and he asks me for my name.

I can't resist it, of course. I wave my hand in front of his boat and go, 'You don't *need* to know my name,' but then he's suddenly looking over my shoulder, going, 'Hey! Big Juice! How *you* doing?'

Big Juice goes, 'Guido? Guido Roselli? Is that you in there?' and suddenly it's all hugs and talk of old times and some old mate of theirs who was found chopped up like a tomato and floating around in a fifty-five-gallon drum off the coast of Miami. Of course, Ronan's face is lit up like he's just met Santa Claus.

Guido eventually radios upstairs, then he says Christian will be down in a minute.

I'm still looking around with my mouth open – an actual Land Speeder goes by – when the next thing I hear is, like, footsteps and suddenly there's, like, eight stormtroopers

morching towards us in two columns of four, with two Royal
Guards on either side – and there, smack bang in the middle
of them, is Christian.

JP storts giving it the Dorth Vader theme music. 'Dom,
dom, dom, dom-de-dom, dom-de-dom . . .' and the rest of
them join in, knowing that this is probably the proudest
moment of the dude's life – *after* beating Newbridge in 1999,
obviously – showing off this thing that he's, I suppose you'd
have to say, created?

I don't join in, though, bad and all as that sounds. 'I'm
tempted to tell you that I'm proud of you,' I go to him,
'except you haven't been returning my focking calls.'

I can't help it.

He sort of, like, squints his eyes at me and goes, 'Ross? Is
that you?' and of course the rest of them react like this is the
funniest thing they've ever heard. 'Sorry,' he goes, still checking my face out, 'the last episode of the show I saw, you still
had the bandages on.'

I'm there, 'Maybe I'd have told you if we'd spoken to each
other in the past two months.'

He's there, 'Ross, it's been manic, with the baby, and then
. . .' he looks around him, '. . . all this.'

And I'm nodding, roysh, because I'm suddenly getting the
message. Lauren's convinced him that what happened by
the shores of Lake Ewok that day was *my* actual fault and
she's using it as a reason to break us up.

The rest of the goys haven't seen Christian for, like, nearly
a year, so it's all hellos and high-fives and whatever else, but
I have to admit, roysh, I'm hanging back in a serious way
while he's giving us the whole guided tour.

I crack on not to be even impressed when he shows us the
cocktail bor, which has been modelled to look exactly like
the one in Mos Eisley in the first movie – they've even got

those freaky-looking fockers with the saxophones. He says there's another bor on the second floor that's modelled on Jabba's sail-borge.

The goys are all like, whoa! But I'm like, whatever!

'And *Time* and *Newsweek* are both putting us on their covers,' he goes, which I take as a definite dig at me – as in I only made it onto the cover of *Us Weekly* and one or two others you wouldn't wipe your hole with.

'*Time* and *Newsweek*?' I hear myself go. 'Who the fock reads *them*?'

Behind me, roysh, I can hear Ronan banging on to Fionn about parameters and variables and Fionn's banging on about residuals and blahdy blahdy blah blah.

Christian asks us if we want to meet the little fella and all the goys are like, 'Cool,' and, 'Thought you'd never ask,' and whatever else. But I'm there, 'Er, I actually can't. I've got to pick up Sorcha and Erika from, like, the airport,' even though they're not in for another four hours. I just don't want to face Lauren again. 'In fact, I'd want to stort thinking of making tracks.'

'Oh, okay,' he goes.

Then, roysh, his face is suddenly all serious.

He's like, 'Ross, you know your nose is bleeding?'

I put, like, my palm up to it. When I take it away it's, like, covered in blood. 'Yeah,' I go, 'it does that.'

Sorcha says she's thinking of having the electricity in her shop converted to, like, wind power. I tell her I wonder how the Powerscourt Townhouse Centre will feel about that and she says she doesn't *actually* care? In fact, she's – oh my God – never listening to negativity again. 'Remember what Karl Lagerfeld said about Stella,' she goes, 'when she started in Chloé?'

We're sitting in the Eiffel Tower Restaurant, the one in Paris – as in Paris, the casino? – staring across at the fountains of the Bellagio, watching all these jets of water dance to a tune that Sorcha immediately recognizes as 'Rhapsody on a Theme of Paganini' by Sergei Rachmaninov, while I'm thinking about that CD she bought years ago – *The Best Classical Album of the Millennium . . . Ever!* – and how it really focking paid for itself in the end.

I feel fat as a fool here, having had the blue cheese soufflé and the duck two-ways and having polished off most of Sorcha's braised salsify and what Erika left of her Israeli cous-cous with mint pistou. I'm thinking, a brandy could be just the thing to settle the old Malcolm. 'Armagnac?' the waiter goes.

I check my pocket, make sure I've got the old man's cord.

I go, 'Armagnac, *oui, oui.*'

Erika says the last time they were here was in 1999 and this place had only just opened. The funny thing is, roysh, I remember that myself. They spent the summer in Mortha's Vineyard, working as chambermaids – totally focking miserable. Yeah, Sorcha used to ring me in tears, telling me about the shit she used to find in people's rooms. Then, at the end of the summer, they came here for, like, a week's holiday.

Erika goes, 'Remember those two guys we met?' and Sorcha looks at me – I'm pretty sure it's *not* a word – but *guiltily*?

See, we were technically still going out at the time.

'They were acrobats,' Erika goes, 'with the Cirque du Soleil,' and I know from the way she says acrobats exactly what's being implied.

Sorcha smiles sadly at me, but who am I to make her feel bad? I went through her friends that summer quicker than the Ugg boot craze. I look at her as if to say, it's cool – it doesn't matter now, which it doesn't.

'Rhapsody on a Theme of Paganini' finishes with an un-believable – I'm *still* pretty sure the word is – crescendo? On the very last note, the water shoots, like, three hundred feet in the air, then all the lights go out and in the dorkness, roysh, you can hear all the wows and the whoas and the oh my Gods, and then the lights come on again and everyone just claps.

It's, like, you'd *have* to?

'Hey, we went to see Lauren,' Sorcha goes – meaning obviously Christian's Lauren – just as the dessert trolley rolls by. She thinks she might have the crème brûlée, but then she changes her mind and waves the dude on.

I'm there, 'How was that?' except I look at Erika when I say it. See, she's always had a thing for Christian, which I *still* find weird – and I'm saying that these days as her brother. She shrugs as if she doesn't know what I'm banging on about. 'Little Thomas is gorgeous,' she goes.

'*Or* Edward,' Sorcha goes, 'because they still haven't decided what it's going to be. I still think I'd prefer Edward Thomas to Thomas Edward.'

Erika's there, 'Lauren's *so* happy, though. It's *so* lovely,' and I stare at her for, like, ages afterwards, I suppose for signs that she's being a bitch?

'She was asking for you,' Sorcha suddenly goes.

I'm there, 'Yeah, well, I'm going to be avoiding her. I'm sure she's going to want to give me the big lecture – don't fock up Christian's big night, blahdy focking blah blah. To be honest, I'm sick of her treating me like a piece of dirt.'

I stand up and knock back the rest of my brandy. Sorcha says she has the babysitter until midnight. They're going to see *Phantom* at the Venetian if I want to come. I tell her no, but thanks anyway, then she asks me if I'm okay and she says it like she really means it? I tell her I'm fine and I'll see her in the morning. We're taking Honor to the Mirage to see the dolphins.

Before *they* all get here.

'And cut!' Johnny goes. 'Beautiful! *Beautiful!* Okay, Sorcha,

I want to get a shot of you looking all Marlene Dietrich to close the scene. I've got Heather Nova singing an acoustic version of Gwen Stefani's "Cool".'

I stort walking away. 'Hey, Ross,' he shouts, 'stick around. I want to cut a short piece into the middle of that scene. Erika's going to mention Charles and Helen arriving for the wedding tomorrow and you say something like, "There's not going to be a wedding!" Can you do that?'

I keep walking.

'Ross,' he shouts, 'do I have to remind you that you are contractually obliged . . .'

I hear Erika telling him to let me go.

I don't know what's suddenly wrong with me. If I'm being honest, maybe it *is* this whole wedding farce.

I find our waiter and hand him my cord. '*Et cinquante dollars pour vous,*' I go.

He's there, '*Ah, merci, Monsieur!*' and I'm like, '*Ne rien,*' and it's being suddenly fluent at French that gets me thinking – maybe *that's* it. Maybe I just need my Nat King Cole.

I ring Fionn – ask him where he is. He's across in the Bellagio – him and JP – playing roulette. I tell them I'll be straight over.

They're in flying form, the two of them – delighted to see me, of course – and they've got, like, loads of chips piled up on the table in front of them. I've no idea how many they storted with, of course, but, judging from the banter, I'd say they're probably up overall.

'Isn't gambling a sin?' Fionn's asking, because JP still believes in all that, even though he's not going to be a priest anymore.

JP's there, 'I think it's pretty much down to the conscience of the individual church-goer,' and the two of them crack their holes laughing.

They're on the old sidecors, which is, like, brandy and triple sec. I ask a passing waitress for one for myself.

The bird spinning the wheel is a ringer for Olga Kurylenko and I can tell she has an immediate thing for me.

'So where's Oisinn?' I go.

The goys are, like, suddenly serious. JP's there, 'We haven't seen him.'

'He's not in his room,' Fionn goes.

JP's there, 'I came down for breakfast at, like, eleven o'clock this morning and he was where we left him last night.'

He means playing Caribbean Stud. I ask him was he winning and he says he's not sure, but people who don't move off their stool for, like, fourteen hours, generally *aren't*?

Fionn's there, 'We think Oisinn might have a problem, Ross.'

I'm like, 'I know. JP said,' and all I can think to say after that is, 'Fock!'

I get a load of chips in anyway – three hundred snots worth? I scatter a few around the place. Then I turn around to the bird, holding a ten-dollar chip between my finger and thumb, and go, 'Go on, what's your lucky number?'

She just goes, 'Gentlemen, please place your bets,' totally blanking me. I suppose they have to at least *pretend* to be professional?

Fionn, I notice, is doing this thing where he puts one chip down on red. Then if the ball lands on black, he puts two on red for the next spin. If black comes up again, then he puts four on red, pretty much doubling his stake every time. I haven't a clue what it's about, but it looks pretty boring. Me, I just stick with, like, numbers?

Anyway, at some point in the evening, three or four drinks in, Fionn turns around to me and goes, 'Ross, I wanted to talk to you about Ronan?'

I look the croupier bird dead in the eye. 'Who?' I go.

Fionn's there, 'Ronan – your son, Ross.'

'But I'm still single,' I tell her, 'just in case you're wondering.'

She doesn't bat an eyelid. She's good.

Fionn's there, 'Were you listening to what he was saying yesterday? About algorithms?'

I'm there, 'Look, you don't want to pay any attention to that. He's just showing off in front of that Big Juice – he told me this morning he wants me to call him Icepick.'

'Ross,' he goes, 'I was going to say this to you on the phone. I – and, well, one or two other teachers in the school – we think Ronan might be gifted.'

'Okay,' I go, still wondering where this is going.

'I'm talking about *really* gifted. He may even have a genius IQ.'

I'm there, 'A genius IQ?'

Then I ask the question that I suppose any father would ask in those circumstances. 'How's this going to affect his rugby?'

He pulls a face, roysh, like he's losing patience with me.

He's there, 'All I'm saying is that he appears to display a higher than normal rate of concentration, memory and problem-solving capacities.'

'Oh,' I go, trying not to sound *too* disappointed?

'He came to me a few weeks ago,' he goes, 'and said he was interested in joining the Maths Club. I set it up a few months ago for the fifth and sixth years.'

'But *he's* still in the junior school,' I go. 'I'm not sure if I approve of that.'

'Well, I told him – rather patronizingly, as it turns out – that it might be a bit *too* advanced for a boy of ten.'

'Good. I don't want him turning out a geek – no offence.'

JP smiles at that. Secretly, they all love watching me hammer Fionn.

He goes, 'That's when he told me he'd been giving quite a bit of thought recently to the Collatz Conjecture – in other words the $3n + 1$ problem. I said to him, "What do you know about the Collatz Conjecture, Ronan?" and he said, "Only that it's one of the great unsolved problems in mathematics." Then he went on to explain it to me in perfect detail. "Well, you let f (n) be a function defined on the positive integers, such that $f(n) = n/2$ if $n = 0$ and $f(n) = (3n+1)$ if $n = 1 \ldots$"'

I'm there, 'This is Ronan we're talking about?'

'Yes,' he goes. 'Ross, he understood that when you form a sequence by performing this operation repeatedly, starting with any positive integer and taking the result at each step as the input at the next, the process will eventually reach the number 1, irrespective of what positive integer is chosen at the outset.'

'And you're saying this makes him a genius?'

'I don't know. He certainly should be tested.'

'Fair enough. Are we talking, I don't know, opening his actual head up here?'

He laughs in my face. He's got balls, I'll give him that.

'No,' he goes. 'What the school would like is for Ronan to see a child psychologist, one with expertise in performing either the Wechsler Intelligence Test for Children or the Stanford Binet Test . . . Ross, my suspicion is that, mathematically at least, Ronan is inside the top 0.001 per cent of the population.'

Which *can't* be bad.

Something suddenly occurs to me, roysh, and it must occur to Fionn at exactly the same time because he storts, like, shaking his head before I even open my mouth.

'So, you're saying . . .' I go.

He's there, 'No!'

'. . . that this scam he's been banging on about – with the roulette wheel – *could* actually work?'

'Ross, what I'm saying is, we owe it to him as a school to help him discover whatever extraordinary abilities he might possess and see to it that he gets an education commensurate *with* those abilities . . .'

I'm there, 'Er, that sounds like it might end up actually *costing* me money. No, fock that – we're going to take a casino for a lot of money . . .'

The croupier bird looks at me. 'I'm not saying necessarily this one,' I go.

JP gets in on the act then. 'Ross, it's not *Rainman*.'

I'm there, 'But who says it can't be?'

Fionn shakes his head. 'So you're going to exploit this talent your son has for your own financial gain?'

'Well,' I go, 'sometimes you've got to bet big to win big. I mean, I've been looking at *you* tonight – what the fock are you doing, betting on red the whole time? It's actually storting to piss me off.'

'I'm playing to a strategy,' he goes, 'based on minimum risk and slow but steady gains.'

I'm there, 'Yeah? Well, you play roulette like you played rugby – in other words, safe.'

Of course, I know how bang out of order that is – Fionn was one of the best backs I've ever seen play the game, although you'd never admit that to his face.

Even JP's giving me daggers. It's, like, there *is* a line – and he knows I've crossed it.

'So what's *your* strategy here?' Fionn goes, all pissy with me now.

I'm there, 'Me? I'm doing birthdays – mine, Honor's, Ronan's . . .'

He has the actual cheek to laugh. 'I've just watched you lose three hundred dollars in ten minutes,' he goes.

Of course, I reach into my pocket and whip out a wad bigger than he'll ever see in his life. I go, 'Well, there's plenty more where that came from.'

He just, like, stares at it and, needless to say, he's bulling – focking schoolteacher.

JP goes, 'Come on, guys, this is stupid – we're all mates. We're over here for Christian, remember?'

I'm there, 'Fock Christian! Where is he tonight? Probably off having dinner with George focking Lucas. He doesn't want to know *us* anymore – have you not copped that yet?'

Fionn tells me to grow up.

I peel off two twenties and slap them down on the, I don't know, felt table. 'Get yourselves a focking drink,' I go. 'I don't want you saying that, as well as exploiting my son, I also never stand my round.'

Then I walk back to the *Star Wars* Casino.

Ro's still awake. He's actually sitting up, looking through the Yellow Pages with the little Reggie Kray half-glasses that I got him for his birthday a couple of years ago. Clear glass.

'Alright, Rosser?' he goes.

I'm there, 'Cool. Nice meal with Sorcha and Erika actually – you should have come.'

'Ah, I ate with Big Juice,' he goes, not even looking up. 'Doorty big steak.'

'You *are* coming with us to see the dolphins tomorrow, aren't you? We're bringing Honor.'

He's there, 'Yeah,' but he sounds kind of, like, distracted?

I'm there, 'Hey what are you up to?'

'It's mad,' he goes, finally looking at me over the top of his glasses. 'Prostitution is illegal over here, but they get around it by calling themselves entertainers. Here, have a listen to this, Rosser. *Slim and petite. Thin and busty. Firm and friendly. Tyra and Christy. Tammy and Barbie. Former model. Private dancer. Feminine passable.* Can you believe this?'

'Mad,' I go, playing along. He's only doing it to put the shits up me anyway.

He's there, *'Ebody dream girl. Leather fetishists. Soccer mom. Amber and Kimi. Trish the Dish . . .'*

He storts laughing then. *'Lusty Heather – Light as a Feather!'* I laugh along *with* him.

Then I go, 'Get some sleep, Ro. We've a long day ahead of us tomorrow.'

'He's wising off at me again.'

Big Juice is back from the breakfast buffet, towering over me.

'I wasn't,' I go, sounding – I admit it – like a focking twelve-year-old girl. 'I'm actually just sitting here eating my pancakes and drinking my coffee.'

Ro goes, 'Ah, he was flapping his mouth off, Big Juice – like he was down the precinct.'

It's like Ro's been given one of those dolls, where you pull the cord and it, like, says shit.

'Sir,' Big Juice goes, 'how 'bout I punch your jaw loose, then pull out your fucking intestines?'

Ro cracks his hole laughing. He's like, 'Pull out your fooken intestines! Ah, I need to be writing these down.'

I'm there, 'Okay, whatever. Can we be serious for, like, five minutes here?'

'Go on, so,' Ronan goes, still shaking his head. 'What's on your mind?'

I'm there, 'Okay, that scam you've been banging on about – are you serious about it?'

He looks at Big Juice, like he's trying to decide whether

373

they can trust me or not. They were obviously discussing this over dinner last night. Eventually, Big Juice nods at him and Ronan goes, 'Okay,' then whips a pen from behind his ear and storts scribbling on, like, a napkin?

When he's finished he pushes it across the table to me. It's like:

$$\sum_{i=1}^{n} (Y_i - \hat{Y}_i)^2 = \sum_{i=1}^{n} \left(Y_i - \sum_{j=1}^{k} \hat{\beta}_j X_{ij} \right)^2$$

'This equation minimizes the sum of the squares of all the residuals,' he goes.

Of course, I don't even know whether I'm looking at it the right way up.

He's there, 'Or to put it more simply . . .' and he takes back the napkin, flips it over and writes on the other side:

$$\hat{\beta} = (X^T X)^{-1} X^T Y$$

'This one works with an ordinary least squares estimator,' he goes, and I'm sure I don't need to tell you I'm storting to feel faint again.

'Are you still with me?' he goes.

I'm there, 'Errr . . .'

He laughs then. 'I'm only pulling your wire, Rosser. We're not gonna be needing maths – which I have to tell you I'm pretty sad about. No, see, it's computers these days.'

I'm there, 'So explain to me – and imagine for a minute that you're the adult and I'm the ten-year-old child – how it actually works.'

'Okay,' he goes, 'it's like this. Most people think that roulette's a game of random numbers. But it's not, Rosser. By feeding certain data into a computer about the speed at which the ball and the wheel are travelling, it's possible for a computer to predict, with a high level of certainty, where the ball is going to land.'

I'm there, 'Okay, first of all, how do you measure the speed of the wheel and the ball?'

'By putting a camera on it.'

'Er – and how do you propose to do that? These casinos have got, like, surveillance everywhere. I mean, they've even got their own cameras on the tables.'

'Exactly,' Ronan goes. 'We're going to use one of those.'

I actually laugh. 'You'd need to be, like, an expert computer hacker.'

'Or know someone,' Big Juice goes, 'who works in security.'

I look at him. I'm there, 'Your mate Guido?' and he nods.

It's immediately obvious that it's Christian's casino we're talking about hitting.

Ro goes, 'See, we were racking our brains about how we were gonna do it. We were looking at maybe sticking a filament camera on a pair of glasses. But the picture was too grainy. Then Big Juice had a beer with Guido last night.'

'He's an electronics man,' Big Juice goes. 'Owes a fortune in back alimony.'

I'm there, 'So he's obviously no qualms about this?'

Big Juice laughs, like it's the stupidest question ever. 'We pick any table in the house,' he goes, 'and he can have the live CCTV feed diverted straight to a laptop computer.'

'I got a programme,' Ronan goes, 'Nudger and Gull got it for me, that'll study the feed . . .'

I'm there, 'Nudger and Gull? Is this what you goys have been doing in the den?' and suddenly, them hiring Big Juice to look after Ro makes a lot more sense to me.

'The programme will calculate the speed of the wheel, and, by observing, say, a hundred spins, where the ball is likely to land when travelling at different speeds . . .'

I'm actually getting excited listening to this. It's kind of like one of the *Ocean's* movies?

'I'm going to be sitting in our room,' Ronan goes, 'with the laptop. Big Juice is going to play the table. The ball spends an average of fifteen seconds in the outer rim of the wheel before the croupier says, "No more bets." The computer will give us the number in approximately five seconds, which leaves us with ten seconds to get a message to Big Juice and for Big Juice to cover the predicted number.'

'And how do you propose to do that?' I go.

'There's a broad I know,' Big Juice goes. 'Name's Chelsy. Works as a cocktail waitress. Ronan's going to talk to her on a radio mic. Most casinos sweep for these things, but only the gaming floor, never the bar. I'll be able to see her from the table. We've worked out a system of signals – a combination of cocktails and trimmings – covering every number on the wheel. Three variant glasses, multiplied by three colours of liquid – clear, red, dark – multiplied by four trimmings – umbrella, one straw, two straws, cherry – gives us thirty-six combinations.'

'If it's zero,' Ronan goes, 'she puts nothing up on the bar.'

I shake my head. They've certainly got it all worked out. 'So, like, how much do you reckon you could actually win here?'

Ro looks around him, I suppose for, like, dramatic effect? 'Depends how we want to play it,' he goes. 'Do we just bet big on the predicted number and risk them smelling a rat? Or do we extend the chord by two or three numbers on either side and buy ourselves more time at the table?'

'And, hey,' Big Juice goes, 'it also depends on the stake, of course.'

I'm there, 'Okay – what could you do with, like, twenty Gs?'

Now it's their turn to be impressed. They both look at each other, then back at me, their mouths wide open.

'You heard me right,' I go. 'Twenty focking grandingtons – what could you do with it?'

Big Juice turns to Ro. 'Even in a brand new casino, I reckon we got a four-, five-hour window before they figure something's up. In that time, playing cautious, we could turn that into . . . two million?'

Ronan nods, I suppose you'd have to say, thoughtfully?

End of focking conversation. I stand up. I'm there, 'I'll go get you the focking money.'

As I'm walking away, roysh, Ronan goes, 'You've no problem with it being this casino?' meaning Christian's casino.

Big Juice goes, 'There's no better time to make a run on a joint than in the first week it opens. They're worrying about all sorts of other shit, see. The fucking paint job in the lobby.'

I think about it for, like, three seconds. 'Look, it's not even Christian's money?' I go. 'It's George focking Lucas's. And it's not like *he's* short of a few bob.'

I tip upstairs then to get the old man's cord from the safe in the room. It's as I'm keying in the combination that I happen to notice the phone book, lying open on the floor, still on Entertainers. My eyes for some reason fix on Lusty Heather – Light as a Feather. The words obviously, but then the face. And I laugh. I actually can't stop laughing, because I realize that I know her.

I whip out my phone and ring Sorcha. I tell her I'm feeling a bit Moby and would she mind taking Ro and Honor to see the dolphins without me. She goes, 'Oh my God, poor you! Although, don't forget, your mum and Trevion are arriving this afternoon. And so are Helen and your dad. We're all meeting in the cocktail lounge at six.'

Which I already know. MTV want to talk to us about the so-called wedding tomorrow.

'You poor thing!' Sorcha goes. 'Maybe try and get your head down this afternoon.'

I *could* say something funny in response to that. In the end, I don't.

I tell her I hope she doesn't mind me saying this, but she doesn't *dress* like a hooker?

'All my gear's in the bag,' she goes, meaning her Millie hobo, which I know because Sorcha has the exact same one. I like her use of the word gear – conjures up all sorts of images in my head.

'You can't exactly walk into The Strip's hotels in thigh-boots and a thong,' she goes.

Which is also why I had to go down to the lobby to pick her up, crack on we're, like, boyfriend-girlfriend?

On the way up in the elevator, I tell her I wouldn't imagine she gets many 11.00 a.m. call-outs. She says I'd be surprised.

We go into the room. She's straight down to business because she heads immediately for the bathroom with her bag. I'm there, 'Hey, let's just chill out for a second.'

She goes, 'Hey, this isn't *Pretty Woman*, friend. Believe me, you can't afford to keep the meter running.'

I'm there, 'You don't recognize me, do you?'

She looks at my face. But she doesn't *really* look? She goes, 'Sure I do,' but she obviously presumes I'm just, like, a regular client?

She throws me a Zeppelin. 'You remember I'm a safety girl?'

She unbuttons her coat and drops it on the floor, then takes her top off over her head, so she's standing there in her bra.

I smile.

'The last time I saw those puppies,' I go, 'I was jumping out of a second-storey aportment on La Cienega Boulevard.'

She reacts, roysh, like she's just seen a ghost. I'm there, 'Hello, Sahara. Er, it's *Ross*, by the way?'

She nods, roysh, but for ages it's like she can't actually speak? 'You look . . . different,' she finally goes.

I'm there, 'Yeah, I had, like, a nose job – among other things.'

She stares hord at it, then checks it out from, like, various angles. 'It suits you,' she goes.

I'm there, 'Yeah, I'm getting used to it – although I'm still getting the odd nosebleed.'

That sort of, like, shocks her? 'You could have a septal perforation,' she goes, suddenly sitting down on the bed. 'That can happen if the surgeon doesn't know what he's doing. You remember Trevion?'

She obviously hasn't seen the show. I expect she works most nights.

'Well,' she goes, 'he had this friend from, like, Ecuador?'

Something tells me I'd be happier not hearing the rest of this story. I sit down beside her and rub my hand up and down her bare orm.

'I take it the Ayaan Hirsi Ali musical didn't happen,' I go. 'Broadway, blah blah blah?'

She shakes her head. 'The guy was just . . . stringing me along,' she goes.

I tell her it's great to see her again. The tension – and we're talking *sexual* tension? – is electric and I've a feeling that no amount of yoga or talk of septal perforations is going to hold back the tide.

She suddenly throws the lips on me. Which is worth repeating – *she* throws the lips on *me*? – and, well, if anything I'm a gentleman, so I'm not going to give you the gory details, other than to say that I ended up giving her the magic *and* in a major way.

She literally gasped when she saw the new bod, by the way.

Anyway, roysh, where all this is going is, we're lying there, post-match, her trying to get her breath back, me sweating like a man on ten penalty points, when she turns around to me — her face all flushed — and goes, 'I'm sorry, by the way — about that night?'

I tell her to forget about it. 'In fact,' I go, 'and this is one of those definite small-world stories — Trevion and my old dear are getting married.'

She's there, 'What?' except the way she says it, it's more like, '*What!*'

I tell her that was my exact reaction. 'And you haven't even met her,' I go. 'I can tell you this, the poor focker doesn't know torture yet.'

At first, roysh, she laughs.

Then she's suddenly looking at me, propped up on her elbow. She's there, 'You don't believe those stories, do you?'

I look at her. She's being actually serious. I'm there, 'Are you saying they're, like, exaggerated?'

She laughs. 'I'm saying they're invented. Trevion was never *in* Korea. I shouldn't tell you this . . .'

Now *I'm* propped up on my elbow. I'm like, 'What?'

'I don't know . . .'

'Come on, Sahara — you can't, like, half tell somebody something like this. He's going to be my stepfather, remember?'

'Okay, you've got to promise that it goes no further.'

I'm there, 'I give you my word of honour,' which obviously means fock-all.

'Trevion never went to Korea,' she goes. 'He deserted.'

I'm there, 'What?'

'Yeah, he deserted — soon as they told him he was going.

He went AWOL. Disappeared for years. His name isn't even Trevion Warwick – it's Trevor Warwick.'

I actually laugh. 'That's some deep cover,' I go. I'm suddenly racking my brains for, like, movies I've seen? 'Isn't that, like, illegal – in other words, deserting?'

'Oh, yeah! He could still be court-martialled. But you won't say anything, Ross, will you?'

'What do you take me for? So, like, what's the Jack with all the scors on his face?'

'It's psoriasis.'

'Psoriasis?' I go. 'Oh my God, that's focking hilarious.'

We get up then and fix ourselves. I tell her it was great to see her again and of course then there's that whole dilemma – if a hooker ends up making the first move on you and then obviously enjoys herself, do you still have to pay?

In the end she only chorges me half.

I kiss her goodbye at the door, then I go back into the room and, like, punch the air. Not only have I got the goods on the man my old dear's supposedly marrying, but I realize that my mind is back to normal again. I try to think in French, then Irish, and it hits me all of a sudden that I know absolutely fock-all of what I accidentally learned at school.

And I can't tell you how good it feels to be free of that curse.

I run into Oisinn in the corridor outside the room. He looks like absolute crap. He's, like, still in the clothes he arrived in two days ago. He's white in the face and his eyes are, like, sunk into his head.

I ask him where he's been, but he just stares through me. It's like he can't even see me?

I grab him by the shoulders. 'Oisinn!' I go, literally shaking him.

He's suddenly with me. He's like, 'Oh, Ross,' and I'm there, 'Forget *oh Ross* – Dude, what's going on?'

He stares at a point on the wall, over my right shoulder. 'I've got to . . . not be here,' he goes. 'It was a mistake coming.'

'So it's true,' I go, 'what JP said – as in, you've got, like, a gambling problem?'

He looks down at his clothes, as if that should be an answer in itself.

I'm there, 'Is it a stupid question to ask whether you're up or down money-wise?'

It is, roysh, because he laughs, then he just brushes past me on the way to his room. I follow him, going, 'Dude, talk to me,' but he just keeps walking.

He slips the key cord in the door and goes into his room. I follow him in and watch while he opens his bag and storts shoving clothes into it. 'How much?' I go. Except he doesn't answer? I'm there, 'Dude, how much?'

He stops what he's doing, looks me dead in the eye and goes, 'One point three million dollars.'

It honestly takes my breath away. I'm like, 'One point . . .'

'One point three million.'

'Fock,' I go. 'I thought you were going to say three or four Ks. I was going to give it to you out of my own sky-rocket.'

'Well,' he goes. 'Now you know.'

I still can't get my head around it? 'One point three million? You could nearly buy a decent house in Dublin for that.'

He finishes packing – if you could call it that – zips up his bag and swings it over his shoulder.

I'm there, 'Where are you going?'

He's like, 'I think Vegas is the worst place in the world for someone like me to be.'

'You're going to miss Christian's grand opening,' I go.

He nods like he's already thought of it. 'Tell him sorry for me, will you?'

I've never seen the focker this down about anything.

I'm there, 'You *are* alright for dosh, though, aren't you? As in, generally?'

He shrugs. 'Might need to sell a property or two.'

I'm thinking, fock, that doesn't sound good.

'Can I ask you something?' he goes. 'It's a bit embarrassing. Can I borrow twenty dollars? For my taxi fare.'

I'm straight out with the wad. I'm like, 'Dude, take fifty.'

He shakes his head. He goes, 'Please, Ross – don't give me any more than I need.'

'Oh, hello there,' he goes, not a focking clue who I am – his own son. He actually asks me for a brandy and perhaps some of these nut things.

It's Sorcha who ends up having to go, 'Charles, it's Ross.'

I'm there, 'Yeah – as in your only son? Oh, unless there's others – which we can't rule out, of course?'

'Oh,' he goes, sort of, I don't know, scrutinizing my face. 'This is the famous nose. Look at that, Helen! Oh, I wouldn't have known you, Kicker.'

They're all sitting around the cocktail lounge like it's happy focking families all of a sudden. We're talking the old dear and Trevion, the fraud, then Fock Features and Helen, then Erika, Sorcha, Honor and Ro.

Erika and her old dear are holding hands, I can't help but notice. 'Hello, Ross,' *she* goes.

I'm there, 'Hey, Mrs Joseph – how are you?'

She smiles. Other people's old dears have, like, *always* had a thing for me? 'Ross, it's Helen,' she goes. 'I've been telling you that for years.'

I nod at their two hands. 'That's nice to see,' I go, 'as

in genuinely,' and they turn to each other and just, like, smile.

Of course, the old man has to blunder in then with his big hobnail boots and ruin the actual moment. 'Trevion here's just been telling me some of his war stories,' he goes. 'Where was it, old chap – South of Suwon?'

Of course *he* doesn't need any encouragement. 'We was outnumbered,' he goes, 'four to one. We was getting pounded. But *our* order was to delay their advance while more troops was flown in. We had no anti-tank guns. We're using divisional artillery against T34s – can you believe that?'

The old dear's all pleased with herself, listening to him.

Of course, I'm just staring at him, going, 'That must have been shit for you, Trevion. Like, really shit. As in, absolute shit.'

'A boy of eighteen!' the old man goes.

'The day they crossed the Kum river, I'm sat in a slit trench – the bastids – cleaning my weapon. The next thing I look up – twenty feet away, there's a tank. And its turret . . . is slowly turning on my position . . .'

'Unbelievable,' I go. 'Literally.'

The old man's, like, shaking his head, looking at him in, like, total awe. 'Well, Fionnuala,' he goes, 'you've always had a thing for war heroes. What about that chap you went out with when you lived in Paris? Fought in Algeria!'

'Oh, yes,' she goes, cracking on to remember, except she probably doesn't because it's almost certainly horseshit as well.

He turns to Helen. 'Tortured by the ALN, if you don't mind. To the point where he lost the use of both arms.'

'Which is why he couldn't push her away,' I go.

Nobody laughs, although I'm sure one or two are dying to.

I sit down next to Trevion. I have to – it's, like, the only free seat? I cop the old man's iPod on the table. I pick it up and laugh, then I turn the clickwheel, expecting to find, I don't know, Andrea Bocelli and all sorts of shit on it. Instead, it's all Keane, Killers and the Kings of focking Leon.

'When have *you* been into this kind of music?' I go.

He's there, 'Oh, Helen lent me one or two of Erika's CDs. Hope you don't mind, Erika. We, em, what's this they say – *imported* them. Quote-unquote. Lot simpler than it sounds.'

It's pathetic – he ignores his daughter for, like, twenty-seven years, then he's suddenly desperate to get all in with her?

'It's "Sex on Fire",' I go, throwing it back across the table at him. 'Not "Your Sex is on Fire".'

'Are you sure?' he has the actual cheek to go.

I'm there, 'Er, I think *I'd* know, don't you?'

The next thing, roysh, who arrives on the scene only Lauren. On her Tobler. Christian's looking after the little lad. They make such a focking fuss over her, of course. It's all congratulations and blahdy-blah and the old man says that Hennessy sends his love and he hopes to get over in a week or two to meet his little grandson.

Lauren goes, 'Hi, Ross,' and if I didn't know her better, roysh, I'd say she was actually being nice. I'm just there, 'Hey, Lauren,' thinking there's no way I'm going to suddenly stort feeling guilty about this scam we're pulling.

'Hey, Ro,' I go, 'tell you, soon as we're finished here, let's head down to the MGM to see the lions,' and he's there, 'Fair enough, Rosser, if that's what you're into,' and I turn to Sorcha and ask her can I bring Honor as well and she says – oh my God – of course, even though, she makes sure to add, she doesn't exactly approve of animals being kept in captivity and Stella would probably kill her if she found out that she went to see the dolphins earlier.

I'm like, 'Ro, how much water have you drunk today?' and he shrugs and goes, 'Ah, a glass or two,' and I'm there, 'Well, you better drink some more. It's a hundred and ten out there and it's, like, desert heat? You shouldn't even go out without at least a litre inside you.'

'Reet enough,' he goes.

I'm there, 'And Sorcha, you might put a bit more suntan lotion on Honor's face and legs, would you?' and she goes, 'Oh my God, I would have *totally* forgot!'

I look over at Lauren and she's just, like, staring at me. Again, there's no way I'm going to stort feeling bad about shit?

Johnny Sarno finally arrives. I'm thinking, okay, let's get this over and done with. He goes – major fanfare, of course – 'Ladies and gentlemen, I'm happy to tell you – we've found a venue for the wedding!'

I'm just there, 'Except it isn't an actual wedding.'

'Where?' the old dear goes.

He's like, 'The Chapel in the Clouds. It's at the top of the Stratosphere . . .'

Everyone's giving it, 'Whoa!' and 'Oh my God!' and all the rest.

'Eight hundred feet above the ground. It's the highest wedding chapel in the United States and we'll be able to get some wonderful footage of all of you against the backdrop of the city lights.'

I stand up, thinking, cool – now I know where *not* to be tomorrow afternoon?

I'm like, 'Yeah, whatever,' and I take Honor out of Sorcha's orms and I go, 'Come on, Ro, let's go,' and Honor claps her hands together and goes, 'Daddy! Daddy! Daddy!'.

It's just as we're reaching the front doors of the casino that I hear a voice call me. I whip around, roysh, and it's, like, Sorcha. She turns to Ro and she goes, 'Ronan, do you mind if I have just a quick word with your father?' and he goes, 'Not a problem,' and he takes Honor out of my orms and brings her over to meet an Ewok.

Sorcha goes, 'Why don't you and the guys take Trevion out tonight for a bachelor party?'

I'm there, 'A bachelor porty? You're pulling my wire!'

'Why not?'

'Because the whole thing's a farce, Sorcha. I mean, what was all that about back there?'

'What?'

'Well, him and her for storters. *You've always had a thing for war heroes, Fionnuala.* Then *her* with her Chapel in the focking Clouds . . .'

She looks at me, I suppose, sympathetically? 'Look, everyone's had a lot to deal with, Ross. New relationships. New configurations. But we're all making the effort to adjust. It's like your mum says, Ross, there isn't a person around that table who can say they've lived a perfect life. We've all made mistakes. But you have to let them go if you want to go on living.'

'Meaning?'

'Ross, you said it yourself – look at us. You let *me* go – and look at us now. It's different, but who's to say that what we have now isn't better than what we had?'

I turn away from her.

She's there, 'Why not your mother, Ross? Why can't you let Fionnuala go?'

And what I can't bring myself to say is that I never *had* her. I never had *her* and I never had *him*.

Fionn wants to know if it's true. I knew I couldn't trust JP to keep his trap shut. I don't bother my hole answering him and he takes what he wants from that. 'Your best friend,' he goes, 'you're going to screw him over on his big night?'

I'm there, 'I'm sick to the teeth saying this – it's not *his* money. It's George Lucas's. And the amount of *Star Wars* shit I've bought for Christian over the years – birthdays, Christmases, blahdy blahdy blah – I reckon the focker owes me. And anyway, the way Christian's been running around after him, it's about time he remembered where his priorities lie.'

He tells me there's a bad streak in me, which of course is news to no one.

Of course, there's shit I could throw at him – as in, what's he doing out on the stag of the dude who's marrying my old dear? Not just him either – JP as well. It's, like, where's *their* loyalty? We're *supposed* to have played rugby together?

'There he is!' is the next thing I hear. 'The greatest outhalf *never* to play for Ireland!'

I don't focking believe it. *He's* out as well.

I'm there, 'I'd hordly have thought this was your scene,' meaning The Rum Jungle in the Mandalay Bay. It's, like, a young people's bor?

He suddenly slaps Trevion on the back. 'Well, in normal circumstances, I'd be tucked up with a bloody good Tom Clancy. Except, well, just after you left this evening, Trevion here asked me if I would do him the signal honour of being his best man.'

I'm like, 'Whoa back, horsy. You're going to be best man at the wedding of the woman you're still actually married to?'

Trevion orders shots, including one for me, which I've no intention of drinking. I stare at the old man and realize I've never seen him so hammered.

Fionn says there's still no word from Oisinn. JP tells him to keep trying his room.

'Too late,' I go. 'He's gone.'

'Where?' JP goes.

I'm like, 'Presumably home. I put him in a taxi this

afternoon. And you're right, he has got a problem. One point three million of them.'

Their jaws just drop.

'He says he's probably going to have to sell one or two aportments.'

Fionn takes, like, a deep breath. 'I tried to talk to him,' he goes, 'the night before we came away. But he's like you, Ross – he can't be told anything.'

The funny thing is, roysh, on *some* level, I realize that Fionn is right? Without trying to come across as all intellectual here, there are times in our lives when we've got, like, two roads in front of us. One of them is, like, the right road and one of them is, like, the wrong one.

Deep down, I probably know that the right road will take me back to the *Star Wars* Casino and up to my room to tell Ro and Big Juice that the scam tomorrow is off.

But then I hear Trevion telling some total randomer at the bor about his escape from Pyongyang and the road I *actually* take is suddenly decided for me.

I walk over to him. 'Can I have a word?' I go.

He looks at me sort of, like, half-eyed. Hammered, of course. 'What is it, Bambi?'

I look at the dude he's talking to. I'm there, 'Believe me, you don't want me saying this in front of actual people,' and I flick my head in the direction of this, like, seating area.

He shrugs, then just follows me – obviously hasn't a bog what's coming. I can see Fionn, JP and the old man looking over, wondering what the fock. I'm straight out with it.

I'm just there, 'I know, by the way.'

'Know what?' he goes.

'Pretty much everything. I know your name's not Trevion Warwick for storters – it's Trevor. And I know you were never in Korea. Unless it was later, on your focking holidays.

I know you're, like, a deserter and a focking traitor to your country.'

He goes suddenly white. It's the first time I've ever seen him stuck for words. He doesn't call me Eeyore or Pocahontas or any of that shit. He just goes, 'What are you going to do?'

I'm there, 'I'm going to ring, I don't know, whoever it is you ring.'

'Unless . . .' he goes. 'I can feel an *unless* coming.'

'Oh, there is an unless – don't you worry about that. Unless . . . you do another of your famous disappearing acts. We're talking tomorrow morning, first thing . . .'

He nods. He looks sad, but at the same time totally, I don't know, resigned? The only thing I could compare it to is looking into the eyes of the Newbridge players as they collected their losers' medals in 1999.

'Will you explain it to your mother?' he goes and I'm there, 'Probably not.'

He nods. He knows he's in no position to ask for anything. He says he's just going to go and finish his drink. Then he heads back over to Fionn, JP and the old man, walking with an air of something that I couldn't put my finger on at the time, but which I would later come to recognize as dignity.

11. Bringing down the house

Two imperial stormtroopers walk by. Ronan tells me to relax – I'm making *him* nervous. It's just, I don't know, I could have sworn they looked at us. He turns around to Big Juice and says this is why he never works with amateurs. Then they go back to staring at the wheel, their eyes sort of, like, rolling around, following its spin. This is what they call the final recce.

Ro's there, 'It's not fifteen seconds.'

'You're right,' Big Juice goes. 'It's more like twelve.'

'Which means,' Ro goes, 'that Chelsy's really going to have to be on her game.'

We all look up. There's, like, a middle-aged woman behind the bor, maybe twenty, thirty yords away. She's focking cat, in case you're wondering. A real Minger the Merciless.

She's putting up various drinks on the bor. 'Cocktail glass, clear drink, one straw,' Big Juice goes, then quick as a flash, 'number eight . . .'

It's funny, roysh, I always presumed that if I was ever going to make a fortune off my son's back, it would be by selling him to one of these *soccer* clubs. As in, Alex Ferguson or one of that crowd would roll into the estate one day – in a limo obviously – watch him do a few, I don't know, keepie-uppies, then go, 'Okay – we'll take him,' and throw Tina and me enough money so that neither of us would ever have to worry about working again.

Not that either of us ever *has* worked – it's just the worry alone would actually wear you out.

But never in a million years did I think that it would be Ronan's *mind* that would be my basically meal ticket.

The casino is focking rammers, which allows us to sort of, like, blend in, in as much as you *can* standing beside someone like Big Juice. There's, like, TV cameras everywhere, reporting on the newest addition to The Strip, which, just three years ago, I hear one reporter go, was just a vacant dirt lot.

If I wasn't so pissed off with Christian, I'd actually be proud of him.

'Would Sir care for a drink?' I hear someone go.

I'm thinking, I'd know that voice anywhere. I whip around and it's, like, C-3PO. *And* R2-D2, of course. I suppose you never see one without the other.

It's, like, two o'clock in the afternoon, roysh, but then it's never too early for champagne.

'Can I get, like, a glass of Cristal?' I go.

I look at Ronan and Big Juice and they're just, like, shaking their heads – disappointed would probably be the best word?

'I'm terribly sorry to inform you,' C-3PO goes, you know the way he talks, 'that your nose appears to be bleeding.'

I touch it with my middle finger. He's right. It's, like, a heavy one this time? I tip my head back.

R2's carrying, like, a tray which has, like, napkins on it and 3PO hands me one, in fairness to him, and I hold it hord against my nostril, trying to, I think the word is, like, *staunch* the flow?

Then he goes off to get my champers.

I'm there, 'The first thing I'm going to do with my winnings is get this thing fixed. Find a proper plastic surgeon this time – one at home, not even here – and just get it put back the way it was.'

Big Juice loses it with me then. 'You're talking about winnings?' he goes to me, through – it has to be said – gritted teeth. 'You're drinking champagne. What are you, *looking* to be busted?'

Of course, Ronan takes *his* side as well. He's there, 'Tone it the fook down, Rosser.'

The next thing, roysh, I look up and who do I spot on the far side of the gaming floor – only focking Christian. He's giving instructions to a bunch of Jawas. I try to subtly hide behind, like, a Wookie, but he sees me and I have to suddenly tell Ro and Big Juice that he's on his way over. Ro tells me to stall him.

I'm there, 'How?'

He's like, 'Just fooken stall him, Rosser!'

'So, Christian,' I go, walking straight up to him, 'what's the story – are those Jawas slacking?'

'Hey, Ross,' he goes. 'You're in early. I didn't expect to see you until tonight.'

'Ah, it's just the excitement,' I go. 'I don't know if I actually mentioned it the other day, but I'm actually proud of you, Dude.'

He just nods, roysh, and doesn't say the same thing back to me. Then, totally out of the blue, he's there, 'Hey, do you want to come up and see the little guy?'

Of course, I'm caught on the hop.

'Lauren wants to talk to you as well,' he goes.

I'm, like, humming and hawing and I'm just about to tell him that I have to shoot off when C-3PO and R2-D2 arrive over with my champagne. 'Er, cool,' I end up *having* to go, then the next thing I know, we're in the focking elevator, on the way up to their suite.

There's, like, an atmosphere between me and Christian – there's no doubt about that.

One thing I can definitely say for me is that at least fame, success, whatever you want to call it, didn't change me?

'Hey, what time is the wedding?' he goes.

'So-called,' I go. 'It's supposed to be, like, six o'clock?'

He's there, 'Oh. Will you all make it back here for the official opening – it's at, like, half-eight?'

'Don't you worry,' I go. 'I've, er, a funny feeling that the wedding's not even going to happen.'

He doesn't get a chance to ask me why, roysh, because the next thing the elevator doors open, then we're suddenly walking into the aportment?

It has to be said, roysh, that I'm expecting Lauren to be pretty frosty to me. So you can imagine my surprise, roysh, when she steps out into the hall and ends up giving me one of the biggest hugs and warmest smiles anyone's given me in my pretty much life. She's there, 'Hi, Ross,' and you can imagine me – I'm like, 'Er, hey, Lauren.'

Christian tells me to come in. It's some penthouse, I can tell you that – modelled, he makes sure to mention, on Senator Amidala's aportment on Coruscant.

Lauren tells me to sit down, which I do, on this huge cream leather couch. There's still a port of me expecting her to, like, flare up at me any minute. I somehow get it into my head all of a sudden that she knows what Ronan and Big Juice are up to downstairs.

She's there, 'Will you have something? Tea? Coffee?'

I sort of, like, hold up my glass and tell her I'll stick with the champagne.

Christian goes, 'I'll leave you two alone, then,' and he disappears – the focker – into one of the other rooms. I'm suddenly telling myself to keep calm and play it cool. And remember the old rule – never admit or deny anything until you've been actually accused. And even then, deny, deny, deny.

'I owe you an apology,' she all of a sudden goes. You can imagine, that totally wrongfoots me.

I'm there, 'Em, okay – apology accepted.'

She's there, 'You don't want to know what I'm apologizing for?'

'Not necessarily, no.'

'You know I've never been a fan of yours?'

I'm there, 'Well, I know you've never been a rugby fan in general.'

She closes her eyes, roysh, like she's counting to ten in her head. 'But I've been especially hard on you recently,' she goes. 'The way I treated you, when you came up to visit us that time. I could blame hormones . . .'

I *told* Christian it was hormones.

'But that wouldn't be completely true. But when you're pregnant, there are all sorts of changes that happen . . .'

My eyes automatically go to her belly. I can't actually help it?

'Yes, physical,' she goes. 'But also psychological. I suppose I was looking at Sorcha bringing up her daughter with a man who wasn't her father and, being pregnant myself, it really got to me. I blamed you for the fact that you weren't all together as a family. Bringing a child into this world is the most terrifying thing you can do. I think you became the focus of all my worst fears. I was looking at you thinking, what if Christian turns out like *him* . . .'

This has for some reason *stopped* sounding like an apology?

'What if he's a bad husband? What if he plays around? What if he leaves me to bring up this child on my own?'

I'm gagging to say something back to her, but then I think, no, leave it. I knock back a mouthful of champagne.

'Because I never thought much of you, Ross, despite all the lovely things that Christian says about you . . .'

I get this sudden stabbing pain in my stomach. It could well be guilt.

'I wouldn't listen to him. I thought you were a bad father, a bad husband . . . And the person who finally helped me see the light was Sorcha.'

I'm there, 'Sorcha?'

'She and Erika came to see me the other night.'

'I heard.'

'She said you've been very upset. She said you felt I'd driven a wedge between you and Christian.'

'I, er, might have mentioned it to her, yeah.'

'She said I'd been unfair to you, Ross.'

'Sorcha said that?'

'Yeah. She told me how supportive you'd been during her break-up with Cillian. She reminded me of all the times you've been there for Christian as well. And she made me see that you are a good person, deep down . . .'

I suddenly think about Sorcha and Erika, putting on their bridesmaid dresses for a wedding that's never going to happen.

'Then I saw you yesterday, the way you were around Ronan and Honor, and I thought, Lauren, you're wrong about this guy. How could someone who loves his children so much be all bad?'

I think about the old dear, standing around in the Chapel of the Clouds, waiting for Trevion to arrive.

'And I know that my husband loves you like a brother – and that, Ross, is good enough for me.'

I think about Ronan and Big Juice and how we're about to ruin one of the happiest days of his life.

'Christian!' Lauren shouts.

Suddenly he walks in carrying a little bundle. He smiles at me, like he knows something that I don't. He's there, 'You two still haven't been properly introduced.'

'Ross,' Lauren goes, 'we'd like you to meet . . . Ross.'

It's like I've suddenly been punched in the chest. I try to say something, but I can't actually speak. Christian puts the little goy in my orms and I sit there just staring at him while he looks up at me. He even smiles.

'Hey,' Christian goes, 'he likes you.'

I have that feeling you get sometimes, that if I open my mouth to speak, I'm just going to, like, break down?

I have to just hand the little goy back to Lauren, jump up off the sofa and literally run for the door. 'Where are you going?' Christian goes, but I don't even answer.

The next thing I know, roysh, I'm pegging it past Sandpeople and Bounty Hunters, past tables full of Jedis and Sith playing Texas Hold 'Em and a Biker Scout giving out shit to a croupier and I'm thinking how I have to find him before he makes this terrible, terrible mistake. A bird in a Princess Leia slave-girl outfit asks me if I want my champagne topped up, but I don't even answer. I keep running towards the West Tower and the elevator that will take me to *his* room, hoping against hope that I'm not too late.

I *am* too late. The door's open and I can hear voices inside the room, even from down the corridor. Sorcha and the old man – one saying that the chap must be suffering from post-traumatic stress disorder, capitals P through D, the other saying that the whole thing is like, *Oh my God!*

'What's going on?' I go, standing in the doorway, cracking on not to know.

They all look at me at exactly the same time. The old man is pacing the floor. Sorcha and Helen are sitting on the edge of the bed, either side of the old dear, who's already in her wedding dress – even though the ceremony's, like, hours away – and she's got, like, tears streaming out of her eyes, making shit of her make-up.

Erika's there as well. It's actually Erika who goes, 'Trevion's gone, Ross.'

Her and Sorcha's dresses are nice actually. They must have all been having a final dress rehearsal when they found out.

I'm there, 'Gone? What do you mean, gone?'

The old man's there, 'Decided he couldn't go through with it and had it away, like the proverbial thief in the night.'

He really does love the sound of his own voice.

'I'm sorry,' I go, actually being sincere. 'As in, sorry to hear?'

The old dear just looks up at me – an Emo gone wrong – but she doesn't *say* shit? She just, like, stares me out of it.

The old man's there, 'You didn't say something to him, did you, Ross?'

I'm like, 'Meaning?'

'Well, it's just I saw the pair of you having a *tête-à-tête*, pardon the French, last night. Well, I was just telling your mother. It was immediately after – Trevion walked over to bar, *knocked back* his bourbon – as they say in the movies – and said that's it, he was gone. I said, "Well, this is a fine how-do-you-do – you bowing out of your stag at, what, half-eleven?" He gave me a good old hug and he said, "Goodbye, Charlie." At the time, I thought he meant goodnight – the whiskey talking and so forth. But no. Came to check on him about an hour ago and he was gone . . .'

'Fock!'

'Leaving nothing but a note.'

'A note?' I look at the old dear and I'm like, 'Er, what did it actually say?' trying *not* to sound worried? 'As in, were there any clues in it, as to why he, you know, whatever . . .'

Sorcha answers for her. 'Ross, I think that's between your mum and Trevion, don't you?'

The old dear hasn't taken her eyes off me for the last thirty seconds and the way she's looking at me, roysh, it's as if she's trying to read my face? And what I'd imagine she's thinking is, what did I ever do to make him hate me like that?

Sorcha says that Johnny Sarno's on his way up. He wants to shoot the scene where Charles discovers that Trevion's gone, then when he breaks the news to the old dear. She's there, 'We better get you in the bathroom, Fionnuala. Fix up your make-up.'

I turn to go. Erika says that I need to be here for this. I tell her I don't. I really don't. What I need to do is find Ronan and stop myself from focking up Christian's life and probably Ro's as well. I step out into the corridor and try his phone. It's off.

I go back downstairs and make my way back to the roulette table. There's, like, no sign of Ro or Big Juice anywhere. I ring both their rooms, then try Ro's mobile a second time – again, nothing.

It's at that exact point, roysh, that I feel what I immediately know is another trickle of blood coming from my nose. It's the worst bleed I've had yet and I have to put my hand up to my actual face to stop it. Luckily, roysh, there's a gents, like, ten feet away. I walk over to it, push the door and go into Trap One. I pull off maybe twenty sheets of toilet roll and sit on, like, the lid of the jacks with my head back, trying to stop the bleeding. I'm sniffing like a focking madman as well, trying to stop it getting all over my clothes.

It takes, like, ten minutes, roysh, but eventually the bleeding stops. I put the paper in the jacks and flush, then I open the door of the trap . . .

I end up nearly shitting myself there on the spot.

There's, like, three security gords outside the door. And these goys aren't dressed like focking stormtroopers either

– they're the real deal. We're talking nightsticks, we're talking guns, the lot.

One of them sort of, like, throws me out of the way, then rushes into my cubicle and takes a look in the bowl.

'Looks like he flushed it away,' he goes.

I'm there, 'What the fock *is* this?'

'Sir,' he goes, 'we've had a complaint from a member of staff that someone was snorting cocaine in here.'

I catch my reflection in the mirror behind him. There's all, like, dried blood on my upper lip?

I'm there, 'I wasn't snorting anything. I had, like, a nosebleed?'

'Sir,' he goes, except he says it, like, really firmly, 'I'm going to have to ask you to calm down!' the way bouncers do when they're looking for an excuse to deck you.

I'm there, 'But I'm not even into that shit.'

'Let me see some ID,' he goes, like he's not going to take any shit from me.

I hand him my driving licence.

'This you?' he goes.

I'm there, 'Of course it's me.'

'JP Conroy?'

'Yeah.'

One of them sort of, like, grabs my elbow from behind, then another one grabs the other and the third dude goes, 'Sir, we're going to ask you to accompany us to the front of the casino – the police *have* been called.'

I'm like, 'Police? Whoa – you're making, like, a major mistake here.'

They literally pick me up and carry me out of the jacks and I'm suddenly like the coyote out of the *Road Runner* when he goes off the cliff – as in my legs are moving but they're just, like, treading air.

Out of the corner of my eye, I cop C-3PO, over by the craps tables, trying to look all innocent. There's no prizes for guessing who the member of staff was.

I'm there, 'You're a focking grass, 3PO!' except I'm not sure if he hears me, roysh, because I'm moving pretty fast now and all I can see is the blurred faces of the old man and Darth Maul and Sorcha and Erika and Bib Fortuna and Helen and a couple of Gamorrean Gords and Ronan and Big Juice and the old dear in her wedding dress, tears still streaking her face, then finally Christian, Lauren and little Ross, staring at me open-mouthed as I'm carried, like a battering ram, through the gaming hall and the lobby and into the back of a waiting cop cor.

'Fourteen hours!' I'm banging on the cell door, going. 'Fourteen focking hours! Either chorge me or release me.'

I don't know where that line comes from – probably *CSI* or one of those.

The cell's got, like, a bed, a table and two chairs, although the only thing you really need to know about it is that it smells of piss.

The door swings open and a cop walks in. His name's, like, Pat Patterson. I met him earlier and he told me his great-great-grandfather was from Limerick, like this was something to be proud of? I cracked on to be impressed, of course, and told him that Limerick was a beautiful port of the world.

He leans against the wall. 'We picked you up at three this afternoon,' he goes, then makes a big point of looking at his watch. 'It's ten to seven.'

I'm there, 'Yeah? And your point is?'

'My point is, JP, that's not even *four* hours.'

I'm like, 'Facts and figures – whatever. *My* point is, why am I still here? What did the medical examiner say?'

He checked me out just after I got here.

'Quite a bit,' he goes. 'Did you know you've got a septal perforation?'

I'm like, 'Yeah, I'm *kind* of aware of that at this stage? But what did he say about the whole, I don't know, coke thing?'

'Well, from his examination of your pupils, and the swabs he took from your nose, it was, in his opinion, highly unlikely that you ingested any illicit drug in the previous twelve hours.'

'Dude, that's what I told you – my life's a natural high . . .'

He laughs – Pat's actually sound?

'So, like, what am I still doing here?'

'The Federal boys want to talk to you,' he goes.

I'm there, 'The Federal boys? That sounds suspiciously like The Feds to me.'

'That's right.'

'Er, do you mind me asking why?'

I'm suddenly kacking it, thinking they've obviously searched the room and found the laptop and the radio mic.

But it's not that at all.

'It seems there's an arrest warrant outstanding for you since 2001.'

'For me?'

'Yeah, a complaint you slapped a kid around in some toy store in New York?'

My hort nearly stops. Of course, the obvious thing to do is to tell him that I'm not *actually* JP Conroy? But I know one or two goys from Clongowes who did jail time over here for carrying fake ID and it's a generally accepted fact that I'm too pretty to go to prison.

'I'd hordly say *slapped around*,' I go. 'If anything, it was just one good slap?'

'Well, whatever – the kid's coming up here with his parents. Hey, do you have any objection to taking part in a line-up?'

I'm there, 'Er, no.'

He nods. 'Hey, speaking of kids,' he goes, 'yours is here.'

I'm there, 'Ronan? Look, whatever he did, it was my idea,' automatically thinking the worst.

'He didn't do nothing. He came to see you.'

'Oh – well, that's one good thing.'

'Hey, what a great kid . . .'

'Yeah, he definitely has a way with, like, people?'

'The sergeant here – been here forty years. Got some great Mob stories. They're sitting out there for hours talking.'

His voice drops to, like, a whisper. 'Look,' he goes, 'I shouldn't really do this. But like I said, the boys all love him. I'm going to let him in to see you.'

I'm there, 'Really?'

'Hey,' he goes, 'what harm can it do?'

I'm tempted to tell him to frisk him for explosives. Knowing Ro, he's come with an escape plan.

So off he goes and ten or fifteen minutes later, roysh, the cell door swings open again and in walks Ro, looking majorly pissed off with me. 'You're some fooken tulip,' he goes.

I'm there, 'What?'

He looks over his shoulder. 'I feel it only fair to tell you, Rosser, Big Juice is not a happy man.'

I'm there, 'So you didn't go ahead with the whole, I suppose, scam?'

'What, with the heat you drew on us? What do you think?'

He sits down at the table, opposite me, and sighs, I think the word is, *wearily*?

Something suddenly occurs to me. 'Hey, what name did you use when you asked for me?'

'JP Conroy. Don't worry, I'm wide. I remembered you talking to that speed cop and I thought, "I know what this bag of piss is going to do." What are you at, Man? Tell them who you are.'

I'm there, 'No focking way. I could end up getting, like, six months – do you know what they do to pretty boys in the prisons over here? Even best case, I'd be, like, deported? Which'd mean no second series of the show.'

'So, what, you're gonna take the fooken rap for what JP did?'

'Ro, there isn't going to be any rap. I'm just thinking here, they're setting up, like, an ID parade? So they send the kid in. He walks the line. If he doesn't pick me out, they *have* to release me? I'm telling you, I'm going to be back on The Strip in time for the big porty.'

The funny thing, roysh, is that as I'm saying it, I'm storting to relax more? I'm even looking forward to hearing Christian's speech and wondering will I get a mench.

'Take my advice,' Ronan goes, 'tell them the fooken troot.'

I'm like, 'Ro, forget it. Now this scam of yours, is it fixable – as in, could we do it somewhere else?'

He shakes his head. 'I think Big Juice was getting cold feet in anyhow. Ah, we're gonna do something diffordent, even if it's just counting cards?'

'Counting cords? Like Dustin Hoffman?'

He goes, 'You don't have to be autistic, Rosser, to track the ratio of high cards to low cards in a deck and determine the probability advantages . . .'

It's only now, roysh, sitting there in the cop shop, that I suddenly realize how proud I am to hear my son talking like that.

'It's just a matter of assigning a positive, negative or null value to each card in the deck,' he goes, 'then adjusting the running count as each card is dealt. Two to six are plus one. Tens, aces and paints are minus one. Seven, eight, nine are zero . . .'

'Fionn said they think you're gifted,' I go. 'In other words, freakishly intelligent?'

He nods, roysh, like he's taking it all in his stride.

'Don't you worry,' I go, 'I'm not going to let them experiment on you.'

The door suddenly opens. Pat's back. 'You ready for this line-up?' he goes.

I'm there, 'Right with you, Pat.'

Ronan looks me dead in the eye. 'Just fooken tell them, Rosser.'

I actually laugh. 'Ro,' I go. 'Piece of piss.'

So the next thing I know, roysh, I'm in this room with, like, five or six other dudes, who are all around my age? We're actually having a bit of craic because it turns out they're all, like, students and they do this just for the shekels. I stort telling them some of the shit we did for dosh when we were over here on our J1ers and they're cracking their holes laughing – really loving me, if that doesn't come across as, like, too big-headed?

'Hey, aren't you that guy from that show?' one of them goes.

I'm there, 'Er, yeah – but do me a favour, keep it to yourself.'

'Man,' he goes, 'I love that fucking show,' and he high-fives me.

Another cop comes in and tells us to quit talking and to line up against the wall. There's a whole *The Usual Suspects* vibe to it? They've even got the, like, height measures painted on the wall behind us.

'Okay, bring him in,' the cop shouts.

I turn to the dude beside me and tell him they should all come to the casino opening tonight – as in, the new *Star Wars* casino? I happen to be best mates with the dude who project-managed it. He even named his kid after me, if you can believe that. He says that'd be awesome. I tell him I'll be out of here in, like, fifteen minutes.

And then in walks the kid.

I feel my body go instantly cold. I'm thinking, no way. No *focking* way. This has got to be someone's idea of a joke.

He walks the line, roysh, spending a good four or five seconds studying each face. I'm shitting Baileys, of course. Not only am I trying to *not* look like JP, I'm also trying to *not* look like me.

Then I'm thinking, there's a good chance he won't recognize me with the new nose. But I'm sweating like a fat bird writing her first love letter.

He's suddenly standing in front of me, staring hord at my face. I'm doing all sorts of shit, like squinting my eyes and pouting my lips to try to, like, throw him off the trail – but there's obviously something familiar about my face.

It's just he can't place it.

He's just about to move on to the next dude when he suddenly stops and I watch the – I suppose – realization dawn across his face. Our eyes sort of, like, lock, for ten, maybe fifteen seconds, then I watch *his* eyes narrow. He suddenly smiles at me, the little prick.

'Number six,' Danny Lintz goes. 'It's number six.'

Pat Patterson says he's sorry he has to cuff me. I tell him it's cool. He pushes my head down to make sure I don't bang it getting into the back of the cor.

He gets in and storts the engine. He turns on the siren, roysh, but then changes his mind.

The gate rolls upwards and we come up from the underground cor pork. There's, like, a crowd waiting outside. They're mostly, like, reporters, but then I stort picking out one or two familiar faces as well. Sorcha and Erika. Fionn and JP. Christian and Lauren. The old man and Ro. And Honor. All standing by me, no matter what.

There's no sign of the old dear, though, and that sort of, like, winds me like a kick in the stomach.

They're all waving at me. But with my hands cuffed, I

obviously can't wave back. Honor recognizes me even through the glass. 'Daddy!' she's going. 'Daddy!'

Johnny Sarno's loving it, of course. He's got, like, two cameras trained on the cor and two or three more on the crowd. I suppose he's thinking – like we all are – what a focking series finale.

The cor makes its slow way through the crowd, Pat shouting at people through the speaker on the roof, to get out of the way. There's a lot of flashbulbs going off in my boat.

Then, all of a sudden, we're clear of them and I'm looking back through the rear window at the madness, getting smaller and smaller, until it finally disappears and I'm left thinking, so that was it then – that was fame.

I feel suddenly, I don't know, empty, although I do realize I'm getting off lightly here. It took twenty-four hours for me to persuade them that I was Ross O'Carroll-Kelly, not JP Conroy.

The District Attorney wanted to chorge me with all sorts. It turns out his son is, like, a major fan of the show. Two nights ago he called his mother a focking truffle-hunter and I don't need to tell you who they blamed.

'Hey, you're lucky the sergeant took a shine to that kid of yours,' Pat goes.

I laugh. If only they knew.

Soon, we're taking the slipway for McCarron International Airport. Pat suddenly turns up the radio. There's some shit on the news about home repossessions. 'Hey, that's only going to get worse,' he goes. 'You hear Bear Stearns said today they got serious problems with two of their hedge funds?'

I turn around – as anyone would – and I go, 'Er, this affects me *how* exactly?'

Acknowledgements

I would like to, very humbly, thank the wonderful team that continues to support me in my endeavours. Rachel Pierce is more than just an editor to me – she's my director, and a truly great one, too. Rachel, thank you for working so tirelessly, while never allowing the quality to suffer. Thank you, Faith O'Grady – I'm truly blessed to have you as my agent and friend. Thank you, Michael McLoughlin, Patricia Deevy, Cliona Lewis, Patricia McVeigh, Brian Walker and all the Penguin Ireland team – it's a pleasure and a privilege working with you. I'd like to thank my friend Paul O'Kelly for allowing me to pick his enormous brain on the subject of mathematics. Thank you, Alan Clarke, for your quiet-spoken genius. Thanks to my father and my brothers for their love and support and all the fun years. And thank you, Mary, for making me happy.